WINTER

at

MEDORA DOWNS

Anne Rouen

A catalogue record for this
book is available from the
National Library of Australia

Anne Rouen
PO BOX 116
Manilla NSW 2346

Paperback ISBN: 978-0-9924036-5-2
eBook ISBN: 978-0-9924036-6-9

Cover Images:

'Young woman with suitcase'—Copyright: Vladimir Nikulin—
via Dreamstime

Cover Design by Felicity Matthews of Web Etch Design and
Editing

Editing by Felicity Matthews of Web Etch Design and Editing

DEDICATION

For my sister, Jeanne.

Chapter One

March 1987

Sarah leant against the bathroom door, gazing blindly at the white, blotched face and anguished eyes that stared back at her from the mirror opposite. She was twenty-two and her world—her whole life, in fact—had just come crashing down around her to lay shattered at her feet. She flinched as the furious tirade and continued banging and thumping suddenly escalated. *Oh, God! Will he never stop?* 'I can't believe it!' she whispered. 'I *can't* believe it!' Yet, according to her friend Jo, just now bandying words through the closed door with gusto, the signs were all there and had been for some time.

Safely locked in the bathroom, Sarah moved to the basin. *Safe? Am I safe?* she wondered as a particularly savage blow battered the front door. Stifling another sob, she told herself fiercely, 'I will not cry! I will *not* cry! He is just not worth it!' Pushing back a curtain of pale gold hair, she leant over to splash cold water on her tear-drenched face. But a small voice within her, which would not be silenced, cried incessantly. *What will I do? What can I do? How will I go on?*

Head bowed over the basin, Sarah pressed a cool washer to her eyes and began to relive the nightmare into which she had so suddenly and disastrously been plunged.

Embracing with joy an unexpected opportunity to go out shopping for a wedding gown, Sarah had spent most of her evening in various boutiques trying on creations that ranged from elegant simplicity to frothy confections of embroidered lace, dripping with pearls and crystals. With a train or without a train? Off the shoulder or sleeves? High or low neckline? Waist or princess line? Unable to make a decision, she went out onto the street.

And then it happened: As she passed the door of an opulent restaurant, it swung open, held by an invisible hand for departing guests. Sarah involuntarily glanced inside and, gasping with shock, stood transfixed on the pavement, all colour draining from her face, her eyes dark pools of misery. There before her sat David. *Her* David! And he was holding the hand of his beautiful dinner companion across the table.

In those few confused moments, Sarah received an impression of chic elegance: black hair, shining and immaculate, and a flawless complexion enhanced by skilfully applied make-up. She recognised her, too: It was Chantal, David's personal assistant. And she was wearing an orchid! *David always brought me an orchid,* thought Sarah. *Because he said he loved me so much.*

Sarah wanted to run, but she could not seem to move. She could only stand and watch the cruel tableau before her. And as she watched, David raised his glass in a silent toast and passionately kissed the fingers he was holding; a waiter ushered out the departing guests, and the invisible hand closed the door.

Sarah chewed her lip and tried to find a reasonable explanation for what she had just witnessed. David had told her he was working on a new curriculum and that Chantal was staying back to help him. Maybe she should give him the benefit of the doubt? After all, they work together and may have snatched a quick bite. *What?* said a cynical inner voice. *In this cordon-bleu restaurant? Dressed like that? Don't be a fool!*

A woman murmured an apology as she brushed past. Sarah moved and began to turn away. Then, rocked by a fury completely foreign to her, she made a small exclamation, swung back to the door and swept inside.

Driven by the same impetus, she achieved an airy tone: 'David, *darling* … Hello, Chantal. I was passing and I saw you, so I thought I may as well join you. Do you mind?'

'*Sarah!*' He so obviously *did* mind that it was laughable. Both of them looked as though they were sitting on an ants' nest. 'I thought you were tutoring …'

Tell me something I don't know! 'Did you, really?' She smiled. By now she could see that his PA was not exactly dressed for work, in a low-cut, clinging lace evening gown that left little to the imagination: *From top to bottom and everything in between!* Sarah thought, glancing from one to the other with icy calm. *I'm doing this well. I can't believe it is me.* 'Well? Aren't you going to offer me a drink?' she asked, pulling out a chair and picking up David's wineglass. She met his eyes. 'What are we celebrating?'

A look passed between David and his assistant; a look that was as old as time itself. *I'm not that much of a fool*, thought Sarah. But she listened politely while he said with his charming smile, 'Look, sweetheart, we're working. We just stopped for something to eat. I don't have the time to explain now, but I will see you later.'

Once, she would have believed the oily insincerities that dropped so easily from his lips, but as she saw through him, a sudden, gale-force gust of anger smashed her frozen calm. 'No, you won't,' she said, leaping up and ripping off her engagement ring. 'You've made it more than clear, already.' Without hesitation, she dropped the ring into the wine and dashed it down the décolletage of the PA. Then, hauling the bottle out of its silver ice bucket, proceeded to empty the exclusive *chablis* over her fiancé's well-groomed head.

'Sarah!' he got out through gritted teeth, cruelly twisting her wrist to force her to drop the bottle. 'You are making an *exhibition* of yourself!'

'Oh, am I?' she said, using her other hand to jerk the tablecloth so that all the expensive crystal and china—and the wine bottle—crashed to the floor. 'What a shame!' She threw the bundled-up tablecloth at the startled waiter who had arrived with all speed and an expression of ludicrous alarm. 'A little accident, *Garçon*. I am so terribly sorry. Monsieur will pay for the damage.' Then, she stalked out in a magnificent rage. Her fury sustained her all the way home where she collapsed just inside the door; her slender frame convulsed by great, racking sobs. Her flatmates, Jo and Wendy, found her on the hall floor when they came back from their session at the gym.

'Sarah! My God! What is the matter?' asked Jo, dropping down beside her.

'Come on, love,' said Wendy, tugging unavailingly. 'Get up off the floor.'

'Let me do that. You're littler than she is,' said the tall brunette, hauling Sarah to her feet and pushing her onto the couch. 'She's in shock. You get her a whisky.'

'I … You know I d-don't drink,' mumbled Sarah, watching her diminutive red-headed friend pour a measure into a tumbler.

'Shut up and do as you're told,' said Jo, taking the glass from Wendy and holding it against Sarah's chattering teeth.

Sarah took a gulp, choked, coughed and doubled over. 'No … more …' she gasped, waving her hand like a drowning swimmer.

'Sip it, you fool,' ordered Jo, unmoved. '*Now* tell us!'

Jo and Wendy had been her friends since she was six years old. There was nothing they did not know about each other. Sarah took a deep breath, told them that her tutoring had been cancelled because her pupil was ill and gave them a brief account of what she'd seen, adding that she'd confronted David in the restaurant and given back his ring.

'Perhaps it *was* innocent,' offered Wendy when she finished. 'They *do* work together.'

'*Innocent?*' scoffed Sarah. 'Don't give me that! She had enough make-up on for a drag queen! And you know that Zampatti number we saw last week? The one we thought was a little too much, or rather, not enough? Well, she was wearing it.'

'Doesn't sound like a work outfit to me,' said Jo, frowning at the glass. 'I mean, even if there was a school do, you wouldn't wear *that* in front of your principal, would you?'

'Not unless you wanted the sack,' agreed Sarah. 'Not to

mention what the parents might say. I mean, I *did* wonder if they might have been grabbing a bite to eat, but they were in Bondi's classiest French restaurant drinking two-hundred-dollar-a-bottle wine!'

'*Were* they?' said Jo. 'Well, when you put it like that, it looks pretty grim. Look, I didn't say anything, but I have seen him out to dinner with his PA. It was none of my business, and it may have been work related, but now, with the evidence stacking up … What did he say to you when you walked in?'

'He said he could explain.'

'Oh, yeah? Go on.'

'And I said he couldn't and gave him back his ring.'

'And?'

'He said I was making an exhibition of myself, and I walked out.'

'Why?'

Sarah shrugged. 'I didn't think there was anything else to do.'

'Not that, you nit! Why did he say you were making an exhibition of yourself?'

'Oh, that!' Sarah looked vaguely ashamed: pink and defiant. 'Well, it was the way I gave back the ring.'

'Oh, yes?' Jo glanced at Wendy. 'Tell us more.'

'You *didn't!*' gasped Wendy, pummelling the chair arms with glee, when Sarah had told them just what she'd done with the ring.

'Well, good for you!' approved Jo, trying to keep a straight face.

'I suppose it *was* a bit over the top. But something just snapped, you know.'

Her two friends looked at each other and fell about laughing. Sarah was so sweet and forgiving; she drove them mad with her saintliness. They'd even begun to think of her as a mouse. She was so meek that unconsciously, all their lives since boarding school, they had formed a protective cult around her. Both had deplored her awed obedience to David's every decree.

'I'd love to have seen their faces!' Wendy got out, tears streaming down her cheeks. She shook her head. 'Oh *my God!*'

'Oh, Sarah, it is about time!' said Jo, when she could speak. 'Wow! I can't believe it. Grrr! Sic him, girl!' She gave Sarah a considering look. 'And now: what's the plan?'

'I haven't had time to think of one. I would give back the ring if I hadn't already done it.'

'Yeah, it's a rock,' sighed Wendy. 'If it were me, giving it back would be the hardest part about the whole relationship.'

'Well, I've already done it,' said Sarah, still in her defiant mood, 'and I didn't think twice about it!'

'Yes, and what a way to do it,' laughed Jo. 'I wonder what Chantal thought about having to fish it out of her cleavage? She might never find it,' she added, waggling her eyebrows. A thought crossed her mind, and she turned to Sarah, suddenly serious. 'I suppose you *do* know that David is going to be furious?'

'Yes, I feel a little uneasy about that,' she admitted. 'You see, I've never made him angry before.'

'No, because you always do as he says.'

'Don't worry,' said Wendy. 'We'll protect you.'

'She's right to be worried,' said Jo. 'The man's a control freak. He won't take it well.'

'But, surely …'

'Have you ever crossed him?'

'No, but …'

'Well, I have. Over the way he treats Sarah. You'd be surprised how he can turn: A real Jekyll and Hyde.' She turned to Sarah. 'You're well out of it, you know, little though you may think it now.'

'What do you mean?'

'Violence, my child. Against women. He's too cowardly to try it with someone his own size.'

Sarah had no time to question or challenge this accusation because the words were hardly out of Jo's mouth when there was a frenzied banging on the door. 'Sarah, you crazy *bitch*! I know you're in there! Open the door!'

'David,' said Jo, raising her eyebrows. She leapt to her feet and snatched up a hockey stick out of the umbrella stand. 'And he's dead drunk, by the sound of him. Quick, lock yourself in the bathroom. Leave this to me.' She looked back and mouthed, 'I hope the door will stand it.'

'Open the door, I said!'

This was followed by a string of epithets that made Sarah gasp. It was David's voice, but she had never heard him say such words or speak in such fury. Shaken to her foundations, she allowed Wendy to propel her to the bathroom and leant against the locked door. When Jo had told her her assessment of David, she really hadn't believed it. But she had to now! *What a way to be enlightened!* She listened, in shocked disbelief, to the altercation between her friend and her ex-fiancé conducted through the locked door.

'Go away, David. You're drunk!'

'I want to see Sarah. And I am staying until I do.'

'Sarah's not here.' She chuckled. 'What happened to your dinner?'

David ground his teeth at the provocation. 'Chantal was so upset that she had to go home. She told me I should come round and see Sarah.'

'Big of her.'

'Well, it was, considering Sarah ruined her dress and humiliated both of us.'

'Oh, boohoo,' mocked Jo, her eyes alight. She caught Wendy's disapproving glance and subsided: as a one-liner, even she had to admit that it was pretty crass. 'Sarah doesn't want to see you.'

'I want an explanation!'

'*You* want an explanation? Oh, that's rich!'

'She tipped wine all over me!'

'We know. I can't think of anyone who deserves it more. Now, *go* away!'

An even more frenzied assault on the front door brought Sarah to her senses. *What am I doing skulking in here like a coward?* she asked herself. *Leaving Jo and Wendy to fight my battles. I'll have to go out and help them. Perhaps he'll calm down if he sees me?*

At this rate, it was only a matter of time until the latch gave. Sarah unlocked the bathroom door and stepped out into the hall.

Wendy caught her arm to hold her back as David shouted in a blind fury: 'I'll break down this door if she doesn't come out!'

'You can try!' Jo beat a rat-a-tat-tat with her hockey stick. 'But I'd be a bit careful if I were you. You know what will be waiting for you, don't you? And, let me tell you, I'll be happy to break the shoulder rule! Along with your head! Now, buzz off, or I'll call the cops. In fact, they might already be on their way—*if* you've disturbed the neighbours enough.'

This gave him pause.

'You have until the count of ten,' warned Jo. 'One … two …'

'Okay, okay, I'm going. But I'll be back. I am going to come every day until I see her. She's not going to get away with treating me like that! Don't think it! Do you hear me, Sarah?' he shouted. 'You will pay for this! I'll make you pay—if it's the last thing I do!'

CHAPTER TWO

'Come on, love,' said Jo, waiting until she heard the last of the retreating footsteps before tossing her hockey stick back into its repository and shepherding Sarah into the kitchen. 'We all stand in need of a bit of refreshment after *that*! Let's get some coffee and toast.'

'You and Sarah sit down. I'll get it,' said Wendy, reaching for the kettle and the bread packet. 'Sarah looks done in. And if you aren't, *you* should be, after all that shouting.'

'You were enjoying yourself!' Sarah accused Jo, when she'd recovered a little and all three were seated around the kitchen table eating toast and drinking coffee. 'Going at him like a fishwife!'

'No, I wasn't!' Jo protested, a reminiscent sparkle in her eye. 'Well … just a little bit. I enjoyed that the mongrel has shown his true colours before you found yourself tied up in marriage to him.'

'What did he do to you, Jo? To make you hate him the way you do?'

'Do you remember when he started choosing all your clothes? And threw out your beautiful designer jeans?'

Sarah nodded—a look of pain in her eyes.

'Well, I tackled him about it one day when you and Wendy were grocery shopping. He twisted my arm up behind my back and told me to mind my own business or I'd be sorry. I knew then.'

Wendy choked on her toast. 'Do you mean to say you let him get away with *that*?'

'No,' said Jo. 'When he let me go, I showed him out with my hockey stick.' She sipped her coffee with a complacent smile. 'I didn't hear any more about it.'

'I didn't think you would. You're a tough cookie,' said Wendy, eyeing her friend with affection. 'You don't take any prisoners.'

'Got to be if you're a sportsmistress,' said Jo, who was also member of the state hockey team. She wasn't masculine, but she was tall, athletic and very, very capable: discomfiting men who were not sure of their masculinity *and* teenage girls who didn't want to exercise. She did have quite a few male friends and admirers, but no-one she took seriously.

'But, Jo …' Sarah put a hand on her arm. 'Why didn't you tell me about David doing a thing like that to you?'

Jo turned to her; the sparkle quenched. 'Would you have believed me if I had?'

Sarah ducked her head. 'No,' she said, at last.

'Would you have *even* listened?'

Sarah thought of how much under David's influence she'd been; how she'd believed him implicitly when he gave even the most glib and improbable explanation for his actions. 'Probably not, no,' she concurred.

'No. Out of loyalty to the prat, I suppose.' Jo snorted. 'Or one of his oily explanations might have got to you.'

Sarah said nothing.

Jo looked at Wendy. 'We can't let her stay here. I have a feeling the worm has turned with him: he will hurt or even kill her if we give him the chance.'

'No, Jo!' objected Sarah. 'He's never laid a finger on me. *Never!* I think you're overreacting …'

'No, I'm not. You fool, didn't you *hear* him?'

'Yes, but you said yourself that he was drunk.'

'And you think that he wouldn't be again? No, Sarah, we have to get you out of here. Right away, somewhere. I've got a bad feeling about this. I think we've had our warning.'

There was a strained silence, unbroken for several minutes, while both girls looked at Jo. Her words had all the more effect because Jo was no doomsayer. Full of commonsense, she was more likely to say, 'Pull yourself together, you fool!' than to make a dramatic pronouncement like this.

'I have some kind of second cousin in the Queensland Outback,' said Wendy, after a while. 'Mum was saying the other day that she was looking for a governess.'

'Perfect,' said Jo. 'Go and ring her and find out if she still wants one. That will be *perfect*.'

Wendy glanced at her watch. 'It's a bit late now. I'll ring her tomorrow.'

Sarah sat, heartbroken, trying not to think of David. But it was no use: memories crowded, jostling for space. Into her mind jumped a vision of their first meeting at a college dance: she a raw fresher, and he a sophisticated third-year student. He had walked over to where she had been standing with some other equally overawed first-year students, smiled his dazzling smile, looking so handsome that she had caught her breath.

'Hey, fresher,' he'd said, a teasing light in his eye. 'Like to dance?'

'Lucky you!' an envious voice had breathed behind her as he led her onto the dancefloor. Their relationship had blossomed from there.

The romance lasted through her three years at college. After the first year, David had been appointed to an exclusive private college in another suburb but had always found time to take her out once or twice a week.

Tall, fair David: handsome; well-dressed; a first-rate sportsman; the most popular man in college, and now, at his school, being noticed by his superiors as a man who was going places. Already, he was master of a large department with his own personal assistant. Sarah's lips twisted wryly. She had been so proud that he had chosen her instead of one of the many beautiful girls that had thrown themselves at him. Sarah stirred, trying to hold back tears as she thought of the night, only last month, when David had produced the magnificent diamond ring (she'd so furiously flung back) and placed it reverently on her finger. She had been speechless with joy. What happiness was hers! What bliss! And now it was all finished. All ruined. *Somehow, I must find a way to get over it,* she thought in despair.

Finally, with a little hiccough, she spoke: 'Is anyone going to ask me what I think?'

Both girls looked at Sarah. 'All right, I'll buy it,' said Jo, leaning back. 'What do you think?'

Sarah sat for a minute looking into her cup. 'Perfect or not, I will go if I'm given the chance, because I don't want to have any more to do with David, whether he's just a cheat or ——'

'He's a psychopath!'

'You may be right, Jo, although it seems a bit over the top.' Sarah sounded forlorn. 'I will miss you girls, but I think I do want to start a new life away from …' she burst into tears.

Jo and Wendy hedged her about, supporting her, making plans, extracting promises to write.

The next day, Jo rang her school and took a sick day. Wendy—a freelance designer and her own boss, who could do as she pleased—went to work on the telephone. She was able to report that, although her cousin Elisabeth Andrews had already found a governess, the neighbouring station was in desperate need of one. Two recently orphaned children needed loving care and attention. 'I told them you would be just the person they should have and why,' said Wendy. 'They'll be sending your tickets by express and want you to leave as soon as possible.'

'Oh, the *poor* little darlings!' said Sarah. And from then on, her own troubles took a back seat, her tender heart rent by the plight of poor little children left without the love and direction of their parents.

'I hate to interrupt your very proper sentiments,' said Jo, eyeing her thoughtfully, 'but we'll have to be out of here by four thirty. Otherwise, all hell will break loose.'

'Won't it be all right if *I* just go somewhere else?'

'No, you fool, it will not.' Jo was nothing, if not forthright. 'Neither Wendy nor I want to be subjected to your ex's bullyboy tactics to prise your whereabouts out of us.'

'Would he ...?' But Sarah said no more. The answer was written in the other girls' faces and her own heart.

After a little discussion and another hurried telephone call, the girls packed all Sarah's things, a few of their own and went to stay with Wendy's parents in their gated mansion in Wollstonecraft until the day of Sarah's departure.

§

Wendy came running in, waving an express envelope. 'It's here, Sarah. It's here!'

'You open it,' said Sarah. 'I feel all jelly legged.'

'I'll make the coffee,' said Jo, bounding up the stairs and into the hall behind her. 'Sarah needs something to brace her.' She smiled at her. 'Have you made arrangements?'

'Yes,' said Sarah, indicating the rose-patterned white china telephone, reposing elegantly on a polished cedar table. 'Diane, from our old boarding school, will take over my share of the flat, and Shelley, a first-year-out teacher, will take over my tutoring.'

'Perfect,' said Jo. 'What's in the package?'

Wendy slit the envelope and emptied its contents onto the table while Jo handed round the coffee. 'Two airline tickets,' she announced. 'An accommodation voucher—ooh, for a posh hotel in Brisbane!—and a train ticket. Oh, and a letter for you, Sarah.'

'What does it say?' muttered Sarah, holding her coffee mug in both hands and sipping as if her life depended on it.

'It says: "You appear to be exactly the person we have been looking for." Then there's a bunch of instructions of how to get there. Then he says: "We look forward to making your acquaintance. Sincerely, Devin Mainwaring." Devin Mainwaring!' repeated Wendy, in awed tones. 'As far as I can gather, he's rather a big shot out there.'

'What does your cousin say about him?' asked Jo.

'Oh, you know: Decent bloke, blighted in love. Confirmed bachelor after being jilted by the girl next door, years ago. Bit of a looker, too, apparently.'

'Oh, that's all right, then,' said Jo, at her most flippant. 'He should be just right for Sarah. They can console each other.'

'Hey! *You two* …' protested their victim.

'Come on,' said Jo, putting down her cup. 'Get your skates on.'

'Where are we going?'

'To Charltons Saddlery in St. Leonards to buy you some jeans and jodhs, love. Now, that I *will* enjoy!' Jo's eyes were bright with laughter. 'No fear of meeting David in a place like that! *But*, I'll take my hockey stick, just in case …'

Chapter Three

Sarah was in the air, on her way, still suffering from the emotional farewell with Jo and Wendy at the airport. *No-one could have better friends*, she thought, dabbing at red-rimmed eyes. She had an uneventful flight to Brisbane, made her way to the luxury hotel named on her voucher and presented herself in the plush reception office where she received her key from a chatty and admiring young man at the desk, who summoned a bellboy to carry up her luggage.

Early next morning, at the busy airport, she boarded the plane for Longreach in western Queensland. According to the travel brochures she had obtained, Longreach was a gateway to the Outback and the home of the Stockman's Hall of Fame—a monumental tribute to the pioneers of the largest part of Australia known as the Outback. Consulting her timetable, she realised, with a pang, that she would not have time to visit it, since there was less than an hour between the arrival of the plane and the departure of the Midlander for Winton.

As the plane winged its way from Brisbane, Sarah noted the changes in the landscape as they flew farther west. Once over the Great Dividing Range, covered in thick, green forest, there was the emerald-green, brown, black and yellow patchwork quilt of the Darling Downs. *Oh,* thought Sarah, *Wendy would love these beautiful colours!* Then there was some poorer, scrubby country as they penetrated farther inland; some hills and mountains, old and eroded as they passed the Central Highlands; followed by a glimpse of grey-green mulga scrub with red, sandy soil as the plane touched down at Charleville. The plane serviced the west and landed at many of the western towns en route to Longreach, so it took much longer than Sarah had expected. She understood that on the return trip to Brisbane the plane landed at the towns it had missed on the way out.

Sarah looked out over the dry, red, dusty paddocks and the thick mulga scrub and wondered, for the first time, how she would react to the landscape when she arrived at her destination. She had read somewhere that at first sight of the real Outback one either thrilled to its vast magnificence and fell instantly under its spell or—afraid of its challenges—ran back to the smaller country where the horizons were closer and gave a feeling of security. She had read, also, that Outback people, accustomed to the far horizons, felt claustrophobic when surrounded by the hills and forests of the softer country. She felt a stab of excitement and apprehension as she wondered which sensation would be hers. Somehow, she felt that the former would be true for her: she loved the freedom of the wide-open spaces, and she would wear jeans again—fast becoming her own personal symbol of freedom now that she'd escaped from David and his domination of every aspect of her life. Why had she never thought to resent it? It had taken a shocking occurrence to awaken her to what he was. And even now, she only half believed it, though she had seen and heard for herself.

Sarah tried to close her mind to thoughts of David and his controlling nature. *He took advantage of my love,* she thought, tears squeezing between her lashes, *and used it to his own ends.* It was all too painful. She must relegate him to the past, and he must stay there; she was determined on that.

The roar of the plane's engines startled Sarah out of her reverie as it rose in the air for the last time before landing at Longreach. The red soil and the mulga gradually gave way to open, rolling downs, sectioned at intervals by tortuously winding, tree-lined channels. A shiver of apprehension seized her as the plane banked and descended at last to the airport at Longreach. There could be no going back from here. She was past the point of no return.

As Sarah stepped down from the plane, the heat rising from the tarmac hit her with an impact that pulled her up short. So hot, and it was April! Momentarily, she wished she'd opted for a shorter skirt than the comfortable maxi she was wearing. However, after she had walked across to the tin shed where she would be able to collect her luggage and obtain a taxi, she noted with relief that she had begun to adjust to the heat. *It's always a shock to step out of air-conditioned comfort into the open air,* she thought, trying to be positive.

While she waited for the trolley with her luggage to come over from the plane, Sarah looked around at the small patch of lawn adorned with palm trees and bougainvillea that bordered the entrance to the airport and farther out to the flat, brown paddocks that surrounded the town.

Having obtained her luggage, she went to a waiting taxi, where she was greeted by a cheerful, middle-aged woman. 'Where are you going, luv?'

'The railway station, please. I am catching the Midlander.'

'Okay, we'll have to hurry, then. Hop in.'

§

Seated on the train, Sarah was beginning to wonder if her journey would ever end. Another four hours or so to Winton. And then, how far? She didn't know, but it must be a long way. She had looked up a map of Queensland after she had received Devin Mainwaring's letter, and the distances had indeed seemed vast. She knew from the letter that Medora Downs was on the Diamantina River, but really, that was just a wriggly line on a map. *Until tomorrow,* she thought. *Then I'll know.*

As the train rocked and clattered over the downs, Sarah caught her breath at the vast emptiness of the land. Miles and miles of tall, waving grasses, dotted here and there with an occasional mimosa bush or whitewood tree; interspersed at intervals with wandering lines of coolibah growing in channels. From time to time and very far apart, Sarah saw a windmill or a clump of unusually luxuriant trees—denoting a homestead.

The morning wore on into the afternoon with no visible change in the landscape, except for some unusually coloured low hills in the distance, and Sarah began to think that she would never stop travelling: there was nothing in her whole world but the rhythmic clickety-clack and rocking motion of the train on its shining, silver tracks.

Eventually, the train pulled in to a small, tidy railway station. Sarah was here, at last! Soon, she would meet someone from Medora Downs. Devin Mainwaring had mentioned in his letter that he would try to come himself to collect her from the station, but if that were not possible, she could expect his overseer. *Who will it be?* she wondered as she prepared to leave the train. *And what will my employer be like?*

Sarah stepped down and looked around her. The street was empty, and the handful of other passengers had gone their separate ways. Hot, tired and dusty, she was left alone on a deserted Outback railway station. For a moment, she almost panicked until her commonsense reasserted itself. Medora Downs was a long way from Winton, and they may have been delayed. She sat down on a seat in the shade and schooled herself to wait patiently.

Finally, Sarah heard the sound of a vehicle and looked around as a battered old utility pulled up in a swirl of dust. She gave a gasp of disbelief—her eyes widening. Surely, they had not come to collect her in that old thing! It looked as though it could hardly get around the town, let alone the miles of Outback she still had to cover.

A spry old man climbed out of the utility, his hat as battered and ancient as his vehicle. His seamed face was burnt to a walnut hue and had the appearance of fine leather. From between the weather-beaten folds of skin, he surveyed the world through a pair of twinkling eyes, the bluest of blue. He strode rapidly into the station—his small, wiry frame containing hidden reserves of energy—and halted before Sarah, his expression thoughtful.

'Day, Miss,' he said, lifting his hat. 'You be Miss Sarah Johnston?'

'Yes, that's right. Are you from Medora Downs?'

The hand that held the hat scratched his head; the blue eyes twinkled more than ever. 'Nar, Miss,' he said with a chuckle. 'Don't think Bessie 'ud get us that far. I'm from The Gregory.'

'Gregory?'

'Yair. North Gregory Hotel—the only one we've got left in town. Useter be three or four. But that's progress, fer ya.' He spoke out of the corner of his mouth in staccato, like a machinegun firing short bursts. 'Mary sent me to pick you up. Good sort, Mary. Do anythin' for ya. Been a radio message from Medora Downs: Can't get here today. Says you're to stay at The Gregory an' they'll pick you up, termorra. Mary'll tell ya all about it.'

'Oh,' said Sarah, slowly. 'I see.' So, she still wouldn't meet her new boss and the children. 'Oh, well ...' she shrugged fatalistically and followed the old man, who had picked up her cases and was walking to his vehicle.

Safely stowed in Bessie, they lurched off down the street to draw up with various squeals and rattles in front of an imposing hotel.

'I'll take yer bags up ter yer room fer yer, Miss. Me name's Bert. I'm the yardman here. Mary said ter tell yer she'd have a nice cuppa waiting fer ya in the dining room. Through there, Missy,' he added, gesturing to his right.

Sarah thanked him and stepped into the cool atmosphere of the hotel with its gracious proportions and huge glass doors etched with Outback scenes and the *Waltzing Matilda* swagman.

At the far end of the room was a moulded staircase leading to the guestrooms upstairs. The whole effect was that of having stepped onto the set of a 1950s movie.

Just then the dining room doors swung open, and a motherly, middle-aged woman appeared. At sight of Sarah, her face creased into a welcoming smile. 'Hullo, dear. I thought I heard someone. Come on in to the dining room and have a cuppa,' she said, leading the way. 'You got the message? Good. Something about a bore breaking down. They can't leave the stock without water, you know. Ah well, these things do happen. Dev said to tell you that he is very sorry, and Jim, the overseer, will be here first thing in the morning to pick you up. Jim Barnes, that is. About seven, he said, so I'll get you an early breakfast. He'll leave about four: that way, it won't be too hot for you. You'll like Jim, he's a bit of a character, has everyone in stitches with the things he says, has the whole bar laughing sometimes. But he's a good man and knows his job. Else he wouldn't be where he is. I'm Mary, by the way.'

Mary did not seem to require a reply to any of this, so Sarah smiled politely and let the motherly clucking flow over her while she drank her tea and ate the delicious sandwiches her hostess had provided.

'I suppose you'd like to freshen up a bit, dear? Those trains are horrible things! And you've come such a long way, too. You go along to your room and rest. Dinner's at six, dear. In the dining room. And now I'll show you to your room.'

Mary shepherded Sarah up the stairs to a large, airy room with double doors opening onto a balcony; pointed out the bathroom; smiled her warm, friendly smile and bustled away.

After a refreshing shower, Sarah went out to explore the town. She found a street of quaint, old-fashioned stores of the type that had long ago vanished from the city. Enchanted, she went into one and was greeted with old-world courtesy by an elderly shopkeeper. *Just wait until I write to tell Jo and Wendy about this,* she thought. *This is a bit better than a chrome-and-plastic supermarket with its overworked check-out girls!* She spent a few minutes chatting to the shopkeeper before resuming her exploration.

Sarah dined in solitary state and retired early to her room. Tired as she was, she still found it impossible to sleep. A quiver of excitement ran through her as she thought of what tomorrow might bring. Endless questions raced through her mind. If she'd given it even a passing consideration, perhaps it may have surprised her that not one of her many thoughts was concerned with the past—only the future.

Finally, all the tensions and exertions of the last few days caught up with her and she slept deeply.

Chapter Four

When Sarah, dressed in well-fitting jeans and a fresh pink-and-white checked shirt, came downstairs at seven to the sounds of convivial banter and much laughter, there was already a man seated at the table. He had a pleasant, round face; a thatch of reddish-fair hair and blue eyes alight with mischief. He rose, shook Sarah's hand as Mary introduced them and told Sarah to help herself to an array of dishes, containing a mountain of grilled sausages, lamb chops, steak; tomatoes and other vegetables; fried and scrambled eggs; toast; and two steaming pots, one containing coffee and the other tea.

He helped Sarah to a plate, asked what he could pass her, then resumed his badinage, gazing worshipfully from his own loaded plate to his hostess. 'Mary, you sweet, beautiful darling! How did you know I was starving?'

'I *wonder* …' she said with a wry smile.

'This is the *best* meal I've seen since I was here last,' he announced with boyish enthusiasm. 'When are you going to marry me?'

Mary chuckled and swiped him with her tea towel. 'When you show me that you're more in love with me than my cooking, you wicked young devil! Besides, aren't you forgetting someone?'

'If you mean Ernie, he can come, too. I'll find a back shed somewhere.'

'I am sure he will be thrilled about that—*no end*. And what about Mattie? You'd have to be a brave man to cross her. Braver than you—*or* me!' Her eyes twinkled. 'But thanks for the offer, Jim. I appreciate it.' She flicked her tea towel again. 'At its true value.'

'By the Lord Harry, you're right!' said Jim, making a grab at the end of the tea towel and grinning at the latter part of her speech. He heaved a comical sigh. 'The path of true love is ever fraught with obstacles.'

'Yes: like *my* husband and *your* cook!' Mary turned to Sarah and shrugged. 'We go through this every time he comes here.'

'Well, you shouldn't feed me so well,' he countered.

'Go on, *cheeky!*' Mary deployed her tea towel to good purpose, making him yelp. 'You'd better eat up and get out of here, before Sarah decides the Outback is peopled by a bunch of lunatics and takes the first available train out of town.'

Sarah, who had been consumed by laughter throughout the whole exchange, could only make a negating gesture between paroxysms and wondered if she would even be able to eat at all if they didn't let up. But finally, Jim applied his energy and amazing appetite to his meal, giving Sarah the respite she needed to tackle hers; though, she could only handle toast and coffee at that hour. Then they said a fond goodbye to their jovial hostess and climbed into the Range Rover parked outside—Bert having thoughtfully loaded Sarah's luggage.

'And what's your story, Sarah?' asked Jim with easy camaraderie, just after they turned off the highway and headed west on a dirt road. 'What made *you* run away to the Outback, eh?'

Sarah went red, then white and looked out her window. She hadn't expected a question as direct as that and was struck dumb. She moistened suddenly dry lips, wondering what she could say.

'Oh, have I hit a nerve? I'm sorry,' said her tormentor, with an apologetic smile. 'It was just my way of asking what brought you here. I'm a bit of a blunderer, not known for my tact.' He flicked her a serious glance. 'We're all running away from something, you know.'

'Are we?' Sarah finally found her voice and her wits. 'Well, then, what are *you* running away from?'

'Ah …' he said with an exaggerated sigh. 'I thought you'd *never* ask.'

That made her giggle, and he gave an answering smile. 'Actually, it was more that I was running *to* something.'

'Well, so am I. If you want to put it that way.'

'Oh, yes? What?'

'No,' said Sarah. 'You first.'

'All right.' He settled his shoulders against the backrest as if to set in for a yarn. 'I've always been mad keen to run an Outback station, and there is no room for two bosses at home, so my old man sent me to jackaroo for a friend of his: old Jonas Neumann, up in the gulf. That's what jackaroos are, you know, managers in training. Learning the trade, so to speak. And there was no better teacher than old Jonas … And no place like the gulf, really,' he added thoughtfully.

'What made you leave him?' Sarah was seeing a different side to this man—the *serious* overseer—though she had no doubt that his endearing sense of humour was all part of his ability to get the best out of his men.

'I would've liked to stay, but the word went out that Dev was looking for an overseer. Jonas thought I was ready to make the step up and recommended me. Yes, I got lucky,' he reminisced. 'I learnt a lot from Jonas, and Dev's a great boss.' He slanted a glance at her. 'Now it's your turn.'

Sarah had decided to tell a partial truth. 'I was orphaned quite young,' she began, adding, at his sympathetic murmur, 'I don't remember my parents. So, when I heard about this job, I decided to try and help some other orphaned children.'

'By Jove, yes, that was a sad business. Dreadful, really. Well, young Sarah, I think you're a godsend, after what's been ——' He reacted suddenly. 'Hold on to your hat!'

Before Sarah could take in what he meant, he jammed on the brakes, controlling the resultant effects with effortless command. She grabbed the panic rail, staring in amazement at the flock of emus racing across the road in front of them, as the Range Rover, with a protesting scream, almost stood on its nose to avoid a collision.

Jim looked over at Sarah with a rueful grin. 'Whew! That was lucky: no casualties. Are you okay?'

'Yes, fine. You did a good job. You know, I've never seen emus in the wild before.'

'Haven't you? There are plenty of them out here, so I'd better stop gasbagging and watch the road. We're getting closer to the channels, so the next few Ks could have a few surprises for us. Shout out if you see anything.'

Sarah agreed and glanced at her watch. They had been travelling for just over an hour and a half. Obedient to his wish for silence, she covertly studied his profile as he concentrated on guiding the vehicle over the rough and dusty road. His cheerful, happy-go-lucky disposition was at variance with his firm chin and stubborn jawline. He was a fast driver. He had proven himself to be a capable one, not only by avoiding unexpected carnage with his lightning reflexes, but by the dexterity with which he avoided the larger potholes and deep tracks without slackening speed.

They had both been silent for some time while the vehicle bounced across a brown, rolling plain of ironstone ridges, dotted here and there with flat, paler-brown claypans. Occasionally they passed reddish, flat-topped hills, worn down and ancient.

The overseer met her eyes briefly before transferring his gaze back to the road. 'How are you travelling?' he asked. 'All right, after your scare?'

'Oh, yes, thank you: Fine. I wasn't scared. You're a good driver.'

'Just lucky,' he said, giving her his friendly smile. 'It's not far to The Crossing. You'll be able to get out and stretch your legs if you like.'

'The Crossing?'

'Yes. Properly speaking, it's called Adeline Crossing, but everyone here calls it "The Crossing". On the Diamantina,' he explained.

'Is it a town?'

He shook his head. 'Couldn't call it a town. Just a pub, fuel bowsers and a store with a few essential supplies. The publican owns the lot, and the store's a room on the side of the pub. Tom Wills, his name is. We have to stop there because I have a parcel for Jenny, his wife. What do you say to a cool drink, eh? You can see the pub now.'

Sarah looked ahead to where, shimmering in the heat haze, a silvery-white object was coming into view. Everything looked so strangely distorted at a distance that it was not until they had come fairly close that the outlines of the buildings became distinct.

Close up, the pub was an unprepossessing building, rather like a shed of corrugated iron construction, covered in traces of peeling white paint. It stood on an uninviting patch of dusty, bare ground. A couple of straggly trees overhung the petrol and diesel bowsers, otherwise there appeared to be no living plants whatsoever. About five hundred yards away were some half-dozen winding, tree-filled channels. The larger one in the middle was flanked by smaller channels that weaved their way around it. *The Diamantina?* wondered Sarah. *Surely not!*

As she stepped out of the air-conditioned vehicle, Sarah was once again conscious of the almost physically overpowering force of the heat. Jim ushered her in to the relatively cool darkness of the bar and set up a shout for the publican. 'Hey, Tom! Where are you? Hurry up, man. Before we die of thirst!'

'Okay! Okay!' yelled a gravelly voice from the dark recesses of the building. 'I'm coming, Jim. Don't get yer knickers in a knot.'

'Watch it, Tom! Ladies present,' protested Jim in a shocked voice, winking cheekily at Sarah.

A short, stout man in a Hawaiian-print shirt and bermuda shorts suddenly appeared behind the bar. He grinned bashfully at Sarah and apologised, 'Sorry, Miss.'

'This is Sarah,' said Jim, introducing them. 'Medora's new governess.'

'Pleased to meet yer, Sarah. What can I do yers for, Jim?'

'I'll have a Four X and …?' He cocked an expressive eyebrow at Sarah.

'A squash, please.'

'And a squash, thanks, Tom.'

Tom disappeared into the depths of the coldroom and returned with two cans, a straw and two glasses, which he placed on the counter. The squash was cold and delicious, and Sarah thought she had never felt so thirsty. *I'm absolutely parched*, she thought. *I suppose it is the hot, dry air.*

Jim nodded towards the Range Rover. 'Got a parcel for Jenny, out there. Picked it up in Winton. Came in on the Midlander,' he said, getting up and going out.

'Gee, thanks, Jim. Jenny's been breakin' her neck to get that parcel. Dunno what's in it, but she seems to want it awful bad. She'll be real pleased.' He raised his voice: 'Jen! Hey, Jen! Come and see what we've got here!'

Jim returned with the parcel, which he placed on the counter in front of the thin, dark woman with enormous, solemn eyes who had entered the bar in his absence. 'G'day, Jen,' he said. 'I hope this is what you've been looking for?'

Her eyes lit with pleasure, and she hugged the parcel reverently to her chest; her low, cultured voice vibrating with joy as she replied, 'Oh, it will be, Jim. It will be!' Then, to Sarah's amazement, she turned without another word and vanished through a door at the back of the bar.

The publican gazed apologetically at Sarah and spoke in a soft, comforting drawl. 'Jenny's a bit shy. Doesn't see too many strangers: scared of people, really. But she'll come good once she's seen ya a couple more times, aye.'

Sarah smiled understandingly and finished her drink. Jim looked at her and said, 'Well, we'd better get going, Sarah. Won't get very far sitting here, driving the bar. The Boss'll be on the radio thinking we've broken down somewhere. See ya, Tom.'

As they crossed the channels Sarah had seen in the distance, Jim grinned at her. 'That's the Diamantina. We've just crossed it.'

'Truly? The Diamantina River? Those little channels? But which one …? Oh, you're joking!'

'Not this time.'

'But there's no water!'

The grin broadened. 'Not many of the Outback rivers have, most of the time; there are waterholes in places, but this one only runs in the wet season. And we didn't get one this year.'

'But what about the sheep and cattle? How do they survive without a wet season?'

'Well, Medora Downs has been lucky,' he replied. 'There has

been enough water from storms to grow feed, but not enough to run the channels. Some haven't been so lucky, though. They've had to either sell their stock or send them away on agistment.'

Sarah looked out the window at the golden, waving grass. She had noticed many areas with no grass cover at all, only bare brown earth and red gibbers: the unlucky places that had missed the storm rain.

After another half an hour, they crossed a white-painted grid. 'The front gate. Welcome to Medora Downs, Miss Johnston,' intoned Jim, mock-solemn, his eyes dancing.

'Thank you, Mr Barnes,' replied Sarah, in the same tone.

They looked at each other and laughed.

Sarah suddenly felt lighthearted. *What good company Jim is,* she thought as she began to take particular note of the countryside. 'I suppose it won't be long before we see the homestead?' she ventured.

He threw her a teasing glance, brimful of mischief.

He looks just like a leprechaun, she thought and giggled like a schoolgirl. *I am as bad as he is.*

Today was the first day she had felt like laughing in a long time, and the closer they came to Medora Downs, the more a burden seemed to lift from her shoulders, and the dark cloud of misery that was never far away began to recede into the distance. Suddenly, she felt a rush of gratitude for this man's innate kindness and cheerful good nature.

Grinning from ear to ear, he said, 'It is forty Ks to the homestead from the boundary grid.'

'You're joking!' gasped Sarah. 'Aren't you?'

'You'll see,' he replied. And with that she had to be content.

It did, indeed, seem a long time before the ephemeral outlines of the homestead and outbuildings mysteriously loomed on the horizon. *Every bit of forty kilometres,* she thought. For what had seemed like hours, there was nothing but open downs, waving grasses and ridges clad in reddish pebbles. Then, like magic, the buildings appeared: strange silvery ships on a shimmering ocean.

Sarah felt a quiver of excitement as they passed a group of raw, red mesa-topped hills, rising starkly out of the plain. *What a magnificent land this is,* she thought. *Such far horizons; such unexpected features rising eerily out of the vast sameness!* She loved it already—this harsh, often cruel, yet extraordinarily beautiful land. Something within her rose to meet its challenge, and curiously, she felt as if she were coming home. She shook off the impression and sat up to get a better view of the homestead, which was growing steadily nearer.

Eventually, Sarah could see a clear outline of the homestead and the verdant garden surrounding it. *How lovely it must look from the air: an exquisite, brightly coloured jewel in a setting of grey, brown and ochre. Oh, how much Wendy would appreciate it!*

The Range Rover crackled to a halt on the gravelled circular drive, in front of an imposing entrance as a bent and bowed figure rose from one of the luxuriant garden beds and turned towards them.

'That's Reuben, the gardener,' said Jim as they alighted. 'He created this garden—carved it out of an ironstone ridge—tends it on his own and loves it like a baby. He may look blind, but they say there's never a weed that escapes his eye. Doesn't miss much else around the station, either, come to think of it! Well? What do you reckon?'

'Oh, it's *gorgeous*', breathed Sarah as her eyes drank in the orderly riot of colour before her. 'A feast of colour!'

Bougainvillea of all shapes, sizes and colours waved brilliant masses of petals in the autumn breeze. They tumbled over the stone walls of the garden; climbed lovingly up the verandah posts; stood alone and proud, trained magnificently into weeping standards; or clipped into thick bushes. Almost without exception, their leaves were hidden by the massed petals of red, white, apricot, orange, pink and purple. Flowering trees and shrubs, hibiscus, frangipanni, plumbago, bird of paradise, oleander and others Sarah did not know were set out to show to best advantage, each surrounded by a small bed of profusely blooming succulents, petunias and other groundcover plants.

As if this wasn't enough, bordering the circular drive, the house and the stone walls, were formal flowerbeds similarly filled with the hardy flowering plants—vinca, marigolds, zinnias, petunias, nasturtiums and many others—all vying colourfully for attention. And setting all these off to perfection: a dazzling green lawn, rolled and clipped to within an inch of its life; Reuben's pride and joy, and the envy of all who set eyes on it. Larger, hardy trees and shrubs surrounded the entire garden wall, an effective barrier from the worst of wind and sun.

In the centre of the circular drive, Sarah was surprised to see a small fountain playing into a lily pond: an oasis, indeed, and rarely to be seen in an area where water was valued much more highly than gold. Sarah later found that a large permanent hole in the river with a well sunk beside it allowed this extravagance.

Over the years, Reuben had received many tempting offers

from envious station owners, Jim had told her. But he had remained true to his first love: his masterpiece—his own gem of creation—the Medora Downs' garden.

Jim called him over, 'Hey, Reub, come here. Got someone you'd like to meet.'

The old gardener arched his back, rubbed his lumbar region with gnarled old hands and shuffled over to greet them. The corded sinews of his arms and neck stood out like pieces of rope beneath the burnt, leathery skin. 'G'day, Jim,' he said in a tired voice.

'Reub, I'd like you to meet Sarah: our new governess.'

Sarah looked into the wizened, walnut face; the faded, rheumy eyes; and saw past them to the beauty-loving, artistic soul beneath; because, in his own way, Reuben was as much an artist as Michelangelo or da Vinci.

He removed his battered old felt hat and spoke politely, 'How do you do, Missy. Glad to have you here.'

'Your garden,' said Sarah, 'it's so beautiful! Jim says you do it all yourself. How wonderful!'

Reuben was not proof against the admiration in the shining blue eyes or the angelic fairness of the slight, graceful figure. He darkened under his tan and said gruffly, 'Thanks, Missy. You remind me of a flower yourself. Well, I gotta finish this bed. Take her inside, Jim, out of the heat.' He turned and shuffled away.

'Yes, and that'll be enough of your flirting, too, you old devil,' said Jim, grinning after him.

'Jim! That's outrageous!' protested Sarah, but as Reuben, with great dignity, had pretended not to hear, she said no more. The last she saw of him was his bent old back as he continued to plant out his seedlings. Sarah felt a surge of fondness for this dear old man, who could not only create, but maintain such magnificent beauty in the teeth of the harsh, unyielding climate of the Outback.

'Do you know,' said Sarah, surprised, 'it isn't as hot here.'

'No, it's not,' agreed Jim. 'It's the effect of the garden. It creates a microclimate.'

They turned to enter the house. It, too, was magnificent in its own way. Built in colonial style; surrounded by wide, cool verandahs; trimmed with wrought-iron lace onto which double doors from every room opened. The house was a T shape with a wide hall down the centre of each part. It was very large; the main part being constructed of wood with an iron roof. The walls of the kitchen and four other rooms, forming a large part of the stem of the T, were built of interlocking stonework, two feet thick. Sarah was later told that the stone part of the house had been built by the first Mainwaring to settle here, over one hundred years ago. The rest had been added by succeeding generations; the last about thirty years ago, if one didn't count the bathrooms that had been recently modernised and the air-conditioning ducted to all rooms.

Sarah followed Jim into the cool dimness of the main hall. As her eyes adjusted from the bright sunlight, she was conscious of polished wood floors; thick-piled rugs; a carved antique hallstand; chest and chairs; light, panelled walls with an old-fashioned picture rail and carved layer-glass light fittings.

'Yoo-hoo, Aunty! Mrs Brennan,' called Jim.

'Coming, Jim,' answered a woman's voice—high-pitched and

youthful—as a tiny, silver-haired lady with bright, expressive eyes entered the hall through one of its many doors. She smiled warmly as she came towards them, holding out her hands. Sarah did not think it could have been she who had answered Jim's call. The voice seemed to belong to a much younger woman. 'You must be Sarah,' she said in the same high, girlish voice. 'Welcome to Medora Downs, my dear. I hope the trip hasn't tired you too much? Jim, you naughty boy! I hope you have been looking after Sarah?' she added, with mock severity.

'Of course I have, Aunty,' he assured her, grinning broadly. 'You know me!'

'I do! That's why I asked,' she said, twinkling, and turned to Sarah. 'Has he?'

'Oh, yes, Mrs Brennan. He has been very kind.' Sarah almost stammered in surprise.

'Well, I'm glad to hear it. And you can call me Aunty or Aunt Fay, if you prefer it, like everyone else does. I hate being called Mrs Brennan because I'm a Mainwaring—first, last and always.'

'Amen,' said Jim. 'Back up a little, Aunty. You're frightening Sarah.'

'Am I?' She looked at Sarah, the twinkle more pronounced.

Sarah shook her head.

'Mattie has some tea and sandwiches for you.'

'Now, that's someone who *will* frighten you …' muttered Jim under his breath.

'Not at all,' said Aunt Fay, straight-faced. 'Just because your palaver cuts no ice with her.' She mouthed behind her hand to Sarah: 'She hates men,' adding in a normal voice as she led the way to a spacious sitting room, 'Mattie regards tea and sandwiches as a cure for all types of fatigue and stress.'

'I'll be off then, Aunty,' said Jim. 'Where's the Boss?'

'Out at number fourteen bore. Mattie has packed a smoko for you boys. You might pick it up in the kitchen as you go.'

'Will do, Aunty. See you later. See you later, Sarah. I'll catch up with you soon. I'll leave your bags on the verandah, outside your room.' A cheery wave, a carefree grin and he was gone.

Sarah felt a little strange and lonely at his leaving, although she could not but respond to the warm friendliness of the woman beside her.

'Won't you sit down, my dear? When we've had our tea, I'll show you your room and the bathroom where you can freshen up and rest until lunch. And then, this afternoon, you can meet the children and explore your domain. How does that sound?'

'Wonderful!' said Sarah, who was about to speak again when a door at the far side of the sitting room opened to reveal a massive woman with a loaded tray, which she set down on the coffee table.

'Mattie, I'd like you to meet Sarah Johnston. Sarah, this is Mattie: our wonderful cook.'

The big woman straightened, and Sarah found herself looking into a pair of brilliant dark eyes, full of character and expression. Mattie carefully scrutinised Sarah for a nerve-racking moment, then apparently satisfied with what she saw, held out her hand, speaking in a rich, mellow voice: 'Glad to meet you, Sarah. Thanks for the compliment, Mrs Fay.' She smiled at Sarah. 'The kettle's always on in the kitchen, Sarah, any time you want to pop in for a cuppa.'

Sarah thanked her and thought what a remarkably pretty face she had, especially when she smiled.

Mattie turned and surged out of the room, unusually light on her feet for one so large.

'She likes you,' whispered Aunt Fay, beginning to pour the tea. 'Not everyone gets an invitation like that, let me tell you.' She passed Sarah her cup, indicating milk and sugar, then stirred her own, saying, half to herself, 'We only have two staff here now. It was different, once.' Recollecting herself she added, 'Sue, our housemaid, is the other one. I try to help them where I can, but this house is a lot of work.'

Sarah glanced around at the gleaming wood floors; the carved, antique furniture and agreed that it must be so. 'I'll look after my room and the schoolroom and help where I can,' she offered.

'Thank you, my dear. It may be necessary from time to time, but mostly we get it done.'

'I'd like to do my own room, anyway,' said Sarah, firmly.

'Oh, you *do* sound like a governess!' The older woman's eyes twinkled, surprisingly blue and youthful and always ready to appreciate a joke. 'Very well, my dear,' she said, proffering a plate. 'Do have a sandwich. They are quite delicious. And we shall forget about such mundane topics as housekeeping.'

Sarah took one and bit into it, suddenly realising how hungry she was, since excitement had prevented her from swallowing more than a cup of coffee and a slice of toast at breakfast.

Aunt Fay was speaking again: 'I have arranged for us to lunch together privately, Sarah, so that I can tell you a little of the children's background. The men are lunching at the bore, today. Mattie and Sue are looking after the children this morning and will give them lunch in the kitchen.' She was silent for a moment, then continued, 'The children did have a nanny ...' Her face puckered in distaste. 'Let us just say that the arrangement ... was not a success. So, you may have some extra problems to overcome ...' Her voice trailed off. Suddenly, she was brisk again. 'Well, if you're ready, my dear, I will show you to your room. We will talk later.'

Sarah followed her down a passage that led off the main hall between the sitting room and the formal dining room that gave access to all the rooms on the eastern wing. On the other side of the main hall were the breakfast room and a lounge large enough to double as a ballroom. A similar breezeway to the one in which Sarah found herself ran the length of the western arm of the T.

Aunt Fay stopped at one of the doors, threw it open and gestured to Sarah to enter. Sarah looked around the charming room and gave a gasp of pure happiness. Lacy curtains hung at the windows and decorated the high canopied four-poster bed. The bedspread matched the curtains, sheepskin rugs were scattered on the highly polished floor and the carved furniture gleamed in the light from the window and double doors that led onto the verandah. 'What a *lovely* room! Thank you.'

'Well, I hope you'll be happy here. Sue spent quite a while yesterday doing out the room for you. She unearthed the bed hangings from somewhere and washed and ironed them, so they'd be fresh. I'll leave you now, dear. Lunch will be served at one o'clock in the breakfast room. Someone will show you the way.'

Twenty minutes later, Sarah, refreshed from a shower, sat in the padded bedroom chair, considering all that had transpired during the morning. She loved her room. It gave her a feeling of peace, and the idea that she had come home washed over her again. In fact, the whole house had the same effect, as though it were a house that had known much love and laughter over the years, as well as its tragedies. She still had not met the elusive Mr Devin Mainwaring, her employer, and wondered, for the umpteenth time, what he would be like. If he were as easy to get on with as Aunt Fay seemed to be, it would be all right.

Sarah gave a sudden start. Was that someone scratching at the door? Checking her watch, she saw that it was nowhere near one o'clock. She relaxed once more. No, there it was again! A hesitant scratching. Crossing to the door, she flung it open.

Two children, who had jumped back like startled fawns, stood, looking up at her, round-eyed with apprehension. The little girl, who had scratched at the door, was about six years old, and a smaller boy, clutching a large, battered teddy bear, stood behind her.

The little girl, whose huge, dark eyes wore an expression of anxiety mixed with determination, spoke in a high, nervous voice. 'Are you a nanny?' she asked breathlessly.

The little boy clutched his teddy tightly and kept his large, solemn eyes fixed on Sarah's face as he waited with bated breath for her reply.

'No, I'm a governess,' she answered. 'Would you like to come in, and we'll talk about it?'

The little boy breathed a tiny sigh of relief and slightly loosened his grip on the teddy. He advanced a little way into the room and peered up at Sarah. 'Do you smack kids who cry?' he asked, in a gruff little voice.

'No,' said Sarah. 'I usually cuddle them.'

He turned away. 'Don't like cuddles,' he muttered, almost inaudibly.

'I only cuddle people if they want me to,' Sarah assured him gravely, her lips twitching.

He gave another tiny sigh and allowed his teddy to trail on the floor, holding him by the arm, his eyes once more fixed on Sarah.

'Is your name Miss Johnston?' asked the little girl, braver now.

'Yes, but you can call me Sarah. What are your names?'

'I'm Naomi and he's Adam.'

Adam spoke suddenly, 'This is Sam.' He held out his teddy.

Sarah walked forward and, kneeling down near Adam, shook the teddy's moth-eaten paw. 'How do you do, Sam?' she said, and then held out her hand to Adam. 'How do you do, Adam?

The little boy gravely shook her hand.

'How do you do, Naomi?'

The little girl replied politely, then returned to another pressing matter. 'Are you going to teach us to read? In the schoolroom?' she breathed, in awe.

Sarah nodded.

'Yes, that's what Uncle Dev said.' Naomi looked at her brother. 'What about Adam?'

Sarah nodded again.

Then Adam spoke up: 'What about Sam?'

'Yes, Sam, too,' said Sarah, straight-faced.

'And are we going to do School of the Air?'

They were suddenly interrupted by a raised voice, 'Naomi! Adam! Where *are* you two? Mattie's got your lunch ready. Come *on!*'

Naomi looked a little guilty. 'That's Sue,' she said. 'We're supposed to be in the rumpus room.'

Sarah put her head around the door into the hall. 'The children are here with me,' she said, smiling.

Sue, a slim woman of about thirty, similar in build and colouring to Sarah, wore an expression of anxiety on her thin, sallow face. She smiled in return. 'Thank Goodness! You must be Sarah. How do you do? I'm Sue.'

'We said that, too,' said Naomi. 'And told her our names.'

'Did you, darling?' asked Sue, stroking her hair. 'That's good.'

'Thank you for the lovely job you did on my room,' said Sarah, smiling warmly.

'That's all right. A pretty room makes all the difference, I reckon. Come on, you two,' she added, holding out her hands to the children.

'Goodbye, Sarah,' they chorused. Then, each taking a hand, they skipped away with Sue.

Sarah stood for a moment, looking after them—a thoughtful expression on her face—before going in search of the breakfast room.

Chapter Five

Aunt Fay and Sarah were chatting over their coffee, having finished a light lunch of cold meats, delicious salads, and fruit and cheese.

Aunt Fay took a deep breath and became serious. 'I have a lot to tell you, my dear,' she said. 'And I don't know where to start. As you know, the children are orphans. Their parents, Devin's brother and his wife, were killed last December in a light-plane crash.' Her eyes clouded with pain, and she swallowed before continuing, 'They were going on a second honeymoon, which is why the children weren't with them. One learns to be thankful for such mercies,' she added. 'It was our own plane, and Darcy was flying it himself. He was a very good pilot. They were over some rough country to the east of here and sent out a mayday call that the engine was on fire: That was the last anyone heard from them. They crashed into the side of a mountain.

'The children were devastated; we all were. Devin, in particular, idolised his brother. They got on so well. He was an older version of Dev, very tall and handsome. Jane, his wife, was small and dark, very vital: a warm, loving wife and mother.' Her eyes glittered with unshed tears. 'I am afraid nothing has been quite the same since then.'

Sarah made a sympathetic sound, but Aunt Fay put up her hand.

'The children cried themselves to sleep every night, missing their parents dreadfully.' Aunt Fay took another deep breath. 'So, we got a nanny. She was an older woman and had been recommended by the people over at Nairobi.' Her normally soft expression hardened. 'The children became more and more tense and nervy: Naomi in tears all the time; Adam in uncontrollable tantrums. We thought it was reaction to the loss of their parents. Finally, we discovered that, far from giving them the love and attention they needed, the woman was smacking them for crying and locked them in their rooms, while she sat, reading, in hers.

'Naturally, Dev packed her off as soon as he found out what was going on. But, I am afraid, the damage had been done. The children could not bear the sound of the word "nanny", and the mention of another one produced such fear! Which was why we decided on a governess.' She smiled. 'A very special one. The only thing is …' Her brows knit with worry. 'I don't know how they will accept you, just at first, after the trauma of the nanny.'

'I think I can set your mind at rest there,' said Sarah, a little quiver in her voice. 'I have already met the children, and once we'd established beyond doubt that I was not a nanny, but a governess who did not smack children for crying, we got on very well.'

'Oh, for goodness' sake!' exclaimed Aunt Fay. 'And how did

this come about?'

Sarah told her of the morning's events, laughing a little as she did so.

'The enterprising little devils!' said the older woman, her eyes dancing. She leant across the table to press Sarah's hand warmly. 'I knew the instant I saw you that you were right for them.'

Sarah blushed bright pink. 'Oh, I do hope so,' she said.

'By the way, you may have noticed how attached Adam is to his teddy? That has only come about since he lost his parents. For about six months before that, the teddy had been relegated to the toy cupboard.'

'Yes, I did notice. And I thought as much. Poor little things!' she added, impulsively.

'Indeed.' The older woman started. 'Oh! There is one more thing I must tell you: Since being locked in his room by that dreadful woman, Adam has developed a phobia of sleeping alone. Naomi has a twin room, so he sleeps in the second bed. We have been trying to encourage him back to his own room, but with little success, I am afraid.'

Sarah thought for a moment. 'Would it be possible to rearrange or redecorate his room?'

'Yes, of course. Both his and Naomi's could do with a refurbish. What are you thinking?'

'Just that if we could involve him in redecorating his room according to his own ideas and taste, it really will become his. Then, in the long term, as he gains more confidence, he will want to sleep there.'

'What an excellent idea!' Aunt Fay sat back and smiled at her.

'Well? Shall we go and resume your acquaintance with the children?'

Sarah agreed with alacrity and rose to follow Aunt Fay to the rumpus room.

'Hello, Sarah. Hello, Aunty,' yelled the children, jumping up from the model farmyard they'd been playing with.

'Hello, children,' said Aunt Fay, smiling. 'Why don't you take Sarah and show her the schoolroom?'

'Can we?' Two eager little faces peeped up at Sarah; two little hands crept into hers.

'Come on, Sarah,' said Naomi. 'We won't let you get lost.'

Adam suddenly pulled his hand away and ran to where his teddy lay beside the farmyard. Scooping him up by the paw, he raced back to Sarah and took her hand again. 'Sam wants to show Sarah the schoolroom,' he explained with great solemnity.

Aunt Fay, watching the trust with which the children chattered to Sarah as they proceeded down the hall, suddenly made a wry face and whipped out her hanky.

§

It was not until later that evening, long after dinner, that Sarah finally met her employer. She was relaxing in a comfortable chair in the sitting room, reading a glossy magazine. Aunt Fay, close by, was occupied with her exquisite embroidery, when they heard the sound of voices—one deep and soft, the other, unmistakably Sue's—outside the door.

'Ah …' said Aunt Fay, raising her eyes from her work. 'Devin, at last. And the tea trolley,' she added, laying aside the doily she had been working on.

The door opened, and Sue pushed the tea trolley into the room. A tall, broad-shouldered, dark-haired man stood framed in the doorway behind her, and Sarah caught her breath at the penetrating grey eyes set under strongly marked, arched brows; the sun-browned, finely modelled planes of his face; strong chin and well-built lines.

In those first few confused moments, Sarah received an impression of quiet strength, controlled power and an aura of vitality. Instinctively, she knew that this was a man who would always be in charge—could always be relied upon.

He moved forward into the room and greeted his aunt.

'Dev, what happened to you?' asked Aunt Fay, a little querulously. 'I have been very worried.'

'A problem with number twelve bore, Aunty,' he said, easily. 'We were just checking it on our way home from number fourteen, when we noticed a leak in one of the outlets from the tank, so we thought we'd better fix it straightaway. There was no need to worry,' he assured her and turned cool grey eyes on Sarah.

'Devin, this is Sarah Johnston.'

'How do you do?' he asked with chilly reserve. Then reversed the effect by adding, with a twinkle, 'Call me Dev. Aunty only uses my full name when I'm in trouble.'

Aunt Fay made a tut-tutting noise while she poured the tea, and Sarah almost lost her voice, such a strange effect he had on her when she met his eyes. She murmured a conventional reply and thankfully received the cup that Aunt Fay was holding out to her.

Her employer was speaking again: 'I am sorry I was unable to meet you in Winton. I trust that Jim looked after you?'

'Oh, yes. Very well … Thank you.'

'Good. Tomorrow, in my office, after breakfast, we will discuss the terms of your employment and the children's education.' He turned to his aunt. 'I'm sorry I can't stay. I have some invoices to attend to. Mattie has sent a tray to my office.' He bade them goodnight, his light eyes unreadable as they rested briefly on Sarah.

For some reason, Sarah hardly knew why, the room seemed to lose some of its brightness with his exit.

§

It was the week before Easter, and Sarah and the children were in the schoolroom, fully absorbed in making Easter cards for Aunt Fay, Devin, Mattie, Jim, Sue and Reuben. Sarah had drawn some Easter bunnies, eggs and chickens, and the children were busy colouring them in, before cutting them out and pasting them on folded pieces of thick drawing paper.

A soft knock fell on the door, and there was a scuffle as the children hurriedly tried to hide their work before Sarah called, 'Come in!'

Devin appeared in the doorway. Sarah wondered why a room seemed to suddenly become smaller the minute he entered it. It wasn't really his size—he was tall and well-built, but not excessively so. She decided it must be a sort of presence.

'Go away, Uncle Dev! We're making a surprise,' commanded Naomi, trying to cover her work with her hands.

'Yes, a surprise,' echoed Adam, solemn as ever.

'Naomi, please don't be rude. We will still have time to make it after we talk to Uncle Dev,' reproved Sarah.

Naomi flushed but looked Devin fearlessly in the eye. 'I am sorry, Uncle Dev,' she said.

'That's all right, my pet. I could sense something momentous was going on when I came in, and I'll leave you to it.' He turned to Sarah. 'I really wanted to speak to you privately for a minute, if I may?'

'Of course,' said Sarah, her heart beating unevenly. *What can it be?* 'I'm going out for a few minutes, children. I want you to carry on with your colouring, and then I'll help with the cutting out when I return. Is that okay?'

The children nodded but kept their work well hidden until Devin had followed Sarah out of the room.

'Let's go into my office, shall we?' he said, indicating a door just a few steps farther down the hall. 'I don't think we need worry about the children losing concentration for a little while yet.' He ushered Sarah into the room and shut the door, gesturing for her to sit down in one of the padded leather armchairs and followed suit. 'Sarah, I should have spoken to you before this, but I've just realised that this weekend will be Easter. Would you like to take the holiday and spend it somewhere else? There would still be time to arrange air transport for you, if you wish.'

Sarah hesitated for only a second. She wanted to see her friends, tell them what a wonderful place she'd found, but she knew it would be madness to put herself back within David's reach. 'If you don't mind, Dev, I think I'd like to stay here. My friends are in Sydney, and I feel that it is just too far to go for such a short time.'

'That's all right, then.' Devin appeared to be satisfied with her answer and seemed about to close the interview.

'Um, there is just one thing …' Sarah hesitated again.

'Go on,' he said, giving her all his attention.

'The children would like to have a party on Easter Sunday. Is that okay?'

Devin smiled. A heart-stopping, beautiful smile that left her feeling slightly breathless. 'That would be lovely,' he said warmly, suddenly abandoning his cool reserve, the way he had unexpectedly done once or twice before. 'By the way, Aunty has some chocolate Easter eggs for the Easter bunny to leave in the night. Get her to give them to you.' He rose and held the door open for her. 'See you at the party, then,' he said, smiling, and walked rapidly away.

Sarah was left feeling stunned. Irritable with herself for her inexplicable reaction to her employer's presence, she mentally shook herself and retraced her steps to the schoolroom to give her pupils the good news. *Jo and Wendy would giggle and tell me it's because it is the first time I've met a real man,* she thought. *And maybe it's true.*

The next few days were fully occupied with preparations for Easter. The children spent the better part of their time in the kitchen under the guidance of Mattie, and helped by Sarah, in making chocolate eggs; marzipan sweets in the shapes of bunnies, chickens and eggs; and homemade chocolates filled with glacé cherries, caramel and marshmallow.

At other times, Sarah read them the story of Easter from a

huge old book of illustrated children's bible stories that she found in the schoolroom bookcase. They learnt why Good Friday was a time of sad remembrance and Easter Sunday was a day of celebration to Christian people the world over.

On Good Friday morning, they all went to Ilona Downs for an Easter Mass. The priest, who was a pilot and visited his flock in his vast parish in a light plane, landed at the airstrip just as they arrived. Denominations did not count out here: everyone went to worship whenever there was a visiting cleric, no matter to what church they nominally belonged.

After mass, morning tea was served on the wide verandah. And while the adults chatted, all the children played in the garden on the swings and trampoline.

Back at Medora Downs, lunch was a quiet affair. Mattie served delicious salmon quiche and delectable salads. Devin seemed preoccupied, saying little, and soon left the table to check on one of the young horses that had hurt itself earlier in the day.

The children were impatient for Sunday to arrive, and most of Saturday was spent painting designs on hard-boiled eggs and making decorations and party hats for the Easter party. Naomi had spoken shyly to Reuben, and he had promised her as many flowers from the garden as was necessary to decorate the room and table.

On Saturday night, as Sarah tucked them into bed, they sighed happily at the thought of tomorrow. Sarah read again the story of Easter from *The Book of Children's Bible Stories*. Then, as their eyelids drooped, she crept away to her own room. She waited another hour before arranging a little basket of chocolate Easter eggs beside each bed and tiptoeing away.

Easter Sunday dawned bright and clear. Shrieks of discovery issued from the children's room as each found their mysterious basket of eggs with fluffy chickens perched on the handle. They came tumbling into Sarah's room.

'Look, Sarah! Look!' squeaked Naomi.

'Goodness! Where did they come from?' asked Sarah, a smile tugging her lips.

'Here's the card.'

'Happy Easter Day from the Easter bunny,' read Sarah.

'Ooh!' breathed Naomi.

But Adam looked suddenly sad. 'He forgot Sam,' he said.

'Perhaps he thought that you might like to share yours with Sam,' suggested Sarah. And Adam's gloomy expression brightened.

After breakfast the children ceremoniously handed out their Easter cards to everyone amid much admiring exclamation over their handiwork. Then began the all-important task of decorating the dining table for the party. After that there was just enough time to change into their party clothes before helping Mattie carry in the lunch dishes.

Mattie had excelled herself. There was a creatively decorated ham, roast chickens and, of course, an array of her famous salads. The sideboard was creaking under the weight of assorted tarts, gateaux, cheesecakes, sweets, fruit salads and trifles. And her *pièce de résistance*—a magnificent pavlova.

The guests had arrived and were being entertained by Aunt Fay and Devin in the lounge. Bill Richmond had come over, together with John and Elisabeth Andrews from Ilona Downs, their three children and their governess, Jacqui. Naomi had specially requested Jim to come—since he was a prime favourite with her—and he was busy making the punch.

When lunch was ready, Adam went to the door of the lounge and rang a tiny silver and crystal bell. In a well-rehearsed tone, he announced importantly, 'Lunch is served, Ladies and Gen'lemen!' Only stumbling over the last word and looking so anxious and solemn that most of the guests could not help a fond smile or two as they moved obediently to the door.

Naomi was waiting in the dining room to hand out paper baskets of homemade chocolates and marzipan sweets and a party hat to the guests as they filed in. When everyone was seated, a short Easter prayer was recited by Naomi, and the party began.

After lunch the two governesses took the children into the rumpus room to play party games. Some of the adults, who had come to watch, soon joined in, and a hilarious time was had for the next few hours.

Later that evening, long after the last guest had departed and the children had gone, exhausted, to bed, happily declaring it to have been the best party in the world, Sarah was having coffee in the lounge with Aunt Fay and Devin, listening to one of Aunt Fay's soothing records and generally relaxing. She was startled to see the door swing slowly open, apparently of its own accord. Then, two small, dressing-gowned figures appeared in the aperture: Naomi carrying a large, brightly wrapped parcel; and Adam clutching a long, white envelope.

'For you,' he said breathlessly, thrusting it at Sarah.

She took out a beautiful Easter card and opened it to read the message: '"Happy Easter, Sarah. From Adam, Naomi, Aunt Fay and Devin." Oh, *thank* you. How lovely!' She took the parcel Naomi was holding out to her and undid the wrapping to reveal a rich array of chocolate Easter eggs, presided over by a gorgeous pink, fluffy rabbit.

Sarah felt a lump rise in her throat. She hugged the children and glanced towards Aunt Fay, surprising a knowing and slightly wavering smile. Looking up, she met Devin's eyes and almost flinched at their hard, brooding expression, before he turned away and went to the record player to select another song. *Does he dislike me?* she wondered. *To look at me like that?* A chill rippled down her back. Sarah felt exactly as though someone had just thrown cold water over her. When a moment before, she had been so warm and happy—so fulfilled. She managed to smile and say in a slightly shaky voice, 'Thank you so much, everyone. I will cherish my Easter bunny.' Then, excusing herself, she took her two lovable charges back to bed and retired to her room.

It was long before Sarah slept. She was haunted by that hard, daunting expression in Devin's grey eyes each time she closed her own, wondering what she had possibly done to deserve it.

Chapter Six

Sarah had been at Medora Downs for almost six weeks—totally involved with the children, loving the relaxed lifestyle of the Outback—when she realised, with dismay, that she had not written a word to Wendy and Jo since she had dashed off a short note to tell them of her safe arrival with a promise to write more fully, later on. She resolved to sit down that very night and write them a long, newsy letter. She wrote:

Dear Wendy and Jo,

I am enjoying life in the Outback very much. The children, Naomi and Adam, are the dearest little things, and I adore looking after them.

Devin's aunt, who runs the domestic side of Medora Downs, is an absolute darling, and she and I are fast friends, already. I have learnt quite a lot about the people and history of the station from her, since we always have tea together while the children take their afternoon nap.

This is a magnificent house, and you should just see my room!

There followed a description of the house and garden.

I will give you a quick sketch of my fellow occupants of the homestead: Aunt Fay; Mattie, the cook; Sue, the housemaid; Devin, the Boss; and, of course, the children, Naomi and Adam. It seems that, having lost both their parents, as you know, the children had been mistreated by the nanny who was engaged, so that is how I come to be here.

Naomi is an elfin-faced, quicksilver creature, already showing great beauty and charm (like her mother, I am told). She is also very intelligent and a joy to teach, very advanced for her six years. Adam, at four, is a sturdy little boy with enormous, solemn eyes and is absolutely lovable. He has a teddy called Sam that he takes with him everywhere. Heaven help us if ever Sam gets lost!

Mattie has been here for over twenty years. According to Aunt Fay, she was only a slip of a girl when she came and so pretty. Since she weighs about twenty stone now, that's hard to believe, but she's still very pretty with the most incredibly beautiful and expressive eyes. All the stockmen for miles around used to come courting, but she would have nothing to do with any of them. Apparently, she was jilted once in her teens and became a confirmed man hater. The only men she tolerates at all are Devin and old Reuben, the gardener. And we think that's because she has known Dev since he was a little boy of nine, and the fact that Reuben produces the raw materials for her fantastic vegetable dishes. (You should taste her salads!)

Sue is kind and capable but is a very private person and keeps to herself a lot. Aunt Fay says that she was born here at Medora Downs—the daughter of the then head stockman. She left home at sixteen, made a bad marriage (of which she never talks) and turned up here again four years later with a small son. That was eleven or twelve years ago, and she has been here ever since.

I haven't met her son, Colin. He is at boarding school. When he finishes, he will be apprenticed to Reuben, who has been here for nearly fifty years. He is an amazing old man, and so ugly he is gorgeous! Anyway, Colin apparently shows a lot of aptitude for gardening and has always followed Reuben around since he first came here.

And now we come to Aunt Fay herself. A Mainwaring of Medora Downs—Dev's father's only sister—she had married a man much older than herself, but unfortunately the marriage was not happy, her husband succumbing to uncontrollable fits of temper as he grew older. So, it is perhaps with relief that she returned, a youngish widow, to Medora Downs to take care of her boys, Darcy and Devin, when their parents died. She insists that we call her Aunt Fay or Aunty because she doesn't wish to be known by her married name. There is a whisper that she married on the rebound because her fiancé broke her heart when he returned from the war with a

French wife, but I haven't heard that from Aunt Fay herself.

Dev's parents died when he was nine. They were drowned trying to cross the flooded Diamantina. (A contradiction in terms when I tell you that, at the moment, it is bone dry except for a few waterholes.) Dev's mother's horse slipped as they were crossing the river on the way home from shifting some sheep to higher ground, and she was swept away down the river. Dev's father galloped down to a bend in the river and went in after her, but tragically, they were both lost. Anyway, Aunt Fay came to look after them and has been here ever since.

And now, the description you've been waiting for! My employer! Well, in the words of the old cliché: he's tall, dark and handsome with dark brown, almost black hair and grey eyes. And he's the undisputed boss of this outfit! He's remote and embittered against women because his heart was broken years ago by some neighbour's daughter. However, he always treats me with courtesy, but I rarely see him, except when he pops in to visit the children for a few minutes whenever time permits.

There's something about him, though, that makes one feel safe, somehow, when he's around. The children adore him. But, don't worry, I am not about to lose my heart to him. Don't forget to envy me as I sit on the verandah, graciously sipping tea, while you're bustling like ants along the concrete pavements of the city!

Sarah finished her letter and walked out onto the verandah into the moonlight. She caught her breath at the beauty of the night. How lovely everything looked in the pale silvery light; the trees making black, lacy patterns against the deep-blue sky. She heard the sound of movement and spun around, straining every nerve to see into the darkness of the verandah.

'It's all right, Sarah.' A quiet, deep voice spoke out of the shadows. 'It's me—Dev. Come and sit down.'

Sarah breathed out a sigh of relief. 'Oh,' she said. 'It's you.'

As she approached, she saw he was sitting in a comfortable squatter's chair by the wrought-iron table where she and Aunt Fay often had their afternoon tea.

Devin indicated a similar chair beside him. 'Sit here,' he said in the tone of one used to command. 'How are you?'

'Well, thank you, Dev. Fine.' Why did she, all at once, have to feel so breathless and inept?

He gestured to a covered jug on the table. 'Like a drink?'

'No … thanks.' *What is the matter with me?* she wondered. *He'll think I'm an idiot!*

There was a short, surprisingly comfortable silence. He said softly, 'I want to thank you for what you have done for my … brother's children, Sarah.' His voice deepened slightly after the pause. She did not know how to answer and was relieved when he continued: 'They have returned to the happy, carefree children they were before the … accident. Believe me, words cannot express the depth of my gratitude for your loving care of them.'

Sarah felt overwhelmed by some emotion that she dimly recognised as joy. Devin no longer seemed so cold and remote;

he had, at least, shared some of his feelings with her, something that she sensed was very difficult for him—even if they concerned the children and nothing else. Besides, Naomi and Adam were the most important people in the world, just now. They were like delicate young plants: if they were neglected and mistreated in any way, the resulting scars would affect them their whole lives.

She suddenly found her voice, 'But it's easy, Dev. You see, I love them. They are so easy to love.'

'Yes,' he said quietly. 'I can see that you do. I think you find it easy because you are such a loving person, yourself, Sarah. We were so lucky that you came to us.'

Sarah could hardly believe her ears. Could this be the cool, aloof man she was used to, speaking to her in such a way? Her heart fluttered wildly; she was only thankful that the shadows hid her hot face. Her whole being was suffused with warmth and joy at his praise.

After another companionable silence, Devin spoke again: 'By the way, do you ride?'

Sarah was a little surprised at the sudden change of subject. 'Yes, I do. We all learnt at boarding school as part of the curriculum, although I haven't been on a horse for a couple of years, now.'

'No matter,' he said. 'Once you've learnt to ride, you never forget—even if the muscles protest a little, at first. How about coming down to the stables in the morning for a ride, then?'

'Oh, yes. That will be lovely!' said Sarah, instantly.

A thought struck him. 'Have you your riding gear?'

Sarah mentally blessed her visit to the saddlery, engineered by

Jo. 'Yes, I brought my jodhpurs and riding boots.'

'Good girl. Well, off to bed with you now, and I'll see you in the kitchen at a quarter to six for a quick cuppa before we ride.' He rose and wished her goodnight.

Sarah walked to her room in a happy daze. He had said such lovely things to her. Then he had ordered her to bed like a child, and still, she didn't mind. *Once a boss, always a boss,* she thought with fond amusement. Somehow, it was easy to obey his orders without question or resentment. He was *that* kind of man. It wasn't that she'd got used to meekly obeying David. He was nothing like David. Her face puckered with concentration as she tried and failed to grasp the subtle differences between them.

Later, as she drifted off to sleep, she could still hear his deep, soft voice saying, 'You are such a loving person, yourself, Sarah.'

§

The next morning, Sarah was awake very early. She watched the sky slowly lighten and become tinged with red. Quickly, she dressed in her jodhpurs, riding boots and a cool cotton shirt. She tied her hair up into a ponytail, which made her look young and vulnerable, and went to the kitchen.

Devin, tall and broad-shouldered in his blue countryman shirt and moleskins, was making toast when she entered the large, stone-walled kitchen. He greeted her with a smile and a nod towards the huge scrubbed-pine table, which was already set with china and cutlery.

Sarah returned his greeting and sat down, looking about her. One entire wall was taken up by a vast, old-fashioned iron range with an open fireplace beside it, swept bare and obviously unused. Set into the cupboards on the adjoining wall was a modern gas wall oven and below it, on the benchtop, were six large hotplates. Beside them, a double sink was placed under a window, which looked out over the vegetable garden. In the hazy distance, Sarah could see the tree-lined channels of the Diamantina. A sturdy door in the wall opposite the old range led to a cavernous pantry and a coldroom where perishables were kept. A second door opened onto a covered walkway that led to the men's dining room.

Devin set the teapot and a pile of toast on the table and smiled at Sarah. 'Tea?' he asked, picking up the pot again.

'Please.'

'You look like a schoolgirl with your hair like that,' he told her with a hint of amusement.

Sarah flushed and busied herself buttering the toast.

Just then, Mattie came bustling in, and Sarah was glad of the diversion. The cook cast a disapproving glance at the table and snorted. 'Hmph! Looks like I'll have a mess to clean up before I even get started.'

'I didn't think you'd mind, Mattie,' said Devin, his humble tone belying a lurking twinkle. 'Besides, I've already made the tea for you. That should count for something.'

Mattie's brilliant eyes lit with laughter. 'Get away with you, Boss! You wouldn't care whether I minded or not.'

'Well, that's where you're wrong: because I *would*.'

'Great boast; small roast,' she sniffed. A cunning look came into her eye. '*Unless* I *make* you …'

'Mattie!' Devin exclaimed in shocked reproach, with just the tiniest flicker of an eyelid in Sarah's direction.

But Mattie wasn't fooled for a second. 'Yes, well, you can keep your conning tactics for those that may want them,' she informed him. 'They're wasted on me.'

Devin laughed. 'You're a terrible woman, Mattie. But I don't know what we'd do without you.'

Mattie snorted again. 'Those that have no business here should eat up and be on their way. *Some* of us have work to do!' Her eyes were twinkling, and she was hard put to hide a smile. 'And *if* I have to put up with you coming in here and messing about, you might as well pour me a cup of tea while you're waving that pot around. And Sarah can pass me the toast. I don't know why you're sitting about like a couple of dummies!'

§

Walking down to the stables in the early morning, Sarah found the air fresh and cool.

'How do you like Medora Downs, Sarah?' asked Devin, breaking a long silence.

Sarah turned to him impulsively. 'Oh, I love it! The vastness, the magnificence of it! It is all so *beautiful!*'

'I'm glad,' he muttered in a tone that suggested otherwise, relapsing into silence.

Sarah suddenly felt uncomfortable, as if he had raised a barrier between them. *He didn't like me gushing like that,* she thought. *Perhaps I embarrassed him? There's only so much that Dev will let you see of him,* she acknowledged. *One minute, there seemed to be a closeness; then, all at once, he froze you out.* She glanced at Devin, striding along beside her, remote and silent. How tall and handsome he was! She could see the outline of his lean, muscular frame beneath his thin cotton shirt. He looked so fit, due, she supposed, to all the hard physical work he did. Aunt Fay had told her that his men respected him because he did not ask them to do anything that he could not do himself just as well, or better, than they could.

Yet, in repose, he had about him an aura of helpless grief— almost palpable in its intensity. A strangely endearing weakness in so strong and self-contained a man. Sarah's immediate impulse was to offer comfort, and she understood why the others in the house hovered about him so anxiously. But the wall of reserve he'd built around himself made it impossible to reach him.

They rounded the corner of the stable block and were greeted by Johnnie, the groom, who had two horses saddled, ready for them. Johnnie was responsible for the Medora Downs Brahman Stud, as well as the thoroughbreds and stockhorses bred and raised on the station. From the fine herd of stud Brahmans, Johnnie selected the best bulls and heifers, which he prepared for the shows and sales.

The walls of Devin's office were lined with ribbons, and a cabinet that ran the length of one wall was packed with trophies—all won by their stud stock at agricultural shows from Mount Isa to Rockhampton, and even some from the Ekka (the Brisbane Exhibition). Sarah had seen them on the odd occasions she had been there to consult with Devin about the children or her position as governess. He'd told her that they bred the bulls for use in their main herd and sold a fair number of quality stud cattle, either privately or at their annual stud sale, which was a big occasion with a barbecue and dance at the end of the day.

'Mornin', Miss. Mornin', Boss,' said Johnnie, handing Devin the reins of a tall brown horse.

'Good morning, Johnnie. How is Bold Rover, this morning?'

'Aw … feelin' his oats a bit, Boss. I reckon you'll have to watch him for a while.'

'Like that, is it, boy?' murmured Devin, stroking the nose of the elegant brown thoroughbred.

'What about this one?' asked Sarah.

Johnnie smiled tolerantly. 'Old Persian Prince won't give you no trouble, Miss. He's a real ladies' horse.'

'Please, call me Sarah,' she said, stepping back to look at Persian Prince. He was a bright coppery bay with two white hind feet and a star on his forehead. He had a very pretty head and was surveying her with huge dark eyes that held a world of wisdom and kindness. Sarah straightaway felt attuned to him and knew that she was going to enjoy her ride.

Devin looked at Sarah. 'Mount up,' he said. 'We'd better get going or we'll miss breakfast with the children, and that really will upset Mattie.'

Sarah took the reins that Johnnie was holding out to her, carefully drew them over Persian Prince's ears to gather them on his neck. Then, placing her other hand on the pommel of the saddle, she stepped into the stirrup and swung neatly onto his back.

Johnnie nodded approval. That was a good start, anyway. Maybe she did know how to handle a horse. So many people thought they could ride until they got onto a real stockhorse, and then one had to rescue either them or the poor, confused horse.

Devin mounted easily onto Bold Rover, even though the horse was plunging and curvetting. After a few mandatory pigroots and sidesteps, the big brown consented to move forward, and they rode off down the track that led to the river channels. After a short while, he put his mount into a trot, watching Sarah out of the tail of his eye as he did so. She rose easily to the trot, enjoying the rhythm—hands and legs still. *They make a nice picture*, he thought. *The small, neatly made girl on the pretty thoroughbred. She's a graceful rider, too*, he noted with pleasure.

Bold Rover bounded forward in a gallop, but Devin controlled him, and he dropped back to a steady canter. Persian Prince began to canter, too—a slow, rocking-horse canter that was, oh, so comfortable. Sarah felt as though she had never enjoyed anything so much in her life. Her mount blew gently through his nostrils; he was enjoying himself, also. It was not often he carried so balanced and tactful a rider. Being well-known for one's tolerance and kindness was not all joy, when one was a horse.

Sarah glanced at the man beside her on the tall brown thoroughbred. *How well they suit each other*, she thought. Her gaze lingered on his hands holding the reins. How strong, yet gentle they were; never interfering with or hurting the sensitive mouth of his horse; but in control, just the same.

Suddenly, as if he sensed her eyes on him, he looked at her and smiled. 'Like to try a short gallop? Just to the rise?' he asked, pointing to the top of a gently sloping ridge, ahead.

Sarah nodded, shortened her reins, leaning slightly forward

over her horse's withers. Persian Prince needed no more urging than that. He shot forward after Bold Rover, who had bounded away in front of them.

Sarah was exhilarated. The wind whistled past her face, blowing little strands of hair and whipping colour into her cheeks. Faster and faster went Persian Prince, as he strained every muscle to catch Bold Rover. But before he could overtax himself, they reached the top of the rise where Devin was already reining in.

Sarah followed suit, breathless and laughing. 'That was *fun!*' she exclaimed, patting her horse's steaming neck. 'Just look at the old fellow, prancing and champing his bit. He feels young again.'

'We'll walk them down to the river to cool them off,' said Devin, seeming not to notice his horse's strongly expressed wish to keep galloping as he cantered almost on the spot. Meanwhile, Persian Prince dropped into a sedate, long-striding walk.

The early morning sun touched the leaves of the trees, edging them with gold, and the shadows were long black fingers stroking the earth as they followed the cattle pad that wound along the edge of the meandering river channels.

'You know,' said Devin, making conversation, 'Persian Prince was a very good racehorse, once. He's well-bred, too. The sire of his dam was Persian Lyric, and he is by Wilkes. It is unusual that he is not a chestnut.'

'He's a beautiful horse,' agreed Sarah, 'and he can still go like the wind. How old is he?'

'He's about sixteen, now. He retired from racing when he was six, and he won a good many, too. Then, we used him as a stockhorse for another six years, but we look after him a bit, now that he's older. Johnnie mainly uses him when he moves the stud Brahmans around. Other than that, he's kept for visitors or someone that wants a quiet ride on a reliable horse.'

By this time, Bold Rover had tired of his ineffectual efforts to get his own way and strode out on a long rein, just as his companion was doing.

'And what about him?' asked Sarah, indicating Devin's horse. 'He looks like a good type.'

'Yes, he's been a good horse. We've just retired him from racing. He won several races at Eagle Farm, but the weight beats him after he's won a few. His mother, Bold Miss, was a good racemare by Bold Ruler. He's by Gypsy Rover—a horse Bill Richmond had—a good racehorse, but unfortunately, he suffered an accident and had to be put down before he'd ever reached his potential. We were lucky to have got this fellow— there were only three foals by him, since he was still in training when Bill lost him.'

'Oh, that was sad,' sympathised Sarah, thinking of Bill Richmond's kind old face. 'It would have hurt him badly to have lost a horse like that.'

'Yes, I think it did,' said Devin. He shrugged. 'You have livestock: you have dead stock. You have to be prepared to take the bad with the good.' When next he spoke, it was to change the subject: 'You're a very good rider, Sarah.'

Sarah murmured a confused, 'Thank you!' Flushing with pleasure at the compliment.

Devin went on, 'Well … now that I know that, I would like to ask you if you would be prepared, as part of your governessing duties, to give the children weekly riding lessons on their ponies.

They have already been on them but have only been led at the walk.' He looked down at her, his eyes glinting into hers. 'What do you say?'

Sarah was conscious of an overwhelming and surprisingly bitter rush of disappointment. Devin had not asked her to ride with him because he wanted her company, it was only to see if she were a capable enough rider to take charge of two small children on their ponies. She felt crushed and humiliated to think that she had believed that he had wanted to know her better. Sarah couldn't understand why she felt this way. Almost without exception, in the presence of this man, she ended up feeling small and somehow inept. She chided herself severely. *What else should I expect? If I had been in his place, wouldn't I do the same?* The children were precious to him, more so because they were all that was left of his beloved brother. *Of course they can't be entrusted to the care of an incompetent rider!*

Sarah agreed to his request in a muffled voice, unconsciously straightened her shoulders and, very quickly, recovered herself.

'By the way,' added Devin. 'Since you seemed to enjoy your ride, I have no objection to you taking Persian Prince out any afternoon you like. The exercise will do him good … As long as there is not too much galloping,' he warned.

Sarah laughed. 'I won't gallop him. But thank you, Dev. I would like to ride as often as I can.'

'All right, then. Just tell Johnnie when you want him, or if you don't mind saddling him yourself, just go and get him.'

Sarah nodded, well-satisfied with such a treat to look forward to.

It had been arranged by Devin and Aunt Fay that she should

have every afternoon off between the hours of two and four while the children had their afternoon rest. Sue and Aunt Fay would look out for them during this period, which would give Sarah time to ride. They had assured Sarah—who had protested—that this was only fair, since she had charge of them from seven in the morning, when they rose, until eight thirty at night, their usual bedtime. Although their lessons in the schoolroom only occupied five mornings a week, another one would now be taken up with riding lessons, unless they cut short the schoolwork on a weekday morning, which Sarah didn't want to do. She could have one day off a week if she chose, or she could save them up and take them as a block. Since Sarah had nowhere to go, she had not availed herself of this offer. And since she really loved the children, having them with her on weekends was no hardship.

Devin looked at his watch. 'Well, we'd better get back, or we'll have Mattie up in arms,' he said, touching Bold Rover with his heels. Obediently, his horse broke into a trot, and Sarah allowed her horse to do the same. When they pulled up in the stable yard, the groom came out to take their horses.

Johnnie had watched them trotting up from the river. 'She'll do,' he said to himself as he hung up the leather headstall he had been oiling and came out into the sunlight. 'Enjoy yourself, Missy, er, Sarah?' he asked, grinning all over his comfortable, honest face.

'Oh, yes!' said Sarah. 'He's beautiful. Aren't you, boy?' And she stroked the bay's velvet nose. He lowered his head and rubbed his forehead on her shoulder, blowing softly.

'Looks like you've made a friend,' he commented, taking both sets of reins.

'Sarah's going to ride in the afternoons.'

'Good-o, Boss. I'll put him in his stable, lunchtimes, for her.'

'Yes, and Johnnie? I'll be back after breakfast to see you about that consignment of stud bulls for Emerald Hills.'

'Rightio, Boss. See you later, Sarah.' Johnnie disappeared around the end of the stable block, followed quietly by the two horses.

As they walked up to the house, Devin told Sarah about the children's ponies. Snowball, the Shetland, was quiet, lovable and well in his twenties. He had taught many children to ride. The other, Binny, was an Australian pony—a little larger and younger—but also suitable for beginners. As Yalara Bindi-i, she'd had an illustrious career in the show ring before her retirement.

'The only thing you'll have to watch,' said Devin, with a rueful smile, 'is Naomi's insistence that she *can* gallop. It happened when Johnnie took her up in front of him on Persian Prince one day and went for a canter. Since then, she has only one thought in her head as soon as she gets on the pony.'

'Well, in that case, I think I'll give them a few lessons on the lunge first, and then, once she's got her balance, it won't matter if she does canter.'

Sarah felt that Devin looked at her with new respect, but he only said, 'Good idea.'

When they arrived at the homestead, Sarah thanked Devin again and hurried away to change and get the children ready for breakfast. She finally tracked them down, fully dressed and playing in the rumpus room.

Naomi and Adam looked up from their game, smiles lighting

their faces. 'Hello, Sarah. We have a surprise for you!'

'*Have* you? Ooh, what is it?'

'Well …' began Naomi, giggling. She looked at Adam whose shoulders were heaving.

'Who do you think dressed us?' demanded the little girl.

'Um, Sue? … Mattie? … Aunt Fay? … Reuben?' she guessed.

To each of these, the answer was a chorused 'No!', except for the last, which they couldn't get out for the screams of laughter it produced.

'You're funny, Sarah,' said Adam. 'Reuben never comes into the house.'

'Yes, he does!' corrected Naomi. 'He has tea in the kitchen with Mattie!'

A stormy look crept into Adam's eyes. 'But he doesn't come *through* the house,' he objected. 'Only to the kitchen door. The kitchen's not the house!'

Seeing that Naomi was drawing breath to hotly defend her statement, Sarah intervened: 'Why don't you tell me who *did* dress you?'

'Well …' said Naomi, forgetting her quarrel. 'We got up at seven o'clock and looked in your room, Sarah, but you weren't there, and we didn't know where you were. So …' She took a deep breath. 'We dressed *ourselves!*' she finished, triumphantly.

Both children closely watched the effect of this on Sarah.

'Oh,' she said, standing back to admire them, 'that *was* clever!'

'Of course,' the little girl confided importantly, 'I had to put Adam's shoes on for him.'

'No you didn't!' Adam wore an expression of indignant outrage. '*I* put them on. You only did the laces up!'

'You had them on the wrong *feet … Silly*!'

Sarah judged it wise to interrupt: 'Do you want to know what I think? *I* think you were both very clever children. *But …* if we don't hurry up, we'll miss breakfast.'

Argument gave place to hunger, and they trooped into the breakfast room; greeted Aunt Fay and Devin, already at the table; and climbed up into their places to wait for Sarah to serve them scrambled eggs and toast from the warming dishes on the sideboard.

'Hello, Sarah. Did you enjoy your ride?' asked Aunt Fay.

'Did you go *riding*?' asked Naomi, round-eyed and envious. 'With Uncle Dev?'

'You didn't tell *us*,' said Adam.

'Don't talk with your mouth full,' said Aunt Fay, automatically. 'Sarah doesn't have to tell you everything.'

'She used to say that to me, too,' said Devin, out of the corner of his mouth to the boy beside him.

'I would have told you, but ——' began Sarah, about to say that they hadn't given her a chance, when she was interrupted.

'Sarah knew that I wanted to tell you myself,' their uncle finished with a wink.

'Your ride, Sarah? Did you enjoy it?' repeated Aunt Fay with a quelling glance at her nephew.

'I did,' bubbled Sarah, her face aglow. 'Very much, indeed.'

Aunt Fay nodded, looked at her for a moment, then turned

her attention to her scrambled eggs with a peculiarly satisfied expression.

Devin glanced from her to the children. 'Naomi, Adam,' he said, 'what do you say to a surprise?'

Naomi giggled. 'Another surprise?'

Devin looked at Sarah and raised an eyebrow.

'It was their surprise for me. They dressed themselves.'

'Well done, you two!' he praised. 'What do you say to learning to ride?'

'Ooh!' gasped Naomi.

Adam's eyes grew as round as saucers. 'Will you teach Sam, too, Uncle Dev?'

'Sam might have to sit on the fence and watch, just at first, like the stockmen at breaking-in time. But Sarah is going to teach you, not me,' he said.

'Oh, goody!'

'Today?'

'Not today: Saturday,' he told them with stern emphasis. 'Now, eat your breakfast. And if you don't do exactly as Sarah tells you, no more riding. Okay?'

'Yes, Uncle Dev.' The children bent docilely to their breakfasts, but Naomi's face was flushed, and Adam's eyes huge from excitement.

Devin's lips quirked, and his eyes met Sarah's in a fleeting, silent message of shared amusement. She felt her cheeks grow hot and turned hastily to the sideboard to pour herself some coffee.

§

Four or five afternoons a week, Sarah managed to get down to the stables to ride. She and Persian Prince soon became firm friends, and he began to whicker softly whenever he saw her coming.

If Johnnie happened to be around and saw her walking down from the house in her jodhpurs, Persian Prince would be saddled, waiting, and Johnnie would come out and pass the time of day with her before returning to his duties. But if the bay horse was standing, unsaddled in his stable, Sarah would take down the small saddle that had been provided for her use, and Persian Prince's bridle, and groom and saddle him herself before riding down to their favourite trail along the river.

Here, along the winding channels, there were some logs that Sarah and her mount enjoyed jumping as they went. Then, pleasantly tired, they would return to the stables; Sarah wrapped in thought, and Persian Prince, no doubt, thinking of his dinner, striding out in a fast walk.

Sarah would mostly return in time to change and have tea on the verandah with Aunt Fay before taking charge of the children once more. As she managed to convey to her sympathetic hostess: the times she spent riding were golden, happy hours in the bright autumn sunshine, and she revelled in the chance to practise a sport that she loved but had previously had little opportunity to pursue.

Sarah began to feel that, not only had she lived here forever, she wanted it to go on forever. She had no idea that at least one of her actions was about to precipitate her back into a nightmare that had become just a distant, unpleasant memory.

Chapter Seven

Aunt Fay put down the microphone of the two-way radio and stood for a moment, a troubled crease between her brows, before turning to see who had entered the room. She greeted Sarah with, for once, no trace of a smile on her face.

'Is something wrong, Aunt Fay?' ventured Sarah, observing her unusual gravity.

'Well, yes,' she admitted. 'Something may very well be wrong. You see … Louella Richmond is home again.'

'You mean the woman that broke her engagement to Dev and married someone else?'

'That's right. And what's more, if I am not mistaken, she's more than ready to renew old acquaintance. However,' added Aunt Fay, pensively, 'she may not find Dev so easy to bring to heel as she thinks.' She sighed and walked restlessly to the window. 'And she's coming here, tomorrow.' She lapsed into a silent consideration of the bougainvillea overhanging the window and, after a few minutes, appeared to come to a decision of some kind. 'Oh well, Sarah, we can do nothing about it. We must just take things as they come. Let's go and have our tea. I've asked Mattie to take it onto the verandah again, since it is such a beautiful day.'

Over tea, the older woman returned to the subject of Louella Richmond. 'As a young girl, Louella was very beautiful: tall and willowy, like a model. She used to help with the big musters, and she and Dev would ride together. They made a handsome couple. Bill and Esmé encouraged it. You see, Louella is an only child, and Medora Downs and Emerald Hills would have become one huge aggregation. The Richmonds were close, lifelong friends of Devin's parents, and when Bill did not have a son, he set his heart on Dev as his son-in-law. Of course, I don't think Dev gave any consideration to the property; he was so completely wrapped up in Louella. Obsessed was more the word,' said Aunt Fay, warming to her tale. 'He couldn't see what others saw—that she was spoilt and utterly self-centred.

'Ten years ago, when he was twenty-one and she was eighteen, they became engaged. After a few months, she ran away with a wealthy American she met when he came out to look at his oil company's research project. She sent Dev a telegram informing him that she was married. It broke his heart—completely changed him. He became so bitter! I don't know if, even then, he saw what she was really like.' Aunt Fay bowed her head.

'And what is she really like?' asked Sarah, driven by an uncharacteristic urge to know more of this woman who had been able to ensnare the heart of the enigmatic man who was her employer.

Aunt Fay shot her a searching glance and dropped her eyes to the tablecloth. 'Under that beautiful façade … cold as ice and hard as nails. There is very little she will stop at to get what she wants,' she said, deliberately. 'And now she is home again, divorced from her American and ready to take up where she left off. And I am just a little afraid that Dev will be taken in by her again.' Her gentle blue eyes met Sarah's. 'You see, he has never spoken of it, and I just don't know how she will affect him. One thing is certain: She will only cause unhappiness. She always has …'

Sarah was silent. There was nothing that she could say. Her heart ached for the young Devin who'd had all his hopes and dreams so carelessly trampled in the dust by a spoilt and heartless beauty. Suddenly, she felt an inexplicable sense of foreboding, as though she, too, shared Aunt Fay's premonition that, somehow, this woman spelt trouble for them all; that the quiet, restful atmosphere of Medora Downs would be disturbed by a malevolent presence, generating unease and, perhaps, even fear. Sarah shivered with apprehension.

Aunt Fay's gaze sharpened momentarily, then she sighed. The moment passed. They returned to happier topics of conversation, and their anxiety faded into the background, almost, but not quite forgotten.

§

The next afternoon, while the children were having their nap, Sarah was engaged in arranging some fresh flowers in a bowl in the lounge. She had not gone riding this afternoon because yesterday Persian Prince had cast a shoe and was slightly lame.

And Johnnie, busy with some bulls that were being prepared for sale, had not had time to shoe him.

Sarah heard the door open and turned to see Devin shepherding a tall, elegant and truly beautiful woman into the room. From the top of her fashionably streaked, dark honey-blonde hair to the soles of her strappy Italian leather sandals, she shrieked wealth, chic and luxury. Large, emerald-green eyes were, just now, turned on Devin in a melting gaze, and her linen-clad shoulder brushed his chest as she preceded him through the doorway.

Glancing at Devin, Sarah thought that a little flame seemed to kindle and leap in his eyes before being quenched as he looked down at Louella (for this must surely be she). But whether it was suppressed anger or passion of a different sort, she hardly dared speculate.

The gorgeous creature looked at Sarah, eyes narrowing slightly as she noted her slender fairness and delicate features. 'Oh, *my*, Dev,' she drawled in a husky, bored voice that held the trace of an American accent. 'Is this your new housemaid?'

What a bitch! Inwardly, Sarah began to seethe at this insolent remark—calculated, she knew, to have this precise effect—but outwardly, she made no sign.

'That's enough, Louella,' said Devin, brows snapping together. 'You already know that Sarah is our governess.'

'Oh well …' she yawned, gold charm bracelets jingling as she delicately covered her mouth with long fingers, on which were crowded several sapphire and diamond rings. 'Servants are all the same, anyway. I could do with a drink, Dev,' she added plaintively, completely dismissing Sarah. 'You know what I like.'

She threw over her shoulder as she swayed across the room and began, idly, to fiddle with the stereo.

Sarah, torn between anger, amusement and disgust at this blatant rudeness, looked at Devin and found him watching her with a distant, unreadable expression in his eyes. Was it helplessness that darkened their grey depths? Or was it something else? He shrugged apologetically and went to the bar to mix Louella her favourite cocktail. 'What will you have, Sarah?'

'Nothing, thanks, Dev.' Sarah placed the last flower in the bowl and gave it a final twitch into place. 'I was just doing this for Aunt Fay. I must go to the children now.' She left the room, enveloped in an aura of quiet dignity that did not go unnoticed.

Aunt Fay, uncurling herself from the depths of a wing chair behind the bookcase at the other end of the room, exited, unseen, through a curtained French window at the same time as Sarah left by the door. *Surely, Dev can see what Louella is like from that: the contrast is … Sarah is everything she is not. Surely, he can see! He's not twenty-one any more. But is he still love-smitten?*

Out in the corridor, Sarah expelled a silent breath of relief. *So, that's Louella. Well, she doesn't like me, that much is obvious!* After that first narrow, assessing glance, the woman had behaved as though Sarah did not exist.

Aunt Fay entered the kitchen with much the same thought, tut-tutting at the rudeness. 'Ill-bred, that's what she is! That woman! *Something …*' she said to Mattie, shaking her fluffy, silver curls, 'will *have* to be done!'

'I suppose you mean that hussy from the Hills?' replied the cook, attacking a mound of dough with her rolling pin. 'Nothing we *can* do, Mrs Fay. Mind you, I'd like to oblige you, nothing better, but it's the old story. Dev *might* see sense, but men don't as a rule. Always the same!' she snorted. 'Lead them about by the ——' Her eyes flashed with loathing. 'What do *you* want?'

'Take it easy, Mattie,' said Jim, edging into the room, subdued but unfazed. 'The boot's on the other foot. I got a message that Aunty wants to see me.'

'Yes. I do, Jim,' said the lady with decision. 'Come out onto the verandah where we won't disturb Mattie.'

Mattie sniffed and belaboured her pastry with renewed vigour.

§

In the weeks that followed, it seemed to Sarah that Louella practically haunted Medora Downs. She was always coming to lunch or dinner—or riding over on an exquisite, black thoroughbred mare and demanding that Devin show her the stud bulls so that she could make her choices. Once, Sarah had been moved to comment on the beauty of the mare and immediately wished she had kept her mouth shut when Louella replied in that detestable, bored voice, 'Cinders? Well, Emerald Centura to the likes of you. Yes, indeed, she is. No doubt, your life's salary would not buy such a mare as this. So have a good look at her. It's as close as you're likely to get.' She rode off without a backward glance, expecting Devin to follow on his brown gelding. Sarah looked at him to see what he thought of this piece of disgraceful hauteur, but though his lips tightened, he said nothing and rode away slowly in her wake.

Nothing changed. Louella continued to treat Sarah with cold disdain. But once, at dinner, Sarah looked up to catch Louella's eyes on her, and the expression in their green depths sent shivers down her spine. The light emanating from them was not coldness, but a burning flame of jealousy and the realisation the Sarah was the embodiment of all the fine integrity and loving warmth that she herself lacked. Something within her dimly registered this, and she hated her all the more, with an implacable fury that was not the least abated by its irrationality.

Good Heavens! She hates me. I wonder why? She's much more beautiful than I am, thought Sarah, amazed. But Sarah did not realise that her beauty, which sprang from within, was so much more appealing than Louella's coldly beautiful façade, which masked the self-centred, calculating soul beneath.

Both looked down at their plates and became instantly absorbed in their meal, but the air seemed to vibrate with the tension that the startling revelation had produced.

After this incident, Sarah, unused to such overt animosity as Louella displayed, did her best to avoid having to run into her and succeeded fairly well for several weeks. She wondered what Devin thought of the other woman's behaviour, but he appeared not to notice, treating Louella with unfailing courtesy.

A few evenings later, after dinner, Devin retired to his office with Jim to discuss the approaching picnic races over a quiet beer; Aunt Fay followed the children to bed complaining, unusually, of a headache and fatigue; and Sarah was left alone to read in the sitting room. She looked up at the sound of arrivals in the hall.

'Yoo-hoo, Sarah?'

Sarah jumped up. Was that honeyed voice Louella? *I can't believe my ears,* she thought, going out into the hall to find Devin's neighbour all smiles.

'Sarah,' she purred. 'I have a little surprise for you. Look who I found on the road to Emerald Hills. The silly man took the wrong turn-off.' She laughed as Sarah whitened at a tall blond figure behind her. 'I'll leave you to it. I'm sure you have a lot to talk about.'

David! Sarah had to grasp hold of the Victorian hallstand to keep upright. Out of the nightmare, she found her voice: 'David! But how did you …?'

'Get your things, Sarah. You're not staying here a minute longer. You're coming home with me. You can't serve me a trick like that and get away with it. Don't think it!' The handsome face was red and suffused, the eyes glittering almost as if drugged, the mouth taut and mean.

Why did I never notice what a mean mouth he has? wondered Sarah. *David! Still furious! Bullying, already.* She turned and fled for the kitchen. 'Mat-*tie!*'

Sarah's desperate call brought the cook to the door, carving knife in hand, from where she'd been slicing a brownie for the men's supper. 'What's the matter, Sarah?' She saw the man and accurately sized up the situation. 'In here, behind me,' she said, dragging Sarah through the doorway and shoving her behind her massive form. 'Now, you!' she said to David, her magnificent eyes flaming with contempt. 'What's all this?'

'Sarah is my fiancée.'

'And this is *my* kitchen,' said Mattie, waving the knife in his face. 'And that doesn't sound like a good enough reason for me to let you in. Because you look like an *ex* to me. And if you aren't, you ought to be.'

'Look! This is ridiculous. I have to talk to her.'

'Not in my kitchen, you don't.' She pointed the knife suggestively. 'Now, get out!'

True to Jo's description of his treatment of her, he made a panther spring, grabbed Mattie's wrist and twisted her arm up behind her back. 'Not so clever now, are we?' he crowed through clenched teeth. 'Drop the knife!'

But David hadn't bargained for the woman's massive bulk. She bore him backwards against the pantry door and, quite literally, crushed the breath out of him. Weak and fainting from lack of air, he slid to the floor as soon as she took her weight off him.

'Get up!' yelled Mattie, still brandishing the knife. 'Get out before I bury this knife in your gut, you lily-livered woman-basher! *Poor* little Sarah!'

'Sarah?' he said, entreating her with a pathetic travesty of his old charm. 'Don't you care? I just want you back. I *love* you!'

Mattie made a choking sound, but Sarah had recovered enough to say, '*Me?* You love *me?* What about Chantal?'

'Chantal was a mistake.'

'I'm sure she'd love to hear you say *that*,' said Sarah, eyes flashing.

He reddened, but before he could reply, Mattie shouted, 'Oh, you two-timing son of a rattlesnake! You viper! Let me at him, Sarah! I know just what to do with him!'

'No, Mattie, please! He's not worth it!'

The commotion had, by this time, penetrated the walls of the office.

'Listen!' said Devin, leaping up and making for the door with long-legged strides. He looked at Jim. 'A strange man in Mattie's kitchen?'

'Better get down there, Dev, before she kills him, and we'll have to find another cook.'

'We'll never find one like Mattie.'

'No, thank the Lord,' mouthed Jim, following his boss down the hall to stand, round-eyed, in the doorway. His quick glance took in the cook standing over a man on the floor, holding a knife, looking as though she were deciding where in his torso to plunge it; the man, blond and good-looking, cowering away with a look of terror; Sarah, white and distressed, apparently pleading with the cook not to kill him.

'What's all the racket, Mattie?' asked Devin, his eyes on the knife.

Mattie straightened, sighed and dropped it on the table. 'You're just in time, Boss. I was about to commit a murder.'

'I can see that. But why?'

'This slimy goanna has come here threatening Sarah. That little witch from the Hills brought him over. Said she had a *surprise* for Sarah.'

'I lost my way,' said her victim, struggling to his feet.

'Shut up, you! Then Sarah ran to me for protection, and *he* came in here and tried a bit of his domestic violence on me. But the swine bit off more than he could chew, there.'

'I'll say,' muttered Jim. 'A true optimist!'

Devin sent him a warning glance, walked over to pick up the

knife, threw it in a drawer and closed it.

'Boss,' said Mattie, with dangerous calm. 'You'd better get this *canaille* out of my kitchen, or I won't be answerable for the consequences!'

'I didn't know you were French, Mattie,' said Devin, with a lightness he was far from feeling.

'I'm not, but I can talk it. And I'm winding up for some that's *not* in the dictionary!'

'Okay, okay. I get the picture. But who is this bloke? What is he doing here?'

'I came to see Sarah. I ——'

'God grant me patience!' snapped Mattie. 'Sarah can do better than a slimy toad like you!'

'I'm from Sydney, I … Sarah's my fiancée. Please, I just need to talk to her,' he pleaded. 'We had a misunderstanding ——'

'Misunderstanding? *Mis*-understanding?' marvelled Mattie. 'The only thing you don't understand is that it won't be good for your health if you don't get out of here.' Then, shouting in his face: '*Right now!*'

'Boss,' said Jim in an urgent under voice, elbowing Devin in the back. 'Look at Sarah!'

Devin shifted his gaze and frowned in concern. Sarah was swaying on her feet. He started forward but stopped when she put up her hand to grasp the shelf above the range. He couldn't know her thoughts, but he had a fair idea of the shock she must be experiencing.

Sarah stood there, white to the lips, battered by so many

emotions that she could not begin to voice them. The contrast she had just witnessed in David's conduct when he was alone with women and when he was in the presence of men—*Real men*, thought Sarah—was mind-boggling: from bullying and standover tactics to crawling and wheedling. *He's disgusting and contemptible,* she thought. *Not even a man! How could I have ever thought I loved someone like that?* Such a brutal exposure of his mean and cowardly disposition was truly shattering.

Devin may not have understood all that was going through Sarah's mind, but he could see that there was something she was struggling to put into words.

David and Mattie began to speak at once: Mattie hotly; David in a pleading, whining tone.

Devin made a gesture to shut him up and spoke to the cook. 'Hang on, Mattie. I need to get to the bottom of this. We've heard a lot from you and this fellow. Now I want to hear from the person most nearly concerned.' He turned to the pale, trembling figure supporting herself against the mantelpiece over the range and said with gentle firmness, 'Tell us what *you* want, Sarah. Do you want to talk to this bloke or not?'

'*Not!*' she said, unable to conceal either her distress or her revulsion. 'I *never* want to see him again.'

'Right,' said Devin. 'Well, I think that's pretty clear, isn't it, Jim?'

'I'd say so, Dev.' Jim's face wore a thoughtful expression. 'Tell you what, why don't we give him the bum's rush?'

'Why not?' said Devin. 'It's an idea, Jim.'

Their eyes held the same devilish twinkle. Both men

descended, each took an arm, lifted their victim off the floor, bore him backwards out of the house and threw him on the gravel. 'Now, get out of here,' said Devin. 'Johnnie! Are you in there with Reuben? See this fellow off the place, will you? He's being a nuisance to Sarah.'

'Gladly, Boss,' came a voice from the dark. Johnnie came into the light, and David whitened as he saw the shotgun over his arm; almost fainting, he heard the click of both barrels being cocked. Then Reuben stepped forward, carrying a light chainsaw. He was fiddling with the starting cord and grinning like a vicious monkey.

'Ever see them horror movies, Mister?' asked Johnnie. 'You know, the ones with a madman sitting on the roof of your car with a chainsaw? Yeah? Get what I'm sayin'? Now, you better get back in that fancy Merc of yours and get going while you can. I'll try to hold off this madman while you get away, but I don't know how much luck I'll have.'

David scrambled to his feet, leapt into his vehicle and roared off. Johnnie and Reuben exchanged wicked glances, climbed into Reuben's old runabout and followed him for a few kilometres before returning. Both of them had heard at least a part of the altercation and had a fair idea of what was afoot.

'Standover merchant,' muttered Reuben. 'Poor little Sarah.'

'She's okay now she's got us,' said Johnnie, watching the receding tail-lights. 'He won't be back. Gutless!'

Devin and Jim went back inside to find Sarah and Mattie in the hall. 'He's gone,' said Devin with a glance at Sarah's face. 'Come into the sitting room and we'll talk. Can you liven up the coffeepot for us, Mattie? Then you can go off to bed if you like.'

His lip just quirked. 'You've had a big day. We'll wash up.'

'Oh, that's likely!' snorted Mattie, back to normal. But she went out and came back with a tray of coffee and the sliced and buttered brownie. 'Leave them on the sink when you're done. I don't trust men with my china. And I utterly forbid Sarah to lift a finger! She should be in bed, so don't keep her up too long,' she added with a minatory glare and went out.

'Whew!' said Jim, rubbing his neck. 'That woman ...'

'Oh, don't abuse her.' Sarah's lips were trembling. 'She ... she saved me!'

'Pour Sarah some coffee, Jim, and stop gassing,' ordered Devin, going to Sarah and putting long, gentle fingers under her chin to make her look at him. For once, his grey eyes held an expression she *could* read: tenderness and kindly understanding. 'He broke your heart, didn't he?' he murmured, letting his fingers slide away to press her shoulder. 'Never mind. I know.'

But it was Jim who had the last word. 'I knew you were running away from something,' he told her as he brought her coffee. 'But it wasn't something, it was *someone!* You should have told us, Sarah. We could have saved you all this—headed him off at the pass. He wouldn't have got beyond Winton if we'd known. That's the Outback: it's big, but it's also small.'

'What's this?' asked Devin, brows raised, as he turned from the coffeepot.

'Just something Sarah and I talked about when I picked her up in Winton, Boss. But we'll have to discuss it another day. I think Sarah has had enough for now, don't you?'

CHAPTER EIGHT

Early next morning, there was a phonecall for Sarah. It was Jo. 'Sarah, I am *so* worried! Your letter came when Wendy and I were away for a week, and David strongarmed Diane, forced his way in and took it, so we never got it. I've only just got back and found out. I had to let you know straightaway: He has your address, Sarah. He *knows* where you are!'

'You don't have to worry, Jo. He can't hurt me now.' Sarah knew that it was true, and her heart sang with joy. 'He came last night and got thrown off the place and told never to come back.'

'Oh, thank goodness! What happened?'

Sarah described the evening as she remembered it, and Jo almost went into convulsions when Sarah described Mattie's solution to having her arm twisted. 'She almost killed him,' Sarah told her, 'by crushing him so he couldn't breathe.'

'Oh, Sarah, you crack me up! Tell me that again. I don't think I could've heard you properly … Oh, *perfect!*' she gurgled, when

Sarah explained that Mattie weighed about twenty stone, had backed David up against a door and simply leant on him with all her strength. 'Served with his own sauce!'

And when Sarah told her of Johnnie and Reuben's reprehensible escort, it was a little while before Jo could stop laughing enough to speak.

'Too good for the brute!' she gasped between wailing bursts. 'It sounds like you're well protected. The *perfect* spot for you.'

'Yes.' Sarah's heart thrilled at another truth.

They talked for a little while longer. Then Jo rang off, and Sarah went, with a light step, to get the children ready for breakfast.

§

Midmorning, when Sarah took the children into the sitting room for morning tea, Aunt Fay was entertaining a visitor.

'Hello, Sarah,' said Louella brightly. 'Did your friend have a nice visit with you, last night?'

'Friend?' said Aunt Fay, looking from one to the other. 'What friend?'

'He said he was Sarah's fiancé,' replied Louella, concentrating on smoothing her skirt.

'Sarah?' queried Aunt Fay, her eyebrows disappearing into her hairline.

A cold voice spoke from the doorway: 'He is neither Sarah's fiancé nor her friend. And I would appreciate it,' said Devin, stepping into the room and frowning at Louella, 'if you would call or ring before dumping someone on my doorstep at that hour of the night.' He poured himself tea and explained to his aunt, 'All this happened after you had gone to bed, Aunty. He, er, made the mistake of wandering into Mattie's kitchen.'

'Oh, no, Dev! Was it …?'

'It *was*. But … no harm done *in the end*. Was there, Sarah?'

'Oh, no. It was all fine … in the end.'

'Oh, that's good,' said Aunt Fay. 'Mattie can be rather difficult about strange men.'

'Why don't you sack her and get a normal cook, Dev? I wouldn't put up with her for a second!' exploded Louella, who had, ten minutes before, received a contemptuous look and sniff as Mattie slapped down the tea tray.

She was dealt an unexpected snub. 'You won't be required to, will you?' he returned with a satiric smile. 'And when I *do* want your advice on whom I employ, my dear Louella, rest assured, I will ask for it.'

'Oh.' Louella, finding herself on the backfoot, tried to change the subject by making friendly overtures to Adam. He backed away, swinging his teddy as protection. A loose paw pad snagged one of her expensive nylons and holed the knee. 'You little *horror!*' she breathed, tight-lipped. 'Now, look what you've done! I'd know what to do if you were *mine!*'

The silence positively crackled with ice.

Louella read condemnation in three pairs of adult eyes and laughed. 'Well, you didn't think I *meant* it, did you? Of course, I've no intention of touching the little beast.' Her eyes wandered to Naomi, large-eyed with reproach. '*Either* of the little beasts.'

'Come on, children,' said Sarah, rising and holding out her hands. 'It is time we went for our nature walk. Miss Richmond wants to talk to Uncle Dev.'

'Is she going to marry Uncle Dev, Sarah?' asked Naomi, brows wrinkled, when they were out of earshot.

'I don't know,' said Sarah. 'Look over there in that tree. What is it?'

But Naomi wouldn't be swerved from her topic. 'I *don't* like her.'

'Sam doesn't like her either,' said Adam. 'But he didn't mean to break her stocking.'

'I know, darling. Of course he didn't. Bring him over here to look at this tree.'

Back in the sitting room, Aunt Fay continued to foil any chance of a *tête-à-tête*, supposing that, if Devin really wanted one, he could take Louella off somewhere. She hovered over her nephew, so much like the goddess Diana or the mythological Avenging Fury, that Devin had to hide a grin. She hardly spoke, but when she did, it was in such frosty tones that her visitor finally took the hint and left.

'I'm going now,' announced Louella in a loud, bored voice; her eyes snapping. 'I'll come back when you're all in a better mood—especially Aunty!'

After this, even Devin seemed short-tempered and moody; the children reflected this by becoming slightly nervous and needing constant reassurance; Aunt Fay, watching them, seemed thoughtful and preoccupied. Sarah often found her sitting perfectly still, contemplating whatever was in front of her unseeing gaze. *Louella's abrasive presence affects us all,* thought Sarah. *Wears us all down.*

§

One evening, unable to sleep, Sarah walked out onto the verandah and sat in the squatter's chair, gazing restlessly out over the moonlit garden. She was about to go indoors when she heard voices, and Devin and Louella came into view, strolling in the garden.

Sarah heard Devin say, 'It's late, Louella. You shouldn't have come at this hour.'

'But, Dev, darling,' replied his visitor in plaintive tones, 'it's the only time I can prise you away from your limpet of an aunt. And we have *so* much to catch up on!'

Sarah shrank back in her chair, out of sight in the deep shadows of the verandah. Every nerve was screaming for her to exit this scene, but the last thing she wanted was to advertise her presence and expose herself to Louella's caustic tongue, so she sat still and quiet in the shadows, willing them to move on, so she could leave without attracting attention.

Devin's reply was indistinguishable, since they had passed by her. In another minute, it would be safe for her to get up and go back to her room without being seen.

Unexpectedly, Louella turned to face Devin with a little pent-up exclamation, flung her arms around his neck, pulled his head down and passionately kissed him on the lips. Sarah drew in a painful breath and stayed only long enough to see Devin stand rigid for a moment, putting his hands up to Louella's shoulders, before she whisked herself into her darkened room and shut the door.

Every time she closed her eyes, Sarah saw the passionate embrace she had inadvertently witnessed and wondered at her reaction. Why did she feel such cold dismay? What was it to her if Devin Mainwaring fell once more into the clutches of a ruthless, calculating woman? He was a mature man, and it would be by his own choice, after all.

Even though she chided herself in this fashion, Sarah knew that she could not bear him to be hurt again—the way he had been ten years ago. How much worse to be married to someone vain and selfish and completely uncaring, than to be jilted by them?

Tears flooded her eyes as she remembered how tenderly he had spoken to her when David had gone. How gently he had taken her chin in his long fingers; how kindly had been his expression. He knew exactly what it was like. Yes, he knew: *exactly.*

The thought flashed into her mind that she'd had a lucky escape, and suddenly, she saw that Louella, except for the violence, was a female version of David: both of them cloaking their selfish vanity in a crumbling veneer of charm but, nevertheless, going all out for what they wanted. *But was Louella violent?* Sarah thought, sometimes, that she could be. Perhaps she was more like David than they knew.

Sarah caught her breath at the revelation: Louella was to Devin what David had been to Sarah. That was the reason he'd said what he had to her. She could only pray that Devin would have the kind of awakening she had *before* any wedding and not after. Another amazing realisation hit her: somewhere along the line, during her weeks at Medora Downs, her bruised heart had been healed; the dull ache of loss had miraculously left her. It still hurt her that she had loved so empty and shallow a person—had mistaken the dross for the gold, in fact—but the agony was gone.

Oh, Dev, she thought. *I wish it could be the same for you.* But she knew his hurt was buried so deeply under the scarring of his soul that it would be a miracle if he could be freed.

Why, then, did she feel vaguely restless and not quite happy, as though there were a gap in her life waiting to be filled? And why was her employer so often in her thoughts? She admired him, yes—even felt that there was something special about him— but in his presence, she often felt gauche and tongue-tied. She wasn't usually like that, so why? She had no answers, only a sad little premonition that, emotionally, he was unreachable.

Sarah sighed, pounded her pillow and turned restlessly, yearning over she knew not what and, eventually, drifted off to sleep.

Sarah had left the verandah so precipitately that she did not see Devin reach up and unwind Louella's arms from around his neck and put her from him.

'Louella,' he said quietly—his face set and stern. 'All that was finished ten years ago. By *you*. And, as far as I am concerned, it is going to stay that way.'

Louella pouted up at him, her eyes huge, dark pools in her blanched, moonlit face. 'But, Dev, darling, *I* haven't changed. Are you going to punish me for a youthful mistake I once made? I was overwhelmed by the exciting promises Charles made me, of seeing the world and living in the jet set! I realised almost at once that I'd made a mistake—that it was you I really loved. But what could I do by then?' her voice was low and appealing. 'And look,' she added, holding out her left hand. 'I still wear your ring.'

He shrugged. 'You can wear it whenever you like. I told you to keep it.'

'But, darling, doesn't that *mean* something?' An expensive, heady fragrance wafted upwards, filling his senses.

Yes, she was beautiful and alluring still: he had to give her that. But he realised, with relief, that she no longer had any power over him. She could neither move him nor hurt him any more. Yet, paradoxically, her words made him impulsively angry. How could she think that, after having so cruelly dismissed him ten years ago, she could casually walk back into his life and take up where she'd left off?

'Didn't you punish me, Louella? For loving you?' he said. 'But don't you understand? You took my love and destroyed it, trampled it under your pretty feet. And then you rubbed my nose in it,' he added with brutal candour. 'And now there's nothing left. I have nothing left to give you.'

Louella quailed before the finality in his voice and the coldness in his demeanour, walking away without another word. He stood, looking after her—his face a mask in the moonlight—until he heard her car start up and roar down the drive, scattering pebbles as she tramped viciously on the accelerator.

He straightened his shoulders and went into the house.

Aunt Fay moved from behind the curtain of the open window, and her lips curved into a little smile of satisfaction. Would she tell Sarah about this? She spent a few minutes in profound thought before shaking her silver curls. No, probably it was best that she should never know. She smiled again. *It could be difficult for me to explain how I know ...*

CHAPTER NINE

It was early morning. Sarah was standing on the verandah outside her room, looking out over the paddock to the racetrack where Devin was exercising his horse in preparation for the Medora Downs Picnic Races, which were to be held in two weeks' time. The station staff had been talking about it for weeks, and there was an air of anticipation and excitement over the whole place as the big event drew closer.

Members of the Medora Downs Picnic Race Club had been coming and going for several weeks now, as working bees were held to prepare the track and amenities. Small yards had been erected or repaired, as was necessary, for the many racehorses that were expected to contest the rich prize money. Several of the stations in the area had donated valuable trophies for races that were named after them.

Sarah had never experienced a picnic-race meeting, and even if she had, it wouldn't have been one like this. She was told that, even though there were only two days of actual racing, the festivities often went on for as long as five days. This she found difficult to believe, but the Outback people really knew how to turn on a celebration. They may not have had many events on their social calendar, but when they did, they made the most of it. And this was, by all accounts, one of the biggest. Sarah was looking forward to her first major social occasion in the Outback.

Sarah's lips curved upwards as she watched Devin riding his highly strung thoroughbred, Bold Rover. She'd got into the habit of coming out on the verandah at first light when she knew that he had started to train his horses for the races. She loved the easy way he sat his horse, his gentle but sure handling of the reins, his complete mastery over the excitable animal. His calm confidence that seemed to reassure his horses and bring out the best in them.

Bold Rover, she knew, was favourite for the Emerald Hills Cup—the richest race of the meeting and sponsored by Louella's father—but the odds would have been shorter were he not such a difficult horse. Yet, Devin rode him with a light hand, holding him with his legs, controlling his flighty impulses with hand and voice, never shifting in the saddle as his horse pranced and curvetted, champing his bit and snorting with impatience at the restraints so skilfully applied.

The other horse in training was the sweet little mare, Gracious Lady: a lovely chestnut, her gleaming flame-red coat in striking contrast to her mane and tail of pale gold. Sarah itched to ride her but dare not ask. She thought Devin's horses regarded him in much the same way as his men did: he was the boss and they respected him, but he also engendered in them a love and loyalty that went beyond the call of duty. Sarah had no doubt that she and Bold Rover would give him their best on the day.

Lost in her reverie, she did not notice that Reuben had been watching her for some time, grinning broadly. 'Reckon you fancy the boss a bit. Eh, Missy? Fine lookin' fella, ain't he? But, by heck, you've got a bit of competition. Reckon someone else has got her claws well into him.' His frame shook with mischievous chuckles. 'Or *thinks* she has.'

'Oh, *Reuben!*' gasped Sarah. Scarlet and almost speechless with embarrassment; she fled down the verandah into the hall, pursued by a wheezy cackle. 'Oh! The *horrid* old man!' she exclaimed, putting her hands up to her hot cheeks. '*Urrgh!*'

Mattie poked her head around the kitchen door. 'What was that?'

'Oh, nothing. Reuben was just teasing me.'

'The old beggar! Come in and tell us about it. Sue's here with me. We're just grabbing a cuppa before the madness starts. Have one with us. Now, what's up?'

'Oh, I was on the verandah watching Dev train his horses, and without me knowing, Reuben was watching *me*. Then, he said — —,'

'Yeah, I know what he would've said. He's a man, what do you expect? Mind you, he's got more sense than most of them. But that's not saying much. The old devil gets these bees in his bonnet from time to time. Don't let him embarrass you.'

Sue chuckled. 'Probably fancies you himself.'

'Oh, Sue … Please!'

'Who do you think leaves the flowers for the teacher every morning on the schoolroom desk?'

'I thought it was you!'

Mattie snorted. 'Well, he'd be better than her last fellow—one foot and all in the grave as he is.' She shot Sarah one of her sparkling glances. 'All the same, it mightn't hurt to listen to him. I hate to admit it, but he's more often right than not. But don't you go telling him I said so. I've got my reputation to maintain.' She sniffed. 'But they're all the same, whether they're nineteen or ninety: keep their brains in their —— What are you cackling about, Sue? Should I be looking for an egg?'

'*Poor* Sarah!' exclaimed Sue, almost choking with laughter at Sarah's expression. 'Look what we've done to you! Have some more tea and settle down. It'll all be the same in a hundred years.'

Mattie gave another snort. 'God, Sue, you say some silly things! I've got enough to do thinking about the next hundred minutes, let alone the next hundred years when we'll all be dead and gone.' She looked at the clock. 'And so's Sarah, I'll be bound.'

Sarah's bemused gaze followed Mattie's. 'Oh, look at the time!' she said, bolting the last of her tea. 'I'll have to go to the children.' She gestured thanks and fled.

Sarah forgave Reuben when she saw the bowl of fresh flowers on her desk and knew she should thank him for his daily offering, but it was a few days before she had enough *sangfroid* to face him. She found him on his knees in a bed of flowers he was preparing for spring colour.

When she thanked him with her sweet smile, she realised she'd turned the tables on him because he became a dull red and rose creakily from his knees to stare into the distance. *He's as embarrassed as I was*, she thought. *I wonder if anyone ever thanks him?*

'That's all right, Missy. A pleasure,' he said, glancing at her and away again. 'It's hard for a young girl to come here from the south, right enough.' He paused to contemplate a bougainvillea spray, then said gruffly, 'Reckon girls need a few flowers to keep them happy when they come so far to a hard land. Reckon a young girl 'ud be used to flowers down south.'

'Well, it's very kind of you, and I do appreciate it so much.'

'No trouble, Missy,' he said, sinking to his knees, apparently absorbed in tending his tiny plants.

Between them, Reuben and Mattie might have given Sarah something to think about, but she was not about to admit it. *I'm not in love with Dev: I'm not!* she told herself angrily. *What does it matter what an old gardener says? And what a man-hating cook thinks? I've only just got out of one disastrous entanglement. I'm not about to plunge into another!*

What was the point of falling in love with a man who had shown that he had no possible interest in her, aside from her duties as governess? A man whose heart had been broken and turned to stone years ago by a woman—and not just any woman—the same woman that was here now, pursuing him with a determination that knew no bounds: not even those of manners or taste.

I'd be a fool to try and compete with her, Sarah told herself. *And I am not that much of a fool!*

§

On Saturday, after breakfast, Sarah and the children dressed in their riding clothes and walked down to the stables. They were riding quite well now, and Sarah felt that today was a milestone:

Adam had relinquished Sam into Mattie's care while they had their lesson, due to the cook's masterly strategy.

'I'll teach him how to cook fairy cakes for your morning tea,' offered Mattie. 'Sam doesn't want to get all dirty down in the dust of the stables.'

Adam had been about to object, but the mention of Mattie's mouth-watering fairy cakes changed his mind, and he left him surprisingly readily. In Sarah's mind, this was proof that Adam was healing and advancing in confidence. To have left behind, even for an hour, the one unchanging comfort amidst the trauma of chaos and despair into which his young life had been plunged was progress, indeed. Sarah felt such joy that she wished she could tell someone; then bit her lip when she realised that there was only one person with whom she wanted to share it.

Johnnie had the ponies and Persian Prince saddled ready for them. Sarah's heartbeat quickened when she saw who was with him, deep in conversation. *Think of the devil ...* Sarah took a sharp breath as the men greeted the children and turned to her.

Devin looked her over as she approached, and she felt her colour rise under his measured gaze. 'Hello, Sarah, we've just been discussing you,' he said.

Sarah greeted both men and raised her brows in enquiry. 'Should I be worried?' she asked lightly.

'Not necessarily: you get to have the last word. Johnnie tells me that he'll be needing old Prince for a few weeks, and he has suggested that you might like to take over the exercising of Gracious Lady instead.' He gave a deprecating smile. 'She might prefer it. She's not really up to my weight.'

'Gracious Lady? But ...' Her eyes blazed with light. 'Oh, Dev, *thank you!* I can't think of *anything* I would like better!'

'And also, I wondered … provided you get on with her, of course!' He paused and looked into the hazy distance before bringing his light eyes back to hers. 'Whether you might like to ride her in the Ladies' Bracelet at our picnic races?'

'May I, really? How *wonderful!* Oh, I don't know how to thank you!' Sarah's eyes began to sparkle. Now, she could *really* look forward to the picnic races.

Johnnie turned to Devin, a huge grin splitting his homely face. 'What did I tell you, Boss? I knew Sarah 'ud want to ride her. This'll be the first time ever that Medora Downs has an entry in the Ladies' Bracelet. And she'll win, too. You mark my words!' He added with satisfaction, 'There's not another mare for a thousand miles that can hold a candle to the little Lady.'

'Yes? Well, *that* remains to be seen,' said Devin. 'Sarah hasn't been on her, yet.' He bade them goodbye with a forbidding glance and strode away to his four-wheel drive. In another minute, he was gone in a cloud of dust.

'Whew! The Boss *has* got his tail feathers on fire,' commented the groom—adding as he saw his companion's face, 'Don't worry, Sarah. You'll ride her all right. She just needs gentle aids because she's very sensitive. She'll like the way you ride.'

'Sa-*rah!*' called a plaintive little voice, and Sarah turned to the children waiting patiently with their ponies. She and Johnnie helped them mount; Sarah swung up on Persian Prince, and they rode out of the stable yard.

Sarah took the children for their ride in a mood of happy anticipation. How often had she watched Devin riding the exquisite chestnut and wished fervently that she could ride her herself? And in a race, too! Her very first competition! For Sarah, the sun seemed to shine just a little more brightly and the day seemed to be made of pure gold. She and the children sang joyful nursery rhymes as they rode along the river channels.

Her exciting news did not prevent Sarah from keeping a keen eye on the children's riding positions. No bad faults must be allowed to creep in; otherwise, it would be so much more difficult to correct them later. She smiled, thinking how sweet they looked in their hard hats and jodhpurs on their dear little ponies.

Adam's ride was Snowball, a living Thelwell pony. He had a huge, bushy mane and forelock through which just peeped the tips of two tiny, pointed ears; occasionally, as it swung aside, a soft, dark eye was glimpsed. His snowy-white coat was long and fluffy, and his thick tail almost brushed the ground as, head tucked in, he minced along with short, quick steps.

Binny was a very pretty black pony with a narrow blaze and two white hind socks. She reminded Sarah of a miniature thoroughbred. She was well-educated and stepped out proudly under Naomi, with arched neck and pricked ears. Even now, at nineteen, Sarah could see why she had set the show ring alight in her prime.

Although Sarah was conscientious in her riding instruction, a little part of her mind could not help returning to that incredible conversation earlier in the morning.

Johnnie had explained to her that the Ladies' Bracelet was a race in which only mares ridden by ladies could be entered. It had been sponsored by Bill Richmond several years ago, in response to cajolery, so that his daughter could ride in (and win) a race against the other women. The prize was a glamorous and expensive gold-and-diamond bracelet—each year, a different design.

Sarah shivered in anticipation. She dare not hope to win; she had not even proved that she could ride Gracious Lady yet.

When the children had handed their ponies over to Johnnie, and Sarah led Persian Prince into his stable, he said, 'The little Lady's had her exercise for the day, but if you want, you can take her out on a slow ride this afternoon, just to get to know her.'

'Thanks, Johnnie, I'll do that.' Sarah gave him her beautiful smile. 'See you at two.' And, taking the children by the hand, she went back to Sam's fairy cakes and tea, wrapped in dreams of winning a race and with it, Devin's approval—replying absently to the children's eager comments.

§

Sarah's heart thudded a little as she took the reins from Johnnie and led Gracious Lady into the stable yard. She stroked the gleaming satin neck, placed her foot in the stirrup and swung lightly into the saddle. At first, Gracious Lady pranced sideways and fiddled with the bit, proudly arching her neck, then, reassured by her calm, still rider, relaxed and stepped daintily out onto the roadway.

Johnnie watched them go with a curious ache in his chest. 'Two little ladies, all right. Same colour hair and all,' he said to the air. 'Ah, and they'll win, too! *And* put a nose or two out of joint, I'll be bound.' At this happy thought, he grinned suddenly and turned cheerfully back to his work.

Sarah took her time to get to know Gracious Lady, who responded to her slightest wish, seeming to know, before she gave an aid, what Sarah wanted of her. She was a soft and willing ride, and Sarah was thrilled with her and could hardly wait for her training session tomorrow.

Every morning until the race, Sarah rose early, and under Johnnie's instruction, exercised Gracious Lady on the racetrack. Sometimes, Devin rode at the same time, and Sarah's heart sang as the horses thundered neck and neck down the home straight for an exciting finish to the requisite three laps of trot and one of canter that constituted the morning training session. Then, they walked them once around the track to cool them off before taking them to the washbay to hose them down.

Devin didn't make any comment about her achievement with Gracious Lady, but Sarah thought his eyes had momentarily gleamed when he had first seen them together. In reality, he had caught his breath at the picture they made: the small, graceful, fair girl on the exquisite red-gold mare with her flaxen mane and tail. Sarah sat relaxed and upright in the saddle as the mare strode out beside her stablemate on their way back home, and Devin thought that the two might have been made for each other—horse and rider appearing almost to merge as one being—since Gracious Lady responded to Sarah's invisible aids without the slightest sign to any onlooker that she did anything but sit there.

§

One day, Louella (who had mercifully stayed away since the scene with Devin in the moonlit garden) arrived in her Mercedes four-wheel drive and drew up with a flourish and a scatter of pebbles at the front entrance.

Reuben raised his head from a garden bed to see who it was and frowned, muttering to himself as he went on weeding. '*That* hussy,' he said, stabbing another weed with his garden fork. 'Nothin' but trouble, she is! Chucking stones all over my floral borders every time she comes, and I don't know what else, besides!'

Louella ran up the front steps to where Aunt Fay and Sarah were having tea on the verandah. 'Hello, Aunty. Have you seen Dev?'

'Hello, Louella,' replied Aunt Fay. 'He's in his office. Why don't you ——' But before she could finish her invitation, Louella had vanished into the house.

Sarah glanced at Aunt Fay and saw that her blue eyes were snapping. 'The ill-mannered witch!' she breathed. 'I told Bill and Esmé many years ago that Louella would be the better for a few *spankings*!' she added, looking so unlike herself that Sarah smiled. She could not imagine Aunt Fay spanking anyone! Although, for a moment there, she looked quite vicious.

Louella opened the door of the office without knocking and caught Devin unawares. As he looked up, she caught so forbidding an expression in his eyes, before he masked it, that she quailed inwardly, and the thought crossed her mind that her visit was unwelcome. It was a look that, had it been directed at Sarah, would have frozen her to the marrow and caused her to flee with a stammered apology. But Louella, supremely confident, brushed it aside as she would a fly. She sat down in the big leather armchair; elegantly crossed long, slender legs and directed an appealing smile at Devin.

'What can I do for you, Louella?' he asked, without returning her smile.

'Well … a drink would be nice, for a start,' she said, settling herself so that her dress rode a little higher up her shapely thigh.

A muscle moved in Devin's cheek as he poured them both a drink and handed one to her.

'Actually, Dev …' Louella smiled charmingly. 'I came to ask you a teeny favour.'

'Yes?' He paused. 'What is it?'

'I was hoping that you would allow me to ride Gracious Lady in the Bracelet.'

'You're too late. I already have a jockey for the mare.'

'Oh? Who is it? Medora Downs has never had a runner in the Ladies' Bracelet.'

'Sarah is riding her,' he replied, such a stern expression in his eyes that the acid comment she was about to utter died unspoken on her lips. 'Besides,' he went on, 'if I'd thought about it, I would have assumed you'd want to ride your *own* mare.'

Louella showed her chagrin at this provocative remark, uttered so blightingly. Colour fluctuated in her cheeks, and she clenched her teeth on her full lower lip as she tried to control her spleen. Devin had touched on a sore point.

Emerald Centura was a magnificent creature and had cost Bill Richmond at least as much as Louella's spiteful boast to Sarah, but she had been an abysmal failure on the racetrack and equally unsuccessful as a broodmare. So, she had come home to Emerald Hills, where she had immediately been pounced upon by Louella as her riding horse.

Louella met Devin's hard, challenging gaze with a bravado she was far from feeling. Her mare did not have a hope of beating Gracious Lady, and she knew it. And what's more, she knew that Devin knew it, too. Her glance became resentful, but she recovered herself to smile sweetly. 'Oh, well … I guess I will be, now. Cinders and I should have the advantage over an inexperienced governess—however good your mare is.'

Devin said nothing in reply to this disparaging remark, and Louella began to think that perhaps she'd gone too far. He was looking almost furious as he returned to his paperwork, shutting her out. She looked at his bent head. What if he had really meant what he said? That he no longer loved her? *No, it couldn't be true. He couldn't have changed that much*. She would bring him around in time. Time—that was all she needed.

'I can see you're busy, Dev. Don't get up. I'll see you at the races, then.'

'All right, then. Goodbye,' he returned absently, already immersed in his bookwork.

Louella fought off an uncharacteristic feeling of despair. He had always seen her out to her car before, no matter how busy he was. She shrugged and went to her vehicle, wrapped in thought. He was angry with her, that was all, for jilting him. Her confidence returned: she'd always been able to twist him around her little finger, and there was still the race ball. She hummed a little tune as she stepped off the verandah, glancing neither right nor left.

Aunt Fay looked at Sarah and made a moue. They finished their tea in silence.

Chapter Ten

As the days of the picnic races drew nearer, excitement and tension heightened to an almost unbearable pitch. Cavalcades of vehicles came and went as members of the Picnic Race Club did all the last-minute chores: washing the floor and decorating the woolshed for the evening festivities; setting up the bar and barbecue; bringing chairs, tables, provisions. The list seemed endless.

The day before the races, Sarah was stunned by the number of trucks, caravans, four-wheel drives towing horse floats and family cars that arrived at the racetrack. The horses were off-loaded into the stalls and yards, and the trucks and caravans retired to the camping area in the horse paddock—on which tents had suddenly sprung up like mushrooms. The ablutions block at the shearers' quarters, a short distance away, was used by the campers.

As far as lessons were concerned, the morning was an abject failure—as first one child and then the other rushed to the window to see what was going on.

Sarah was beginning to feel frustrated, when Aunt Fay popped her head around the door and suggested she take the children down to the racetrack. 'The Ilona Downs children will have arrived by now, with Jacqui,' she told her. 'I've just been talking to Elisabeth on the radio. Why don't you take Naomi and Adam down to join them?'

'Oh, why not?' agreed Sarah, in relief. 'There is not much productivity happening here.' She smiled. 'You must have second sight, bless you.'

'I know what it's like,' said Aunt Fay, backing out of the room. 'Have fun with your friends, children. And you, too, Sarah. Jacqui is a nice, friendly girl.'

The children rushed to the door, almost falling over each other in their excitement. Sarah called them to order, and they proceeded down the hall at a much more decorous pace, but once outside, she let them run free. Her eyes went to Sam, seated in the teacher's chair, and she wondered how soon it would be before Adam remembered him.

Jacqui and her pupils, John Junior, Jennifer and Susan, were waiting for them at the bottom of the horse paddock. Jacqui's smile lit up her face, and she greeted Sarah with friendly cheer. While the children darted ahead, the two governesses strolled along, chatting amicably and keeping an eye on their excitable charges.

'I hear you're riding in the Ladies' Bracelet,' said Jacqui, giving Sarah an admiring glance. 'Good on you!'

'Thanks, Jacqui. Yes, I'm going to have a go.'

'You'll be riding against Louella Richmond.' Jacqui grimaced. 'That's one tough lady!'

Sarah nodded but did not comment.

'Oh, well … If you win the Bracelet, that's one thing—and, believe me, I hope you do! But heaven help the woman who cuts her out with your boss!'

'I beg your pardon?' said Sarah, startled.

Jacqui giggled. 'Haven't you heard? The word is out that *Miss* Richmond—apparently when she discarded hubby, she discarded the name as well—is looking for a new husband. And your boss is *it*.'

If only she knew what I know, thought Sarah. *But I can't discuss Dev's business with Jacqui.*

'And, oh, Sarah! This is really terrible, but Jack Grey is keeping a book on it. Two-to-one on are the odds he's offering!'

Good Heavens! Everyone in the Outback must know about it. How awful for Dev to be the butt of all the stock camp and pub gossip. Sarah's face puckered. Now she knew what Jim had meant when he had said that the Outback was both big and small. Sometimes, it was a good thing—and sometimes not.

'I hope I haven't upset you, Sarah? I know I do rattle on,' apologised Jacqui, after a quick look at her companion's expression. 'Anyway, we've got better things to do than worry about Outback gossip. Let's catch up with our kids.'

As they came closer to the horse stalls and the camping ground, they could hear chatter and happy laughter as people caught up with each other for the first time, perhaps, since the last picnic races, here at Medora Downs.

'Come on over to the van, and I'll make a cuppa,' said Jacqui, after they left the children in the hands of two smiling teenage girls who promised to bring them straight back after they showed them their horses. 'You look as if you need it.'

'Ahoy there, Sarah!' Jim Barnes was approaching with long, rapid strides, his face wreathed in smiles. The two governesses waited for him to come up to them.

'Hello, Jacqui. How's it going, old girl?' He gave her shoulder a friendly squeeze, then slipped a companionable arm around Sarah's waist. 'How's it going, Sarah?' Jim strolled along with them to the van, chatting and joking.

Sarah noticed that Jacqui had gone very quiet and glanced at her, almost pulling up short at her rigid expression. Gone was the friendly smile and sparkling look of a few moments before. Jacqui was looking straight ahead, unsmiling, and there was a spot of colour in her cheek. Dismayed, Sarah disengaged herself from Jim's arm and tried to include Jacqui in the conversation, but she kept her eyes averted and answered in monosyllables.

When they reached the van, Jim stood outside and chatted to Sarah for a few minutes, obviously hoping for an invitation to come in, but when none was forthcoming, he remembered a pressing duty somewhere else and said goodbye to them. 'See you tonight at the barbecue, Jacqui,' he added in a casual tone.

What's eating Jacqui? he wondered. *She's usually a lot of fun to be with; a real good sort!* It puzzled him that she had clammed up and become so unfriendly, and he wondered if, in some way, he had unwittingly offended her. He told himself that he would make it his business to find out before the weekend was over.

Jacqui and Sarah set out the camping table and chairs under

a shady tree and had just finished putting out mugs, plates and biscuits, cake and slices, when the five children arrived, ravenous and full of excited chatter. The two governesses were completely occupied for the next few minutes in handing out food and drink but, eventually, were able to turn their attention to themselves.

'Are you all right, Jacqui?' asked Sarah, looking at her in concern.

Jacqui grimaced. 'I'm just jealous, Sarah,' she said with unexpected candour. 'Jim Barnes wouldn't know if I was dead or alive with you around.'

'Oh, but … Jim is just a friendly kind of person. Truly, Jacqui, you have no need to worry.'

Jacqui's normally sunny nature reasserted itself, and she smiled apologetically at Sarah. 'I'm sorry,' she said. 'Men can be pains, can't they?' When she changed the subject, Sarah followed her lead, but she could not help feeling just a little sorry for Jacqui. It was so sad to love someone that didn't even know you existed. *If I was stupid enough to fall in love with Dev, it would be the same for me*, she thought.

Later that night, Sarah stood out on the verandah and looked down towards the horse paddock. She could almost feel the air of excitement and general camaraderie from here. The bar was open, the barbecue fires were in full swing and, now and again, the breeze wafted sounds of cheerful laughter towards the house. As she turned back to go to her room, Sarah experienced a curious longing to be part of that happy crowd.

§

Friday dawned with the promise of a bright, clear day to follow, and an air of festivity hung over the racetrack. The races were due to start at ten o'clock, and Devin was to ride Bold Rover at one in the Emerald Hills Cup—in which the owner had to train and ride his own horse. Sarah's race was not until Saturday. Her heart contracted painfully at the thought.

At a quarter to ten, Sarah, Aunt Fay, Adam and Naomi—dressed in shady hats and all their finery—walked into the colourful crowd in the grandstand area. Sam had once more been left in charge of the schoolroom. To Sarah, this was one more milestone in the development of Adam's confidence. *But he'll look for him fast enough at bedtime*, she thought with a smile as she looked around for familiar faces. The air was vibrating with anticipation as the racegoers placed their bets for the first race.

In the distance, Sarah caught a glimpse of Devin talking to Johnnie outside Bold Rover's stall. Aunt Fay was quickly becoming surrounded by old friends, as first one, then another recognised her and came over to greet her.

The children were hanging over the top rail of the fence, hoping to catch sight of their uncle. In between this absorbing pastime, they watched three races and complained that they were starving.

Sarah took them off to the barbecue area to find some lunch. As their hunger was assuaged, their excitement mounted, and they asked Sarah to tell them the time at least once every five minutes. At a quarter to one, Sarah allowed them to go to the saddling paddock where Johnnie was already walking Bold Rover around with some other grooms and horses. The children sat on the fence and watched with keen interest.

In a few minutes, Devin—dressed in jockey's silks with the Medora Downs' colours of white with a red star and black striped sleeves—joined him, and they began to talk quietly in a corner of the paddock while Johnnie adjusted the girth and stirrups.

Bold Rover looked a picture of health and fitness. His dark mahogany coat gleamed in the sunlight, and the straight, silken strands of his mane and tail hung in a shining fall, swaying gently with every movement, which, as the time of the race drew closer, became more and more frequent and impatient.

At last, Devin mounted and settled himself in the saddle. The big thoroughbred, though still held firmly on the lead rein by the groom, plunged and reared in his anxiety to be off and running. Eventually, he tired of this and contented himself with shaking his head and kicking out at imaginary enemies from time to time.

'There's Uncle Dev!' called Naomi.

'Uncle Dev! Uncle Dev!' shouted Adam, bouncing up and down so much that he would have fallen into the saddling paddock had Sarah not taken a firm grip on the back of his belt.

Devin glanced over towards them, smiled and lifted his whip in salute. His eyes briefly met Sarah's, and she thought she caught a flash of fellow feeling in their depths, before he turned his attention back to his horse. It was as if he said, 'This is you, tomorrow.'

Everything seemed to move quickly after that. A sea of spectators surged from the saddling paddock to the fenced edge of the racetrack. The horses paraded past the grandstand at a smart trot and followed the starter down to the far side of the track. The starter marshalled them into a straight line at a steady trot; then, when all the heads were level, he gave the signal to race.

Bold Rover got away well and settled down three or four behind the leader, keeping steadily to the pace. Sarah held her breath. The tension was unbearable. The children, jumping up and down, were screaming encouragement to Bold Rover and Uncle Dev. After the turn into the home straight, Devin gave Bold Rover his head, and his big, ground-covering strides just ate up the distance as he overcame his rivals and sped away up the straight—a clear winner.

Sarah, in a daze of excitement, unclenched her fingers from around the race booklet and turned to Aunt Fay, who was brushing away a tear. 'Darcy would have been so proud,' she said in a choked voice and turned away to blow her nose and compose herself. Sarah patted her hand and set off after the children who had run back to the saddling paddock.

After the race, Devin joined them for a short while in the grandstand enclosure, before taking his turn behind the bar. All the male committee members took turns at manning the bar, which operated, as far as Sarah could see, about twenty-two hours out of the twenty-four.

Sarah congratulated Devin on his win.

He thanked her, adding with the hint of a smile, 'Bold Rover and I did our part; it will be your turn tomorrow! Which reminds me of something I had forgotten to tell you: There will be a barbecue and bush dance tonight, which all the children attend. If you will bring Naomi and Adam down about six, that would be good. Oh and, by the way, Mattie will babysit tomorrow night, so that you can go to the ball. Your ticket is paid for, and I'll pick you and Aunty up about nine o'clock.' He handed Sarah the package Aunt Fay had passed to him. 'Wear this tomorrow in the race. And,' he warned, 'no late night, tonight. The Bracelet is the first race tomorrow.' A tender, upward curve softened the rigid set of his lips as his gaze lit on his niece and nephew. They ran up to him with joyous admiration, hugged his legs and darted off after their friends. 'The children are loving this!' His glance, warm and interested, met hers. 'Are you enjoying it, too, Sarah?'

Sarah thought how different he looked when he allowed himself to relax and show expression. How charming he could be when he liked. How kind were his eyes, just now, as he asked his question. She drew in her breath. Her naïve assessment of what she saw there made her heart leap. Then, as she was about to answer, his gaze shifted; he looked into the distance, and she felt that he had forgotten her. 'I have to go,' he said. 'I'm needed at the bar. Right now, by the look of it!' A cool glance of apology, and he was gone. Sarah watched as he wove his way through the crowd and disappeared into the bar.

One minute he was all tender warmth. And then he withdrew it: just like that! *It is just bewildering,* she thought, refusing to admit that her principal feeling was one of loss and disappointment. *But, anyway, why should I care? I mean, he is my boss, after all. And not anything else,* she warned herself.

Sarah looked into the paper packet. It was a jockey's silk in the Medora Downs' colours with a red silk cap to match. Not the one Devin had been wearing, but a new small one. She wondered where it had come from and fell to thinking about tomorrow's race. Sarah hoped with all her heart that she would ride Gracious Lady properly tomorrow and tried to ignore the fluttering of nerves in her stomach. She collected Aunt Fay and the children, and they went home so that Naomi and Adam could have a rest before the exertions of the evening.

When they returned to the horse paddock at six o'clock, the nearby woolshed was a blaze of light and the barbecues, set up at the end of it, were glowing cosily. They met up with Jacqui and the three Andrews' children who were looking out for them as soon as they arrived. Sarah blinked: There seemed to be children everywhere; she had not seen so many before.

Jacqui laughed. 'Children's night,' she explained.

After they had eaten, all the children trooped into the woolshed, eyes suddenly round at the colourful decorations of streamers, balloons, flowers and branches. The committee ladies had done an excellent job, and they had to do it all again before tomorrow night's ball.

The children sat, wide-eyed and shy around the edge of the dancefloor, waiting for the bush band to strike up. Some of the adults organised the children into groups, the band started, and all was joyful concentration while the youthful dancers performed such timeless favourites as the hokey-pokey, the Canadian three step and the polka, then played games of drop the hanky and piggy in the middle.

At last, exhausted, the children made no demur at being packed off to bed, leaving the woolshed floor clear for the adults.

As they were leaving, Sarah caught a glimpse of Devin's broad shoulders over the other side of the barbecue area. Her heart gave a painful lurch as she saw Louella walk up and link her arm through his as he conversed with her father.

Sarah hurried the children to the car. No matter how much she told herself that it was nothing to her what her employer did in his spare time, she found that her enjoyment of the evening had evaporated.

Chapter Eleven

Sarah woke suddenly, very early, her heart thudding with mingled apprehension and excitement. Today she would ride in the Ladies' Bracelet. *I can't believe it*, she thought. *It can't be true!*

She slipped on jeans and a sweater and went down to the stables. But, early as she was, Johnnie was there before her, giving the mare a light breakfast. Sarah was glad that the committee had allowed the horses to be corn fed at this meeting. The rule was that the horses should be grass fed, but owing to the dry conditions prevailing over most of the district, it had been waived this time.

'How are you this morning, Sarah?' asked Johnnie, looking at her closely. 'Not nervous, are you?'

'Oh, a little … Well, yes, a lot,' she admitted.

'You'll be all right, you know. The Boss did a good job yesterday, didn't he?'

'Oh yes, he won really well.'

'And you will, too, Sarah,' he assured her. 'Just hold her back a little, at first, and ease her around the turn. Then, when you hit the straight, give the mare her head. The little Lady knows what to do.'

Sarah nodded and smiled. It didn't sound too difficult put like that, and Johnnie seemed to have confidence in them. *Oh, if only we can win …* 'Except … What about Louella's black mare?' asked Sarah, voicing her most pressing fear.

'Don't you worry about her, mate, that mare can go like the clappers for the first three hundred or so, but after that, she's finished. She's the biggest disappointment I think old Bill Richmond's ever had as a racehorse. Just when you want a bit of speed in the home straight, after the turn, she pulls up so fast she nearly throws the jockey over her head.' He wagged an admonitory finger. 'You ride like I tell you, and you'll have nothing to worry about.'

Sarah stood for a few minutes beside the mare and stroked her gleaming chestnut coat. 'Please, do your best, Lady,' she whispered. But Gracious Lady only blew gently into her feed bin, intent on picking out her favourite sunflower seeds, totally unconcerned about the race or anything else. Giving her a last farewell pat, Sarah turned away and went slowly back to the homestead.

§

Here we are, Lady, thought Sarah. *This is it!* Seated astride Gracious Lady in the saddling paddock, she felt unreal, as though she were living in a dream.

'Remember what I said, now, Sarah,' whispered Johnnie as he

unclipped the lead rein and let her out the gate.

She trotted past the grandstand and back again in a daze, then followed the others to where the starter was waiting.

Louella rode up beside her, Emerald Centura's glossy coat shining blue-black in the sunlight. 'My, my,' she sneered as she passed. 'I didn't think Devin would be silly enough to allow a novice on his good mare. I mean, you'll probably be *stupid* enough to miss the start!'

Sarah flushed, but said nothing, stroking Gracious Lady's silky mane and keeping her eyes firmly fixed between those two delicately curved, pointed ears, which were, just now, flicking nervously back and forth. Taking her place on the outside of a line of five riders, Sarah was surprised to find that Louella had turned from the inside and roughly pushed her mare into the line to range alongside of her as they trotted along, waiting for the starter to give his signal.

'Go!' he yelled, dropping the scarf he was holding.

Suddenly, all was action. Sarah gave a gasp of shock and almost fell off as, without warning, Gracious Lady jumped in the air, leapt sideways and backwards, shaking her head violently. In stunned disbelief, Sarah registered that Louella had hit out viciously with her whip at Gracious Lady's head, striking the mare in the face and causing her to prop and swerve as she flinched away from the cruel blow.

By the time Sarah regained her seat and steadied Gracious Lady, she realised, with a sinking heart, that the rest of the field were well ahead of her. The mare recovered herself, tossed her head and, snatching the bit, fairly bolted after the other horses. Sarah tried several times to ease the pace, then realising she had no control, sat still, crouched over her mount's withers, clinging like a burr as Gracious Lady—hooves flying and tail streaming out behind her—settled down to the job she knew best.

Faster and faster flew the little chestnut, until all that existed in Sarah's world was the rushing of the wind—all but snatching her breath away—and the frenzied drumming of those wildly galloping hooves as the mare relentlessly bore down on her rivals.

She's every inch a racehorse, thought Sarah, suddenly choking with emotion at Gracious Lady's display of raw courage. *This little mare is as brave as they come! Oh, God, please don't let her break down,* she prayed silently and crouched even lower over the mare's withers to help her all she could.

They came around the turn glaringly wide, since Gracious Lady had not slackened her blistering pace. Sarah held her breath, knowing that this was where the mare was most likely to hurt herself, but they straightened up safely and shot after the others.

'And look at Gracious Lady!' The commentator's voice vibrated with excitement, rising higher in pitch with every word. 'She's fairly mowing them down! What a run this little mare has made! And now she's out after Emerald Centura! Emerald Centura! Gracious Lady! She's narrowing the gap, but *can* she do it …?'

Johnnie stood, white-knuckled fists gripping the rail, as he watched the mare's headlong run with troubled eyes.

Devin, beside him, was in the grip of a cold fury. 'If *she* breaks that mare down …' he ground out in a tight under voice.

'She'll be okay, Boss,' responded the groom, but he was worried and miserable. Why hadn't Sarah ridden the mare the way he'd told her? Instead of missing the start like that, and then not sparing her mount in that wild, heart-bursting run?

Dimly, Sarah was aware of flashing past three blurred shapes, and Gracious Lady—finding from somewhere an extra, unbelievable turn of speed—came up beside Emerald Centura a few lengths from the winning post. For several desperate strides, they galloped neck and neck; the little chestnut cocking an ear and keeping well out from that vicious whip, which was just now being applied energetically to the black mare's shoulder; as Louella, lips drawn back from her teeth, grimly pulled out all the stops to prevent her from being overtaken. But Emerald Centura, who had already done more for Louella than she ever had for the best jockey on a city racetrack, was tiring now. Moreover, she resented the whip as her laidback ears and white-rimmed eyes attested. She imperceptibly slowed her pace, and Gracious Lady pulled smoothly away to win by a length.

For the first time, Sarah heard the race commentator, almost screaming in his excitement: 'And it's all Gracious Lady! Gracious Lady by a length! Emerald Centura second. Blue Gum third. What a gallant little mare this is, Ladies and Gentlemen! What a race we have seen today! She missed the start by about thirty lengths, and I didn't give her a chance of catching up, let alone winning. Take a good look at her, Ladies and Gentlemen: This is a *real* racehorse! And I predict a great future for her when she goes off for the Spring Racing Carnival in the city. Ladies and Gentlemen, this is the stuff that champions are made of, and we have seen a champion today!'

After the winning post, Gracious Lady dropped the bit, seeming to understand that the job was done, and allowed Sarah to ease her back to a canter and then a trot. She hoped with all her heart that the run hadn't hurt the mare: she seemed all right at the moment, sweating a little, but not blowing too much. Sarah patted the steaming, delicately arched neck as Gracious Lady fiddled demurely with the bit, inclining her ears slightly back to catch Sarah's softly uttered words of praise. 'Good girl,' she whispered. 'Oh, you good, *wonderful* girl!'

They turned back to the saddling enclosure to be met by a smiling clerk of the course on his grey. As they paraded past the grandstand, the crowd cheered and clapped. Gracious Lady arched her neck even more and pranced daintily beside the sturdy grey—appearing to enjoy the admiration she excited. *She knows,* thought Sarah, with absolute certainty. *She knows what she has done. And what's more, she meant to do it!*

Johnnie was waiting at the gate of the saddling paddock to clip the lead rein onto Gracious Lady's bit as she reached it. He ran an experienced eye over her and heaved a sigh of relief when he saw that no apparent harm had been done by the gruelling race. 'What happened, Sarah? he asked in a low voice, looking up into her white, anxious face.

'Louella hit her in the face with her whip ——'

'God, yes! I can see the mark! She's even drawn blood! Well, *what* a ——'

'And then Lady just took the bit, and I couldn't hold her,' explained Sarah, adding in an agonised whisper, 'Oh, Johnnie: will she be all right?'

'She's all right. Don't you worry, I'll look after her. I don't think any harm's been done. Like I said, the little Lady knows her job,' he reassured her, holding the mare still while Sarah dismounted. She unsaddled with fumbling fingers that wouldn't seem to obey her and walked stiffly to the weighing room while the groom led Gracious Lady into the winner's bay and stood, stroking her velvet nose.

As Sarah was about to enter the room, she glanced over to where Devin stood, and she flinched at the hard, angry expression in his eyes, before he turned on his heel and strode away. Sarah's victory, righted somewhat by Johnnie's assurance that Gracious Lady hadn't injured herself, now turned to ashes. Never had she felt so miserable. *Dev's furious with me! But how can I blame him,* she wondered, *for thinking that I carelessly missed the start and then rode Gracious Lady into the ground to catch up?* He didn't know that the mare had taken over—virtually bolted with her—because she didn't want to be beaten. *And would he believe it if I told him?* He knew as well as she did that Gracious Lady was so sensitive that a slight tug on the rein was normally all that was necessary to control her speed.

While she was waiting to step on the scales, Sarah marvelled again at the fighting spirit of the little mare who, after such a cruel blow, could shake her head and gallantly go all out to win. No-one could have seen Louella's action because, not only were they on the other side of the racetrack, but Sarah had been on the outside of the other four horses. And the mare was so small that she would have been well hidden behind Louella's big black. *And how can I tell Dev something like that, anyway? I just can't, that's all.* Her face puckered. *He will just have to think badly of me.* This conclusion could have made her feel even more miserable if it were possible.

Sarah stepped out of the weighing room and stood beside Gracious Lady for the presentation. The mare wore a handsome pale-blue ribbon around her gleaming neck, and Sarah was presented with the lovely gold-and-diamond bracelet. But, after the look Devin had given her, all the glow had gone from the day, and it was a hollow victory.

Bill Richmond smiled, shook her hand and clasped the bracelet around her wrist. 'That was a great run,' he enthused. 'A well-deserved win! That little mare is a real treasure.'

Sarah glanced from him to his daughter, standing next to him, and the glittering malevolence in those sea-green eyes made her quake inwardly for just one tiny moment before she turned back to Bill to murmur her thanks and gratitude for the bracelet and his kind words. She turned to walk with her horse and the groom to the hosing bay.

'Sarah! Sa-*rah!*' called joyful voices from the fence, and she looked around to see the beaming faces of Naomi, Adam and Mattie.

'Mattie's won fifty dollars on you, Sarah!' shouted Naomi; Adam jumped up and down so much that he nearly fell off the fence; and Mattie, holding him with one hand, jubilantly waved a fistful of banknotes in the other.

Sarah waved and smiled, then followed Gracious Lady's retreating form into the hosing bay and held her for Johnnie to hose her down and carefully check her legs. Then, she tied her to a piece of string on the rail.

Johnnie cast an anxious glance at Sarah's white, strained countenance. *Taking it hard,* he thought with compassion. 'Don't worry, Sarah. The little Lady's all right.' He cleared his throat, keeping his attention on gently sponging the mare's injured face. 'The Boss won't be cranky when I explain to him what happened.'

Sarah swallowed; her eyes stricken. It was a moment before she answered. 'It doesn't matter, Johnnie ...' choking on any further words, she made a helpless gesture and started back to the homestead to change.

Johnnie watched her go with a worried frown. 'Like *hell* it doesn't matter!' he muttered as he scraped the water off the mare's coat and expertly wiped her down with a towel. 'I can't have that cow-handed floozy from the Hills moving in over here and ruining the mouths of all the horses on the station! So, I can't!'

Gracious Lady stamped her hooves and tossed her head, as if in agreement.

'Ah, you know, don't you, girl? Just look at that welt on your poor little face! Well, we'll have to set things straight, won't we?' He was thinking hard as he led her back to her stable.

§

'You busy, Boss? You'd better come and look at this mare.'

Devin excused himself from the gathering and went off to the stables with the groom. 'Has she taken hurt, Johnnie?'

'Well, yes and no. Nothing that can't be fixed. But there's something you need to see.'

Without preamble, Johnnie showed him the welt on Gracious Lady's face and the nick over her nostril, still oozing blood, where the whip had cut into the tender skin, passing on just what Sarah had told him. 'And it explains everything, Boss: Why she missed the start like that. Why Sarah couldn't hold her. The lot.'

Devin was speechless, running a gentle hand over the mare's

face. 'I can't believe this!' he said at last. 'But I have to, don't I? Sarah doesn't lie and nor does this.' He indicated the swelling running from eye to nostril with the small red strip at the end.

Johnnie shook his head. 'You'll pardon me if I'm speaking out of turn, Boss. But you had a lucky escape!'

Devin screwed up his eyes, then looked at him with the flicker of a smile. 'I've known that for ten years, Johnnie.'

'Yeah?' Johnnie gave him a dry glance. 'Funny,' he mused, 'I would have sworn she cut you up bad.'

'The head can believe what the heart can't accept,' said Devin, as if to himself. Then he looked straight at the groom. 'Don't worry; she won't get another chance at something like this.'

Johnnie whistled in relief. 'You're all right, Boss, and so's the little Lady. Sarah did the only thing she could. Fighting her would only have made it worse, and then she *might* have injured herself. A bit of a spell, and she'll come back better than ever.' He took a deep breath … It was now or never: 'The one I'm worried about is Sarah. She took it hard, you know, what happened.'

'I know—and I'm sorry.'

'She's fretting over the little Lady. Worried about whether she's hurt her, or whether she could have ridden her better. Worried about what her boss thinks, too, if I'm not mistaken.'

'Okay, I'll talk to her. Let her know the mare is okay.'

'Good on ya, Boss.' Johnnie gave him an engaging grin. 'I can look after this little blonde, I reckon. I just need you to go and make your peace with the other.'

Chapter Twelve

Sarah sat on the verandah, blinking back tears and staring out over the garden with unseeing eyes. She did not feel equal to going back down to the races and facing Devin's condemnation. The memory of his furious expression—the contempt in his hard gaze—lashed her senses, making the tears flow in earnest. Annoyed at her weakness, she dashed them away with the back of one hand, refusing to give in to them.

The day had been spoilt from the moment that Louella had made her incredibly cruel, unsporting attack on Gracious Lady at the start of the race. Sarah reflected that this was an aspect of the woman's character that she had wondered about. *It was a dreadful way to find out, but now I have my answer: Yes, she is just like David, cowardly violence and all! Not that it does me any good!* So engrossed was she in her thoughts that a light, firm tread on the verandah went unnoticed.

'Sarah!'

Startled, she turned her head to see Devin striding towards her. He sat down in the squatter's chair beside her and placed his hands on the arms, curling his long fingers around them. Absently, she noted how strong and capable they looked while her mind grappled with his presence and the fear of what she would read in his eyes.

As if compelled, she slowly raised her own to his to find that they were warmly regarding her, and her treacherous heart quickened its beat.

'Why aren't you down at the racetrack having some lunch?' he enquired, lifting an eyebrow.

'I …' she began, then shrugged. She could not seem to get the words out past a lump in her throat.

'Look,' he said, 'Johnnie told me what happened out there on the track, and I believe you did the only thing you could. Gracious Lady has a heart as big as a house, an unbelievable will to win, and she knows her job. That's why she's such a good racehorse. And she's taken no harm,' he added gently.

Sarah knew in her heart that he wouldn't mention Louella to her and was painfully aware that she could not do so, either. She said, 'I am so glad Lady wasn't hurt. I couldn't bear it *if* she had been.'

'I know you couldn't. But all's well that ends well.' Suddenly, he smiled. A warm, breathtaking smile that lit up his eyes, transforming him instantly from a reserved stranger into a vital, magnetic personality—making Sarah's eyes widen and her heart suspend its beat. 'Anyway,' he said, rising to his feet and holding out his hand. 'I came to get my winning jockey and take her to lunch. How does a steak sandwich and champagne sound?'

'Just beautiful, Boss,' said Sarah, placing her hand in his and allowing him to pull her to her feet. She smiled up at him and thought of Jo's favourite word. '*Perfect!*' she added, walking with him in the bright sunshine to the car.

Everyone was waiting for Sarah in the barbecue area. Someone pushed her into a chair, and somebody else handed her a glass of bubbly and a steak sandwich. Then, they all toasted her with champagne. At last, Sarah felt as though she belonged here with these generous, warm-hearted people, and she was so happy that, momentarily, she was afraid—before shaking off a warning from an inner voice that such happiness could not last.

Adam and Naomi came to her and put their arms around her as she sat in the folding chair. 'We think you're terrific, Sarah,' they whispered.

'Thank you, my darlings,' she said, hugging them back, her heart overflowing, laughing as she almost spilled her champagne. Involuntarily, she glanced over to where Devin was standing with Jim and John Andrews and saw that he had been watching this exchange. He caught her eye, smiled and raised his glass to her, and Sarah smiled back, feeling in her heart that they were on the edge of something wonderful. A warm glow spread through her, and she didn't think that it was just the champagne. The memory of the expression in his eyes stayed with her all that afternoon and while she was dressing for the ball.

§

Sarah luxuriated in a warm, scented bath, soaking away the aches and pains from her exertions in the race, while she dreamt in happy anticipation of the evening to come. The mood lasted while she applied her evening make-up, dressed her hair with jewelled combs and stepped into the one good evening gown that she had brought with her.

It was a beautiful dress, its soft silver-grey folds falling to mid-calf and enhancing her fair loveliness. Modest yet provocative, it subtly hinted at the details of her slender figure. Clinging, yet not revealing, it was a masterpiece of understated elegance. It had cost an arm and a leg at an exclusive fashion house in Sydney, and Sarah had only bought it at David's insistence.

Now, incredibly, she was glad that he had chosen it for her, and she hoped that Dev would notice her in it. Soon he would be here, handsome in his dinner suit, to escort her and Aunt Fay to the ball. Butterflies turned cartwheels in her stomach, and she laughed at herself. *Anyone would think I'd never been to a ball! Come on, Cinderella. Pull yourself together!* With a last appraising glance in the mirror, she left the room.

Halfway down the hall, Sarah put her hands up to her ears and realised she had forgotten her earrings. The car arrived just as she ran lightly back to her room. Hurriedly, she placed diamond studs in her ears to match the diamond bracelet, which, of course, she must wear, and retraced her steps, wondering at her state of mind. Her heart began to pound as she neared the door of the lounge, and she hesitated a little before entering. *I can't be nervous,* she thought, *can I? Surely not!*

Aunt Fay stood talking to Jim, and Sarah was ashamed of the sudden and intense pang of disappointment that assailed her.

Jim turned to greet her with his wide smile. 'Dev's behind the bar for the next couple of hours, so I hope you two beautiful ladies don't mind coming with me?' His eyes told Sarah how much he appreciated her dress.

As they turned to leave, there was a knock on the door, and Reuben stood there, bashfully clearing his throat. In his left hand were two lovely pink orchids. He gestured to them with his right. 'For the ladies,' he said.

'Oh, Reuben!' squeaked Sarah. 'How *utterly* gorgeous! But ... where did you get them?'

'Ah, Missy ...' His old eyes crinkled up in amusement. 'I keep a few things in my shadehouse that I don't tell everybody about. Grew 'em 'specially for tonight,' he added with pride as he watched them fix the glowing blooms onto their gowns.

Aunt Fay, small and dignified in black, added her smiling thanks to Sarah's, both almost moved to tears by the thought of all the love and care that had gone into the raising of these two delicate beauties Reuben had so proudly presented to them.

'Enjoy yourselves,' he said, watching them walk out of the room and down the hall. Then, he sighed and turned away, thinking how lovely these two women were—perfect settings for his orchids. A thought struck him, and he chuckled as he pictured the envy the blooms would arouse in others less fortunate than *his* two ladies who reaped the benefits of his magical green fingers. *And I hope that hussy from the Hills is properly jealous!*

§

The woolshed was ablaze with light when they arrived, and Sarah looked around in surprise and admiration at the decorations. The ladies of the committee had surpassed themselves this time. Sarah had thought last night's decorations wonderful, but they were nothing compared with these. The walls were covered in brightly coloured posters depicting ladies in crinolines and courtly gentlemen in tails and top hats, since the theme of the ball was 'Ye Olden Days'.

The multicoloured streamers that hid the high-raftered ceiling were gathered into hoops—rather like crinolines themselves—at intervals along the centre of the pitched roof from which they suspended, looping gracefully, to the walls. In the centre of each hoop were bunches of balloons, a mirrorball and a chandelier mobile made of wire wrapped in silver foil with hanging brilliants set with tiny mirrors that flashed rainbow patterns of light as they swayed in the breeze. Huge urns of flowers and greenery—courtesy, no doubt, of Reuben—filled the corners of the ballroom and were placed at intervals along the walls.

When Sarah saw how people dressed here for gala occasions, she was pleased that she had worn her model dress. The men were all very different in their dinner suits from their usual attire of drill trousers, cotton shirts and broad-brimmed felt hats. Some of them were unrecognisable to her, since they were usually more or less covered in a film of dust of varying thickness; their faces anonymous, hidden beneath their hats, whenever she had seen them previously.

The women's gowns were brilliant points of colour amongst the press of black suits. Some even wore crinolines, in accordance with the theme of the ball. Everywhere was abuzz with happy conversation as the people of this lonely land threw off the cares and worries of everyday life and prepared to enjoy their special night.

Aunt Fay was claimed for the first waltz by her old friend Bill Richmond, who had obviously been keeping his eye out for her arrival.

Jim grinned at Sarah. 'Well? Shall we dance?' Without waiting for an answer, he swept her lightly onto the dancefloor, joining the throng of people already there. 'You dance well, Sarah,' he said after a few minutes, breaking the silence between them.

'Thank you, so do you,' replied Sarah, smiling at the compliment, then glanced over towards the bar. She caught a glimpse of Devin's broad shoulders as he turned away to mix a drink for a customer, and the now familiar, restless longing washed over her. Making a supreme effort, she maintained a lighthearted conversation with Jim and kept her eyes on him for the rest of the dance.

Sarah danced twice with Jim; once with Alex, one of the young jackaroos; and once with Bill Richmond, who was eager to discuss the breeding, racing ability and conformation of Gracious Lady; before they returned to their table to sit with Aunt Fay. Devin was still busy behind the bar, and Sarah wondered with a little shiver of anticipation if he would ask her to dance.

A jovial voice spoke behind her, jolting her out of her reverie: 'Come on, Sarah, the night's too good to waste sitting around.'

'Oh, Jim! You made me jump,' she said, rising to walk with him to the dancefloor. Her eye was caught by Louella—tall and elegant in a gold lamé strapless evening gown that clung seductively to her statuesque curves. She looked stunning and sophisticated, and Sarah wondered despairingly how Devin would react when he saw her. *What chance do I have, beside her?*

she asked herself hopelessly, and as they danced closer to the bar, her eyes strayed towards it again, unconsciously seeking him.

Sarah drew in a sudden breath, arrested by a man leaning on the bar who was staring at her fixedly, an untouched drink in his hand. A wave of shock swept over her as she became aware of his regard, and she was assailed by a sudden, nameless fear. He was tall and slim—lithe, as many stockmen were—and had a high cheekboned, rather pointed face. His eyes were flat and dull like slate, and his narrow, high-bridged nose flared at the nostrils. As her startled gaze met his, she saw his thin lips twist into a sneer, and she quickly looked away. But she could not repress a shudder at the almost intangible waves of menace that had seemed to emanate from this man when, for that infinitesimal space of time, she had looked into those frighteningly lifeless eyes. Nobody had ever affected her this way before, and though she tried to shrug it off as a silly fancy, she was not successful.

'What's the matter, Sarah?' asked Jim, concerned by her sudden pallor.

'Oh … nothing.' Sarah forced a smile. 'A goose walked over my grave, that's all. I think I must be too hot.'

Jim had felt the tremor that passed through her body, but he said nothing more, waltzing her expertly out onto the landing. They walked down the steps and into the cool night air.

Sarah breathed deeply and felt her nerves begin to steady. *How silly to feel so afraid just because a stranger stared at me!* she thought. Perhaps she had imagined the malevolence in his eyes? It was best to think so, anyway.

They strolled down towards the trees in the channels, enjoying the relative quiet and the freshness of the breeze.

Without warning, Jim stopped and pulled her against him. She could feel the quickened, heavy beat of his heart.

'Sarah, honey! I …' he began and bent his head to kiss her.

'Jim, don't! Please *don't!*' she whispered, trying to struggle out of his arms.

He loosened his hold but looked at her for a long moment. 'Okay, honey,' he said, stepping back with a puzzled frown. 'But I am not just amusing myself, you know.'

'I know.' She swallowed. 'It is just that I ——'

'You're not still pining after that loser we threw out, are you? I know it takes time.'

'No. Oh, no. I've almost forgotten all about him. Please, Jim …'

'Is there someone else?'

'*No!*' Her unwonted vehemence gave them both pause. Sarah was thankful that the darkness hid her hot cheeks. 'I'm not … I don't want to hurt you, but I can't feel the way you want me to.'

It's Dev, he thought. *God help her! Poor little Sarah: I don't know how many hearts he's broken.* 'I'm sorry, Sarah. I won't pry any further,' he assured her, adding with touching humility, 'I don't suppose you *could* come to care for me, one day?'

'Jim, I already do care for you, very much. And I value your friendship. If I could have a brother, I would wish him to be you.'

He turned away and laughed. Yet, Sarah thought it was the saddest laugh that she had ever heard.

'Oh,' he groaned. 'Somehow that hurts more than anything else you could have said!'

'Oh, Jim, I'm *sorry* …'

He stood a minute, pushed his fingers through his hair and took a deep breath. When he turned to face her, he appeared to be his cheery self again. 'Well, honey,' he drawled, 'I can't say I'm not disappointed. But the last thing I want to do is make you unhappy. Kiss and be friends, eh?'

Mutely, Sarah lifted her face, and he kissed her gently on the lips. 'You're very sweet, Sarah,' he said, stroking her hair. 'Will you come back in to dance?'

'No, I'll stay out here for a while. You go.'

'Okay.' He gave her a mock salute. 'See ya, mate.'

Sarah watched him make his way to the barbecue area, where he shouldered his way through the crowd, exchanging jocular greetings as he went. *Poor Jim*, she thought. He was so nice. Why did she have to harbour feelings for someone with no interest in her, when kind, happy-go-lucky Jim was prepared to give her his heart? *But I don't have feelings for Dev*, she reminded herself. *It is just that I can't feel that way about Jim.* She sighed and turned away, gazing with troubled eyes out over the channels.

A sound made her look around, her heart began to pound in earnest and her knees turned to water. Devin was striding towards her, and she knew, instinctively, that it was not for the purpose of asking her to dance. He was angry, but why? She was not to know that he'd seen Jim's farewell kiss and put his own construct on it.

Devin stopped in front of her: his face rigid; eyes dark pools she could not read. 'I want a word with you, Sarah,' he said, moving closer and invading her space.

Sarah fought against the compulsion to step back from his confronting presence, but even though all her nerves seemed to jump and catch fire at his proximity, she managed to speak calmly: 'Yes, of course, Dev. Is there something wrong?'

'Wrong? You tell me! I never thought that I would have to remind you—of *all* people!—that I expect certain standards from my staff.'

Feeling as though she'd been slapped in the face, Sarah took a minute to answer. 'I don't understand. What do you mean?'

'I mean that I won't have you making out with my overseer! It is bad for the other men, and it's no good for the children!'

Sarah gave a gasp of sheer fury, but before she could speak, he made a little sound and pulled her into his arms. Momentarily, he glared down into her face: a tense, angry set to his jaw. Then, he crushed her against his lean body and kissed her: a kiss that drew out all her breath and left her limp and trembling— clinging to him as a drowning man might cling to a raft.

And then, just as suddenly, he released her and stepped back, leaving Sarah feeling bereft and confused, despising herself. She bitterly regretted her response and felt that he must be silently mocking her.

It took some time for the enormity of his words to sink in, but eventually, she found her voice. 'How *dare* you!' she breathed. 'I have no interest in your overseer … or in *any* of you!' she added through shut teeth. For an instant, her eyes blazed—almost as magnificently as Mattie's—into his. Then, wrenching herself free, she ran around the back of the woolshed to the ladies' room.

'Sarah …' said Devin, half to himself—his hand unconsciously reaching out towards her slender, retreating form.

'Sarah …'. Like a man stunned, he stood gazing after her, long after the figure in the shimmering grey dress had vanished around the corner of the woolshed.

Through his preoccupation, Devin became aware of a sinuous form draping itself around him. 'Dev, darling,' purred a voice he knew only too well, 'I've been looking all over for you. They're playing our song. Let's dance, hmm?' Louella stroked his arm seductively.

At first, he didn't seem to comprehend what she was saying, then his lips twisted into a wry smile. 'You never give up, do you? But as it happens, you're the very person I want. You're coming with me.' He took her arm above the elbow and steered her in the direction of the car park.

'What's with the he-man act, Dev?' asked Louella with a speculative glance at the hand on her arm. 'Don't tell me little Miss Prunes and Prisms has been stirring up your manhood?' She laughed. 'Her loss, my gain.'

'Oh, God, *Louella!* Need you be so vulgar?'

'Once, you didn't mind.'

'*Once*, I was a fool!'

Louella drew in a sharp breath. It was a moment before she spoke. 'Well, then, where *are* we going?'

'The stables.'

She tittered. 'If you've got something in mind, darling, I can think of better places than the *stables*.'

'I'm not feeling amorous, if that's what you mean,' he said, glancing at her with a set jaw. 'Far from it! If you must know.'

'Well … Not *yet*, perhaps,' she temporised. '*Why* the stables?'

'To look at my horse.'

'But, darling, I'm not dressed for the stables. And my shoes … *Must* we?'

'You'll survive,' he said, unimpressed, yanking open the passenger door of his Range Rover. 'We're driving. Get in.'

But when Devin showed her the welt on Gracious Lady's face, Louella appeared to be as shocked as anybody. 'Did *I* do that? Surely *not!*'

'My jockey says you did. And I warn you, Louella, that I believe her. Now, I want you to tell me how such a thing as this could have happened!'

Louella saw the revulsion in his face and thought quickly. 'Look, Dev, it was an accident. You know how hard I have to hit my mare so as not to miss the start? Well, the inside horse jostled us, making Cinders jump sideways just as I brought down the whip. It must have caught your horse then, and I didn't know. I *am* sorry.'

'*That* is a very lame explanation.'

'It's the *truth!*'

He shrugged. 'Very well. On the face of it, I will accept it because your father is a valued friend and neighbour. But it had better not happen again. Petty spite and jealousy is one thing—cruelty to animals—quite another.'

'Ooh …' Louella flinched artistically. 'You don't pull your punches, do you?'

'I can't afford to,' he said. And his light eyes shamed her so that she turned away.

Devin let her go and stood, stroking the mare's silky neck. 'What will I do, Lady?' he murmured. 'I know what I should do—*must* do. But can I do it? And if I do, will it serve?'

§

In the ladies' room, Sarah reapplied her lipstick and powdered her nose with a trembling hand. Then, she spent a good deal of time combing her disordered hair into its usual shining fall, making a supreme effort to compose herself before going back into the ballroom.

Hesitating on the edge of the crowded dancefloor, Sarah thought that she had never felt more alone. Aunt Fay seemed to have gone home, her table empty, and Bill Richmond stood talking to a group of men near the bar. Jim danced by with plump, dark-haired Jacqui. They looked to be enjoying themselves. Jim was laughing and Jacqui sparkling as they swept past her. *Jim, cutting his losses,* she thought, making a wry mouth. Momentarily, she wished that she could have done the same.

Suddenly, Sarah had a vision of the Barnes family of the future: cheerful, happy, well-adjusted children nurtured by positive, loving parents, and she was glad that Jim did not seem to be suffering as she was—that kind, friendly Jacqui was his future.

Devin walked in, meeting her eyes across the room. He looked stricken, uncertain. Then, just as he was about to step towards her, was hailed by Bill Richmond. At the same time, Louella came up, putting a confiding hand on his arm. He bent his head attentively to listen to her, and Sarah, who could stand no more, turned and fled into the kindly, anonymous night.

Sarah made her way back to the house—a prey to her tangled thoughts and emotions. Why had Dev kissed her? She touched her lips with her fingers. They still burned from his touch, and the memory seared her like fire. *He had been so angry! Why had he been so angry? Could it be jealousy? Surely, not!* And yet the yearning passion in his kiss had been in direct contrast to the fury in his face.

A hot tide of shame engulfed her as she recalled her inadvertent, equally passionate response. She wished fervently that she could be far away by morning and never have to face him again.

But the children needed her. How could she callously desert those two trusting little ones who had already been deprived of their loving parents and had only just begun to thrive again after being ill-treated by her predecessor. *How can I leave them to the mercy of Louella?* she asked herself, miserably. It was unthinkable that she could even contemplate it. Louella: truly *La Belle Dame sans merci!*

Chapter Thirteen

Sarah paced around the schoolroom, unable to concentrate on the task she had set herself. It was still relatively early after she had showered and dressed in her pyjamas. Sleep was far from her, so instead of going to bed as she had intended, Sarah put on her dressing-gown and came to draw up the progress chart that she had promised her pupils last week.

So much for Cinderella at the ball, she thought. *At least the real Cinderella made it to midnight before her evening fell around her in tatters, whereas I couldn't even manage that*! She dare not even think about the handsome prince!

Sighing, she went out onto the verandah and down the steps to take a walk in the garden, before going back to her room. The trees etched their familiar delicate patterns of black lace against the moonlit sky, and the garden was still and tranquil. Sarah strolled around the silent borders, soaking up their peace and beauty. In a little while, her hurt and confusion began to ease a little, and she turned to go indoors, feeling that, perhaps, she would sleep, after all.

Out of the corner of her eye, as she was stepping onto the verandah, Sarah thought she glimpsed a grey, blurred movement over in the trees beyond the garden wall. She halted and swung around, anxiously scanning the shadows, but she saw no further sign of movement. 'I suppose I'm imagining things,' she said aloud. *It's probably nothing more sinister than a kangaroo.* In dry times, they were drawn in their numbers to the succulent, green garden.

Sarah moved into the room, closed the doors, took off her dressing-gown and turned, yawning, to her bed. Stretching out a hand, she pulled back the covers to stand paralysed with shock and terror. A deadly, chiselled head lay on her pillow; its flat, dull eyes staring sightlessly up at her. For an aeon of time, she stood there, unable to move or speak, then she screamed and screamed again in the grip of an irrational, overwhelming horror.

Her screams echoed and re-echoed through the house. Sarah could vaguely hear the sounds, as if from a long way off, but was hardly aware that it was herself who made them, as she tried to fight back her rising hysteria.

The door burst open, and Sue rushed in, closely followed by Aunt Fay.

'What's the matter, Sarah?' Sue spoke sharply, shaking her a little. 'Pull yourself together and tell us!'

Sarah's screams turned to sobs. She pointed.

'A snake!' Sue took a closer look. 'But it's dead. It's all right, Sarah. It won't hurt you.'

Aunt Fay moved to the bed, delicately picked up the snake by

its tail and turned to Sarah. 'Sue is right,' she said with her gentle smile. 'You see, my dear, once they're *dead* they can't hurt anyone.'

Reuben hobbled in, carrying the golf club he kept under his bed in case of prowlers.

'It's all right *now*, Reuben,' said Aunt Fay, in blithe assurance. 'But I'm afraid Sarah has had a scare. I've just been showing her she need not be afraid of a dead snake.'

'Oh, dear, dear, Missus,' scolded Reuben. 'Give that thing to me. You don't want to be touching it.' He took it from her and draped it over the golf club. 'It's a big 'un. And it's dead, right enough. Looks like it's been run over. Don't you worry, Missy,' he said to Sarah. 'I'll soon have it out of your way. Better get her a brandy, Sue,' he added with another glance at her shocked face before he turned and went out with his macabre burden.

Mattie surged in, puffing—enormous in a pink dressing-gown—just in time to hear Reuben's parting words. 'What Sarah needs is a nice cup of tea. You come along to my kitchen, and I'll get you one. You, too, Mrs Fay.' She looked from the bed to Sue and grimaced. 'Looks like you've got a job to do, first.'

A short time later, sitting over a cup of tea, Sarah had regained her composure. 'I'm sorry,' she said, colour flooding her ashen cheeks. 'You've discovered my Achilles heel. I really just go off the deep end when I see a snake. I don't know why. They terrify me out of my wits!'

'Yeah. We noticed,' said Mattie. 'But how the heck someone knew, and why they would bother ——?'

'It must have been a practical joke, dear,' said Aunt Fay. 'Perhaps someone didn't relish being beaten in the Ladies'

Bracelet today?'

'Yesterday,' said Mattie looking at the clock. 'It's gone midnight.'

Sarah didn't hear this, still pondering the idea proposed by Aunt Fay. But, try as she might, she could not envisage Louella picking up a snake—dead or alive. 'It's a pretty nasty joke,' she said, 'whoever did it.'

'If you're going to live here, you'll have to get used to snakes and things, you know.' Aunt Fay patted her hand. 'When you live in the Outback, you have to be able to kill dangerous pests. We only kill the ones around the house, of course. The ones in the paddock, we leave to nature.'

'Do … Have *you* killed a snake, Aunt Fay?' asked Sarah, eyeing her in awed respect.

'Oh, yes, my dear, lots of them over the years. Oh, yes: any number! You have to be careful, of course.'

'Get away with you, Mrs Fay!' snorted Mattie. 'If I didn't know you better, I'd say you were showing off. *I've* never seen you kill a snake.'

'Haven't you, dear? Perhaps you were busy in your kitchen. But I'm just trying to bolster Sarah up, you know. She'll have to face a live snake, one day.'

'There's no call for you *or* Sarah to be killing snakes, Mrs Fay,' said Mattie with finality. 'All either of you have to do is yell for somebody.' She gestured. 'We all turned up fast enough tonight.'

Sue came in, her face expressionless. 'I changed your bed, Sarah,' she said, taking the cup Mattie handed to her.

Sarah thanked her with simple gratitude. 'I don't know how

you could stand it, Sue,' she told her, shuddering. 'But I am eternally grateful.'

'It's her job,' said Mattie. 'No doubt she's had worse things to clean up. Where's Reuben?'

'He's coming,' said Sue. 'He's just having a quick look around the garden in case of a prowler—human or otherwise. Here he is now,' she added unnecessarily as the gardener shuffled into the room.

Mattie indicated the teapot and he nodded. 'How do you feel now, Missy?' he asked, accepting his cup with a gesture of thanks while looking closely at Sarah. 'You look a lot better, anyway. Ah, the things some people get up to.' He wagged his head and said no more, apparently absorbed in spooning sugar into his tea.

§

When Sarah awoke next morning, all the events of the night before had taken on an unreal quality, as if they belonged in a particularly complicated and very bad dream. The snake episode had only pushed the other to the back of her mind for as long as it took to get into bed. Then, she *couldn't* forget a species of nightmare that made her squirm. At seven, feeling wrung out, she dressed mechanically and went to get the children to take them down to breakfast.

Only Aunt Fay was in the breakfast room when they entered. Sarah breathed an infinitesimal sigh of relief and was even able to relax a little when the older woman volunteered the information that Devin had already breakfasted and gone out for the day.

All that week, Devin drove himself and his men hard, working long hours. He didn't appear at any meals and shut himself in his office when he was in the house. He would probably have eaten less than he did if Mattie had not pounced on him with a loaded tray whenever she set eyes on him, loudly demanding that he empty it. The whole household was affected in various ways: Aunt Fay became introspective and thoughtful, Naomi anxious and seeking assurance, Adam unearthing Sam from the toy cupboard and refusing to be parted from him for a second.

One morning, Sarah was sitting alone at the breakfast table, nursing a headache. The children were in the rumpus room playing a noisy game, encouraged by Aunt Fay who told Sarah that she would take care of the little ones for awhile.

Mattie sailed in with a fresh pot of coffee, her brilliant eyes clouded by a frown. 'Mrs Fay says you're under the weather.'

'It's just a headache,' Sarah assured her with an attempt at a smile. 'It's improving already.'

'Hmph!' snorted Mattie, slapping down the pot and reaching for a cup. 'Seems you're not the only one. Someone else is like a bear with a sore head. Out early again, this morning. Driving himself like the devil, he is.' She looked hard at Sarah. '*Something must have upset him.*'

Him? Upset him? What about me? Sarah moved uncomfortably but said nothing. What was there to say? *He kissed me and it has upset both of us? I don't think so!* She did wonder, just for a second, what Mattie would say to that. *But I'm not going to put it to the test,* she thought.

'I'll be straight with you,' said Mattie, screwing up her eyes as she poured Sarah's coffee. 'I dunno what's eating the Boss, but I can't help thinking that *you've* got something to do with it!'

Sarah's face puckered. 'Oh, Mattie, *don't* …' she implored.

Mattie snorted. 'Don't tell me: *you're* in just as bad a case as he is!' She shrugged. 'Oh well, time will sort it out. *If* he doesn't die of starvation first!'

Chapter Fourteen

When Sarah's headache eased, she took the children down to say goodbye to Gracious Lady, who was returning to her trainer in Toowoomba to be prepared for the Spring Racing Carnival. They came in to morning tea, and because Sarah was still looking wan, Aunt Fay told her to take the rest of the day off—she, Sue and Mattie would see to the children. For once, Sarah didn't argue. She loved the children dearly, but she was labouring under a burden she neither understood, nor knew how to cope with.

Later, feeling she needed fresh air, Sarah went to the stables. A ride on her old friend Persian Prince did much to restore her outlook on life, and she returned to the house in a more philosophical mood. *I have to see Dev, one day,* she thought. *I might as well be civilised about it: strive for a little dignity.* Her mouth twisted wryly. *What little is left to me, that is.*

That evening, Devin appeared at dinner for the first time in a week. Sarah thought he looked thinner and fine-drawn; it was obvious that something was troubling him. He spoke little through that interminable, meal but when they rose to leave the table, he said quietly to Sarah, 'I'd like to see you in my office for a few minutes, please, Sarah.'

'You go on, dear,' said Aunt Fay. 'I'll bath the children and put them to bed.'

Sarah nodded. She hardly heard her through the heavy thudding of her heart, and she followed him out of the room and down the hall—a prey to anxious self-questioning. Was this the decision he had made: To sack her? Had he decided he couldn't bear to have her here, even though the children loved her? Doubts and humiliation crowded and jostled in her mind until, by the time she arrived at the office door that he was holding open for her, she was a bundle of jumping nerves: a sick, lost feeling in the pit of her stomach.

Sarah stood with her back against the door, gazing apprehensively at Devin, who was propped against the edge of the desk—a brooding expression on his face. For a long moment, he did not speak, then raising his eyes to hers, he said irritably, 'Sit down, Sarah. I'm not going to bite you. Let's have a drink: Sherry? With an ice cube?'

Sarah nodded, having embraced this Outback innovation, and lowered herself gingerly onto the edge of the leather armchair as Devin busied himself with the ice bucket, decanter and glasses. He handed her a glass and sat, facing her, on the edge of his desk.

There was a silence that seemed to stretch out to infinity. Ice chinked in his glass as he twisted it round, gazing into its depths, as if he might find there the inspiration of a crystal ball. Sarah was hardly aware of the breeze that fanned her cheeks, ruffled the papers on his desk and lifted silky strands of his short, dark hair. She studied his downcast features with painful intensity, trying to read his mind. As always, he seemed remote, unreachable. One part of her silently begged him to sack her and get it over with: the other wanted to put it off forever.

When, at last, he did speak, his words fell into the silence like stones into a still pond, startling her with their intensity, so that she jumped. 'Sarah,' he said, raising compelling eyes to hers. 'I want you to marry me.'

Shockwaves lapped at Sarah's consciousness, and her heart gave a queer, uneven lurch and began to pound in earnest. Of their own accord, the fingers of her free hand found the arm of the chair and gripped until her knuckles shone white. The ice rattled in her glass. *What does this mean?* she wondered. *Does he love me, after all?*

His next words dispelled any such illusion she might cherish. 'The children love you, and I know that you feel the same way about them. I don't want them to have to lose you, one day. They have suffered enough losses. Yet, it wouldn't be all one way: It would benefit you, too. You would have the security of this home for the rest of your life. I am not offering a short-term arrangement. You have no other ties, have you?'

'You know that I haven't.' Sarah carefully placed her glass on a small table beside the chair because her hands were trembling uncontrollably.

'What about Jim?' he said. 'You let him kiss you.'

'I ...' *What about you? Haven't I seen you kissing Louella?*

Uncannily, he seemed to read her mind. 'So, it *was* you on the verandah that night. I thought it was Aunty, snooping. She does, you know,' he told her with matter-of-fact tolerance and a hint of a smile. 'That's how she knows everything that goes on around here. No, I know *you* weren't snooping, otherwise, you would have known that what you saw was someone trying to kiss *me*: A very different thing. Had you stayed a little longer, you would have seen me push her away. I didn't see any such thing with you.'

You would've if you'd been there a little earlier. 'I had just told Jim I couldn't care for him the way he wanted. And he said, "Kiss and be friends." So I did.' Sarah lifted her chin. 'I am very fond of Jim: I said I wished he were my brother.'

'I'm sure that would've gone down well,' he remarked, but since it tallied with Jim's explanation—*Letting me down lightly, Boss*—when he'd tackled him, he said no more on the subject. Devin reflected that Jim had said something else, too, looking quite unlike himself: *Sarah's a little beauty—if you hurt her, you'll answer to me.*

There won't be any trouble in this camp, he'd said in reply. *If I hurt her, I'll answer to myself.* And he'd grasped Jim's shoulder for a moment and walked away.

Coming out of this reverie, he looked at Sarah. 'Now, about us: what do you think?'

'But, Dev, you … we … I …' she floundered into silence.

'You mean that there has been no declaration of love between us as convention dictates?' he said, raising a sardonic eyebrow.

Sarah stared at him, aghast at his cynicism.

'Look, Sarah …' Devin glanced up at the ceiling, then down at the glass in his hand. 'What happened the other night surprised me as much as it did you. I don't know how it happened. I know it is not the way a …' He paused.

Gentleman? she mentally supplied.

'… Decent boss treats his staff,' he continued after a moment. 'I can assure you that I don't make a habit of it. I know it argues a lack of respect, but that is not so, Sarah. I have the greatest respect for you. I was labouring under a misapprehension and a fear that the children would lose you. And if it is any help, I undertake not to do it again without your consent.' His light eyes met hers. 'But I am not going to apologise because, however wrong it may have been, it told us something about ourselves and each other that we did not know before. Don't you think so?'

Her face flamed. She could not look at him.

He took her hand, played with her fingers. 'I discovered how very … alluring you are. And I think you found me … not unattractive?'

Her cheeks grew doubly hot. She drew her hand gently away. *Oh, Dev … The understatement of the century!*

He waited for her to speak, and when she didn't, went on: 'I believe that a relationship based on our obvious mutual attraction, respect, tenderness, and consideration for each other's feelings and needs will work quite well.'

'But isn't that *love?*' exclaimed Sarah, rising unsteadily to her feet.

'Is it?' Devin straightened; took a step towards her. His hands cupped her shoulders, warm through her shirt. He looked over her head—a bitter twist to his lips. '*Love,*' he said with stark emphasis, 'is a word that no longer exists for me.'

How bitter he was. Bitterness had eaten into his soul and destroyed his capacity for love. Sarah felt inexpressibly sad for both Devin and herself. How Louella must have hurt him: a wound that would not heal. Perhaps he still loved her and could not admit it—least of all to himself. Emotionally, he was frozen, and all the warmth and love of which Sarah was capable was not enough to melt the ice that surrounded his heart.

Devin looked down at her and his face softened. 'I have a *very* great regard for you, Sarah.'

'But, Dev, you hardly know me.' *What a stupid thing to say!* she thought. *The heart can make its choice in an instant. I have found that out the hard way!*

He smiled—this time without cynicism. 'I know enough about you, after living in the same house for three months, to know that you are sweet and fine; a woman of integrity that any man would be proud of. Surely, a marriage based on those qualities should be more enduring than one based on a so-called love that turns out to be no more than a mirage—a mirage that a man follows and can't be brought to believe that it has no substance!' The harsh bitterness was back in his voice, and Sarah could hardly bear the pain in his eyes as he continued, 'Love only means suffering, Sarah. And I've had my fill of that. I want peace and contentment in my life, not trauma.'

'But …' Sarah opened her mouth to say that love didn't have to be like that. Then, remembering her own experience, closed it again. For a long moment, she did not speak, staring blindly at the top button of his shirt while she tried to assemble her chaotic thoughts. Then, raising her eyes to his, she saw that he was looking at her intently, as if he would read her very soul.

'Yes?' he prompted her. 'But … *what?*'

Sarah shook her head. 'Nothing.' *What*, she wondered desperately, *is he offering me? What does he want from me?* She wanted nothing more than to be married to him and spend her life at Medora Downs, watching over the children she had grown to love. *Yes, I do!* she thought, bitterly. *I want him to love me!* That was what she yearned for more than anything. Marriage without love was foreign to her, but on the other hand, how could she turn down an offer that would keep her here by his side: Mistress of Medora Downs and guardian of those two beautiful children?

At last, Sarah spoke in a husky voice, completely unlike her own: 'Please, Dev … May I have time … to think this over?' Her eyes pleaded with him.

'All right,' he said, withdrawing his gaze. 'How long do you want?'

'I'll tell you tomorrow,' she said, slipping out of the room. *I must go somewhere quiet,* she thought. *Somewhere I can think!*

Naturally, she went out into Reuben's garden.

CHAPTER FIFTEEN

Walking amongst the trees and flowers, arguing back and forth with herself to exhaustion, Sarah finally came to the conclusion—the extremely reluctant conclusion—that she could not marry Devin.

I can stay with the children until they go to boarding school, she decided. *I can look after them until then without being married to Dev. They won't need me forever.*

And then what would she do? Leave this beautiful place? This place that felt like the only home she had ever known and go … where?

But there's no way I can marry him without love. It's hard enough, anyway, from what I hear, even with all the love in the world and the best of intentions. If he doesn't—or can't—love me, she thought, biting her lip, *there's no way it can possibly work.*

As she made her way back to the house and prepared for bed, Sarah wondered why her decision had not eased her pain or brought any peace to her tumultuous heart. *You fool!* her inner voice said. *Now you'll have to watch him marry someone else. Half a loaf is better than nothing. Take what you're offered and be thankful.* But Sarah tried not to listen, and for the first time in many weeks, cried herself to sleep.

When Sarah brought the children in to breakfast, Aunt Fay looked from her drawn, pale face to Devin's tired, strained one and said, 'Goodness me! Whatever is the matter with you two?' She laughed in gentle amusement. 'You haven't—what does Mattie call it?—been having a night on the tiles, dears?'

'Not this morning, please, Aunty. I'm not in the mood,' said Devin, pouring himself a coffee. He glanced across the table. 'And I don't think Sarah is, either. And now, if you'll excuse me, I'll take this with me. I've got some work to do.' He glanced at Sarah. 'I'll be in my office if you want me.'

Sarah watched him go. *If I want you!* She almost laughed at the irony of it, then looked up to find Aunt Fay's eyes upon her, bright and curious. 'I think you should go, dear. Get it over with, whatever it is. I'll take the children to the rumpus room. You can collect them from there when you're ready.'

Somehow, Aunt Fay had managed to force Sarah's hand, even though she didn't feel ready to face Devin, and she found herself standing outside his office door, feeling as though she might suffocate; the blood sang unpleasantly in her ears in time to the heavy thudding of her heart. *I don't want to have to refuse him,* she thought. *But I must.* She unclenched her fingers, suddenly realising that her nails were digging into her palms, took a deep breath and knocked on the door, entering at his command.

He rose from behind his desk, his light eyes holding an

expression she did not understand. And then she realised it was tension. Then, she saw something else: Devin was afraid of her answer and was steeling himself. *But is he afraid I will say yes? Or is he afraid it will be no?*

'You've made your decision?' he asked, his voice deep and soft.

'Yes,' she whispered.

'And?'

'I am sorry, but it is … It must be …' Sarah took a rasping breath. 'I have to say …' Under his compelling gaze, her refusal stuck in her throat, and she could not utter the word. 'All right, then, I will,' she heard herself gasp to her own amazement and disgust.

His rare, warm smile lit his eyes. He moved around the desk to gather both her hands in one of his. With the other he stroked her cheek. 'I don't know what you're saying you're sorry for! You won't be sorry. I'll see to that.'

Her head drooped. 'I … I meant to say … no.'

'You didn't really?' He looked at her intently. 'You're not going to take it back now?'

'No, I won't take it back,' she said, raising her eyes to his. 'I think it must be meant.'

'I'm damned sure it is! Now I don't have to be worried you'll go off and marry someone else and leave us.'

'Oh, *Dev* …'

'Sarah …' He said her name as if to savour it on his tongue. 'Did Aunty tell you my mother's name was Sarah?'

'No, was it?'

'She wasn't like you, though: tall and dark with blue eyes—*set in with a smutty finger*—as the Irish used to say.'

'She must have been beautiful.'

'She was. Or, at least, I thought so.' He stopped; touched her hand. 'Sarah, we'll have to do something about a ring. You must tell me if you don't like my idea.'

'Of course. What is it?'

He reached into the desk drawer to take out a small red-velvet case, opening it to reveal a dainty ring blazing with a cluster of diamonds in the shape of a rose. 'This was my mother's engagement ring.'

'Oh, that's *gorgeous!*'

'Do you think so? Would you wear it?'

'Oh, yes! I *love* it.'

'Try it on,' he said, holding her hand to slip it onto her finger. 'It's a little large. My mother wasn't as fine-boned as you. Darcy offered it to Jane when they got engaged, but she wanted to design her own.' He stepped back to look at her. 'Are you sure you don't want to come with me to the Isa and choose a new one for yourself?'

She did love the ring, and sensitive to his feelings, she knew that, at heart, he wanted her to prefer it. 'I'm *sure*,' she said, and there was no mistaking the sincerity in her voice. 'I can't think of anything more beautiful.'

When he smiled approval, Sarah was glad she'd followed her heart's direction. He pulled back his chair and sat down, picking up a pencil. 'And then,' he said, 'I thought a split wedding band, like this.' He took a sheet of paper and began to draw. *So, Naomi's talent must run in the family*, she thought, a lump in her throat as she studied his rapt profile. He looked up to meet her eyes and hand her the paper. 'See: what do you think?'

'Beautiful, elegant, individual ... Perfect,' she added, seeing that each half of the matching band provided tiny diamond leaves for the central flower.

'Good, then I will take this drawing with me to the Isa. But how to size it?'

Sarah slipped a thin gold band off the third finger of her right hand. 'My mother's wedding ring,' she said. 'This and my pendant is all I have left of her.'

'I won't lose it,' he assured her, placing it in the tiny box with the diamond ring. He smiled. 'That's the ring organised, courtesy of our mothers. Perhaps they both would have approved. What do you think?'

'Oh, Dev, I hope so!' exclaimed Sarah, her brows knit with uncertainty. 'I *do* hope so.'

'Well, you know,' he said, smiling into her eyes. 'I am getting surer by the minute. Now the next problem: which of us is going to break the news to Aunty?'

'Can you do that, please? It will be better coming from you.' Sarah went white. 'I've just thought,' she whispered. 'What about Louella?'

'Louella can go hang!'

Sarah's eyes widened. *Is this why he has asked me to marry him? To save him from Louella?* She should have found it humiliating, but the idea gave her a peculiar satisfaction. *Well, I don't mind,* she thought, amazed to find that it was true. *Except that it is going to be awkward, if not downright dangerous!* 'But, Dev …' Sarah placed an anxious hand on his arm. 'She'll be *furious*. You know what she's like.'

He covered her fingers with his own. 'Only too well!' he said, then his expression hardened. 'Just tell her to bug off!'

'Dev! You can't expect me …'

'I know. You're a lady: she isn't. Louella is impervious to snubs. But she *is* a neighbour, and we'll have to meet with some kind of social grace from time to time.'

'It's not that. I don't know what she'll do in a temper. She's like David. I mean, *look* what she did to Lady!'

'I'll word Mattie,' he decided. 'If I'm not here, go to her. She'll send her to the rightabout. Even Louella won't square up to *her!*' He smiled. 'Or if she does, she'll come off second.'

Sarah tried to pull her hand away. 'You're treating this as a *joke!*'

'Is this our first tiff?' he asked with a disarming twinkle, closing his fingers.

'No,' said Sarah. She could not help her answering smile. 'I don't think so. But she's too much for me, Dev.'

'I know. That's why I'm enlisting Mattie's help.' He pressed her hand and let it go, saying softly. 'It *will* be all right, Sarah.'

She shook her head, unable to speak for a sudden rush of emotion. 'I …I must go and get the children.'

'Of course. I will tell Aunty, talk to Mattie and go straight to Mount Isa, today. I have some business there and will get the ring altered to fit you at the same time. Then, when I come back, we'll announce our engagement officially. I'll only be a few days.' His smile lit his eyes; made her all too aware of his charm. 'You'll be all right till I come back? No second thoughts?'

'Yes. Oh, no,' said Sarah, answering each question in turn. She suddenly felt faint, as if it were all too unreal. 'I must go. The children.' She fled, almost running down the hall in an attempt to escape the thought of the irrevocable commitment she had just made. Then, re-collecting herself, slowed to a more decorous pace and entered the rumpus room. 'Come on, children. Let's go to the schoolroom.'

Naomi and Adam jumped up from their game.

'You're late, Sarah.' Naomi reproached her. 'We missed School of the Air!'

'I'm sorry. Never mind. We'll do painting instead.'

'Oh, goody! said Naomi, well satisfied with this alternative. She was always ready to paint and showed considerable talent with a good eye for colour.

'Sam wants to draw and colour in,' confided Adam. 'He doesn't want to get paint on himself.'

'Yes, he can do that until we get him a painting smock. Get yours, then.' Sarah followed them to the schoolroom, helped them into their smocks and was kept busy overseeing the use of watercolour with the minimum of splashing. In an amazingly short time, the lunch gong went, and there was a rush to clean up.

When they went in to lunch, Aunt Fay was already at the table. She beamed at Sarah. 'I believe I have to congratulate you, my dear.' She patted her hand. 'And I couldn't be more pleased!'

Sarah thanked her, annoyed with herself for blushing.

Naomi pricked her ears. 'What do you mean, Aunty?'

'Sarah is going to marry Uncle Dev,' Aunt Fay told her with an apologetic glance at their governess.

'Oh, goody! Now Sarah will stay with us for *always!*'

'Oh, *wow!*' said Adam. 'Sam is *really* happy, too.'

'I hope you didn't mind me telling them, dear?' said Aunt Fay with a little deprecating smile as the children jumped down from their chairs and rushed to Sarah—their faces alight with joy.

'Not at all,' said Sarah, hugging them both. *It's worth all the pain*, she thought, *to see the children so happy.*

After lunch, Sarah went riding, and Aunt Fay retired to the lounge to work on her embroidery. It was here that Louella found her as she walked in, unannounced, looking for Devin. 'I'm afraid you're out of luck, Louella,' she said with dry emphasis in answer to the other's curt enquiry. 'Dev's gone to Mount Isa. He won't be back until the day after tomorrow.' Aunt Fay gave her a smiling glance that held the hint of a challenge. 'By the way, have you heard our news?'

'No, I haven't heard anything.' Louella shook her head. 'But I can see you're big with news, Aunty, so give.'

'Really, dear, there's no need for such an inelegant expression. I am afraid that your poor mother would turn in her grave if she heard you.'

Louella lit a cigarette and blew a long stream of smoke. 'You can leave my mother out of this discussion *if* you don't mind.'

'Of course, dear. Of course,' murmured Aunt Fay. 'Now, what

was I saying?'

'News?'

'Ah, yes, of course. Let me get you a drink, and I'll tell you. Whisky?'

'On the rocks, please. Now, what is it?' asked Louella, accepting the drink with a gestured thanks.

'You'd better sit down, dear,' said Aunt Fay with the ghost of a wry smile. 'I am afraid this may come as a shock to you.' She paused for dramatic effect. 'Devin and Sarah are going to be married. The engagement will be announced officially when Dev returns from Mount Isa.'

Louella drew in a hissing breath, eyes narrowing to glittering slits as she stared unseeingly at Aunt Fay. Her fingers clenched hard on the glass she was holding, the whitened knuckles in stark contrast to their scarlet lacquered tips. For a moment, she was frighteningly still and white. Then, with a violent expletive that made the other woman flinch, she hurled the glass into the fireplace and flung herself out of the house.

§

'And so,' said Sue, sitting at the kitchen table, 'Mrs Fay went up to rest, and I cleaned up the broken glass.'

'She's got a temper, that girl!' Mattie shook her head. 'I don't know what the end of it will be.'

'It's a crying shame,' lamented Sue. 'That crystal glass was part of a set given to Darcy and Jane as a wedding present. Fine lead crystal it was, too. And the set ruined! All because a spoilt witch can't control her tantrums! I mean, she had no right to break the glass like that. Threw it in the fireplace, she did, and took off. It upset Mrs Fay, I can tell you: that lovely crystal glass, shattered into smithereens!'

'Crystal glass?' said Mattie, on a rising note. 'Lord, Sue, you do drivel on! If that's the only thing that breaks before this is over, we can think ourselves lucky!'

'What do you mean?' asked Sue, draining her cup and holding it out for more tea.

'I'm not sure what I mean,' said the cook, pursing her lips as she wielded the teapot. 'But I'm not easy in my mind. No, not a bit.'

§

Louella walked into the homestead again; a different person: cold and calm. 'Where's Aunty?' she said to Sue.

'She's gone to lie down.'

'Well, then, where's your governess? She'll do, instead.'

Mattie came out of the kitchen in time to hear this. She folded her arms across her massive bosom. 'What do you want with her?'

'That is *not* your business.'

Mattie smiled grimly. 'I suspect it isn't yours either, *Miss* Richmond. In fact, I think it is a sight more *my* business than it is *yours*.'

'Well, of all the cheek!'

'She's gone riding. I don't know when she'll be back, so if I were you, I'd take myself off home,' recommended the cook, turning back to her kitchen.

Louella was still staring at the doorway, her eyes darting emerald-green daggers of fire, when Sarah walked in.

'You wanted to see me, Louella? If it is to apologise for what you did in the race, I will accept it. Otherwise, I don't see what you can possibly wish to talk to me about?'

'Oh, don't you: you sly little *cat!* Swanning about with your saintly expression! And all the time … I *know* he's not in love with you. It has always been *me*, but he's angry just now and has become engaged to you just to spite me. But this is not the end of it! Dev is mine; do you hear? *Mine!* He was here waiting for me to settle down: my rock I could depend on. And you, you little *tramp*, you've sneaked in and grabbed him behind my back. Well, all's fair in love and war! And don't you forget it.'

'Having a good gossip, dears?' said Aunt Fay, coming in, a faint smile on her lips. 'There's tea and scones in the kitchen if — —?'

'No, thanks. I've got to go to town.' Louella turned to Aunt Fay. 'Anything you want? No? Then, I'll say goodbye.'

'Was she imposing on you, my dear?' asked Aunt Fay with her gentle smile. 'I always found her rather spiteful. Like her mother: hard and brittle.'

'Oh no. It is just ——'

'Dog in the manger, dear. She knows very well she ruined her chances with my nephew long ago.' Aunt Fay put a kindly hand on her shoulder. 'Come on. Let's go and try Mattie's scones— fresh out of the oven.' She sighed. 'Always a treat.'

Chapter Sixteen

The Range Rover sped over the dusty road that led to Medora Downs. Some time ago, it had passed through Boulia, turned eastwards and was now negotiating The Hamilton Channels. Devin sat behind the wheel, a slight frown of concentration in his grey eyes as he guided his vehicle over the rough track, avoiding the larger ruts and potholes.

A little later, approaching the turn-off to Emerald Hills, he saw a vehicle parked in the middle of the road. 'Uh-oh,' he said to himself. 'This looks like trouble: Trouble with a capital T,' he added when he was close enough to see who was waiting for him, perched on the bullbar of her Mercedes, smoking a cigarette in a long holder. *Or a capital L!* There was no getting past with a wave, much as it would have been the easiest way since it was impossible to get around her without going over some ugly looking rocks. Besides, however much he preferred to avoid this meeting, she might, just *might*, be broken down and in need of assistance.

'What's up, Louella?' he said, drawing up and cutting the engine.

'Oh, nothing. I'm just waiting for some people to show up. I promised I'd meet them at the turn-off. But if they don't come soon, I'm going to leave them to it. By the way,' she added, carefully stubbing out her cigarette on the shining chrome of the bullbar. 'Johnnie told me you're looking for an extra ringer for the muster?'

'That's right: I am.' He got out and strode over to lean on her mudguard.

'We've got a good man here if you want him. He was only temporary while our jackaroo was sick, but now Will's back in action, we don't need this fellow. He is an excellent man with stock, and it would be a shame to let him go if you need someone.'

'All right. Send him over when you're ready, and we'll give him a trial.'

'Since he was vouched for by your aunt when he came to *us*,' said Louella, giving him a dry glance, 'I should think you jolly well ought to!'

'Well, thanks for that,' he told her, starting to walk to his vehicle. 'You've saved me a major problem. I couldn't find a man at all in the Isa. I'll get along home, then.' *Either she hasn't heard, or she's going to be civilised about it, after all,* he thought with a little inward sigh of relief.

Her next words seemed to scotch that idea. 'You know, Dev, I never thought of you as a *coward*.'

'Neither did I,' he said, turning to face her. 'Can it be that you've heard of my engagement?'

'Heard of your engagement! That two-faced old aunty of yours couldn't wait to tell me. Laughing all over her mealy-mouth, she was. "Devin and *Sarah*," she said. "Devin and *Sarah!*" But if you think that I am going to let you escape me by hiding behind that little milk-and-water miss, you're very much mistaken!'

'I suppose it would be too much to expect you to have grown up enough to accept that I may just have a motive for my engagement that doesn't include you?' he said with crushing irony. 'The same motive, in fact, that most men have when they ask a woman to marry them?'

'Damn right, I don't! I know you don't love her!'

'Oh, you do, do you? And how do you know that?'

'Dev, you *can't!* You love *me!*'

'I am sorry, Louella, we've been through all this. But there's no talking to you, is there? Now, would you like to move your vehicle, so I can pass?'

'Go *round* me!' she snarled. 'I am waiting for some people.'

'As you like.' He turned to walk back to his vehicle.

'Wait! I didn't mean it, Dev. You know I'm a sore loser.' Louella ran after him to put a hand on his arm. 'Let's kiss and be friends.'

'You'll pardon me if I don't take you up on your charming offer,' he said, shaking her off and opening the door of the Range Rover. 'Sorry, I have to go. I'm running late as it is.'

Baffled by his coldness, Louella said in a little girl voice:

'Don't *go*, Dev.'

'What now?'

'Nothing. I don't want you to be mad at me. We need to talk about this.'

'I'm not going to stand here and argue with you in the middle of the road. It is neither the time nor the place.'

Louella eyed him speculatively. 'All right: give me a time, and I will be any place you want.'

A slow boat to China? Yesterday! He did not allow his exasperation to show but told her in quiet, firm tones: 'There *is* no time or place. *We* are a closed book. I thought you knew that?'

Louella seemed to calm down, draw back into herself. He turned to go. But the venom in her next words shocked him, though he gave no sign. 'You may have ditched *me* because you fancy a *cheap* little blonde,' she spat, 'but don't think you've stuck down the page on me—on *us!*—because you haven't!'

'Are you saying that I should do the same thing to Sarah that you did to me?' He curled his lip. 'I *don't* think so!'

'But it wouldn't be the same!'

'You're right,' he said with a grim smile. 'It won't be.'

'I mean it!' Louella reiterated. 'The page isn't stuck down. *Far from it!*'

When this forceful statement produced nothing but a shrug and a wry smile, she opened her mouth in a furious expletive, then glanced behind her. 'Oh, *blast!* Here comes Daddy. I'm going!'

Devin watched her drive off in a cloud of dust and scattered gravel with a lift of his shoulders. He had known it wouldn't be nice, but the unpleasantness had exceeded even his expectations. He waited courteously for his neighbour to draw up.

Bill Richmond greeted him with a friendly smile and a knowing eye. 'Been copping it, haven't you?' he remarked gently. 'You must forgive my little girl. She's disappointed, as am I. But, as I told her, she has only herself to blame. Give her time and she'll get over it.' He gave him a warm handshake. 'My congratulations to both you and Sarah. I hope you'll be very happy. She's a lovely little thing.' He passed on to more general discussions, and Devin was at last able to get away without giving offence.

§

Devin walked into the dining room just as lunch was being cleared away. Mattie reset a place at the table and brought in the meal she had prepared and kept hot for him. Then, she set the coffeepot on the table and went out.

Aunt Fay poured coffee for herself and Sarah and asked Devin how he'd enjoyed his trip to Mount Isa.

'All right,' he said. 'Where are the children?'

'Gone off with Sue somewhere,' she said. 'So, just the three of us.'

Devin picked up his knife and fork and shook his head at Aunt Fay. 'You've been busy, Aunty.'

'Louella snaffle you, did she?'

He raised his eyes to the ceiling. 'Did she what! I could have done without it,' he assured her. 'Did she come here giving you a hard time, Sarah?'

'Well …' Sarah looked at Aunt Fay.

'We took evasive action, dear,' said Aunt Fay with a reminiscent smile. 'We had all our meals in the kitchen until she'd gone.'

Devin laughed and shook his head. 'You're a wicked woman, Aunty.'

'Needs must …' she said demurely, her eyes on her cup.

'Speaking of which,' he said, 'Louella told me you recommended a ringer to Bill a few months ago.'

'Did she say that?' Aunt Fay looked vague and shook her head. 'I don't remember doing that, no. What was his name?'

'I didn't ask. No matter.' He made a small sound, searched in his pocket, smiled at Sarah and held out a tiny, gift-wrapped parcel. 'For you.'

Aunt Fay looked at Sarah. 'Well, go on, open it,' she said.

The wrappings hid a small chamois-leather bag containing Sarah's mother's wedding ring and a new ivory velvet case. Sarah glanced at Devin, unconcernedly eating his lunch, touched a tiny clasp and the case sprang open.

Aunt Fay gasped, 'But that's ——'

Her nephew glanced up, a quizzical lift to his brow. 'Sarah's?' he suggested.

'Splendid, dears. Simply splendid,' said Aunt Fay, making an instant recovery. 'Well go on, let us see how it looks on your finger, dear.'

'Let me,' said Devin, wiping his hands on a table napkin and rising. He took the ring out of the case and slid it onto Sarah's finger. 'A perfect fit. Suits you very well, doesn't it, Aunty?'

'Oh, yes. Yes, indeed. Now, if you will excuse me, I must go and rest. I'm sure you two have plenty to talk about.'

Sarah sat over her coffee, while Devin finished his meal in silence. Finally, he said, 'If the ring is not what you want, it is not too late to get you another.'

'Oh no, it's perfect,' she assured him. 'I know I could never find anything I like half as much.' She met his eyes. 'Thank you.'

'My pleasure,' he said, smiling as he rose from the table. 'I'd better go and see what's been going on while I've been away.' He looked at her. 'By the way, I sent the notice of our engagement to the papers … Is everything all right?'

'Oh yes, just fine,' said Sarah, dropping her eyes. She would have to write to Jo and Wendy. She had been putting it off but could do so no longer.

He gave her a searching glance, nodded and went out. Sarah poured herself another cup of coffee, which she did not want, and sat on at the table. From time to time, her eye was caught by a flash of fire from the sparkling diamonds on her finger, confusion uppermost in her mind. One part of her exulted at the thought of being engaged to Dev—the other despaired for the lie that seemed to be her life. Sarah took off the ring and shut it in its case. Then, she rose and went to change for her ride.

As always, the anticipation of a ride improved her mood, and it was with relief that Sarah escaped from the house into the warm sunshine of a perfect winter afternoon. Winter mornings were usually windy and a little nippy, but by lunchtime, the wind dropped and the afternoons were pleasantly warm and sunny.

She stopped in the garden for a few minutes to speak to Reuben and admire his latest profusion of flowers.

'Congratulations, Missy,' he said. 'I reckon you did the right thing, there. The Boss is all right.'

Sarah blushed and thanked him, remembering his shrewd, if tactless, assessment of her feelings a few weeks back, although it seemed like a dream from the long ago past. After a few more words, she strolled down to the stables, savouring the beauty of the afternoon.

'Hello, Johnnie!' she called. But there was no answer. *Johnnie must be busy with the stud bulls*, she thought, making her way to the end stand where her saddle was always kept. She collected Persian Prince's bridle from its peg and a saddlecloth from the clean pile in the cupboard and hung them over the rail outside her horse's stable. Then, she fetched a bag of grooming gear and opened the stable door.

Persian Prince whinnied to Sarah as she entered with the treats she always managed to wangle out of Mattie. He lipped up the pieces of apple and carrot she gave him and gently nudged her for more. Sarah sang softly as she groomed the horse, who stood, head down, eyes half-closed, enjoying the attention. Then, she deftly saddled and bridled him, automatically checking the girth straps and stirrup leathers as she did so.

Persian Prince seemed eager for the exercise and stepped out briskly along their usual track. Sarah decided not to go that way for a change and turned him in the opposite direction. Persian Prince started to argue, but after tossing his head a couple of times in disapproval, he remembered his manners and willingly strode along the track that led to several of the bores and, eventually, to the Emerald Hills' boundary.

Sarah had never ridden this way before, and she did not know why she had suddenly decided to change her habit. 'Just restless, I suppose. Looking for change,' she said aloud, and set Persian Prince into his slow rocking-horse canter.

The warm air caressed her cheeks and ruffled her hair as they cantered on and on, her horse blowing rhythmically through his nostrils. Sarah sang softly to him, patting his neck. She loved the exhilaration of riding, and it was marvellous exercise after a morning in the schoolroom. Soon, in deference to her mount's age, they slowed to a walk, and Sarah was free to mull over the incredible events that had occurred since the picnic races.

§

A figure that had been lying against a tree root, hidden in the curve of a channel, eased cramped limbs a couple of times and then lay still. In about half an hour, an arm was raised, and the face of a wristwatch consulted. The figure swore softly, quietly rose in the shadow of the tree and, looking this way and that, gathered up the length of rope that lay on the ground across the track.

Nimble fingers—long and slender, like a pianist's—untied the rope from the bole of a mimosa bush on the other side of the track and deftly rolled it into a neat coil. Then, casting another furtive glance around, the figure walked swiftly away along the channel, keeping well in the shadow of the trees.

§

Riding back to the stables, Sarah felt much more at peace with herself than she had been. The children were so beautiful, and she would never have to leave them. Dev always treated her with gentle courtesy *if* she didn't count the episode at the ball—and he had promised such a thing would not happen again. Sarah did not know if she was glad or sorry: his touch had aroused such sweet agony. But better to bury such feelings, since they caused her so much distress and confusion, and get on with life as it really was. Although, what life was *really* like was a confusing enough issue at the moment, in any case. *Better to count your blessings,* she told herself, *than to mourn over an unreachable star.* Finally, Sarah had to admit to herself that she loved Dev and hoped that, perhaps, in time, he would grow to love her too. She tried to wipe unpleasant thoughts of vanished pride and possible further humiliation from her mind.

If I am going to make a success of my future life here at Medora Downs—which Sarah was determined to do since the day her unbelieving ears had heard herself utter that irrevocable, 'All right, then, I will'—*I am going to have to develop a philosophy of life that allows me to give unstinting love to Naomi and Adam,* she decided.

Sarah knew that children were very sensitive to atmosphere, and if anyone was unhappy or on edge, they would sense it and be made unhappy themselves. There was no point in the course she had taken if that were to be the case. It had never so much as entered her head to go back on her word to Devin. She had given him her answer, and now she must abide by it. *There is no other option,* she thought.

Sarah felt suddenly optimistic as she rode into the stable yard, as if everything would work itself out. And the smile she flashed at Johnnie as she dismounted and handed him the reins made his tough old heart beat just that little bit faster.

'Sorry I wasn't here to saddle up for you, Sarah,' he apologised.

'Oh, it was no trouble,' she answered. 'Instead of riding along the river channels, I went out to the first bore, just for a change. I had a good ride.'

'That's good,' he said, then he cleared his throat. 'I heard your news, and I'm real pleased.'

'Thanks, Johnnie.'

He watched her walk away up the path to the house before he turned to lead the old horse into his stable and speak curtly to the man lounging in the shadows. 'As long as you're here, you may as well make yourself useful and unsaddle this horse and hose him down. And, tomorrow, we'll try you out in the bronco yard. Then, if that works out, we've got a dozen or so young horses to break in for the muster.'

Johnnie watched the man go to work on the horse, and his severe expression relaxed a little. The fellow evidently knew his job. *Well …* Johnnie shrugged. He looked capable enough, moved swiftly and quietly, but the bronco yard would sort him out. *I'll make up my mind tomorrow*, he resolved. *And I'll let the Boss know then.*

§

Over the next few weeks, the station was abuzz with preparations for the big muster. The men aired their swags and bed-rolls, and Johnnie brought in the workhorses and started feeding them oats and corn—working them to get them fit.

The young horses were run in and breaking in began in earnest. Despite Johnnie's reservations, the new man turned out to be a very good horse breaker and a wizard in the bronco yard. Devin was pleased when he saw him in action: tall and lithe with fast, economical action. *He's a good man, all right!* So, Louella hadn't been trying to get at him, after all.

When Sarah, Naomi and Adam went down for their usual Saturday riding lesson, they found the stables crowded with stockhorses and all the stockmen sitting on the fence of the nearby horse yards.

The young horse in the yard was making determined attempts to dislodge his rider, amid hoots of laughter and encouraging cheers from the top rail. After a few minutes, the youngster stopped his gyrations, snorted gently and stepped out in an active trot; his rider gently stroking his neck and murmuring soothing words of approval.

'There's Jim!' called Naomi.

'Jim! Jim!' yelled Adam.

Jim looked around, grinned broadly and swung down from the rail. 'How's my best girl?' he asked, swinging a giggling Naomi high off the ground and around before putting her down. 'Put up yer dukes, mate!' he growled at Adam, crouching and shaping up to him.

Adam grinned delightedly and tried to lob a punch over his guard.

Jim ruffled his hair and stood up to greet Sarah with no trace of a smile. 'So, you're going to marry the Boss?'

'Yes.' Sarah lifted her chin.

'That was pretty quick work, wasn't it?'

'Jim!' she protested. 'Well, if that's *not* the pot calling the kettle …?'

He grinned. '*Touché.*'

'Then, what's your problem?'

'Nothing. As long as you're happy. *If* you are?' he added, looking at her closely.

'Of course I am!' she assured him with a little laugh. 'And what about you?'

'Oh, well …' he said with a bashful grin. 'I might be expecting someone to congratulate me and Jacqui one of these days, soon.'

'Oh, good! Jim, I am *so* pleased for you.'

Naomi tugged at Sarah's shirtsleeve. 'Johnnie's waiting with the horses,' she said, her eyes full of reproach. 'He's been there for simply ages!'

Sarah's eyes met Jim's, and they both laughed.

A short time later, she and the children were cantering along the track that led to their favourite ride along the river channels. They reached a place where there were a few fallen logs on the ground and reined in. Sarah had promised to start their jumping lessons today, and they were eager to begin.

Having tied her horse to a tree, Sarah cleared some rubbish and arranged three small logs in front of a larger one to make three trotting poles and a small jump. She then explained to the children what she wanted of them, ending by demonstrating with Persian Prince, who had difficulty adjusting his stride to the pony-sized spaces.

The children spent a very happy half-hour, each feeling that they had achieved something wonderful. Devin had promised that they could go to pony camp in Winton next year if they did well with their riding, so they were anxious to improve.

They rode back into the stable yard laughing and singing, taking their feet out of the stirrups, as Sarah had taught them, and swung down from their ponies.

Sarah looked on with approval. 'Very good,' she said, doing the same herself.

A man walked forward to take their reins. 'I'll take the horses, Miss,' he said deferentially, his eyes on his polished boots.

Sarah startled. It was the man who had sent chills up her spine on the night of the ball, but he did not look very sinister now. Quite the reverse, in fact, with his downcast eyes and humble manner. Relaxing again, she asked, 'Where's Johnnie?'

'Busy doctoring a horse. A young'un hurt itself,' he mumbled, still looking at his boots.

Sarah nodded with understanding. It was said that Johnnie was as good as a vet. He had a way with sick animals: they quietened miraculously under his gentle, healing hands. 'Who are you?' she asked.

'New man, Miss. Col Jones,' he said, respectfully touching his hat but still not meeting her eyes.

Shy, she thought sympathetically. A lot of Outback men were like this with women because they so seldom saw them. Sarah smiled and handed him the reins, then she and the children went home to have morning tea with Sam.

Since the children had been told of the engagement, Sarah noticed that Sam was no longer indispensable to Adam's comfort in the daytime, but he still could not sleep at night without him. *Poor Sam*, thought Sarah. *He is becoming so tatty now. I hope Adam outgrows his need of him before he wears out completely!*

As they walked into the house, Sarah nearly collided with Sue as she was backing out of a door into the hall with the floor polisher. Both apologised, and as Sue looked over her shoulder, Sarah received a shock. Sue's face was white and strained, her eyes dark-circled, her body hunched protectively as though she were ill.

'Sue! Are you sick?' exclaimed Sarah.

'It's nothing, Sarah. I've a lot to do, that's all,' replied Sue, going into the next room and closing the door with an unfriendly bang.

Disturbed, Sarah followed Naomi and Adam into the kitchen for morning tea and, when the children went off to the rumpus room, stayed behind to watch Mattie making bread. Despite her size, the cook's deft, rhythmical movements as the dough magically changed shape made Sarah think of a graceful dancer. Mattie made wonderful bread, and for a few moments, Sarah watched in silence as the cook continued her kneading. Then she said with diffidence, 'Is there something wrong with Sue, Mattie? I saw her just now, and she's as white as paper.'

'Your guess is as good as mine, Sarah. She says not.' Mattie jutted her chin. 'She says it's nothing. Well, it don't look like nothing to me!' She pounded her dough with aggression—an indignant sparkle in her eyes. 'And when I told her so, she ups and walks out on me without another word!' Mattie looked at

Sarah, the brilliance of her eyes clouded with worry. 'I've known Sue since she was a little kid, and I've never seen her moody like this.' She thought for a moment and then said slowly, 'If I didn't know better, I'd say she was frightened, clean out of her wits.'

They looked at each other.

'But, Mattie: what could she be frightened of?'

'That's just it,' said Mattie, throwing the dough into the tins and dusting her hands on the tea towel. 'There's nothing here to be frightened of. Nothing at all.'

Chapter Seventeen

The day before the muster, Johnnie and the new man, Col, trucked the horses out to the first of the mustering camps. Johnnie left Col with the horses and returned with the truck. Tomorrow, he would take the truck out again with the men, their food and gear, and feed for the horses.

Devin spoke to Sarah: 'I'll be staying out on the camp for most of the time and all of this week from tomorrow. How about bringing the children out to the first camp on Wednesday for a picnic lunch? That should be the last day before we move on to the next one. It will be a good change for the children, and you might enjoy the experience, too.' He smiled down at her and brushed her cheek with his fingers, warmth creeping into his eyes. 'I'll see you at dinner,' he said, turned and strode away towards his office.

Sarah watched him go, his tall, broad-shouldered figure dissolving in a blur of tears. She dashed them away and went to find the children.

At afternoon tea, Sarah said to Aunt Fay, 'Tell me about the muster.'

The older woman smiled. 'This one, you mean?' she asked, continuing when Sarah nodded. 'Well, this happens every year at about this time. Medora Downs and Emerald Hills don't have a fenced boundary between them, and a team from each station works as one to complete the muster. Bill and Louella used to go and camp out. Bill still does, but I don't know if Louella will, this year.

'The cattle are sorted out by the stockmen—ringers, we usually call them—and each station brands its own calves. The fat stock for sale and the big calves to be weaned are run off and taken away to a holding paddock where they stay until the muster is completed. Then, they are drafted off and sent to fattening paddocks or sold, depending on their condition and the season.

'It's a very busy time, but the men look forward to it. They are very skilled at catching the calves for branding, too. When we go out on Wednesday, you'll be able to see for yourself what goes on.

'At night, all the stockmen gather round the campfire, singing or telling yarns for a short while and then turn in to their swags. It's early to bed and early to rise on a mustering camp. But it's fun, Sarah, a lot of fun. Everybody loves a singalong around the campfire.

'When they muster the rough country, they use a helicopter as well. The pilot is able to talk to the stockmen on the two-way radio, and he tells them where the cattle are coming out. The muster is a lot quicker sand easier, these days, than it used to be.' Aunt Fay took a deep breath.

'And what else? Oh, yes, the cook! The camp cook is very important. It is often up to him whether or not the men are happy. Fortunately, Jack Grey from Emerald Hills is a marvellous camp cook, and he has been doing the job for the last ten years.' She smiled. 'You'll taste his damper when we go out. *Real* billy tea and damper, Sarah! There's nothing like it,' she declared, her eyes shining.

§

In his flat off the garden shed, Reuben awakened suddenly at a sound that was not one of the usual night noises. He lay still for a moment, straining his ears. *Yes, most definitely a scuffle.* Creakily, he rose to his feet; pulled on trousers and boots. Then, his golf club firmly in one hand, torch in the other, he stepped outside and looked around. *It might be one of those thrice-cursed wild goats at my shrubs,* he thought, *or a hungry kangaroo on the lawn. Hardly be a prowler, out here. Still, you never know, these days, such goings on as there are.* He shook his head. Only the other week, he had heard on the news of innocent campers being murdered over in the Territory.

The sounds were coming from around the corner of the house. Reuben grasped his golf club more firmly and raised it, switching off his torch so as not to warn any intruder of his approach. When he reached the corner, he would switch the torch back on and surprise it—whatever it was.

The gardener stopped short, hearing a low moan. Someone was in trouble. He switched on the torch and hurried towards the sound, heedless now of danger. Out of the darkness, a heavy blow knocked him to the ground, extinguishing his torch. He muttered an oath, felt for his golf club and gave chase after a shadowy form that leapt agilely over the garden wall and vanished into the night. Reuben stopped, chest heaving. Then, he remembered the moan. His heart thudding heavily in fear for the victim of the unknown assailant; he hurried back to where the sound had come from.

Reuben's eyes had, by now, become accustomed to the darkness, and he could vaguely make out a slim, small figure in a dressing-gown lying on the ground, horribly still.

'Oh, no!' he said. 'Not Sarah?' He knelt beside her and felt for a pulse, relief swamping him as he realised she was alive. *I must get help*, he thought, letting go of her wrist and rising stiffly to his feet. He felt old and tired; the blow he had received had knocked him about more than he had thought. He hurried to the backdoor, switched on the outside light and went to wake Devin, banging on his door. 'Boss! Boss! Come outside. Someone's hurt! I think it's Sarah.'

In a very few moments, Devin appeared, in trousers and boots, dragging on his shirt as he ran in the direction the gardener had shakily pointed out. The noise had roused Aunt Fay, and she came out in her dressing-gown and hurried after Devin. Mattie had also heard the disturbance and struggled into gown and slippers to follow.

As Devin approached the slight figure lying on the path in the glare of the floodlight, he experienced a surge of relief when he saw that it was not Sarah. But the relief was short-lived. *Sue—it's Sue! And badly hurt, by the look of her.* One whole side of her face was bruised; blood oozed from a scalp wound and trickled down the side of her head. There was a swelling bruise on her forehead, and her right eye was puffy and closing. Her cheek was rapidly swelling where it looked as if her jaw had been broken, and he glimpsed broken teeth through her split and swollen lips. His shocked gaze could barely take in that, as well as the rest of her horrific injuries, her throat was bruised and mottled. *Poor Sue! Who would want to do this to her?*

Running to his side, Aunt Fay cried out in distress and subsided in an inanimate heap beside Sue's unconscious form.

This seemed to galvanise Devin into action. 'Mattie!' he shouted.

'Coming, Boss!' But when she arrived, Mattie's eyes widened in horror. 'Oh my God! I knew she was frightened. I *knew* it. I shouldn't have let her —— And Mrs Fay! *Not* Mrs Fay!'

'Pull yourself together, Mattie!' he said; his sharpened tone bringing her to her senses. 'Get Sarah up to help you and bring blankets. I am going to call the Flying Doctor. Hurry! And don't move Sue. Just cover her and keep her as still as possible. We don't know the extent of her injuries. I think—*I hope!*—that Aunty has just fainted from the shock.' He strode away to the radio.

At the other end of the house, Sarah had heard nothing, but at Mattie's urgent call, was up and into her dressing-gown and slippers in a matter of seconds. Mattie explained, between gasps, what had happened as they ran down the hall, stopping at the linen press for an armful each of blankets, before hurrying out to the garden.

Devin left the radio to go in search of the gardener. 'Bring the lanterns, Reub. We'll have to get the strip ready for them to land. They'll be here in about forty minutes.'

Reuben nodded and limped away to the shed where he kept the emergency lanterns that were always filled and trimmed, ready for such an occasion as this, though no-one had ever suspected that they would be required for anything other than an accident or a sudden severe illness. Certainly not a deliberate crime.

Devin went back to where Sarah and Mattie, bending over the two unconscious women, had covered them with blankets. Aunt Fay still hadn't come round. Devin felt her pulse. It was weak and fluttering.

'I think it is her heart,' whispered Sarah. 'See how she is blue around the lips? Mattie just told me she had a slight turn a little while back, but thought it was indigestion.'

Devin didn't comment, but the creases between his brows deepened as he looked at the pale, drawn face of the sweet woman who had comforted him and brought him up after his parents had died. A muscle jerked in his jaw, and he went to take Sue's pulse. It was a little stronger now, so if there wasn't brain damage, Sue would probably be okay.

'Ready, Boss,' said Reuben, appearing at the edge of the light. 'What's happened to the Missus?'

'Fainted from the shock,' said Devin, noting the anxiety in his voice and mentally crossing his fingers.

He and Reuben drove along both sides of the airstrip, lighting the lanterns and sitting them on the white-painted drums, placed at intervals to mark the edges. Then they drove to the end and waited.

Soon, the radio crackled, and the call for which they had been waiting came in. The pilot radioed that he would arrive in ten minutes. Was all in readiness?

Devin informed him in a clear voice that all was right and switched on the car headlamps to guide him in. He felt that this could be the longest ten minutes of his life, but eventually, they heard the hum of a light aeroplane. The twin-engined Cessna circled once, then dropped swiftly for a smooth landing. The airstrip was close to the house, so in a few minutes, the doctor and nurse were bending over their patients.

The doctor looked at Sue and made a sympathetic sound, but what he saw in Aunt Fay's face made him look more closely. He examined her first and gave rapid instructions to his nurse, who nodded and began to fill a hypodermic syringe from a small bottle in the medical bag. Then, he bent over Sue and gently began his examination. He took her pulse, blood pressure, listened to her heart and shone a small torch in her uninjured eye. Gently, he began to feel her skull and neck. Then, he stood up and looked at Devin. 'They are both very ill. This woman has been most severely beaten, and an attempt has been made to strangle her. In my opinion, this is a case for the police,' he said and went to take another look at Aunt Fay.

A little colour had crept into her cheeks, and she was breathing more evenly. The doctor took her pulse and nodded. 'Good,' he said. 'What is the BP now?' he asked his nurse and nodded approval when she told him. 'Your aunt has suffered a heart attack,' he told Devin. 'Perhaps brought on by the shock of what has happened here, tonight. The other woman is suffering from concussion and almost certainly has a fractured jaw. She may have skull fractures, too. We won't know the extent of the damage until X-rays have been taken and a scan done. I propose to take them to Mount Isa now. They will both have to go into the intensive care unit in the hospital.'

Devin made a split-second decision. 'Is there room for me, Doctor, in the plane?'

'Yes. As long as you hurry.'

Sarah looked at Devin. 'I'll pack you some clothes while you get them on the stretchers,' she said, hurrying into the house.

He nodded his thanks, watching the doctor and nurse deftly place the stretchers under their patients. Sue moaned and opened her uninjured eye. She stared unseeingly for a moment and then dropped back into unconsciousness. The stretchered patients were then ferried out to the plane on the back of the garden truck.

Sarah came running with Devin's bag and some nightgowns and toiletries for Aunt Fay and Sue that she and Mattie had hastily flung together. She handed them to him, and he clasped her hand for a moment, his eyes clinging to hers. Then, he bent his head, just brushed her lips with his own, turned and followed the stretchers onto the plane—a shocked and troubled man.

The plane rose, banked and roared off into the distance. Sarah, who had been calm and efficient until now, burst into overwrought tears.

Reuben patted her shoulder awkwardly. 'There, there, Missy. Don't you cry. They're in good hands now. You done the best you could. We all did.'

'I know.' Sarah gave him a grateful glance, helping him collect and extinguish the lanterns. Then they drove back to the house where Mattie was waiting for them with her inevitable pot of tea.

Sarah looked at the kitchen clock. It was a quarter past two. *It isn't real*, she thought, sipping the hot, comforting drink. *It can't be real! I'll wake up in the morning and find it was only a bad dream.*

'What about the prowler?' said Mattie suddenly, breaking the silence. She turned her great, troubled eyes on Reuben.

'Yeah,' he said slowly, 'I've been thinking about that. I don't *think* he'll come back tonight. But, if he does, he might get more than he bargained for.'

Sarah gave a start. In the urgency of caring for the two casualties, she had forgotten all about Sue's assailant. Remembering Sue's white, frightened face of the last few days, she felt suddenly afraid.

Mattie grunted. 'Johnnie's cattle dogs?' she asked.

'Yeah. And my trusty old .410, and Johnnie's double-barrelled shotgun,' said Reuben, watching Sarah. 'Don't you worry; I'll go and get Johnnie in a minute, and he and I will take turns to sit up all night, if need be. You'll be okay, Missy.'

Chapter Eighteen

'Oh, *what?* My God! How utterly awful! A prowler, out here? Good *Lord!* Is Aunty going to be all right?' Louella asked a few more questions, listening intently to the answers. 'Very well, keep me posted,' she said, dropped the receiver and turned away from the telephone, her eyes flashing. 'My *God!*' she said again.

'What's that?' enquired her father from the next room.

'That was Dev, Daddy. He won't be here for the start of the muster. Their housemaid was attacked by some prowler, and Aunty had a heart attack because of it, so they're both in intensive care at Mount Isa Base Hospital. Can you believe it? A *prowler!* Out here! Dev's staying with them until they're off the danger list.'

'Fay?' said Bill Richmond, visibly shaken. 'Did you say *Fay* has had a heart attack?'

'Yes, but she is improving,' Louella answered absently, drumming her long scarlet nails on the table. She was too

211

preoccupied with her own thoughts to notice the expression in her father's eyes as he got up and went quickly to the telephone.

§

Two detectives and a doctor were standing by Sue's hospital bed, deep in murmured conversation. After listening to the doctor's description of her injuries and the details of surgical intervention, Detective Briggs moved to gaze with pity on the bandaged face of the assault victim, pressed the limp fingers and went to look out the window.

Inspector Kingston followed. 'I know we'll have to wait until she regains consciousness to tell us what happened …'

'And what if she can't?' asked the detective, turning from the window to lead the way out the door.

'Then, we're running blind.'

'I wouldn't count on her remembering. They don't sometimes, you know, even if they do come out of it.'

'I know. That's why I want you out there conducting a surveillance operation.'

Detective Briggs gave the inspector a long level glance that caused him to cower with exaggerated fear behind a raised arm.

'I wish you wouldn't do that!' he complained.

'Why not? You know how much I *love* camping in the bush!'

'How long have you been out here, Briggsy? It must be twenty years! You're not going to tell me you're still a city slicker?'

Detective Briggs grinned. 'Past praying for, aren't I? But I'm glad you brought me to see this poor woman. I can reconcile myself to any amount of discomfort, just to get the swine that did this.'

'I thought you'd say that,' said the inspector. 'I feel better already, knowing you'll be keeping a finger on the pulse.'

'I've got to get you out of this hospital,' said Detective Briggs, hustling him down the front steps. 'All that medical jargon must be getting to you.'

'It's that filthy woman-basher that's getting to me. I'm going back out there first thing in the morning. You come in your own time.'

'All right. I'll go and prepare for this bush camp. But you owe me!'

'I know, Briggsy, I know. Put it on the slate.'

Detective Briggs made a small derisive sound between a snort and a laugh.

§

Shorty and Snip, Johnnie's two cattle dogs, roamed the homestead gardens all night. Johnnie slept on the verandah on a shearer's bed, and Reuben slept in his flat with the door open. Both he and Johnnie were able to sleep soundly, knowing the dogs would intercept any intruder and sound the alarm.

About nine o'clock the next morning, Mattie came to the schoolroom, subdued but wide-eyed. 'The police are here to talk to you, Sarah. I'll stay here with the children while you go see them. I put them in the sitting room.' She wagged her head. 'To think it has come to this: *police* at Medora Downs!'

'All right, Mattie. Thank you. I'll be back as soon as I can,' said

Sarah, wondering why Mattie was so upset by police. *Perhaps it's something in her past: like her attitude to strange men?*

Sarah opened the door of the sitting room and found herself confronting three men, two of whom were uniformed policemen: one very large, with sergeant's stripes on his sleeves; the other tall and lean; the third man, older than both, was dressed in a conventional grey suit.

'Good morning,' said Sarah. 'May I help you? I am Sarah Johnston.'

'Yes, Miss Johnston, I hope you may,' said the man in the grey suit in a firm but pleasant voice. He had grey hair with shrewd hazel eyes in a square-jawed face and was large and thickset with an air of calm authority. 'I am Detective-Inspector Charles Kingston, and these gentlemen are Sergeant Riley and Constable Smith, who will keep an eye on things here for a few days. We are here to make enquiries about the assault on Mrs Bryant.'

'Mrs Bryant?'

'Yes, your housemaid.'

'Oh.' Sarah had never heard Sue's surname, and she was a person who discouraged any delving into her private life. 'Of course.'

'Could you show us the scene of the alleged crime? Also, I wish to speak with ...' He consulted his notebook. 'Mr Reuben O'Mara.'

Sarah led the way to the place around the side of the house where Reuben had found Sue—her mind busy. Obviously, Devin had already been to see the police, which was why they were here, asking for Reuben. She found the gardener in his shadehouse, potting ferns, and told him of the police visit and the inspector's summons. He tamped down the soil around the fern he was working on and placed the pot in a bucket of water, before following Sarah to the Detective Inspector.

'I'll speak to you later, Miss Johnston,' the inspector told her. 'And I will also need to interview everybody that was here last night.'

Sarah left Reuben to explain his part in the affair to the inspector and went back to the schoolroom, wondering wryly how he was going to go with his proposed interview with Mattie.

Sarah thanked the cook for minding the children. 'They want to see you next,' she told her. But Mattie's reply surprised her.

'I'd better get some scones into the oven, then,' was all she said.

As Sarah knew was only to be expected, the children were very upset about Sue and Aunt Fay. They had only been told that Sue had had an accident and was hurt, and that Aunt Fay had suddenly become ill.

'But they are getting better,' Sarah assured them with a smile and an encouraging hug each. 'And when Uncle Dev rings up tonight, you can speak to him, and he'll tell you himself.'

They nodded seriously, apparently satisfied. Sarah hoped that this would not bring back their insecurities, and naturally, she did not mention the prowler. But she did notice, with a sinking heart, that Sam was apparently indispensable to Adam again.

When Devin rang that evening, he was able to tell them that Aunt Fay was sitting up, talking and smiling, although still on a heart monitor. But obviously responding to treatment and in great spirits.

Sue had undergone surgery for her broken jaw, had skull fractures and concussion. She had come round for a short time but had been unable to tell them anything of value, having lost all recollection of what had happened to her. She did not even know who she was. The doctors had said that it would take time, and there was a distinct possibility that she would never remember. They thought that there was a good chance that she might recover her consciousness fully, tomorrow, since her vital signs were very good, and she was starting to become restless.

After Devin's call, Sarah felt very lonely, but the children appeared to be reassured to a great degree. She put them to bed, then went to tell Mattie and Reuben the news.

§

During the next two days, the police interviewed the entire station staff. The Detective Inspector told Sarah that they had found a place in the river channel where a horse had stood for some time, tied to a tree. They had followed the tracks to a large, flat rock where they had mysteriously disappeared, although the police had thoroughly scouted around the rock for a great distance. There was no way of telling which way the horse and rider had gone. It was as if they had vanished into thin air once they had reached the rock.

'We're dealing with a cunning customer,' said the inspector. 'We think he has muffled the horse's hooves—tied bags around them—so he won't leave tracks.' He shrugged. 'And the strong wind this morning would have wiped out what little there was.'

At the end of this time, Devin rang in the evening to say that

Aunt Fay was out of intensive care, and Sue had regained consciousness but was still suffering from amnesia. 'I'll be home, tomorrow,' he said. Sarah's heart lifted as she put down the phone and went away to pass on the happy news to the others.

§

Devin arrived home the next afternoon in a chartered light aeroplane with even better news: Aunt Fay could come home in two weeks' time. She would have a supply of tablets that she must keep with her at all times, and provided she did not overdo things, she could expect a reasonably long and comfortable life. Sue was more comfortable now, too. But the doctors would not say when she might be able to come home.

Sarah gave up her riding during this period because she and Mattie did the housework between them in the afternoons. She was dusting books and ornaments and polishing furniture in the sitting room when Devin came in with the inspector. Sarah picked up her dusters and polish and prepared to leave.

'Don't go, Sarah,' said Devin. 'You can hear this, too. Well, Inspector, did you find anything?'

'No. Nothing that we can prove, of course. There is no way of telling where the horse came from or in which direction it went after walking onto that flat rock. One of the horses out at the mustering camp showed saddle marks, but the man with them explained that he had used the horse to bring in the others after feeding them out for the day.'

'That would be right,' confirmed Devin. 'The horses not in use spend the day feeding out and are yarded at night. One horse is always kept back to bring them in just before dark.'

'The other men seem able to account for their movements,' continued the inspector. 'We know the attacker was a tall man, from the position of the blows and the distance between the footprints found beyond the garden wall. But they were so blurred and indistinct that we were unable to get a cast. Looked like an ordinary stockman's boot, average size, from what we could make out,' he added, rubbing his chin. 'Of course, there's no reason why a man couldn't ride in from somewhere else, attack the victim, then ride out again. I am convinced that Mrs Bryant is the key to all this, but until she remembers something, the police are at a standstill.'

'I understand, Inspector,' said Devin. 'But, in the meantime, what do we do?'

'Well … from what I've been privileged to see of your groom and gardener and your two cattle dogs, I'd say you have a pretty good alarm system set up. But I'd like to leave my men here for a few more days. Is there anywhere they can stay where they won't be in your hair?'

'They can use the overseer's cottage if you like. There's plenty of room there. It isn't exactly a cottage,' explained Devin with a twinkle. 'Jim prefers to live with his men, rather than rattle around in it by himself, so we use it for clients and visitors. It can be your headquarters while you're here. Use it whenever you want.'

'Very good of you,' grunted the inspector. 'I will feel a bit better with Sergeant Riley and Smithy here, giving you a hand. Of course, there may be no further trouble. He may have come here with the express purpose of assaulting Mrs Bryant. By the way: what do you know of her ex—Bryant? These things usually turn out to be domestic, you know. Unless, of course, he mistook her for someone else. That's a possibility, too.'

'Bryant?' said Devin, furrowing his brow. 'Well, very little, really. He was here for a short time with the riggers on the oil-research job, and when he left, Sue went with him. Her parents tried to trace her but had no success. Then, four years later, she turned up here—divorced, as far as I know—with a small son. She has never mentioned him, and I haven't asked any questions. I'm quite sure she has not seen nor heard of him since then, and that must be ten or twelve years ago. As far as I know, there is no-one in the district of that name.'

'No, there isn't,' said the inspector. 'I've already checked that. I'm in the process of trying to get a description of him, but if he has no criminal record, it will be difficult. Especially if we can't trace him or find anyone that knows him. Did you ever see him?'

'Not that I know of,' said Devin. 'We didn't see much of the riggers. In fact, the first time I ever heard of him was after he had left with Sue, when her father was trying to track her down.'

The inspector pursed his lips. 'Well, there's nothing much more I can do here. I will have Mrs Bryant moved to a women's refuge or safe house after she leaves hospital, and when she's finished her convalescence, you can bring her home. We might have sorted this out by then. Or, she may have remembered something about her assailant.' He rose and took his leave.

Sarah and Devin stared wordlessly at each other for a few moments.

'What do you think?' asked Sarah.

'I just don't know what to think,' said Devin, slowly. 'Meanwhile, we will all have to be careful at night.

Unfortunately, we couldn't put off the muster, but I think the cattle dogs, Johnnie and Reuben should be enough protection. Lock all the doors and windows at night. And on no account should you or the children go outside unprotected.'

Sarah gave a gasp of shock. She hadn't thought that the children might not be safe.

Seeing her expression, Devin continued: 'It is quite possible, however, that having done what he wanted, the intruder may not return. If, on the other hand, his mission was murder, then he may try to complete the job. Which is what, I think, the inspector had in mind with his plans for the safe custody of Sue.'

Sarah felt a little cold shiver run down her spine. It was like living in a nightmare. She felt that she might choke in the evil atmosphere that had descended over them like a thick blanket of fog.

Chapter Nineteen

The next day, Devin went out to the mustering camp, and those left at the homestead settled back into their daily routine. There were no disturbances at night, the police went home and the occupants gradually relaxed, although Sarah missed the comforting bulk of Sergeant Riley. Devin kept in touch with Sarah by two-way radio and spent every third night at the homestead. She thought that he was looking tired and strained.

One evening, he said, 'It's the last day tomorrow on this camp, Sarah, before we go over onto Emerald Hills, and I *did* promise the children a picnic. Do you think you could bring them out? It's the first turn after the third bore along the Emerald Hills Road. Turn right, there, and keep following the track along the channels. If you leave about nine o'clock, you'll be able to watch some of the cattle work before lunch. By the time lunch is over, the children will be pretty tired, anyway, and ready to go home.'

Sarah agreed to this with pleasure, and the next morning, she, the children (and Sam), dressed in jeans, cotton sweaters and shady hats, picked up a hamper from Mattie and climbed into the Suzuki four-wheel drive that had been set aside for Sarah's use. They sang songs and chanted their times tables as they drove along the track in the golden winter sunshine.

The first indication that they were approaching the mustering camp was a thick cloud of dust that looked like smoke from a raging fire. It was not until they came quite close and could see the cattle through the pall of dust, that they heard the unmistakable sounds of the camp. Cattle bellowed and stamped, horses whinnied, and men shouted to each other in busy, happy tones.

Devin, who had been talking to Bill and Louella Richmond, all on horseback, swung down from the saddle and came over, leading his horse to greet Sarah and the children. Louella followed his progress with narrowed, jealous eyes.

Sarah watched, fascinated, as Devin explained to her and the children the use of the bronco yard. The bronco horse, a thickset, heavy bay that knew his job as well as any man, worked in perfect sync with his rider who skilfully roped each unbranded beast. The horse would then steadily pull the rope up the sloping rail of the bronco fence until it dropped into a slot, maintaining tension while two or three men went into action with ropes and the branding iron.

Sarah wrinkled her nose at the smell of burning hair, but the men were fast and expert at their job, completing the operation with a minimum of stress for the cattle. Time after time, the process was repeated, until all the yarded cleanskins were marked with either the Emerald Hills' or Medora Downs' brand according to ownership, which was sometimes arbitrary.

'Uncle Dev, we're hungry,' said Naomi. 'Can we go and talk to Jack now?'

'All right. Can I trust you with my horse?' he asked, handing Naomi the reins. 'Give him to Johnnie over there, and then go over to Jack. We'll meet you there in a minute.'

'Okay,' she said, leading him proudly—Adam hanging on to the end of the rein. Fortunately, he had been persuaded to leave Sam to watch from the Suzuki.

Bill came over to them, followed by Louella. He took Sarah's hand, kissed her cheek and told her how pleased he was to hear of her engagement and, charmingly, wished her a life of happiness. He stepped back for his daughter to do the same, but she had turned her back and was walking rapidly away. His immediate frown was erased by a good-natured smile as, courteously, he covered for her.

Sarah really didn't mind her rudeness: it was a relief not to have to speak to her after her exhibition the last time they met. She responded to Bill's kind overtures with spontaneous thanks and sweetly spoken observations that pleased him immensely. Or would have done, had it not shown up his daughter so thoroughly.

'Lunchtime, Bill,' said Devin, taking Sarah's hand. 'I'm going to take Sarah over to meet your cook.'

'By Jove, so it is!' he said, looking at his watch. 'Good idea! I'll go and find Louie and meet you there.' But when he ran his daughter to earth sitting on a bale of hay in an Emerald Hills' truck, he shook his head at her. 'Not well done, darling. Not well done, at all. We've talked about this, Louie: You have to let him go, darling. You have no choice, and you *will* have to learn to cope. We have to be neighbours, you know.'

'I know, Daddy. I'm sorry. I will get used to it in time. And I promise that I will go and apologise to Sarah, but not just yet. I just … *can't* do it yet.' She sobbed and buried her face in her handkerchief. 'So-rry …'

'There, there, don't be in a fuss,' he said awkwardly, patting her shoulder. 'I came to tell you that lunch is ready.'

Louella raised red-rimmed eyes. 'Daddy, I *can't*. I've got a sick headache coming on, and I'm going home.' She stood up and tried to smile. 'Make my apologies?'

'Of course, pet. You go home and rest, and don't worry. Do you need someone to drive you?'

'No. I'll be okay. *Really*, Daddy. You go to lunch.'

He put her in her car, watched her drive away; the pain in his eyes unmasked for just a moment before he turned to walk back to the camp. *My poor little girl. Poor, poor little girl.*

Devin had watched Bill walk away with a strange expression. 'Poor old Bill,' he said under his breath. 'Caught between the devil and the deep blue sea …'

'Pardon?'

'Oh, nothing.' He turned his light eyes on Sarah. 'Just … thinking aloud.' He put an arm around her waist and nodded to where the children were talking earnestly to the cook. 'Come on,' he said with a little smile. 'Let's go and try Jack's damper before those two beat us to it.'

They strolled over to the campfire, and Sarah savoured the comfort of his nearness and his arm about her; it made her feel safe and cherished. In that moment, she felt that Louella could do her worst; nothing she said or did could affect her now. Then, she saw that Bill was coming back to meet them—alone.

'Louie's gone home,' he said. 'The poor little girl has a migraine coming on.'

Devin introduced Sarah to the cook: a thickset, middle-aged man with a wry grin. They chatted for a few minutes until Jack told them he'd serve their lunches before the rush if Dev would give him a hand. Devin left her side with a murmured word, and Sarah went to sit on a log under a tree with the children, listening in smiling interest to their eagerly imparted confidences.

Devin came back and handed Sarah a pannikin of hot, sweet tea and some slices of damper for her, Naomi and Adam. And from somewhere, he'd magically produced a bottle of lemonade for the children. He shrugged his shoulders when asked where it had come from. 'Some hidey-hole of Jack's,' he said with a grin, sitting down beside her. 'Better not to ask.'

Sarah looked over at the cook, who was busy slicing slabs from a great piece of corned beef that had been boiling in a huge iron pot. Out of the coals, he pulled another large damper, dusted off the ashes and began to slice it, as well. Each man took a slab of beef and damper, filled his pannikin with hot, black tea from the oversized billy and sat back from the fire against a tree, rock or log.

There was an air of camaraderie, evident when people work as a team; a sense of satisfaction at a challenge met and conquered, in the knowledge that they were experts at what they loved best.

The children saw Jim coming, left their meal and jumped up to run to him. He came over to where Devin and Sarah were sitting—Naomi swinging on one arm and Adam on the other.

'How's it going, Sarah? I see Dev's been taking care of you, as he should. How do you like bush tucker?'

'Lovely!' she answered. 'Really scrummy! Do you know: I've never tasted damper before?'

'Ah, well, there's a first time for everything, they say. But speaking of scrummy, did Mattie send us out some goodies with you?'

'Oh, yes. I'm sorry; I forgot. There's a huge hamper in the Suzuki—over the other side of the yards.'

'Good-o, I'll bring it over. The men might like a feed of Mattie's cakes.' He looked at the children. 'You two come with me to show me where it is.'

In a few minutes, they were back; Naomi carrying a folded picnic rug. 'Look what we forgot, Sarah,' she said, busily spreading it out. Adam plumped straight down on it and demanded a piece of cake.

'Wait a minute, young fella,' said Jim, holding the hamper aloft. 'Hey fellas, look what I've got here. Mattie's come good again.'

The men set up a cheer and surged over to where Jim had set down the basket. With a flourish, he placed a huge sponge cake in front of Sarah and handed her a knife. 'The lady of the house must do the honours,' he said with a merry twinkle.

Sarah cut the sponge into generous slices, placing one on each man's plate as it was handed over. But there was no shortage of cakes. As well as another superb sponge, there were brownies, patty cakes, slices and jam drops.

Jack grinned slyly as the men chiacked him, wanting to know why he didn't produce such delicacies on his campfire. He had his own methods of dealing with those who had the temerity to criticise his cooking. Not that they had any cause: there were those who asserted, many times, that they had never tasted a damper to equal Jack's. But he tucked into Mattie's cakes with the rest of them and, winking at Sarah, told her to present his compliments to the cook.

Adam had become very quiet on the rug beside her, and Sarah looked around to see that he had fallen asleep. She twitched Devin's sleeve and pointed.

He smiled down at him affectionately. 'Too big a day, eh? Well, the camp has to move on today, so we'll have to leave soon, too.' Rising, he picked up the little boy and carried him to the Suzuki, where he deposited him carefully on the seat. Adam did not even stir. Sarah brought the rug and the empty hamper while Naomi skipped over to say goodbye to Jim.

Devin took Sarah's hand and said quietly, 'Take care, Sarah. I'll only be a few more days out here, and then, I think I can go and get Aunty from Mount Isa. And, when I do, I'll bring someone to help in the house. Can you manage until then, do you think?'

'Oh, yes.'

'Good girl.' Devin clasped her hand more firmly for a moment before he turned and strode away. He stopped to speak to Naomi and ruffle her hair, then disappeared into the dust of the cattle yard.

Adam slept all the way home and stirred, but did not wake, when Sarah carried him to his bed. Naomi was tired, too, and went to her room without protest, leaving Sarah free to think over her revealing day in the bush. Devin cared for her; she was sure. Although, how deeply, she could not tell. He had demonstrated his affection for her in front of his men—no small thing—and when he had said goodbye to her, she felt that there were things he would have said, had they been alone.

Mattie was preparing dinner when Sarah brought the empty hamper back to the kitchen. She stopped what she was doing to make a pot of tea, exhorting Sarah to tell her all about her day. Sarah relayed the many compliments and messages that had been sent to her by the grateful men.

Mattie accepted these with composure but laughed when she heard Jack's message. 'It won't worry that old twicer,' she said. 'He'll find a way to get his own again. He hasn't been camp cook for ten years for nothing.' She snorted. 'The sly old so-and-so, he is!'

There were obviously some private undercurrents here, but Sarah, aware of Mattie's opinions on most of the male population, did not enquire as to what they were. Now she understood Mattie's sending of the delicious cakes—so unlike camp food. It was prompted by a desire to needle Jack rather than to please the men, as Sarah had first thought and wondered about.

Sarah gave the children their dinner and bathed them without incident, but when it was time for bed, there was an uproar. Sam was missing.

'Oh,' said Sarah. 'Don't you remember, Adam? We took him with us to the mustering camp but left him in the Suzuki so he wouldn't get dusty. I'll just go out and get him for you.'

Adam's wails turned to sobs and hiccups as he realised that Sam wasn't lost, after all. But when Sarah returned from the car shed, it was with bad news, which started the wailing up again. She had searched the Suzuki from top to bottom, but there was no sign of Sam. Did Adam remember if he had taken him out at the mustering camp? Adam dolefully shook his head and became more and more inconsolable.

Finally, in desperation, Sarah told him that if he would try to sleep, she would go out now and find Sam. Then, when he awoke in the morning, Sam would be with him. Such was his faith in her that he agreed to this but sobbed himself to sleep, just the same.

Sarah explained to Mattie what had happened and that she was going back to find Sam.

'But, Sarah,' objected Mattie, 'it's pitch-dark, out there. Get Reuben to go with you. I don't like you going out there on your own.'

'I'll be all right, Mattie,' Sarah assured her, refusing to give way to her own fears. 'There's no need to disturb Reuben at this time of night.'

'Well, then, take Johnnie. What about the prowler?'

'Johnnie's not back yet. He'll be late tonight, shifting the horses to the next camp. As for the prowler, there's been no sign of him for weeks. And, anyway, no-one knows where I'm going,' said Sarah, reasonably. 'Look, if it makes you feel better, send Johnnie after me if I'm not back in two hours.'

Mattie looked unhappy but agreed to this. Her glance at the kitchen clock showed that it was a quarter to nine. 'Well, I don't like it, Sarah. And if you're not back by a quarter to eleven, I will.

You just be careful, that's all!' she warned.

§

Sarah drove through the darkness towards the camp they had left earlier in the day. She shivered. It was eerie being alone out here at night with no moon to light the way. It was with difficulty that she found the turn at the bore. She had to drive very slowly to see it at all, not knowing the road.

The tree where they had spread the rug loomed up in front of the headlights. Sarah braked. Nothing happened. She pumped the pedal. Still nothing. At the last moment, she swung the wheel hard to avoid the tree, crashing into the bushes on the edge of the river channel. The bushes gave way, and the nose of the Suzuki slowly dropped to the bottom of the channel where it stalled.

Shocked but unhurt, Sarah sat for a moment until the pounding of her heart subsided and she stopped trembling. Then, groping for her pencil torch, she switched off the useless headlights and climbed out to assess the damage.

The Suzuki was hung by its back bumper, wheels clear of the ground and its nose resting against the opposite bank of the channel. She wasn't going to be able to move it tonight, that much was clear. She glanced at her watch. If Mattie kept her word, Johnnie should be here in a couple of hours, so she might as well look for Sam while she waited.

Sarah fought her way up the bank through the mat of bushes, then systematically searched the camp area. And at last, near a pile of huge, flat rocks that reared skyward—having been thrust on their edges by some cataclysmic geophysical force of the Earth's past—she found the teddy. Her overstrained ears caught a noise in the channel, and instinctively, she switched off her torch, desperately trying to identify the sound. It was probably only an inquisitive kangaroo.

Then she saw the flash of a torch, switched on and immediately off again, in the channel and crouched down behind one of the rocks, fear suddenly uppermost in her mind. It rippled along her spine, prickling her skin from the backs of her legs to the top of her scalp and froze the blood in her veins. No-one who did not mean harm would use a torch so furtively. Sarah clutched the teddy more tightly, numb and sick with terror.

She ventured to peer around the rock and gasped as she saw that someone was at her vehicle. He opened the door and flashed the torch briefly around the interior. And in the dim glow, Sarah could see the outline of a tall, slim figure, but she could not distinguish any features. *A man or a woman?* She was almost sure that it was a man.

The man was bolder now. He flashed the torch around and came towards the camp area. Terrified, Sarah inched her way carefully between two of the largest rocks in the centre of the pile, praying that if he came this way, the shadow of the rocks would hide her. She curled herself up into as small a bundle as she could and shrank back, far into the cleft. A vision of Sue's bruised and bloody face rose before her eyes, and she almost fainted from horror and fear. Sobs filled her throat, threatening to choke her. But desperately, she quelled them, knowing that her survival might depend on absolute silence.

Please, God, don't let him find me, she prayed soundlessly, over and over, a refrain beating in her head. When he had attacked Sue (she was sure this was the man), he had been interrupted.

There would be no-one to interrupt him, here. Johnnie would not come for at least an hour yet, and it would not take him that long, whoever he was, to complete his grisly task.

The air was becoming chilly. Sarah had to clench her teeth to stop them from chattering. Cramps tortured her limbs, but she dare not move. The torch flashed over the rocks: once, twice. Each time, Sarah braced herself for the ordeal to come. *Is this why I came to the Outback?* she thought wildly. *To have my life brutally wrested from me on a lonely cattle camp?* Then, as the tension became unbearable, and she felt that she must scream and run— must do something, anything, rather than wait here to be beaten and strangled—the torch moved away again.

For a long time, there was darkness, blessed darkness, protecting her from the evil eyes of the madman out there, searching for her. But why had he come here and flicked the torch over the back of the rocks, yet did not search them for her? The answer flashed into her mind with the clarity of a searchlight, jerking at mind and body. He had been looking for the teddy, for Sam, to see if she had taken him and gone. That could only mean one thing: that he himself had put the teddy there. Sarah had been meant to come and look for him and crash the car. And if she survived that, then he would see that she went no further. Perhaps, he was, even now, searching the road to the homestead for her, in the belief that she had found Sam and started walking home.

A scream rose soundlessly in Sarah's throat, but she fought it back as she grappled with this new horror. And then another thought struck her: The man must be one of the station hands or, at any rate, someone who had been at the mustering camp and knew of Adam's obsession with his teddy. Someone who knew the Mainwarings well. Someone who hated her!

Unaccountably, a vision appeared in her mind of the man she had seen at the ball; his tall, slim figure; dull, curiously opaque eyes; those cruel, contemptuous, sneering lips. And yet when she had seen him again, he had not been sinister at all. And anyway, he was new here—did not know anybody well—certainly not the family. So, how would he know about Sam? And why would anybody want to harm her, anyway?

Sarah wanted, more than anything, to move, to stand up and see where he was, but she knew that could be fatal. Perhaps he was just waiting for her to show herself, so that he could get on with his evil task. She felt her flesh creep at the thought.

The minutes dragged on. And still, she did not—could not—move. She was sick and cold and afraid. *Oh, if only I can last out the time until Johnnie comes ...*

CHAPTER TWENTY

There was a roaring in Sarah's ears, growing steadily louder and louder. She jerked herself awake. *Johnnie! It's Johnnie coming.* But she must not move. Not until he was close enough to see her—to hear her call. Then, perhaps, she would be safe.

Reuben's old garden truck pulled up with a squeal of brakes. Johnnie peered anxiously around the camping area. Then, he saw the back of the Suzuki in the channel and drove over. It was empty. He frowned worriedly. Where was Sarah? He reversed with a grinding of gears and drove towards the pile of rocks. 'Sarah? Are you there, Sarah?' he called. And gasped and jumped on the brake pedal as a white-faced, stricken figure stumbled out from between the rocks and fell in front of the runabout, still clutching Adam's teddy.

Johnnie rushed around to the front of the vehicle and bent over her. 'Oh, God! Sarah!'

'Oh, Johnnie! Thank heavens you've come!' she sobbed—her

eyes huge, dark holes in her ashen face. 'Please, take me home.'

'But what happened, Sarah?' he asked, helping her up. 'You're frozen!' he exclaimed before she could answer as he put her in the truck, tucking a rug around her. He got in beside her and started the motor. 'Now, what is it? What has happened?'

Haltingly, Sarah told him of the failure of the brakes and the man who had come, searching for her.

Johnnie gave a muffled exclamation. 'I thought I saw a torch flash down the road a little way, and I thought it was you. I stopped the truck and shouted, but no-one answered, so I came on. It must've been him, eh? Lookin' for you on the road to home.' He banged his fist on the steering wheel. 'I wish I'd a known!' He mumbled expletives under his breath and drove his foot down on the accelerator.

'Oh, Johnnie, I was so frightened! I thought he was going to kill me.'

'I know,' he said. 'But the main thing is, you're safe now. Mattie'll make you a hot drink when we get you home.' He chuckled reminiscently. 'That Mattie! She's a tartar. She's been that worried about you! She wouldn't wait the two hours to send me. She give me no peace till I come out to find you. And the way things turned out, I'm real glad I did.'

Sarah caught her breath. So, all those long hours she spent crouched among the rocks had not really been hours, after all, thanks to Mattie, who had certainly saved her life. What if Mattie had waited the two hours, and the man had time to ascertain that she had not gone down the road at all and had come back for a careful search of the camp? What then? She expelled her breath on a sigh. 'Yes, I am, too, Johnnie. I am, too.'

When Mattie saw Sarah, she burst into unexpected tears. 'I knew something was wrong!' she sobbed. 'I just *knew* you were in danger.'

'Well, for once, you were right, woman,' said Johnnie, taking advantage of her unaccountable moment of weakness, 'so I don't know what you're blubbing about. Now, how about that cuppa …?'

Sarah was bundled off to a warm bath with orders to return to the kitchen when she had finished, ostensibly for a cup of tea, but in reality, so that Mattie could assure herself that she had suffered no harm.

Warm in her dressing-gown and sipping the hot, sweet tea that Mattie said was necessary for those in shock, Sarah could hardly believe that it was now only eleven thirty. *After all that …* she thought.

All that night, though Sarah was unaware of it, Johnnie sat outside her bedroom door on the verandah—a loaded shotgun over the rug on his knees, and his two cattle dogs at his feet. In the morning, he would call the Boss on the two-way and tell him to come home. He'd know what to do.

An hour before dawn, Reuben brought two mugs of hot coffee and jerked his head to signify that he would take over. Johnnie rose stiffly, took the proffered mug and tiptoed off the verandah, but he signed to his dogs to stay.

Sarah had been afraid that she would not sleep, but Mattie had bullied her into taking a sleeping tablet, which she did, after restoring Sam to his sleeping owner.

But somewhere out in the channels, a cunning, twisted mind full of hate cursed the upset of well-laid plans and determined that next time, there would be no mistake.

§

The Expert eased himself out from under the Suzuki and came to his feet in one lithe move. He pulled off his cap and scratched his head while he thought for a moment, with furrowed brow. Then, he shot Devin a straight look out of sharp black eyes. 'I dunno, Boss,' he said in a worried tone. 'It looks like foul play to me. The brake lines have got small holes in them, just big enough to allow the brake fluid to creep out slowly. One I could believe was an accident, maybe, but not both. And I serviced that vehicle only last week, too. There was nothing wrong with the brakes or the lines then—I'm sure of that.'

'Thanks, Alan,' said Devin quietly. 'Could Sarah have got home from the mustering camp and then got back out there before she lost her brakes, if those brakes had been tampered with at lunchtime?'

The Expert gazed blindly out towards the horizon, eyes unfocused, while he mulled over this knotty problem. He was a small, wiry man who could have been any age from thirty-five to fifty. His proper title was Alan Brownlowe, Windmill Expert and Station Mechanic, but for the last fifteen years, since he came to Medora Downs, he had been known simply as the 'Expert'.

He was thin and nervy and suffered from ulcers: a direct result, some said, of struggling all his working life against Murphy's Law and the treatment that the young jackaroos gave the motorbikes. He had been known, on the odd occasion, to throw his cap on the ground, jump on it and threaten to wrap the handlebars around the neck of the next so-and-so smart alec to bring a bike back in such a condition again. But people like Sarah found him polite and anxious to please.

He had an overworked sense of responsibility towards all the mechanical equipment under his care, and it was a point of pride with him that any vehicle he serviced was safe and mechanically perfect. Hearing of the failure of the Suzuki's brakes and the subsequent accident had caused him to suffer a severe shock, even to the point where he had to inspect it with his own eyes before he could bring himself to believe it. But the evidence was there, no question of that. 'I don't think so, Boss,' he said at last. 'He'd have to do it later, like just before she left or, say, after dark, anyway. Otherwise, she would have noticed when she first tried to put the brakes on, and she says she had them when she turned off at the bore. The car shed's a goodish way from the house. Likely, the dogs wouldn't notice anything that far outside the garden.'

Devin nodded thoughtfully, then helped the Expert tow the Suzuki out of the channel. There was something going on here that he did not understand. First Sue, now Sarah. *But what is the connection?* he asked himself. *Is it a madman loose in the Outback, indiscriminately attacking vulnerable women?* If that was so, no woman was safe while he roamed free. *Or is he after one person—Sarah—and mistook Sue for her in the darkness? Sarah, the victim of a brutal, sadistic killer?* Devin was certain that Sue would have been killed, had Reuben not intervened. *It is unthinkable! But who can this man be?*

The inspector had said that a great percentage of assailants were known to their victims, and it seemed as though this one knew the family intimately, even down to Adam's obsession with his teddy and which vehicle Sarah always drove. And yet, there was no-one that seemed to fit the bill. He drummed his fist impotently on the roof of the Suzuki. *We'll have to get this fellow. No woman will be safe until we do.*

When Devin returned to the homestead, he went into his office and had a long telephone conversation with Inspector Kingston. Then, he drove out to the mustering camp to talk to his overseer. 'Jim, have any of the men been prowling around at night, do you know?'

'Not that I know of, Dev. We're all so bloody tired at night that we sleep like logs, anyway. I'll ask a couple of the boys if they've noticed anything.'

'No, don't!' said Devin in sharpened tones. He added more moderately, 'Just keep your eyes open. What about that new man?'

'Well, I haven't noticed, really. He's a bit of a loner; unfriendly, even. Camps away by himself and goes to bed early. He's always up and got the fire going by the time Jack turns out to start the breakfast. And he's as good a worker as two men during the day—very fast and fit.'

'Okay, Jim. Look, just keep an eye out for anything strange, will you?'

'Yes, of course, mate. But what's this all about?'

In a low voice, Devin told him what had happened to Sarah.

Jim's eyes grew large, and he gave a low whistle. 'Leave it to me, Boss. There won't be a thing that escapes my eagle eye from now on. I'll go round and kick all the swags, if necessary, to make sure they've got bodies in 'em.'

Chapter Twenty-one

When Devin returned from Mount Isa, he brought with him a smiling and surprisingly healthy looking Aunt Fay and a tall, rather tough-looking middle-aged woman with a brisk, no-nonsense attitude, whom he introduced as Mrs Crampton, the temporary home help. As well as her domestic ability, she had some nursing experience, she said, so could keep an eye on Aunt Fay. She had strange, pale-green eyes that seemed to see more than they were meant to; Sarah had read of pale, protuberant eyes described as being like boiled gooseberries, and they were just like that! Sarah felt slightly uncomfortable with her.

When Naomi and Adam saw Aunt Fay, there was an emotional reunion that almost brought tears to Sarah's eyes.

Devin looked on with an indulgent expression. 'Well, Aunty, that's a pretty good welcome,' he said.

'The very best, Dev,' she replied, smiling through her tears and hugging the two little ones.

Sarah kissed her cheek. 'It's lovely to have you back, Aunt Fay. And looking so well! How is Sue now?'

'Oh, she looks well now, too. Most of the bruising has gone, and there is only a very slight scar on her lip. Her jaw will be unwired soon, and she can come home in another three weeks, they think.'

§

Mrs Crampton proved to be as efficient as she looked. But she seemed to have the uncanny habit of working busily somewhere close to Sarah. At first, Sarah thought that this was merely coincidence, but after a while, she began to feel a little wary of her. There was, however, another good thing: having Mrs Crampton meant that Sarah could go riding again, and she thankfully escaped from the house where she had almost felt a prisoner, so closely did her protectors, Mattie, Reuben and Johnnie hedge her about.

Mrs Crampton was sweeping the steps when Sarah went out. 'Going out are you, Miss Johnston?' she said, stating the obvious.

'Yes, I'm going down for a ride.' Sarah smiled with gratitude. 'Thanks to you doing the housework. But, please, call me Sarah.'

'Not at all. A pleasure, Sarah. Where do you ride?'

'Usually along the river. Or, sometimes, along one of the roads.'

'Oh? Well, enjoy yourself. When do you think you'll be back?'

Nosy and wanting a chat, thought Sarah with an inward smile. *Not that she seems that kind of person at all, but you never know.* 'I'm always back a little before four,' she said, 'to have tea with Aunt

Fay.'

Sarah arrived at the stables to find that Johnnie had already saddled Persian Prince, and when she led him into the stable yard to mount, Johnnie appeared with another horse.

'Hello, Johnnie.' Sarah looked at his mount in surprise. 'Are you riding, too?'

'You don't think I'd let you go out on your own, do you?' he replied in gruff tones, his jaw thrust out belligerently.

Sarah started to say that there was no need, but one look at his face convinced her that no words would avail, so she just said, 'Fine,' and mounted her horse.

They rode along the river channels, as usual. Sarah enjoyed her first ride for weeks, but she would rather have been alone with her horse. *Still, there could be someone hiding in the channels,* she supposed. The river, at once, took on a sinister aspect as this unwelcome thought occurred to her, as it had, no doubt, to her companion. She shuddered, suddenly glad of Johnnie's stalwart presence.

Sarah made up her mind that if she rode out alone again, she would go somewhere in the open where no-one could lie in wait for her. All enjoyment of her ride had gone. She turned to Johnnie. 'Let's go back now.'

'Something worrying you, Sarah?'

'Johnnie, it's the river,' she admitted, paling a little. 'I don't think I want to ride along it any more. If I ride in the horse paddock or just around the racetrack, you could see me from the stables, couldn't you?'

'Yeah, I could. If I was outside.'

'I don't want to put you to trouble when I know how busy you are, but I still like to get out for a ride. So that might be a solution that suits us both.'

'It ain't no trouble, Sarah. But, maybe you're right. It could be dangerous down on the river,' said Johnnie slowly. 'Too many hiding places. All right, if I'm busy, I'll look out at the racetrack every so often to check up on you, and if I'm not busy, I'll come with you and watch from the grandstand. How's that?'

Sarah smiled. 'Just like the races. I hope it doesn't give this old fellow ideas!'

'Even if it does, I don't think it will worry *you*,' retorted Johnnie, grinning as he remembered Sarah's last ride on the racetrack. By this time, they'd reached the stable yard, and Sarah dismounted, handed over her horse with thanks to the groom and started walking back to the house.

Tea with Aunt Fay, she thought. *Another welcome change from the last three weeks.* When Sarah reached her room to change out of her riding clothes, she noticed that Mrs Crampton was shaking mats off the edge of the verandah, nearby.

Aunt Fay was outwardly her old cheerful self, but her life had irrevocably changed, and she had to come to terms with it. Sarah was perceptive, and she guessed a little of the conflict that raged within the older woman. But she knew that it was something that Aunt Fay must work out alone. From what she knew of her, Sarah was confident that Aunt Fay would eventually accept this new limitation to her existence and make for herself a new, satisfying life within these bounds. *And, perhaps,* she thought, *the new restricted life might grow to have greater heights and deeper meaning than the old one: Aunt Fay is a fighter!*

§

Life at Medora Downs seemed to go on as normal. In a few days the muster ended, and the men came back to their quarters. All the other mustering could be done on a daily basis, commuting from the home base. Devin seemed relieved to be home and taking some of the strain of guarding the house off Johnnie's and Reuben's shoulders. Bill Richmond often came to visit Aunt Fay, and Sarah continued to ride on the racetrack in the afternoons. She gave the children their lessons there on Saturday mornings in full view of the house and stables.

Johnnie had set up some small jumps for Sarah in an area inside the track, and she often jumped them herself and schooled the children over the smallest of them. Johnnie was as good as his word: if he wasn't busy, he sat in the grandstand, and if he was, he looked over towards the track from time to time to make sure all was well.

As the days went by, Sarah's terrifying ordeal receded to the back of her mind, only surfacing at night in the form of vivid and horrifying nightmares, from which she would awaken, shaking and sweating with the fear of the blank, terrifying figure that relentlessly stalked her. Just as he reached for her, she would try to scream. But no sound would come, and she would wake up just as those long iron-hard fingers closed around her throat. It was always the same dream, and afterwards, she found it difficult to forget her fears and go back to sleep.

Johnnie continued to sleep on the verandah—he and Devin organising themselves, with the aid of Reuben, to maintain regular patrols of the homestead and garden at intervals during the night. The two cattle dogs stayed on duty at all times and the big floodlights surrounding the house ran on a time switch from sunset to sunrise.

Sue had still not remembered anything, so the inspector thought it wiser not to bring her home until her attacker had been captured. She stayed on in Mount Isa, occasionally being moved as the police saw fit, to maintain her anonymity and thus ensure, as far as possible, her safety.

Since the attack on Sue, Sarah and the children had had to forgo their nature study walks, which both Adam and Naomi loved. Their disappointment was patently obvious, and as time went on, they began to ask Sarah to take them out again.

Sarah had explained to them that, with Sue away, she had to help Mattie do Sue's work. But now that Mrs Crampton was here, they could go, couldn't they? Sarah shook her head.

'But why, Sarah?' asked Naomi.

Sarah, having foreseen this question, had had a few minutes of productive conversation with Reuben earlier in the week. '*Because* …' she said, pausing impressively, '*we're* going to learn how to grow flowers and vegetables like Reuben does.'

'*Are* we?' asked Adam: a sparkle of interest in his big, solemn eyes. 'What can we grow?'

'What would you like to grow?' asked Sarah.

'Pretty flowers,' said Naomi, instantly.

'I'm not,' said Adam, looking disgusted. '*I'm* going to grow vegetables. Then, when I've finished, I'll give them to Mattie to cook. Then we'll eat them!'

'What a good idea!' said Sarah.

'Well,' said Naomi, frowning. 'I'm *still* going to grow flowers!'

'And that's a good idea, too,' said Sarah, heading off a squabble. 'We'll have Adam's vegetables to eat and Naomi's flowers arranged on the table to look pretty. The best of both worlds. Come on,' she added, rising to her feet. 'Let's go and see what Reuben has for us.'

Reuben had prepared a plot for them in a corner of the kitchen garden. Beside it were two piles of garden tools, each consisting of a small garden fork, spade and rake, and there was a tray containing packets of flower and vegetable seeds. Sarah divided the plot in half and showed the children how to dig and smooth the soil, forming it into a raised bed. Then, they selected their seeds from the pictures on the seed packets. Finally, they planted the tiny seeds, smoothing and patting the soil back over the furrows. Sarah twisted the nozzle of the hose to make a fine mist and Adam and Naomi took turns in doing the watering.

The children maintained an interest in their garden, anxiously waiting for seedlings to emerge, eagerly measuring and recording on a simple chart the growth and development of their plants, distracted enough to forget about the lack of nature walks. Sarah congratulated herself on such a strategy as they awaited the day of harvest with pride.

§

One evening, Devin and Aunt Fay were having their usual tea in the sitting room, idly discussing the upcoming Medora Downs Stud Brahman sale to be held next month, when Sarah came in after putting the children to bed.

'Sarah.' Devin stood up, holding out a hand. 'Come and sit

here, next to me. No, no, I'll get your tea,' he said. 'The children settle down okay?'

'Oh, yes, out like lights!' Sarah gave a little chuckle. 'I only wish I could sleep half as well.'

'Are you still having trouble sleeping, dear?' asked Aunt Fay with solicitous interest.

'Oh no, much better now, thank you,' said Sarah, accepting her tea from Devin with a grateful smile. 'You're talking about the stud sale?' Sarah already knew from Aunt Fay that it was an annual event, held in early September and that after the sale, there was a barbecue and bush dance.

'Yes, the local B & S—bachelors and spinsters—have asked Dev if they can hold their annual spring ball here in our woolshed in conjunction with our sale, and I was just telling him what a good idea I think it would be. Just think, this year we will have *two* balls to enjoy.'

'Aunty was just saying that we should let them have it the same night as our barbecue on the last day of the sale, instead of our bush dance, and those that want to can stay and party on. What do you think?'

Sarah almost choked on her tea but saved herself in time. The last ball was one that she wished to forget, and she hadn't thought about another one. 'I haven't thought,' she said, truthfully. 'I suppose it is only sensible to take advantage of the number of people here already?'

'Sarah's right. We mustn't forget that the ball is a charity affair, dears,' said Aunt Fay. 'Held to raise money for the Flying Doctor Service.'

'Well, in that case, Aunty,' said Devin, 'you've convinced me.' He smiled at Sarah. 'I know we'd both rather forget the last one. How about we start again: make this a ball we'd *like* to remember?'

Sarah's heart jumped, but before she could collect her chaotic thoughts, she heard a tiny laugh.

'Don't mind *me*,' said Aunt Fay, putting up a coy hand to hide her face.

'I don't. You're coming, too, Aunty.' Devin grinned. 'Your old boyfriend will probably take you if you don't want to come with us.'

'That's enough out of you, Devin,' retorted Aunt Fay—the corners of her mouth twitching. 'I'll see how I feel after the sale.' She turned to Sarah. 'It's very exciting, you know. All the show cattle are paraded first. And if the buyers are early, they can inspect the sale stock in their stalls and look up their breeding and so on in the catalogue.'

'That reminds me,' said Devin. 'I hope those catalogues arrive soon. The agent was on the phone today. He wants to start sending them out to prospective clients. I'll have to get onto it, tomorrow.'

'Oh dear,' sighed Aunt Fay. 'Things are so slow these days, Dev. I hope they get here in time. Now, where was I? Oh, yes, the auction! The auction, Sarah, that's the fun part,' she enthused. 'The atmosphere is just electric! And so many people come! From all over Queensland, New South Wales and over in the Territory! Medora Downs Brahmans are famous, you know!'

'Draw breath, Aunty,' recommended her nephew. 'I know you're the best advertisement the stud's got. I'll have to get you down there on the day to talk to the clients, but you're still convalescing. Isn't it past your bedtime?'

'Oh, yes, how the time flies!' She wagged a finger. 'You're as bad as Mrs Crampton, you know, wanting me to rest. We'll have to do something about dresses, Sarah,' she added, standing up with Devin's aid. 'Do you dressmake?'

Regretfully, Sarah shook her head.

'Well, I do ——'

'The jockey's silks?' exclaimed Sarah. 'You made them?'

'Yes, dear,' corroborated Aunt Fay with a smiling look at Devin. 'And I had a very late night; let me tell you! But it was worth it.' She heaved a sigh. 'Anyway, back to the dresses: it will give me something to do since I'm not allowed my usual activities. Tomorrow, we can choose our materials from some samples I've got. If I ring the order through and quote the sample number, they should be here within the week. What do you think?'

'Well … it is very kind of you, Aunt Fay,' said Sarah, hesitating. 'But will it be too much for you?'

'I don't think so. Not if you'd help with the cutting out?' Sarah nodded, and she went on, 'Sitting in front of a sewing machine doesn't take a lot of energy, and I have enough time, so I can rest if I feel tired. I'll go mad if I can't occupy myself in some way, and I'd enjoy doing it.' She suddenly seemed breathless. 'Think it over. I'm going to bed now. Goodnight.'

Devin helped her to her room and left her in the capable hands of Mrs Crampton. When he came back, he said, 'Aunty started off the night full of fun and gig, but she seems to have knocked herself up. She hasn't been overdoing things, has she?'

'Not as far as I know. Mrs Crampton doesn't let her lift anything heavier than a teacup.'

'What do you think of her?'

'Aunt Fay? About the same, I think.'

'I was talking about Mrs Crampton.'

'Oh.' Sarah hesitated a moment. 'Well, she's very efficient. It is just that she …'

'Yes? It is just that she … what?'

'Oh, nothing, really. She seems a bit of a busybody. And yet … well, it's out of character, really, I suppose. But she's always around, and … and she seems to see right through you, as if she knows what you're thinking. But … perhaps that's just fancy on my part. I mean, she is a wonderful help to Aunt Fay. But she's not an ordinary person, is she? Where did you find her?'

Devin parted his lips but said nothing for a moment. Then, 'I rang a home-help service, and they put me on to her. They said she was a marvel.'

'Well …' conceded Sarah. 'I suppose that is true, really.'

'Inspector Kingston gave me the number. He said they were good in emergencies,' he explained and changed the subject. 'Sarah, I've been looking at the calendar, and I wondered if … How does the tenth of October sound for our wedding date?'

His lips twisted as Sarah blushed in confusion, hiding her face. 'I … I hadn't thought,' she began, then raised her head. 'Yes, I suppose that will be all right.' *So soon, what will I do?*

'That's good,' he said. 'I'll be able to keep a closer eye on you, then.'

Her colour rose even more fierily. She looked down at her hands, writhing in her lap.

Devin regarded her steadily. 'Sarah,' he said softly, freeing one of her hands and holding it. 'Come here.'

Sarah looked up, and their eyes met for a long moment. His were alight with warmth—and something else that she could not define. Mesmerised, she started to rise.

A knock fell on the door, and Mrs Crampton breezed in. 'Telephone for you, Mr Mainwaring,' she said, shooting a knowing glance at Sarah before going over to pack up the tea things.

Devin's eyes darkened at the interruption. Neither he nor Sarah had heard the telephone, but he rose and went to the phone in the hall.

Sarah fled to her room, murmuring an agitated 'goodnight' as she went past him. She sat on her bed; put her hands up to her hot cheeks. What had almost happened back there? *Is he beginning to fall in love with me? Or has he decided to be satisfied with second best?* Sarah did not know if she was glad or sorry that Mrs Crampton had interrupted them. She should be glad—of course, she *should!*—but what if that time alone with Dev had clarified their relationship? Or would she just have made a fool of herself again? What if he had said that he loved her? *What, indeed!*

And she, fool that she was, had fled instead of waiting for him to return. And why? Because she knew that she couldn't bear it if he had kissed her with passion and not with love; could not bear it if he had *not* said those magical words she so longed to hear.

Then why did you say yes when you should have said no? she asked herself. Well, she had puzzled over it often, since the fateful day that changed her life. *And how will you feel about it when you're married—married!—and you find he doesn't love you, but tolerates you for the sake of the children and the convenience of a wife?*

But Sarah refused to acknowledge the validity of these intrusive, disquieting questions from her inner self and clung blindly to the hope that somehow, miraculously, before the tenth of October, Dev would discover that he loved her.

§

Sarah's heart sang as she walked down the path to the stables. It was a perfect winter afternoon in the Outback: the air clear and dry, the sun just pleasantly warm, and nothing had occurred to mar her pleasure in it. She and Aunt Fay had chosen the materials and patterns for their dresses over lunch, and when Aunt Fay phoned the order in, she would ask for samples of fabrics suitable for wedding gowns to be included.

Aunt Fay had been overjoyed when she heard that they'd set a date and insisted on making Sarah's wedding gown. 'A wedding at Medora Downs,' she burbled. 'Just what we need to cheer us up. But you must, you simply *must* let me make your gown for you, my dear.'

'Oh, no: it is too much!' protested Sarah.

Aunt Fay took her hand. 'No, my dear,' she said, her eyes misting. 'You are the daughter I never had. And it was always my wish to make my daughter's wedding gown.'

'Oh, Aunt Fay!' Sarah almost joined her in tears. As an orphan with no family, it meant a very great deal to her. 'Thank you *so much.*'

Sarah glanced at her watch. Aunt Fay was probably ringing the order through now. Even Mrs Crampton hadn't bothered Sarah this afternoon with one of her inquisitions. When she arrived at the stables, she found Persian Prince saddled and waiting for her in his stable. As usual, he whinnied when he saw her, and she gave him his tidbits of diced carrot. Sarah looked at him more closely: he wasn't wearing his usual bridle. Perhaps Johnnie had taken it for repairs? 'Johnnie? Are you there?' she called. But there was no answer. *Of course! Now I remember*, she thought. Johnnie was busy in the cattle yard, drafting out the lots for the sale, making sure that each one was correctly identified by checking brands and tattoos against the stud papers.

It was strange that he had made time to saddle Persian Prince, though. Usually, if he was busy, he left that to her. Sarah could never remember the horse waiting, saddled, without Johnnie there, too. Automatically, she tested the tightness of the girth with a finger. It was tight and did not need adjusting. Her brow wrinkled. *That's another funny thing.* When Johnnie left a horse saddled, he left the girth two or three holes loose for the horse's comfort, only tightening it just prior to mounting. Perhaps he had seen her coming, tightened the girth, then been unexpectedly called away. *That must be it*, she thought.

Sarah mounted and rode slowly down to the racetrack, cantered once around the inside of the track and then turned her horse towards the jumps. They sailed over the first one. Sarah never ceased to be exhilarated by the sensation of flying that jumping always gave her as her horse gracefully cleared each obstacle.

Steadying Persian Prince, Sarah turned to the next jump, measuring the distance. Two strides … one … She felt his muscles bunch as he gathered himself. Then, she was falling. She clutched ineffectually at his mane, and then as pain exploded inside her head, knew no more.

Persian Prince, galloping in fright as he felt Sarah fall, circled around and came slowly back towards her. He put his head down and blew gently at her face, disturbing little tendrils of hair. But Sarah, in a crumpled heap on her side, neither moved nor spoke. Worried, he snorted and stepped back a few paces, where he stood, reins trailing; his soft, brown eyes fixed on Sarah's inert form.

Alone on the verandah, Mrs Crampton watched Sarah riding across the paddock inside the racetrack through a pair of tiny field glasses. *My word, she's a nice little rider*, she thought, watching Sarah take the first jump and steady her horse for the second. Then, 'Holy Moly!' she breathed, thrust the binoculars into the voluminous pocket of her apron and ran to her room. Soon after, first aid kit in hand, Mrs Crampton jumped into Reuben's old garden truck and roared off down to the racetrack.

Chapter Twenty-two

Sarah awoke to a sharp realisation of pain, although everything else was foggy, and her head spinning. Pain was everywhere, radiating through her whole existence, pulsating in her head, her face, her arm—especially her arm—her whole body, and she felt as though she wanted to be sick. She moaned a little before her eyes focused on the face that seemed to be suspended: a nebulous, white orb in the air above her.

'Lie still, Sarah,' said Mrs Crampton in a clipped, authoritative voice—her pale, protuberant eyes fixed in a steady, impersonal regard on Sarah's face as she examined her grazed temple. 'How do you feel?' she asked.

'I ... it hurts ... everywhere,' replied Sarah. 'But there's nothing broken, I think. My arm hurts, but my head's the worst.' It swam muzzily, and the world went dark when she tried to move.

Mrs Crampton nodded briskly. 'Slight concussion, I think,

and a nasty graze on your arm, as well. However, from my examination, I think it is safe to move you.' She looked up as Johnnie came running from the cattle yard.

Breathless, he gasped, '*Sarah!* Sarah! Are you hurt?'

'A little. But I'll be all right, Johnnie.' Sarah grimaced as she tried to sit up, and her head began to pound harder than ever. 'But where's Persian Prince? Is he okay?' She winced as she turned her head to look for him.

'He's fine. He's just waiting here for you to get back on. But what's happened to the saddle?' On an exclamation, he strode quickly to where the saddle lay on the ground and bent over it. When he straightened up, there was a grim set to his mouth.

Johnnie helped Mrs Crampton put Sarah carefully into the passenger seat of the truck and watched while the woman slowly negotiated her way out of the paddock. Then, he picked up the saddle, caught Persian Prince's rein and stood for a moment, stroking his velvety nose, deep in thought. 'It's a bad business,' he said, placing the saddle on the horse and leading him back to the stable. 'A *bad* business.' He frowned. *We'll just have to keep a better eye on Sarah; that's all there is to it. The Boss must be told about this!* But he was over in number six paddock, looking for a stud bull catalogued for the sale that had escaped from the stud paddock. Johnnie sat the saddle on the workbench in the tack room and went to the radio.

Mrs Crampton, having consulted the Flying Doctor Base on the transceiver in Devin's office, took a look around, then made a quick phonecall. That done, she collected two numbered bottles from the medicine chest and went out of the room.

Sarah had soaked in a tepid bath under Mattie's supervision, following instructions from Mrs Crampton who had assumed charge of the household after Sarah's accident: issuing orders in a quiet, calm voice that were instinctively obeyed—another lightning change in character. Sarah was now propped up in bed, her grazed arm resting on a pillow.

Aunt Fay was sitting in Sarah's bedroom chair, watching over her with benign interest, when Mrs Crampton bustled in.

'Now, Sarah,' she said, holding out two tablets and a glass of water. 'Doctor says I'm to give you these every four hours, and you're to stay in bed for three or four days and not do too much for a fortnight. Or, at least, until you stop feeling sore. And if the headache continues, he'll come and take you into Mount Isa for X-rays. I'll check you a couple of times during the night, too, just to make sure you haven't suffered head injuries. But, from what I've seen, I think it is just a mild concussion.' She opened her black bag and set out some bottles, dressings and instruments on Sarah's bedside table. 'Now, if you don't mind, I'll just dress your arm, and then you can be comfortable.' She set to work as she spoke, removing tiny particles of grit that had become embedded in the flesh and swabbing the graze that extended from Sarah's elbow almost to her wrist. In a very short time, she had applied a neat dressing, packed up her things and left the room.

'How do you feel now, dear?' asked Aunt Fay, an anxious air about her. She was looking a little pale herself but had already taken one of her heart tablets at the onset of the dull, spreading pain that signified the beginning of one of her turns.

'Much better now, thanks.' Sarah managed a wan smile. 'Still plenty of aches, though. My arm feels a lot better since Mrs Crampton dressed it.'

'Isn't that woman wonderful in an emergency? We just did not know what to do when she brought you back, but she organised us all. Isn't it *lucky* that she happened to see you fall when she was sweeping the verandah?'

Sarah agreed. Perhaps, she should be grateful for Mrs Crampton's inquisitive ways, after all? Not to mention her nursing training and level-headedness.

'That reminds me: What happened to you that you came off? Did your horse fall with you over the jump?'

Sarah wrinkled her brow with the effort of concentration. 'No, I …' she said at last. 'The saddle moved! Yes, I'm sure …' She looked up, her eyes huge and dark in her white face. 'Aunt Fay, the saddle came *off!*'

Horror dawned in both their faces.

Sarah recovered first. 'Don't look like that, Aunt Fay. It could have been an accident. The girth strap might have given way or something.'

'Did you have the surcingle done up as well as the girth?'

'Yes, I checked them before I got on.'

'Then, it wasn't an accident, dear. That is what the surcingle is for: safety, in case the girth gives way.'

Sarah nodded, fear washing over her again. Was there no escape from the insidious creeping horror of the nightmare that their lives had become since the day that their unknown tormentor had so brutally announced his presence? 'I don't feel safe any more,' she whispered.

'Don't worry, my dear. We won't leave you alone. Didn't you know that either Johnnie or Dev sits guard outside your room every night?'

Sarah shook her head, wincing at the pain the movement caused. 'I knew Johnnie was sleeping on the verandah, but I didn't know Dev … I didn't know he and Dev were sitting up every night.'

'Yes,' continued Aunt Fay. 'And Reuben, being an early riser, relieves whoever it is at about three thirty or four o'clock so that they can get a few hours sleep.'

A lump came into Sarah's throat. How much they all cared for her, and she had not known. All the nights that she had lain awake—straining her ears for sounds, afraid to unlock her doors and go out on the verandah—need never have been. Someone had been there, awake, guarding her.

Sarah sighed. The fear passed. Surely, with all these people who loved her, she must be free of danger? *Love conquers all, they say. Unquestionably, it must eventually triumph over evil. Mustn't it?*

§

Devin and the groom were bent over the saddle that Johnnie had carried outside into the sunlight for better observation.

'And see here, Boss,' said Johnnie, holding up a part of the girth strap. 'All this stitching's been cut. See how the edges of the thread are sharp and clean, not frayed as they would be if they had been worn? Except for the last couple: they would have pulled out when extra strain was put on them, like, say, the jumping. And here, too, Boss. Look at this surcingle strap. Same thing, see?' Johnnie showed him where the stitching had been cut at the point where the leather joined the ring of the surcingle, leaving only the last two stitches that had pulled out when the girth had given way, placing the whole strain of the saddle on it. 'I tell you I don't like it, Boss. Sarah's lucky she wasn't killed.'

A muscle twitched in Devin's jaw, but he remained silent. At last, he spoke, and so serious was his expression that Johnnie's heart jumped. His voice was so quiet that the groom had to strain his ears to make out his words. 'I think we have to face the fact that someone *is* trying to kill her, Johnnie, and until we find him, she isn't safe. I don't know who or why. Perhaps he is a madman. Who saddled the horse for her?'

I don't know, Boss. I put him in at lunchtime for her, like I always do, and he wasn't saddled when I left to go and check the stud Brahmans in the cattle yard. Maybe she did it herself?'

'Maybe. But I think she would have noticed the cut stitching if she'd saddled him herself.'

'Yes, I think she would,' agreed Johnnie. 'She's pretty careful. Always checks her gear.'

'Who was hanging around here, this afternoon?'

'No-one, this afternoon. This morning, the two young jackaroos and Col Jones helped me draft out the sale cattle. And at lunchtime, I heard Jim tell them jackaroos to check all the south waters. I don't know where the other fellow went, but I haven't seen him around.'

Well, I think I'll have a talk to Sarah. Perhaps she saw someone hanging around. If we can find the one who saddled the horse, then I think we've got him, Johnnie.'

Johnnie nodded and locked the saddle away in a secure cupboard in case it was needed for evidence.

§

'Sarah!' Devin crossed to the bed in two large strides and took her hand in a warm, comforting clasp. 'My poor girl! How are you?'

'Much better now.' She smiled. 'The tablets Mrs Crampton gave me have helped a lot.'

'How is your head?'

'Oh, just a dull throbbing on my temple, now.'

'Let me see.' Gentle fingers lifted the silky curtain of hair to expose the large turkey's egg swelling that spread from the outer corner of her left eyebrow to the hairline at her temple. He dropped a tender kiss on her brow. 'Poor Sarah,' he murmured softly. 'In a few days, you'll feel better.' He sat in the chair vacated earlier by his aunt and took her hand again. 'I've just come from the stables. Johnnie and I have examined your saddle, and there seems to be no doubt that it has been tampered with.'

Sarah was not surprised. Hadn't she and Aunt Fay come to the same conclusion earlier in the afternoon?

'Try to think back to when you were walking down to the stables. Did you see anybody on the way?'

'No, I don't think so … No. I'm sure I didn't.'

'What about when you came into the stable block. Can you describe your movements?'

'Yes. When I went in, I called out to Johnnie, but he didn't answer. So, I went on down to Persian Prince's stall.' Her brow creased with the effort of taxing her memory. 'I remember being surprised that Persian Prince was saddled when Johnnie wasn't there. And it wasn't Persian Prince's bridle either, but it was adjusted to fit him, so I thought there may have been a reason …' Sarah touched his hand. 'Another funny thing: When I went to tighten the girth, it was already tightened, and Johnnie never leaves a horse to stand with the girth really tight—he or I do it up before I get on. But then, I remembered that he was busy today. So, I thought he may have seen me coming and tightened the girth and then been called away before I got there. I didn't give a thought to something like this.'

'And you saw no-one?'

'No-one,' she said. Tears sprang unbidden and trembled on her lashes. 'Oh, Dev. Is he going to kill me?' she whispered, raising wide, frightened eyes to his.

'We won't let him hurt you, Sarah. We're doing all we can. He won't get past Shorty and Snip, but if he does, one of us will be guarding you.'

'I know.' She tried to smile, blinking away tears. 'Aunt Fay told me. I had no idea you were all taking such care of me. But, Dev, who is he? Why is he doing this?'

'If we knew *that* …' he said. 'The answer to either of your questions would answer the other. I just don't know. That's why I asked you if you noticed anybody this afternoon. Because, the person who saddled the horse is the one who is doing this to you. And the sooner we get him, the sooner you'll be safe, and we can relax our vigil.'

'Oh, it's all so *horrible!*' she fretted as the enormity of it washed over her once more.

'Try to relax and not worry,' he said. 'Nothing can happen to you in the house. I was just talking to Mrs Crampton before I came in, and she is going to set up a stretcher in here for herself, so she can attend to you during the night, if necessary. So, if you think anyone can get past the cattle dogs, Johnnie or me, then Mrs Crampton can raise the alarm.' He rose to leave and patted her hand. 'You just concentrate on getting well. Okay?'

'Okay.' She did her best to return his smile and watched his tall figure vanish behind the doorpost into the hall. Sarah had felt safe with Devin here, but now that he was gone, all the fears and terrors of the past few weeks crowded in on her again, threatening to overwhelm her. She looked around and could not repress a shiver. Almost, she screamed. Behind every window and door there lurked a man with a blank, evil face: waiting, stalking her, a man with fingers of iron. She drew a frightened breath as a long misshapen shadow fell in the doorway and opened her mouth to scream but could make no sound.

'And how do you feel now, Sarah?' said a brisk voice. Sarah almost fainted with relief as Mrs Crampton came in carrying a stretcher, which she set down against the wall.

She peered closely at her patient. 'Hmm. You look a bit pale. I'll just take another look at you.'

After taking Sarah's pulse; blood pressure; temperature; and shining a torch first in one eye, then the other, Mrs Crampton announced her to be in good shape.

'*Are* you a nurse, Mrs Crampton?' asked Sarah, watching her. Did those pale eyes flicker for an instant?

Mrs Crampton answered readily: 'Was, Sarah. *Was*. I finished my training as a nurse. Then I joined a team of paramedics doing rescue work. And now …' She paused. 'I do this sort of work. It's interesting, and I meet new people. It's a challenge, too, finding your way around a new house.' She smiled. 'Especially one this size.'

'Mrs Crampton?' Sarah plucked at the sheet. She had a sudden urge to confide her fears to this strong, capable woman.

'Yes, what is it?'

'Oh … It's probably nothing. I feel so silly, but when I am alone, I imagine … that man … is here in the house, waiting for me.' She shivered, eyes dilating for a moment.

'That's quite natural after the trauma you've had,' Mrs Crampton assured her. 'But, tell me, what makes you so sure it is a man?'

'Well, I saw him when I … When I crashed the car. You know about that?'

Mrs Crampton nodded.

Of course, thought Sarah. *Mattie would have told her.*

'What was he like? Would you recognise him?' asked Mrs Crampton, back in her role of inquisitive busybody.

Sarah was almost sorry that she had confided in her. 'I didn't see his face, just his outline. He was tall and slim and—yes—I am almost sure it was a man.'

Mrs Crampton nodded again. The mask of inquisitiveness slipped away, replaced by brisk efficiency. 'Your dinner will be ready in a minute. And while you're having that, I will ring Dr Walthorpe and give him my report. Then I'll be back to make up my bed, and you won't have to worry about being alone.' She smiled kindly and left the room.

Shortly after, Mattie arrived with an invalid tray, which she placed on the bed over Sarah's knees. From its covered dishes arose a mouth-watering aroma that made Sarah realise that she was hungry. There was concern in Mattie's big eyes as she flicked them over her.

'Hello, Mattie.' Sarah smiled. 'This smells good.'

'Well, I'm glad to see you looking better than you did this afternoon,' said Mattie, eyeing her severely. 'There's a couple of little tigers out here, fretting over you. So, I told them if they were good and ate their dinner you *might* see them. If you feel up to it?'

'Oh, yes,' said Sarah. '*Do*, please, send them in, Mattie.'

'All right, then. I'll give you half an hour to have your dinner in peace, and I'll bring them when I come back for the tray,' she said, going out of the room.

Sarah turned to her tray and had eaten a bowl of delicious chicken soup and started on her salmon mornay when Mrs Crampton entered the room with an armful of bed linen, her night things and a book. She speedily made up the stretcher, then, moving the chair to the corner of the room nearest the verandah doors, sat unobtrusively reading.

Sarah couldn't finish the salmon mornay and was just pouring herself a cup of tea when she heard a loud whisper from just outside her door.

'Remember, Adam,' admonished Naomi, 'we've got to be quiet and not disturb Sarah. And we're not to jump on the bed because we might hurt her.'

Two anxious little faces peered cautiously around the door. Sarah smiled and held out her hand to them. Caution forgotten, they ran to her bed, almost tripping over the floor rug in their haste to reach her.

'Are you all right now, Sarah?' whispered Naomi.

'Does it hurt, Sarah?' asked Adam at the same time—his sympathetic gaze on her bandaged arm.

'Yes, I am fine now. Still a bit sore, though,' said Sarah, answering both questions. 'My arm hurts a bit and so does my head, but it's much better now.'

Naomi told Sarah all about their afternoon, and Sarah listened drowsily to her volatile conversation, answering when she was applied to. Then, she jerked awake. 'Where's Adam?' she asked, sitting up in alarm.

'I don't know,' said Naomi. 'He was here a minute ago.'

Mrs Crampton started to put down her book—her eyes on Sarah's agitated face—then resumed her reading as Adam rushed back into the room, carrying his teddy. He tucked him into bed beside Sarah.

'There!' he said. 'Sam will look after you now, Sarah. He makes you feel better when you're sick.'

Sarah was touched by his generous sacrifice, and Mrs Crampton's lips curved a little, though she didn't lift her head from the page she was reading.

'Thank you, Adam,' said Sarah, a lump rising in her throat. 'But how will you sleep without him?'

'I've grown up now,' he said, his big eyes serious. 'And I don't need him as much as you do, because I'm not sick.'

Mattie came in to take the tray. 'Come on, you two,' she said to Naomi and Adam. 'Sarah needs to go to sleep. Say goodnight to her, and then we'll go.'

'Goodnight, Sarah. Goodnight, Sam,' said Adam.

'Goodnight, Sarah. Get well soon,' said Naomi.

The children kissed Sarah's cheek and left with Mattie. They hadn't even noticed Mrs Crampton seated in the corner of the room. She came over and checked Sarah's vital signs again and seemed pleased to see that her patient had dozed off. When Devin and Aunt Fay looked in a little later, Sarah was fast asleep.

'Sleep is what she needs,' said Mrs Crampton gently but inexorably ushering them out. 'She'll be much better in the morning, apart from muscle soreness.' She then switched out the light and prepared for bed in the dim glow of the outside floodlights. The stretcher creaked, then silence reigned, broken only by soft, regular breathing.

Devin and Aunt Fay went to the sitting room. Devin stretched himself out in his favourite armchair and tapped his fingers on the arm, frowning.

Aunt Fay reached for her embroidery, settled in her usual upright chair under a lamp, but made no move to ply her needle. 'Dev?'

'Yes, Aunty?'

'Do you suppose ...' she hesitated, angling her position to better gauge his expression. 'That that *Louella* has anything to do with these attacks on Sarah?' Her fingers plucked at the edge of her embroidery. 'I feel that she *could* be capable of doing her a mischief.'

Devin did not answer her immediately. 'I don't see it, Aunty,' he said finally. 'I shouldn't think she would resort to something like this, no matter how disgruntled she may be. The methods so far have been pretty crude and violent. But anyway …' He turned his head to face his aunt, a provocative twinkle in his eye. 'Isn't *poison* supposed to be more of a woman's weapon?'

Aunt Fay's eyes narrowed as she remembered Louella's malevolence when she had told her of Devin's engagement. *Poison? I haven't thought of that.* She opened her mouth to speak but closed it again.

'I think I see your point,' continued Devin. 'You may be right about the spleen, Aunty. But Louella is away. Remember? Cruising in the Whitsundays with some of those jetsetting American friends of hers.'

'Oh, of course! Bill told me. She's due back some time this week—I think he said.'

'Is she?' said Devin with a note of indifference. 'At all events, I believe there is enough evidence to suggest that our attacker is a man. And think of poor Sue!'

'I know! Oh, you don't know how much I *deplore* what happened to Sue!'

'Take it easy, Aunty. I don't want you having another turn. Sue's going to be okay, you know. I was just making the point that only a deranged person could have done that to her. And, whatever else Louella may be, I don't think she is deranged.'

'No, dear,' said Aunt Fay, observing the justice of this. 'Louella is certainly not mad.' *Ruthless and calculating in the pursuit of the object of her desire but, certainly, not mad. Unless her obsession with Dev has become a madness? But poison?* 'Dev,' she said, resuming her needlework. 'She could have *paid* someone to do it for her. You *do* realise that?'

Mrs Crampton, in her dressing-gown, straightened up from where she had been listening at the door and sped silently down the hall: her pale, luminous eyes almost starting from their sockets.

Chapter Twenty-three

The next day, as Mrs Crampton had predicted, Sarah was stiff and sore, but her head had stopped aching, and she no longer felt muzzy and sick. Devin and the children had been to see her earlier, and Aunt Fay had come to have morning tea with her.

Reuben brought her flowers, as he did every day. 'I need to speak to you, Missy,' he said, kneading his old cloth hat between gnarled fingers after she thanked him.

'Of course, come in and sit down.' Sarah threw down the magazine she'd been leafing through out of boredom. 'I am pleased to have some company. What do you want to talk about?'

'Well …' he said, reddening, 'I got another one of them bees in me bonnet that Mattie talks about.'

Sarah chuckled. 'Have you? Is it like the last one?'

Reuben gave a reluctant grin that soon vanished. 'I'm sorry to say it's not.'

'Oh?'

'I got a feeling I've got to warn you that there is someone jealous out after you.'

'Are you saying it is a woman?' Sarah's voice rose in surprise. 'But, Reuben, I am sure it was a man.'

Reuben shrugged. 'Might be a woman, might not. I can't see that far: the bees don't tell me everything.' He stared down at his hat. 'Someone's got it in for you, and it's not, by any means, as straightforward as it seems. Because them that's wicked enough and rich enough can pay others to do their dirty work for them. Just you be careful, Missy, that's all!' he warned, raising his rheumy eyes to hers.

Nonplussed, Sarah thanked him, assuring him that she would be careful, but she could see that he was not at all satisfied with her answers as he went back to wage his eternal war with the weeds.

Over the next few days, Sarah was content to alternate between her bed and a comfortable chair in the sitting room. After the first two nights, Mrs Crampton moved into the room next door and left the connecting door ajar. In the past, it had been part of a suite of rooms—convenient for the home help—now it would be used to hear Sarah if she called.

Devin maintained a solicitous attitude towards Sarah and treated her with a gentleness that brought the ready tears to her eyes. Since her accident, she tended to weep easily and was a little embarrassed by it.

On the third day, Aunt Fay came into the sitting room with a large packet, followed by Mattie with the tea tray.

After casting an appraising eye over Sarah, Mattie said that she was looking better, admonished both of them to rest and went back to her domain.

Aunt Fay smiled at Sarah. 'I am glad it's just the two of us, this morning. Mrs Crampton and Mattie are keeping an eye on the children. I have something that I want to show you.' As she spoke, she drew a large folder out of the packet and laid it on the table. 'The samples of wedding-gown fabric and a pattern book,' she said with satisfaction. 'But we'll have our tea first.'

'Aunt Fay?' Sarah hesitated. 'It ... it doesn't seem real, somehow ... If you know what I mean?' She met the older woman's eyes and smiled tremulously.

'My dear, I know exactly what you mean!' exclaimed Aunt Fay. 'And I am sure that all brides feel the same. I know I did! And it feels even more surreal on the day.'

After morning tea, Sarah, with much helpful comment from Aunt Fay, got down to the serious business of choosing the material and a style for the wedding gown. The fabrics were gorgeous: satin, silk, taffeta, lace, tulle, organza, chiffon. It was difficult to make a choice, but eventually, Sarah decided on an exquisite ivory lace, appliquéd with satin and a matching ivory satin for the underdress.

After much agonising, Sarah chose a pattern with a sweetheart neckline; a fitted bodice with a v-waist; tiny, puffed sleeves and a wide, gathered skirt incorporating a train. Then, having decided on Adam and Naomi as her attendants, she chose a delightful pattern for Naomi, and a frilled shirt, bowtie and burgundy waistcoat and trousers for Adam.

Aunt Fay wrote down the pattern and sample numbers with evident satisfaction. 'I can see you already,' she proclaimed. 'An angel in a breathtaking gown of my creation. No-one will forget this wedding! And they won't forget your gown, either. Not if I have anything to do with it!'

§

In the afternoon, Jim brought Jacqui to visit. Jacqui looked very well and happy but had been most concerned when she heard of Sarah's riding accident and had insisted on coming to see her. 'I'm glad you weren't badly hurt,' she told Sarah. 'You could've been, you know.'

'Yes, I was lucky.'

'By the way, I believe I have to congratulate you?' said Jacqui, brightly. 'Come on, give us a squiz.'

Sarah laughed and extended her left hand to show her the ring.

'Mmm,' said Jacqui irrepressibly. 'That's gorgeous! A rose in diamonds! What it is to be marrying into money ...'

'*Jacqui!*' protested Sarah, laughing.

'Sorry, Sarah. It's that jealous streak again,' she said with a meaningful glance at Jim.

'I told her she has to wait until after the stud sale for hers,' said Jim, hiding a grin. 'Unless Dev will give me a day off before then to take her to the Isa.'

'He might,' said Sarah, holding out her hands. 'But well done, you two. I am so happy for you!'

They chatted cheerfully to Sarah for an hour or so, and she noticed how comfortable they were with each other; how much each appreciated the other's humour. Sarah thought them very well suited and was glad that Jim had realised it. She felt a little pang as she saw that they shared the kind of relationship that she, who had the outward trappings, so craved yet lacked.

After they had gone, she realised how much brighter had been the day for their sunny, uncomplicated presence.

§

In a day or two, Sarah felt quite fit, apart from a few bruises and the graze on her arm. Her head was still tender, but only if she touched it or brushed her hair too vigorously. Lessons with the children were resumed, with touching alacrity on their part, and Sarah's life began to settle down a little.

Dr Walthorpe had decreed that Sarah should not ride for two to three weeks, and Devin told her that he didn't want her to ride at all until they had caught her attacker, since she could not be kept safe from him on horseback. It would be better if she stayed indoors, whenever possible, to minimise his chances of finding her alone.

Sarah recognised the force of this argument and bowed to it without opposition. She spent her spare time helping Aunt Fay with the ball dresses and organising the details for the wedding. And soon there would be the wedding clothes to make.

Sarah thought it ironic that, in one way, time seemed to be passing painfully slowly, yet, in another, it was galloping relentlessly towards that fateful day when she would irrevocably commit herself to a tall, dark stranger and two small trusting souls.

§

Inspector Kingston sat at the desk in the office of his temporary headquarters: the overseer's cottage at Medora Downs. He was speaking on the telephone: 'Yes, I know *that!*' he said testily, listened for a minute, then, 'Yes, I know it's impossible. But that's what you're there for.' There was another pause, then he said, 'Look, I want that information by Monday, at the latest. Understand? Good. Goodbye.' He replaced the receiver with an imperative click and looked up to see Sergeant Riley hovering in the doorway, eyeing him with misgiving. He grinned apologetically. 'You have to talk to them that way or you get nothing done. Come in and sit down, Riles.'

Relieved that his superior was once more his amiable self, Sergeant Riley deposited his bulk in a chair facing the inspector and waited for him to speak.

'I had to call you back to keep an eye on things here. There's been a new development. And Briggsy is saying the matter might be more complicated than we thought.'

Sergeant Riley raised his eyes to the ceiling.

'Another attempt has been made to injure Miss Johnston. She had an accident off her horse. Some of the stitching on the saddle had been cut, and she had a fairly hard fall.'

The sergeant drew in his breath with a whistling sound.

'Yes, that's right. But fortunately, she was not badly hurt. She's in good hands, anyway.'

'Too true,' agreed Sergeant Riley.

'Tell me, Riles: you're a bit of a rider, aren't you?'

The sergeant, who had a shelf full of showjumping trophies from his teen years, grimaced. 'I used to be. I'm a bit heavy now.

Gave up riding out of kindness for the horse.'

The inspector smiled but did not comment, intent on pursuing a line of thought. 'Perhaps, just off the record, you understand, you could tell me this: Would someone who played that sort of trick mean to injure their victim? Or, could it be an attempt at murder?'

Sergeant Riley pursed his lips. 'There's been people killed when the girth has given way. That's why they have a surcingle.' He raised an enquiring eyebrow at the inspector.

The inspector nodded. 'Yes, the surcingle was tampered with, too.'

'Perhaps the perpetrator hoped for a murder that could be passed off as an accident?'

'Perhaps.' The inspector tapped his fingers on the desktop. 'You know, Riles, this is a very odd case. First, we have the brutal attack on Mrs Bryant. By the way, I'm trying to have *Mr* Bryant traced. It's a very long shot, but we've nowhere else to start. Then, we have the brakes sabotaged in Miss Johnston's Suzuki, and it looks as if it was set up for her to go back there that night. She says she thought the man she saw was searching for her to murder her. But, of course, that may or may not have been the case. If it was the same man, perhaps so. But there's no saying that it was the same man.' The inspector took a deep breath. 'The same thing with the cut stitching on the saddle: we don't know if it was the same man, or even if it *was* a man.' The inspector's fingertips were fairly beating a tattoo. 'The attack on Mrs Bryant may be entirely unconnected with the attempts to injure Miss Johnston. On the other hand, there is a possibility that, in the dark, Mrs Bryant may have been mistaken for Miss Johnston. Both of them are small, slim women. However, there seems to be no similarity between the attack on Mrs Bryant and the attempts to injure Miss Johnston that I can see.' He shook his head, baffled. 'Why don't we just go through our list of suspects again? Something may show up that we've missed.'

The sergeant rose and went out soft-footed, returning in a few minutes with a notebook and a sheaf of papers in a cardboard folder. 'There's the ex-fiancé, David Canley ...' he began.

The inspector raised a hand. 'He checked out okay if I remember rightly—was where he said he was. Said he was monstered off the place by a couple of gorillas, and he hasn't cared to come back, and that if there's anybody likely to be a murderer out here, it's the cook.'

'That'd be right, maybe, if the victims were men,' grinned the sergeant. 'But she's very friendly with Mrs Bryant, and I have it on the overseer's authority that she likes Miss Johnston and actually protected her from the ex-fiancé.'

'The overseer? What about him?' Inspector Kingston sat up for a second, then slumped again. 'But he's a solid man of medium height or less, isn't he? Our evidence points to a tall, slim man.'

'Yes,' said the sergeant. 'But I did hear that he had a bit of a crush on Miss Johnston early in the piece. It seems that he was a bit put out when she became engaged to Mr Mainwaring.'

'Hmm. You'd better give me that list and go out and find him. I'd like another chat to him. You can tell him I want his angle on some of the other contenders. No sense in making him feel hunted. He'll only clam up on us.'

'Righto, you're the boss,' said Sergeant Riley. 'Don't know how long I'll be.'

The inspector flapped a dismissive hand, already immersed in the details of his file.

A little later, Jim came in, Sergeant Riley behind him. The inspector waved him to a chair and told Sergeant Riley to go and see what else Briggsy had to say.

'Now, Sir, if you don't mind,' he said to Jim, 'I'd like to go over your statement, if I may, just to clarify one or two points, and then I want to ask you some questions about your fellow occupants of the immediate district. As you know, this is a very puzzling case. A little local knowledge may help.'

'You have my sympathy,' said Jim. 'Naturally, I will do all I can to help you.'

'Do you have any ideas yourself about who this person may be?' asked the inspector when they'd finished with the statement.

'If I did, Inspector, do you think he'd be walking around now?'

The inspector raised his brows at the ugly tone and determined set to the overseer's jaw but decided not to comment. 'Your employer, Mr Mainwaring, how do you find him?'

'He's a good boss and a good friend. If you've got ideas that way, you can forget 'em. Dev's as straight-up as they come.'

'I wasn't suggesting otherwise, Mr Barnes.' There was a moment's silence. 'I understand that you were a bit keen on Miss Johnston, yourself, at one time. That hasn't made any awkwardness between you?'

'No. Why should it?'

'That's for you to tell me, Sir.'

'Fair go, Inspector. Sarah's the kind of girl any man would be proud of, but I'm not likely to blame Dev because she prefers him to me. Where's the sense in that?'

'Quite,' murmured the inspector. 'But I daresay you'd be surprised ...'

'No, I wouldn't.' Jim grinned, his sense of humour back in place. 'There's no end to the stupidity jealousy causes in some people. I've seen a prime case recently. But not me: I've moved on. Now, can *we* move on?'

'Certainly, Sir. Miss Johnston described the man she saw as tall and slim. Do you know anyone who fits the bill?'

'Any number,' said Jim. 'It is a common trait of many people in the district, including Louella Richmond, if you're not set on a man.'

'Louella Richmond? What can you tell me about her?'

'Not to my taste, mate.' Jim shuddered. 'An elemental woman!'

'And what, Sir, do you mean by that?' asked the inspector, eyeing him with speculation. He had his own germinating ideas about the lady.

Jim told him.

The inspector sent him away more convinced than ever that the lady in question—no lady at all, in his opinion—possibly knew more than was obvious about the current situation. *But without evidence?* He shrugged, a downward turn to the corners of his mouth. *Another fruitless morning spent by the police involved in the case!*

On Monday things were no better. The inspector was on the

phone, again. '*What* happened?' He listened for a few minutes. 'All right … I know that … Yes, yes … Thank you. Goodbye.' He replaced the receiver and remarked to the empty air: 'I don't know what we pay that department for. Computers! Bah!'

'Beg pardon, Sir?' asked the sergeant, looking into the room.

'No luck, Sergeant. They traced Bryant to the Territory, where he was a ringer on one of the stations, and then to the Kimberley region of Western Australia, where he was a temporary station manager in the Fitzroy River area. From there he just seems to have disappeared: five years ago! I don't know, Riles, there's something here we've been missing. Look, send Smithy up to see Mrs Bryant again, will you? She just might have remembered something that will help us. Find out if she's got a photo of her ex-husband anywhere. And tell Briggsy to get over here.' He made a moue. 'When it's convenient, of course.' He watched Sergeant Riley gather up the papers and walk out, then sat for a long time, wrapped in thought. When he roused himself, his desk blotter was covered in sharp-pointed stars, triangles and diamonds. Straightening his back, he reached for the telephone.

§

On a far boundary of Medora Downs, a man was leaning against the door of a car, talking earnestly to its occupant. From time to time, he stood back and gesticulated, as if defending his point of view, before resuming his former position. 'How was I to know that flamin' groom was going to come and look for her before she'd been out there half an hour?' he demanded in an aggrieved tone.

The occupant of the car made an impatient movement, and

the man fell silent before a torrent of words.

'But,' he objected, 'I didn't bungle it. I was hiding in the channel, waiting for her to fall off, so I could be first on the scene and finish her off with a rock if need be. I could have said she was dead when I found her, and no-one would've known the difference. If it hadn't been for that nosy new housemaid beating me to her …'

'Well, that's your own fault, after all,' remarked the car occupant, coldly.

The man looked away and shuffled his feet.

'Now, listen carefully,' said the car occupant, sharply. 'You have one more chance.'

The man listened attentively—a grim smile playing over his vulpine features. 'Don't worry,' he said, flexing long fingers. 'There won't be no mistake, this time.'

Some measured words, spoken in a soft, biting tone, made the man flush and step back from the car. He stood, looking after it with narrowed eyes, enveloped in its dust trail as it sped away down the track. Then, muttering angrily to himself, he strode to his motorbike, kicked it into life and roared off in the opposite direction.

Chapter Twenty-four

Sarah knelt on the floor in the midst of a litter of paper patterns and materials in the sitting room, engaged in pinning pattern pieces onto a length of glorious sapphire-blue silk, under instruction from Aunt Fay seated in a comfortable armchair close by.

Aunt Fay had chosen for herself a pleated chiffon in a soft shade of lilac, but no amount of protest on Sarah's part could sway her determination to make Sarah's dress first. 'I'll make yours first,' she told Sarah with decision. 'And if time permits, I'll make mine. I have plenty of other dresses.'

'Oh no, Aunt Fay! No!'

'*Silly,*' chided the older woman in affectionate tones. 'I'll have plenty of time to make it. It's just that I'm more interested in *yours.*'

When all the pattern pieces had been arranged and pinned to Aunt Fay's satisfaction, Sarah began to gingerly cut them out.

'This is the point of no return,' said Aunt Fay, just as Sarah made the first cut. 'Once the scissors go in, it's too late if we've made a mistake arranging the pattern pieces.'

'You're making me *nervous*,' replied Sarah, grimacing.

Aunt Fay laughed. 'This looks quite good, I believe. Anyway, it would be my mistake, not yours.'

At last, all the pieces were cut out and laid in a neat pile. Sarah sat back on her heels and looked a question at her companion.

'Wonderful! I'll be able to start on the sewing after we have our tea.'

As if on cue, Mrs Crampton appeared with the tea tray and set it down on the table. 'That's pretty material,' she remarked. 'Who's it for?'

'It's for Sarah: for the spring ball.'

'Spring ball?' exclaimed Mrs Crampton, looking surprised. 'I didn't know you had one of those. When is it?'

Aunt Fay told her the story, adding, 'We're both having new gowns. What do you think?'

'Lovely,' said Mrs Crampton on her way out of the room. 'Just lovely.' But Sarah thought she had a faraway look in her eyes, as if she were thinking of something else.

There was a companionable silence while the dressmakers drank their tea. The older woman looked pensive before saying, 'I was just thinking of Sue.'

'Oh, yes? Have you heard how she is today?'

'Only indirectly. No-one is supposed to contact her or know her whereabouts. She is quite well now, I believe.'

'That is good to hear. Poor Sue ...'

'Sarah, do you remember ...?'

'Yes, Aunt Fay? Remember what?'

'The last few days before Sue was attacked. Do you remember how she looked?'

'Yes, I do. She looked pale and ill.'

'And she was short with anyone who asked whether something was the matter,' recalled Aunt Fay.

'Mattie said she was frightened,' said Sarah, slowly. 'But, at the time, we didn't think that there was anything to be afraid of.'

'Sarah, do you suppose she could have known the person who attacked her and seen him earlier? Perhaps, *even* knew he was going to attack her?'

'I don't know. I suppose she could have. But she didn't go out of the house, did she? Who could she have seen?'

'It is a mystery, dear.' Aunt Fay shook her head and was silent a moment, her eyes on her teacup. 'I wonder if she's remembered anything, yet?'

§

Things were becoming hectic as the day of the stud sale drew closer. Johnnie roped in the jackaroos to help him clean stalls and spread sweet-smelling wood shavings, teach cattle to lead and generally clean up the sale area and make it worthy of its bovine aristocracy.

The catalogues eventually arrived and were despatched to potential buyers in the very nick of time to avert disaster. The

CWA agreed to serve meals and drinks from a kiosk, and a bar was organised to be set up nearby.

Finally, all was in readiness, and there only remained the last-minute things, such as washing and grooming the cattle and setting up the barbecue: all to be done on the morning of the sale the following Friday.

It was Wednesday and the family and Sarah were at breakfast.

'I don't know about anyone else,' said Devin, looking around the table. 'But I'm taking the day off.'

'Oh?' said Aunt Fay, giving him an arch look. 'You won't know what to do with yourself!'

'Yes, I do,' he said, smiling across the table at his fiancée. 'Sarah and I are going fishing.'

Sarah returned his glance. 'This is very sudden, Dev.'

'Will you come?'

'Oh, can we come, too?' begged Naomi, pre-empting Sarah's acceptance.

'Yes, can we?' chimed in Adam.

'Not this time,' said their uncle. 'Aunty needs your help.'

'Do I? Oh yes! I have a secret I want you to help me with. We'll go fishing another time. You go and wait for me in the rumpus room. I'll be along in a minute.' She watched them run out of the room, then turned to her nephew with an anxious look. 'But, Dev, are you sure this is wise? I mean, aren't you worried about …'

'About?'

'About … Well, about the attacker.'

'No. Sarah has me to look after her.'

'Oh, but what if …?'

'Men who attack women are cowards, Aunty. Didn't you know?'

'But if he sneaks up on you?'

'I'm not worried about that.' He gave her a crooked smile. 'Let me put it this way, Aunty, we're not the only ones going fishing.'

'Oh, I see …' Her brow wrinkled for a moment, then cleared. 'Well, there's nothing to worry about, then, is there?'

'Of course not. You know me.'

'Yes.' Her eyes softened. 'I do.'

'What about you, Sarah? Do you trust me to look after you?'

'Yes,' said Sarah, going pink. 'When do you want to go?'

'Now, if you're ready?'

'Do I have time to change into my jeans?'

'Of course. Take all the time you want. I'll just collect our lunch from Mattie and meet you on the front steps when you're ready.'

Sarah hurried to her room—a curious fluttering in her chest at the thought of spending the day alone with Dev. She slipped into shirt and jeans, swept the brush through her shining fall of hair, gathered up a cotton sweater and a shady hat, let herself out through the verandah doors and went to the front steps where Devin was waiting for her.

Mrs Crampton tut-tutted and relocked the doors that Sarah had forgotten in her haste. Then, picking up her book, she sat on the verandah and began to read. Neither Sarah nor Devin noticed her there as he handed Sarah into the passenger seat of the Range Rover and closed the door. Mrs Crampton watched them drive away and went back to her book. In a little while, she put it in her pocket, stepped off the verandah and strolled along the path. Soon, she vanished among the trees beyond the house.

Aunt Fay also watched them drive off—an enigmatic expression in her eyes. A small hand tugged at hers, and she looked down at Naomi who was eyeing her expectantly.

'Aunty?'

'Can we do it now? They've gone,' said Adam.

'Oh, yes. Come into my sewing room.'

Aunt Fay showed them the material samples and patterns and explained their roles at the wedding. Then, she carefully took each child's measurements. The children were so excited that they found great difficulty in standing still, but at last, all the measurements were taken and written down in Aunt Fay's notebook. Then, they went off gleefully to the rumpus room where Mattie later found them—when she went to call them for lunch—solemnly marching up and down the centre of the room; Naomi delicately holding an imaginary train, and Adam reverently carrying one of the sofa cushions in a way that reminded her of a novice waiter carrying a tray of drinks that he was afraid he might spill.

'We're going to be the bride's 'ttendants!' shouted Adam as soon as he saw Mattie. 'I'm going to be the pageboy, and Naomi's the bridesmaid!'

'Well, you'd better come and have your lunch before you wear a hole in that floor,' she recommended. But she smiled as she followed them to the dining room.

§

There was a crackle on the radio: 'Bait's in place.'

'*Smithy!*' was the admonitory response.

There was the hint of a chuckle before a very correct voice stated, 'They're here, as arranged. Mobile One in position, Sir.' Constable Smith settled into his hiding place among some bushes.

'Where are you, Riles?'

'Watching the line, Sir,' said Sergeant Riley from behind a pile of rocks slightly upriver. 'No sign of any fish rising, yet.'

'Okay. Keep me posted. Out.'

§

Sarah and Devin spent the morning setting handlines along one of the huge waterholes in the Diamantina. Remembering the dry channels at Adeline Crossing, Sarah marvelled at the size of the waterholes here. Devin told her that some of them were reckoned to be as much as eighty feet deep, and they abounded with such delicacies as yellow belly, cod and freshwater crayfish.

Devin seemed happy, relaxed and friendly; eager to introduce her to the art of fishing; patiently untangling her lines from her first inept attempts to cast them into the still brown water. Sarah was secretly amazed at the change in him: 'Dev the relaxed fisherman' was a very different person from 'Dev the workaholic boss'.

They chatted quietly in the bright golden sunlight, dappled with the shadows of the coolibah leaves, and Sarah was conscious of a feeling of companionship that was balm to her heart. She watched his long, tanned fingers deftly thread the worm onto the hook and shuddered, knowing it was something that she could not bear to do herself.

Devin smiled indulgently and baited her hooks as well as his own, telling her that she'd never make a fisherman if she couldn't bring herself to kill a worm.

'It's not that. It's just that they keep wriggling!' she shuddered again.

He laughed. 'Well, how else are they going to attract a fish?'

When the lines were set to his satisfaction, Devin tied them to stakes pushed into the edge of the bank. Then, he sat down and pulled Sarah down beside him. 'Now we wait,' he said, leaning back against a tree trunk and tipping his hat over his eyes.

Sarah looked about her. The land had a timeless quality—still, waiting—a land that tolerated humans much of the time but would always be the master. Out on the horizon, she saw the rough, rocky-topped hills that were thickly populated with mulga scrub at their bases and sides: the raw, red edges rising out of them, sparsely covered by coarse brown spinifex. Cattle disappeared into this country, Johnnie had told her, living off the mulga, drinking from the occasional salt-encrusted mineral spring and, only with difficulty, were brought out. *It's a hard land*, she thought. *Yet utterly fascinating.*

Between the hills and the river channels, the tops of the ironstone ridges glittered brassily in the bright sunshine. Occasionally, dome-shaped or jagged rocks reared their heads above the undulating plain—like icebergs, most of their bulk was below the surface. In places were masses of perfectly shaped spherical and oval rocks, reminiscent of fossilised eggs of some long-extinct bird or reptile. Other flatter rocks were ripple marked, and some even had sandworm trails, such as were found on beaches when the tide was going out. Sarah drew in a rapt breath. What stories these ancient monuments could tell to those who understood the hieroglyphs of nature.

Immediately before her ran the channels of the Diamantina. Here, there was one main, deep channel, flanked by several interweaving smaller ones. Farther down, the river spread out into many smaller channels: a gigantic natural irrigation system that watered a vast expanse of south-west Queensland.

Around her the rivergums and coolibahs thrust their massive, tortured limbs skyward, as if in defiance of the elements, with smaller trees and shrubs clustered humbly at their feet, here and there.

Settling down to drowse in the shade, Sarah heard in her imagination the happy laughter of children as they played and splashed in the cool, brown water while their mothers pounded grass seeds on the bank—keeping a fond eye on their offspring—watching an older boy dive gracefully into the river with hardly a ripple, proudly holding aloft a gleaming, struggling fish on the end of his spear, inspiring a chorus of admiration from the mothers.

Sarah made a small sound as the vision faded, and she was swept by a feeling of profound sadness at the thought of the passing of the proud race that was tied to the Earth Mother by spirit and soul, as well as body.

'What's up?' said Devin, pushing back his hat to look into her face.

'Oh, um … nothing.'

'Divining the spirits of the original inhabitants, were you?'

'Something like that …' She turned to look at him. '*How* did you know?'

'It happens to everyone who comes here and sits awhile: at least, everyone with a bit of sensitivity. As you can see, this would have been a favoured place, just like it is for us. You know what was done to them, don't you?'

'Yes,' said Sarah, and in her fancy, she thought that the spirits of those who had lived here cried out in agony from the rocks and trees at the horror that had been perpetrated on their race.

'They were still here until not so long ago. I can remember them on the riverbank, living in their wurlies: their bark shelters. They lived amicably with the station owners; we gave them food and clothing and general healthcare in return for occasional work; still living on the riverbank as had their ancestors; still free to roam the land as they wished.' Devin's voice became bitter. 'Then some do-gooders came down here from the city. They were horrified at what, to their narrow minds, was the appalling squalor of the primitive living conditions these people had embraced for thousands of years.

'They shouted, "Exploitation!" at the small wage we paid them for their work. I know they meant well, but they didn't understand these people. It didn't matter what we said or how we phrased it, there were two things we couldn't seem to get through to them: the first, that though one man worked, the station might feed and clothe at least fifty of his relatives; and the second, that these people were not materialistic, did not value possessions in the same way as the white man. What would they want with a little suburban house when the whole earth and sky were theirs?' Devin sighed. 'It was very bad, actually. I still seethe when I think of it: herded into trucks like animals, dragged away against their will, crying to be allowed to stay. It was all I could do to stand and watch, but I wasn't much more than a kid ...' He took a deep breath. 'Poor things. Many couldn't adjust to the reserves, fretting and dying in an alcoholic haze because, quite simply, their hearts had been broken.'

'And they still don't realise what they did to them,' said Sarah, honoured that Devin felt he could share with her such a painful memory, yet sighing for those poor, sad people who would never again laugh and play here on the riverbank; for wrongs that could never be put right; for spirits imprisoned by the bars of civilisation; oppressed and yearning for homes they would know no more.

Sarah stirred and changed her position a little, forcing her mind back to the present and the peace of the river. Into the heavy stillness of the day, soft sounds echoed loudly. The water rippled and plopped as a small aquatic animal broke the surface: frogs croaked occasionally, a stick snapped somewhere in the bushes, leaves rustled in a little zephyr that sprang up and then died.

How loud is the silence, thought Sarah, knowing that Devin had been at least as saddened as she was by his recollection.

When next he spoke, the words, though softly uttered, made her jump. 'Grab your line,' he said. 'You've caught a fish!'

Sarah leapt up and ran to her line, which was indeed behaving rather oddly, darting this way and that and jerking madly. Quickly, she began to pull it in, forgetting everything in her eagerness to see what she had caught.

'Careful! Not too fast. You'll lose him!' warned Devin, watching with interest. In his hand he held a large net.

When Sarah, at last, saw the fish, she almost dropped her line in excitement, but Devin's voice brought her to her senses.

'Just hold him there while I get the net under him,' he said, and in one swift movement, scooped a gleaming, silvery fish out of the water. It flipped and panted helplessly in the net, twisting its shining body and flicking its fins. 'A yellow belly. And a good one, too. Well done. If you can get three more like that, we'll have enough for dinner.' Deftly, he killed the fish, cleaned it and placed it in the esky packed with ice. Then he re-baited the hook and threw it far out into the water.

But there would be no more sitting down. Two of the lines were jerking now, and they each ran to one and began to reel it in. Soon, they had six beautiful fish.

'That will do us, now,' said Devin, smiling at Sarah. 'We'll leave some for next time.' As he spoke, he began to pack away the fishing gear.

Sarah smiled back. She felt warm and tingly as she helped him tidy up.

'Feel like some lunch?' he asked, going to the vehicle and taking out a rug, cushions, an esky and a cane basket with a vacuum flask in one of its partitions.

Sarah took the rug and spread it under a shady coolibah. Then, opening the esky and the basket, they set out fresh bread rolls, cold roast chicken, salad and fruit.

'What a feast!' laughed Sarah, settling herself on the rug.

'Mattie must have thought there were a dozen of us.'

Devin's lip quirked in reply as he poured tea from the flask into two large mugs. 'We should have boiled the billy,' he remarked. 'It's much nicer than this.'

Sarah agreed. 'I wonder why it tastes so good? Out of a billy, I mean—when it is so black and strong? Normally I hate strong tea. And I never drink it black or with sugar.'

'I don't know. Maybe it is the smoke from the gum leaves. Something gives it that extra flavour,' he answered, reaching for a roll and a piece of chicken. There was a warm, companionable silence for a little while as they enjoyed Mattie's sumptuous picnic lunch.

Then Devin tucked a couple of cushions behind him and lay back. 'Tell me about yourself, Sarah.'

She was a little taken aback at his command. Never before, not when David came, not even when he had asked—no, *told*—her to marry him, had he questioned her on her past life.

'What do you want to know?' Her clear gaze met his with a hint of laughter. 'You know that I am—*was*—a teacher. You know that, like you, I am an orphan. You even know my awful secret that made me run away to the Outback.'

'A good thing, too. We got rid of him for you.'

'Yes, and I am *so* thankful.'

'Don't mention it. No, I was wondering whether you have any other family: cousins or aunts or uncles?'

'No, I was an only child, and I think my parents must have been, too. They were older than most when I was born. My mother was in her forties and ill. I was what is called a "change-of-life baby". And my father was in his sixties. When my mother died, he died soon after. I was left in the care of his solicitor friend, but he and his wife were elderly, so as soon as I was old enough—six—they sent me to live at boarding school. They're dead now, too. I wish I could remember my parents, but I was just too young. But even though I don't remember them, I still miss them. Which probably doesn't make sense.'

'It does to me,' he said softly. 'You never stop missing them. Time makes you accustomed to the hurt but never entirely allows you to get over it.'

And the comforting thing, thought Sarah, *is that Dev does understand.* He understood exactly how she felt because he had suffered the same loss at an older age than her, although he'd had dear, kind Aunt Fay to help. And she? She'd had her friends Wendy and Jo who had been so wonderful to her.

Uncannily, as if he read her thoughts, he asked, 'What about friends? Do you have some special friends?'

'Yes, I do.' Sarah told him of Jo and Wendy, of how they'd been friends for so long, taking her home in the holidays so that she didn't have to spend them at boarding school, how loyal and dear they were to her.

'Then, they must come to our wedding,' he said. 'Would you like that?'

'I would *love* it!' she exclaimed, her eyes shining. Then her face changed as doubts crept in. 'But it's such a long way. I don't know if they will be able to come.'

'Write and ask them. If they can, I will charter a light aircraft for them.'

'Oh, Dev, no! It will be so expensive!'

He sat up to reach for her hand and held it briefly. 'You must have some of your own people at your wedding, Sarah. It will be a wedding present from me to you. One of them,' he added.

'Oh, *Dev*. That is so kind of you.' Her eyes, luminous with unshed tears, met his.

Devin made a little inarticulate sound and brushed his fingers across her cheek. Sarah drew a sharp breath. Then, trying to control her emotions and her wildly beating heart, she looked away and began to pack up the remains of the picnic with trembling hands.

Silently, Devin helped her. Then putting the esky and basket to one side, he arranged two of the cushions behind her and pushed her back against them. He took the other two cushions and stretched out beside her, taking her hand. 'I'd like you to tell me one more thing if you don't mind: what did your ex-fiancé do to make you run away to the Outback?'

What can I say? she wondered. *He made a fool of me—a mockery of my love—and then offered violence when I took the only action open to me?* 'Dev … It is such a sordid story. I haven't been able to think about it, let alone talk about it.'

'I understand. Tell me if you can. If not, it doesn't matter.'

Paradoxically, with that assurance, she found it easy to tell him the whole humiliating story.

He was silent awhile, studying her face with searching grey eyes. Sarah could not meet his look and lowered her eyelids, her long lashes fanning her cheeks.

'Poor Sarah,' he said. 'What an ordeal for you.' He played with her fingers and cleared his throat. 'Sometimes, even though we know that the person is not worthy of our love, we can't just switch it off like a tap. Do you still love him?'

Her eyes flew open. 'No. You see, the person I thought I loved does not exist. It took that evening here in the kitchen to show me what he was *really* like. And that cowardly, disgusting person—I could *never* love. I realised that I was in love with a dream. *That* took some getting over. And it was a bit of a shock, actually.'

'Yes, I can see that it might be … Well, I *did* see it.'

Then it sank in to Sarah just what he had been saying: that even though someone was not who you thought, you could still be in love with them. She gasped as a sudden pain knifed through her heart and moistened lips gone suddenly dry at the thought of the question she must ask: The question that had subconsciously haunted her since the day Louella had first come to the house. The question she could ask because he had asked her first. Her heart resumed its wild thudding as she began, 'Does that mean that you …?'

'Still love Louella, you mean?' He shook his head, his expression changing from tender sympathy to brooding pain. 'It was different for me than it was for you. You see, I knew exactly what she was under that magnificent exterior: a spoilt brat with the devil's own temper; wilful, intemperate, overbearing. And yet, under all that, she had a conscience and courage of a sort. Or so I believed. And whatever she was, I loved her.' He was silent a minute, reliving his grief. 'Like you, I've never been able to talk about it.' He smiled bitterly, and Sarah saw that his eyes were hard and bright. 'But, unlike you, I haven't been able to come to terms with it or find the answers.'

Sarah looked up at him, and he saw deep into her soul; the hurt and anxiety mirrored in her eyes—and more—her love for him, plainly written in those great, translucent orbs. It was his turn to gasp at a shaft of pain that pierced him, almost, to that frozen thing he called his heart. The hardness in his eyes melted in the warmth of her anxious, loving gaze, replaced by an expression compounded of tenderness and sorrow as he looked down at her. Somehow, she made him feel like that. He found it difficult to drag his thoughts from her and answer her unfinished question. 'No ... I don't love her,' he said and knew, at last, that he spoke the truth.

Sarah heard his voice as if from a very great distance, and the relief was so intense it was almost an agony. His next words ensured her relief was short-lived, but it was only later, when she was alone, that she realised their full import.

'Sarah,' he breathed, his voice vibrating with emotion. 'I wish that I could love you the way that you deserve to be loved ... But I can't.' He could not explain his numbness—his tone reflecting the agony of his soul. So great was his remembered pain from an old scar that he did not even know himself that he was afraid to love again—that the shell of bitterness that had grown around his heart no longer protected him—but crippled his emotions, threatening to ruin his life and that of the girl who loved him.

'Sarah,' he said again, reaching out to her. For a moment, she thought he was going to take her in his arms and kiss her, then: 'Oh God!' he said, rolled away and sat up. 'We can't go into this now.'

Why not? she thought. *If he wants to kiss me, I don't care if the whole world is watching, as long as it means that he loves me.*

A rueful smile just touched his lips. 'I suppose you know that we're under surveillance by the police?'

'I gathered that from what you said to Aunt Fay this morning. And then when nobody else turned up ...'

'It was a plan,' he acknowledged. 'But I refused to ask you to come down here alone.'

'So, I'm the bait?' she said, unconsciously echoing Constable Smith.

'Do you mind?'

'No, not with you here. I don't think I could have stood to come down here alone, and I'm very grateful that you didn't ask me.' Sarah shuddered. 'But he won't come.' She was certain of it. 'For the same reason.'

'We were hoping to lure him out to follow you on the off-chance he might find you alone or far enough away from me to try something. Just to find him anywhere out on the track, even, would be enough to lay him by the heels and ask a lot of awkward questions.' He sprang lightly to his feet and held out a hand. 'Come on. We'd better go.'

Sarah shivered in the chilly breeze that seemed to have leapt up from nowhere. It was as if the shadow of her faceless attacker loomed over her, dimming the golden sunshine—like the hovering wings of some great, menacing bird of prey.

Chapter Twenty-five

Sarah awoke on the day of the stud sale to the sound of the wind howling around the eaves of the house and rushing through the treetops. The sound reminded her of the restless soughing of the sea, and for a moment, she thought that it was raining. But one look out the window showed a pale, brassy sky with not a cloud in sight.

Throwing on her dressing-gown, Sarah went out onto the verandah and stood, looking down towards the stables and beyond to the river channels. The trees tossed their branches backwards and forwards in agony, battered by the strong, gusting wind. Even the plants in the relatively sheltered garden bowed their heads before it. The hanging basket plants on the verandah fluttered and twisted their leaves in such frenzy that she thought they must surely break from their stems.

In dismay Sarah watched eddying swirls of brown dust whip along the road, and on the horizon, it hung in the air, casting a surreal reddish-brown light over the landscape. She shivered in the sudden chill that seemed to be coming straight from the Antarctic and went back into her room with a fine powder on her face and grit between her teeth.

The August winds had arrived late and with a vengeance, and Sarah could only marvel at the strength and persistence of them. Whipping over the dusty plain with neither tree nor mountain to break their velocity, they hurled their massive weight of moving air at whatever stood in their path. The trees; the tall, waving grasses all bowed before their vast power and majesty. Invincible, endless, they filled the house and every available space with soft, choking particles, until all that existed was the wind and the insidious, all-pervading dust.

Reuben trotted around his garden, cursing under his breath and erecting temporary shelters of shadecloth for some of his more delicate plants. Then, with a wheelbarrow, he collected the pot plants from the verandah and put them into the shelter of the shadehouse.

At breakfast, Devin shrugged in answer to an agonised comment from his aunt. 'Not much we can do about it, Aunty,' he told her. 'We should be sheltered from the worst of it in the sale ring, though. You can't control a late season. At least it's still dry. We've got shearing coming up, so let's hope the September storms are late, too.'

'I know, Dev. But the kiosk and the barbecue ...'

'We'll put the kiosk around the back of the stables, sheltered from the wind. By evening, it usually drops. But if it doesn't, we'll have the barbecue in one of the larger sheds.'

Aunt Fay's worried expression lightened a little. 'Yes, that will help a bit. I suppose we should be used to wind, out here. Oh, well … I hope it drops this afternoon. But it *is* going to spoil our day.'

'Only if you let it.'

'What about the children, Dev?' put in Sarah. 'They've been asking if they can go.'

'It starts at two o'clock, so you can take them down for an hour or so then, if you like,' he said. 'As long as they work hard this morning and earn it. Did you hear that, you two?'

'Yes, Uncle Dev.' The children knew better than to make too much noise at the breakfast table and contented themselves with a shared sidelong look brimful of excitement.

Sarah and the children spent the morning in the schoolroom and were busy practising their writing when Mrs Crampton came in with their morning tea. 'Oh, Sarah,' she fluttered—her manner in distinct contrast to her usual brisk self. 'I wonder if you would do me a favour?'

'Certainly, Mrs Crampton,' said Sarah with a smile. 'What is it?'

'I'd like to come with you when you take the children down to the sale.' She rushed on, 'I know it's silly, but I've never been to a stud sale before, and I've asked Mr Mainwaring if I can just take a teeny peek. I'll help with the children if you like and come back when you do. Will that be all right?' Mrs Crampton's strange eyes were alight with some kind of inner glow, and Sarah smiled again.

'Of course, Mrs Crampton. We'll take the children down together after lunch, stay about an hour and then come home. I will be glad of your help.'

'Good,' said Mrs Crampton, resuming her brisk manner. The light went out of her eyes so suddenly that Sarah wondered if she had imagined it. All she could see in them now was the normal satisfaction of an agreement reached mutually.

When morning tea was over, Mrs Crampton went out quietly with the tray, and busy concentration once more reigned in the schoolroom—aided, no doubt, by the warning that if they did not work well, there would be no visit to the sale.

Down in the stables and cattle pens, there had been a frenzy of activity since early morning. Johnnie had woken before dawn, cursed the howling wind and gone out to feed the cattle and horses. After breakfast, he and the men went to wash and brush the cattle and number them according to the catalogue.

'I dunno what's the point of all this,' grumbled Alex as he hosed down one of the bulls. 'Just turns the dust into mud.'

'You just get on with your job,' growled Johnnie, walking past with a huge bull. 'That's all you've got to do.'

The jackaroo grimaced after him. So, the weather was getting to poor old Johnnie, too. His resentment vanished as he thought of the effort the groom had put into this day: the culmination of a year's work and twelve years of selecting bloodlines, and it had to be the filthiest, coldest, windiest September day that Alex could remember in his nineteen years of living in the Outback. He shrugged and began to strip the water from the bull's gleaming hide in long, swift strokes. *Ah, well, them's the breaks*, he thought. *This country doesn't give much quarter, that's for sure.*

The bull—a docile, amiable creature—stood chewing his cud and occasionally flapping his ears throughout Alex's ministrations, and he made no protest now at being led back to his stall and having his tail combed out.

'You'll do, mate,' said Alex cheerfully, giving the bull a friendly slap on the rump before entering the next stall. *Funny, he thought, to go to all this trouble preparing cattle for the sale, when those big shots that buy them—paying pretty long prices for them too, just quietly—turn them out into a paddock and hardly look at them again. If I paid the money they do, I reckon I'd look after them a bit, not just forget about them and hope they turned up in the muster in twelve months' time. And if they don't, what the heck, they'll just come to the next sale and buy another swag of them. Especially those big places over in the Territory.*

But Alex kept his thoughts to himself. He knew better than to say anything out of place to the groom, today. Once the sale was over, he'd be his usual cheerful self. But until then, it paid to watch your step—and your tongue.

§

Lunch was served at twelve o'clock, by which time, thankfully, the wind had eased enough to allow light aircraft to land, and several guests sat down at the big mahogany table in the dining room. Traditionally, the neighbours and several longstanding clients of the stud lunched at the homestead before going down to the sale ring.

Sarah was a little taken aback to find that Louella was one of the guests but felt relieved when the other girl greeted her with civility and every sign that she had forgotten whatever enmity there had been between them. Sarah accepted the proffered olive branch but was secretly dismayed when she discovered that it had been an ongoing agreement that the Richmond family stayed the night of the sale at the Medora Downs homestead. Mrs Crampton had already prepared their rooms for them at the end of the wing opposite to the one where Sarah slept.

Any of the luncheon guests that had not seen Devin and Sarah since their engagement congratulated them warmly as they arrived, several bringing gifts and cards. Towards the end of lunch, Bill Richmond proposed a toast to their future happiness, which was thoroughly endorsed by the other guests. Sarah glanced involuntarily at Louella, who produced a glittering smile as she raised her glass; and if her knuckles momentarily whitened, nobody noticed it.

All through lunch, the roar of light aeroplanes could be heard at short intervals. Upon arrival the occupants made their way down to join the car travellers and obtain lunch from the kiosk and liquid refreshment from the bar. Both of these were set up during the morning; the CWA ladies having arrived with huge baskets of sandwiches, quiches, and delicious cakes and slices.

When Sarah and Mrs Crampton left the house with Naomi and Adam, the wind, though somewhat abated, was still unpleasantly chilly, whipping dust and grit into their faces so that they had to keep them turned away from it. Sarah, trying to hold onto a jaunty red beret and keep her hair under control, began to wish that they had driven the few hundred yards to the stable complex and sale ring. The children, dressed in corduroy trousers and parkas with the hoods covering their hair, were snug and protected against the wind. But Sarah, wearing a grey wool suit with red accessories, and Mrs Crampton in a serviceable navy skirt and blazer, felt the sting of sand particles hurled against their thinly clad legs and the chill of the winds whipping around them. It was hard to talk, too, shouting ineffectually against the wind.

The airstrip enclosure was littered with small aeroplanes: a source of great interest to Adam and ineffable boredom to Naomi, neither having been told the exact manner of their parents' deaths for fear that it would make them unnecessarily afraid of air travel. Adam and Naomi were in high spirits and alternated between running on ahead and having to be called back, explaining in excited voices to Sarah and Mrs Crampton just how a stock auction was conducted, which, in view of the wind, was not very intelligible. Although Adam's phrases, when she could hear them, were such an echo of Devin's that Sarah had to bite back a smile.

Mrs Crampton listened in silence, her gaze fixed on whoever was speaking, but Sarah had the feeling that those protuberant eyes saw much more than anyone guessed. Mrs Crampton seemed to have a trick of seeing things without actually looking at them.

Perhaps it is those bulbous eyes, thought Sarah, immediately contrite at her unkind assessment. Mrs Crampton might be a stickybeak, but she always seemed to be there when she was needed. *And that's what counts. Perhaps her nosiness is just concern for others?* Sarah had not seen it that way before, nor did she know that it was thanks to Mrs Crampton's curiosity that she had not died when she fell from her horse.

When they entered the crowded sale ring, the air was crackling with excitement. Sarah looked upwards around the tiers of seats and caught an impression of a sea of faces and hundreds of fluttering catalogues. Where would they sit? The place was crammed with men in tweedy coats and moleskins and women in expensive winter suits.

In here, at least, the effects of the elements were reduced to an eddy of dust and the chilly bite of the wind each time the outer door opened, but there was a nasty little chill swirling around their feet that stopped it being too pleasant.

A frenziedly waving catalogue caught Sarah's eye, and she looked up to see Jacqui smiling and beckoning from high up in the back row where there was a broad vacant space awaiting them. Naomi and Adam clambered up the steps and sat down beside the children from Ilona Downs, exchanging greetings in loud whispers. Jacqui smiled at Mrs Crampton and Sarah as they seated themselves beside the children.

The buzz of conversation died suddenly as the auctioneer went to his stand. 'Ladies and Gentlemen,' he said, 'we will begin the auction of these fine Brahman stud cattle in a short time. But first, we will parade the magnificent Medora Downs show team, so that you can see what exceptionally fine breeding has gone into the superior cattle for sale here, today.'

A murmur rippled through the assembled company as Johnnie, looking very professional in a dustcoat, shirt, tie and moleskins, stepped into the sale ring beside a huge silver Brahman bull. The bull lumbered majestically around the ring, muscles rippling beneath the gleaming silver-grey hide. Sarah marvelled at the proportions of the gigantic beast. Johnnie was completely hidden behind the massive shoulder as he led him around the ring and out the gate followed by the dustcoated jackaroos, Jim and Col, each leading a shining, healthy bovine aristocrat.

There was a short delay, then Johnnie reappeared with Lot 1:

a young bull of illustrious parentage, causing a flurry of interest. There was some energetic bidding, and Sarah watched in astonishment as it quickly went into four figures. Finally, the bull was knocked down to a large pastoral concern in the Northern Territory for more than thirty thousand dollars.

Aunt Fay had been right about the atmosphere. There she was, a few rows down, seated beside Bill Richmond in pink-cheeked excitement, her knuckles white as she gripped her catalogue. Louella was there, too, in a beautifully tailored tweed suit and a smart hat. There seemed to be no sign of Devin, but Sarah supposed he was busy in the sale office with paperwork relating to the stud stock.

Sarah could hardly bear the suspense as the prices climbed higher and higher, waiting with bated breath while the auctioneer exhorted his clients to make just one more bid. Many times, he raised his gavel to knock down a lot for the third time when a spate of renewed and frenzied bidding interrupted him.

After about three-quarters of an hour, the children showed signs of restlessness, so Sarah, in a whisper, suggested to Jacqui that they take them to the kiosk. Jacqui nodded, gave hushed directions to the children, and led by Mrs Crampton, they filed down the steps and outside. They stood for a moment, blinking at the brightness of the day and shivering in the sudden chill of the wind, before going around the back of the stables to the kiosk.

'This is better,' said Jacqui with her irrepressible humour. 'I thought we were going to get blown away. Come to think of it, if I had an umbrella, now would be the time to do a Mary Poppins.'

Sarah laughed and shook her head at her. 'I don't know where you'd end up.'

'There's that, I suppose,' said Jacqui.

'I've never worked out why her umbrella didn't turn inside out,' said Mrs Crampton—a thoughtful light in her eyes. 'But, my word, it would in this wind! Tea or coffee, ladies?'

They opted for coffee, enjoying the hot liquid while the children had cake and lemonade.

Mrs Crampton was watching the children play a noisy game of tag. 'Kids!' she remarked. 'They never seem to feel the cold.'

'No,' said Jacqui. 'They don't stand still long enough for the wind to catch up with them. At least my three don't.'

'Mine are the same,' laughed Sarah. 'But they'd better go home now for their afternoon nap.'

'Do they really sleep in the day?' asked Jacqui. '*Really?* Half your luck!'

'According to Mattie, it's a custom dating from their babyhood to give their far-sighted mother a little time to herself during the day. And I'm not likely to try and change it.'

'No, indeed!' agreed Jacqui, shooting her an envious glance. 'Why would you?'

The children parted unwillingly, but Sarah's experienced eye saw that Adam was beginning to tire: best to go now, before there were tears and hurt feelings.

Jacqui waved goodbye. 'See you at the ball, tonight, Sarah,' she yelled above the wind.

Sarah mouthed a reply, but the words were snatched away, so with a final wave, the two parties went their separate ways.

It was easier walking home with the wind behind them, but they hadn't gone very far when Bill Richmond's Mercedes purred to a halt beside them. 'Hop in,' he said, indicating the back seat, a smiling Aunt Fay beside him. 'I'm taking Fay home to rest so that she's not too knocked up for the ball,' he said.

'That's a good idea,' applauded Mrs Crampton. 'But I hope you won't stay up too late, Mrs Brennan.'

'No, no,' Bill assured her. 'I'll bring her home the minute she shows the slightest sign of tiredness.'

'Anyone would think I wasn't here, the way you are talking, Bill.'

He flushed under his tan. 'I'm sorry, Fay. It is only that I worry about you.'

'I know,' she said, a little smile curling her lips.

By this time, the car had drawn smoothly up to the front steps. The passengers, two of whom had tumbled out as soon as the door opened and were sitting on the steps, thanked Bill for the lift, but he wasn't listening. 'You make sure you rest, now, Fay,' he was saying. 'I want you to dance the waltz with me, tonight …'

Mrs Crampton thanked Sarah for letting her accompany them to the sale.

'It was a pleasure, Mrs Crampton. Did you enjoy it?'

'My word, I did. Auctions are fun, aren't they? It doesn't matter whether it's household goods or livestock.' She thought a moment, her eyes bulging. 'But I've never seen cattle like that before. Odd, aren't they? With their long, drooping ears and loose flaps of skin.' Without waiting for a reply, she turned and walked rapidly away in the direction of the kitchen.

By this time, Aunt Fay had come in, her cheeks rather pink. 'Well, Sarah, what did you think of it?'

'It was exciting, wasn't it? The cattle looked marvellous. And I couldn't believe the prices!'

'Yes. Dev will be pleased. It's a very good sale. The young bull that brought the big price was rather special, though. He's out of a royal show champion by a top American sire, and his growth and weight gain have been phenomenal. Well, I must go and rest, as *ordered.*' Aunt Fay made a moue. 'But I'm having a cup of tea first. How about you?'

'Yes, I'll just go and see Mattie,' said Sarah, walking off to the kitchen as the older woman turned to go into the sitting room. Aunt Fay sat down, leant back in her chair and closed her eyes with a sigh. Somewhere in her body, there seemed to be a continual drain of energy. *It is hateful being tired all the time. I have so much to do*, she fretted.

Soon, Sarah returned with the tea tray. She looked anxiously at Aunt Fay, wondering if she should call Mrs Crampton but did not voice her thought.

'Ah, tea. Lovely, thank you, dear,' said Aunt Fay, sitting up to accept the tea Sarah poured for her. 'This will buck me up.' She reached for a biscuit. 'Are you going down to the barbecue?'

'No. Dev asked me not to.'

'He's right, of course, dear. You're much safer in the house. It should be all right at the ball, though. I shouldn't think anything could happen in a crowded ballroom.'

'No.' Sarah coloured. 'He said he'll be there to take care of me, whereas he's busy with the clients at the barbecue.'

Aunt Fay nodded. She finished her tea and went off to her room. Sarah poured herself another cup of tea and sat, musing, with a little shiver of anticipation of the spring ball and dancing with Dev. She had never danced with him before, and in thinking about it and all it might mean, she forgot the dangers that surrounded her—forgot the evil presence that hovered over her—and became just another young woman going to a country ball with the man she loved.

Chapter Twenty-six

When they sat down to dinner, Sarah was pleased to see that Aunt Fay seemed to have recovered from her fatigue. There were only the two adults with Naomi and Adam at the table tonight, since Devin and the Richmonds were eating at the barbecue. Towards the end of the meal, Sarah heard Louella's husky tones and the deeper answering voices of Devin and her father as she parted from them to go to her room.

In a little while, the door opened, and Devin looked in. 'We'll go down about nine o'clock if that's all right with you?' he said to Sarah and his aunt after greeting them and the children. After their assurance, he said, 'Good. Bill and I are going to get ready and then have a quiet drink in the lounge. Join us there when you're ready.' His eyes lit on the children, and he smiled. 'Goodnight, you two.'

'Guess *what*, Sarah?' said Naomi after her uncle had gone out and shut the door.

'You're not allowed to tell her!' warned Adam.

'It's not *that*, silly. I don't tell secrets. Anyway, Sarah knows all about that. It's about tonight.'

'Oh, yeah ...' breathed Adam, enraptured.

'What is it?' asked Sarah, amused. 'And it is "yes", not "yeah", Adam.'

'Yes,' he repeated.

'Mattie's got us a video, and we're allowed to sit up *late* and watch it!' announced his sister, her eyes on Sarah and showing satisfaction at her response.

'What is the name of it?' asked Aunt Fay, smiling at Sarah's expression of comical amazement.

'It's called *Snow White and the Seven Dwarfs*, and I bet it's more fun than a yukky old ball,' said Adam.

'You could be right, at that, Adam,' said Aunt Fay, making a moue. 'Hard chairs, crowded dancefloor ...'

'Stay with us, Aunty, if you like?' said Naomi.

'Thank you, my dear. But I had better go. There are people expecting me.'

A quick goodnight, and the children went off with Mattie.

Sarah spoke her thoughts aloud: 'I wonder what Naomi is not allowed to tell me?'

'Oh, that?' Aunt Fay smiled. 'When Dev put me on the spot about the fishing, it was all I could think of to deflect them. I took their measurements for their wedding clothes and told them your plans for them. Of course, I'll have to do it all again closer to the day; but Naomi was right: you do know all about it.'

'Oh,' laughed Sarah. 'It was clever of you to think of it. It certainly stopped them being upset about not coming with us.' She stood up. 'Well, I'd better go and get ready.'

'Yes, dear, indeed,' murmured the older woman, but she sat on at the table, her smooth brow uncharacteristically furrowed.

Sarah entered her room, jumping back with a startled exclamation at the figure seated on her bedroom chair.

'Hello, Sarah,' said a smiling woman in a cream silk dressing-gown. 'I've been waiting for you.'

'Oh … Louella. You startled me. I was expecting Mrs Crampton with my dress. What are you doing here?'

'I've decided that, since we're to be neighbours, we must try to get along, so I've come to apologise for my behaviour towards you. I'm sorry: I've been a bitch,' she said with charming candour and a little rueful smile. 'I have now remembered my manners enough to wish you a happy life with Dev, if not, with perfect truth, at least without rancour. And I do hope you will forgive me for past rudeness?'

Sarah, rather overwhelmed by this speech and the self-deprecating smile that accompanied it, said, 'Oh … well … that's very handsome of you, Louella. Of course, I forgive you.' Touched by the other girl's generosity, she felt that she ought to be no less gracious herself. But there was still one thing. 'My only problem with that is what you did to my horse in the race.'

'But that was an *accident!* Didn't Dev tell you? I was trying to get my horse going when she jumped to the side. I was never more shocked when Dev showed me the poor thing's face.' She looked down at her hands. 'I *am* sorry, truly sorry, it happened. So, now …' Louella paused and looked up—a direct appeal in her eyes. 'Will you be neighbourly and drink a toast with me to our new understanding?'

'Of course, I will,' said Sarah, puzzled by this new side to her neighbour's character, but seeing no other option than to accept it at face value. After all, the other girl did seem to be making an effort. *And it would be awfully difficult for someone like her to swallow her pride and apologise,* she thought. *So, I do appreciate the gesture. But there is one more thing:* 'But before I do—I know it may have been a practical joke—but was it you who put the snake in my bed?'

'Put a snake in your *bed?*' echoed Louella in unfeigned astonishment. 'Good *Lord, no!* Was it …?'

'Oh, it was dead.'

'So, it didn't get there by itself. They do sometimes, you know. Oh, how *utterly* terrifying! You poor thing! If it had been me, I would have gone into hysterics.'

'I did,' said Sarah. 'Snakes scare the wits out of me.'

'And me! Oh, I'd never touch a snake! Ew! The very *thought!* Oh my God! Here, we'd better have that drink before we both go into shock!'

Louella indicated the tray on the side table, which held two small bottles of wine and peach juice, an ice bucket and two crystal long-stemmed glasses. 'It should be champagne, but I could only get a couple of wine coolers down at the bar.' Her voice held a little ripple of amusement. 'And I couldn't convince Aunty that sugar-frosted goblets weren't *quite* appropriate … for either!' she added, going into a peal of tinkling laughter. 'You like ice cubes in your wine, don't you? Not a purist, like me.'

'Thank you, yes.'

Louella was just pouring the drinks when Mrs Crampton erupted into the room, her glassy eyes bulging more than ever. 'Oh, Sarah,' she gasped, 'if you're looking for your dress, I've just pressed it and it is hanging up to air in my room. I'm sorry. I didn't know you had company. Here, let me ...' She scurried across the room to hand Sarah her glass. But, on the way, she tripped over the sheepskin rug and fell full-length, clutching at the edge of the table. Her wildly groping fingers found the floor-length lacy tablecloth, and the bottles and glasses crashed to the floor.

Mrs Crampton picked herself up, gazing regretfully at the shattered goblets and spreading pool of wine cooler dotted with ice cubes. 'Oh, I *am* sorry. I don't know how I could have done that. And your lovely glasses ... I'll just get a cloth and clean it up.'

'Stupid, clumsy, *oafish* woman!' said Louella in a passionate undervoice but managing to control herself. 'Oh, well ...' She shrugged. 'These things happen. But perhaps you'll remember that the thought was there?'

'Of course, I will,' said Sarah, warmly. 'Thank you.'

'Not at all.' Louella made a farewell gesture and turned to the door, her silken robe swishing around her feet. 'See you down there.'

She'd hardly gone when Mrs Crampton came back to clear up the mess. 'I'm sorry, Sarah,' she said, shaking her head. 'I don't know how I could have been so clumsy!'

'That's all right, Mrs Crampton. I know you were only trying to help. And thank you so much for pressing my dress. To tell the truth,' confided Sarah with a mischievous smile, 'I don't like wine cooler much anyway.' She didn't add that, although she was quite happy to do her best to forgive Louella, she was not quite comfortable with her friendly overtures. *However much I try*, she thought. *I don't know if I could be friends with her—ever.*

'I was happy to do it for you. And isn't it a beautiful dress! I'm sure you'll be the belle of the ball. But I think you should go and soak in a nice bath now while I get this room spick and span again. And put plenty of perfumed bath oil in it, mind. I ran it for you just before …'

Her stricken look made Sarah laugh, but she took her advice just the same, pouring scented bath oil liberally into the water and luxuriating in its fragrant warmth. *There is plenty of time, and it is so nice to relax …*

§

Sarah applied her make-up a little more heavily than usual, since it was evening, and outlined her eyes finely with blue eyeliner to enhance their deep colour. Her hair fell in shining waves to her shoulders, caught up at the sides with her favourite jewelled combs. When she was ready, Mrs Crampton helped Sarah into her dress, and they both stood staring at the vision in the mirror. Creamy-white shoulders rose out of the swathed band that formed both the neckline and the sleeves of the elegant off-the-shoulder dress of sapphire-blue silk. The ruched bodice followed the contours of her figure, ending in a band on the hips, which culminated in a provocative bow on one side. From the band, the skirt fell in a profusion of softly gathered folds to mid-calf.

Sarah could not believe it was herself that she was looking at. The dress did something for her that was almost indescribable. Her eyes were a deeper sapphire-blue that matched the dress, her skin seemed to have taken on a pearlescent glow, her features looked more delicate, her hair more angelically fair. It emphasised the slenderness of her waist and gave her the look of a princess. Whenever she moved, the skirt rustled richly and flashed opalescent fire from its shimmering folds. Sarah felt rich beyond desire in this wonderful dress, and her eyes misted at the thought of Aunt Fay and the many hours of fine work that had gone into its creation.

Mrs Crampton made a smothered exclamation: 'Hair! Pins! Quick!'

Sarah indicated her pin box and hairbrush in her make-up drawer, watching in amazement as Mrs Crampton deftly swept her hair into an elegant chignon and, in the space of seconds, expertly pinned it up. Then, almost as if it were sleight of hand, the jewelled combs were placed unerringly in her new coiffure. The chignon set the finishing touch to her air of elegance and emphasised her regal bearing. The upswept hairstyle showed off the swan-like column of her neck and the smooth sweep of her shoulders.

'How did you *do* that?' asked Sarah with an incredulous laugh. 'It's like magic.'

The home help smiled wryly. 'Years of having to pin my hair up under a cap while running to avoid being late for duty in the days when nurses wore such things, and an escaped strand of hair was an excuse for some pretty strong disciplinary measures, let me tell you.'

'I can't imagine you being late, Mrs Crampton.'

Mrs Crampton smiled slightly, a reminiscent gleam in her eye. 'Now,' she said briskly, changing the subject, 'what about some jewellery?'

Sarah put on her diamond earrings, her mother's pearl-and-diamond pendant, clasped the diamond bracelet about her wrist, slid on her engagement ring, thanked her companion and said, 'I think I'm ready now.'

'Yes, I think so, too. My word, I do!' said Mrs Crampton, handing Sarah her lacy white stole and silver mesh evening bag that matched her delicate sandals. 'You *will* be the belle of the ball.'

Judging by the stunned, open-mouthed expressions on the faces of Devin and Bill as she entered the lounge, Sarah's dress had done for her all that Mrs Crampton had prophesied. Aunt Fay smiled in approval, her blue eyes twinkling as she swept them over Sarah, from her corona of gleaming hair and the elegant, jewel-like dress to the dainty silver sandals. The style and colour were perfect for Sarah, just as she had known they would be. She glanced at Louella, and her narrow, dismayed expression made her want to chuckle wickedly. She turned her expectant gaze on Devin and saw that he was still staring at Sarah as if he had never seen her before, and Bill, too, had not quite recovered from the angelic vision she presented. Aunt Fay *did* chuckle wickedly.

All unconsciously, Sarah had made the perfect entrance.

From Sarah's point of view, she was pleasantly aware that the effect of her outfit had created some kind of an impact on the four people assembled in the room. She could see that Aunt Fay was looking palpably pleased with herself and also extremely elegant and feminine in her lilac dress of pleated chiffon, which complimented her shining, silver curls.

Louella was breathtakingly sophisticated in a figure-hugging, flame-red strapless sheath—which had featured in last season's parade at a leading Paris fashion house—that became her admirably. The effect of the glittering mesh fabric, together with her rich tan and dazzling array of diamonds, was only marred by the smile that failed to reach her eyes.

Sarah transferred her gaze to Devin and saw that he was staring at her in a way that made her heart beat unevenly. Time stood still for what seemed an eternity as their eyes locked across the room.

Aunt Fay broke the spell. 'Sarah! How lovely you look! Doesn't she, Dev?'

'Indeed, she does!' he affirmed—his lip quirking at Sarah's heightened colour. 'What will you have to drink?'

'Oh … sherry, please.' Sarah felt her cheeks grow hot at all the attention she was receiving, but secretly, she was thrilled that Devin had noticed her in her new dress. He was not as immune to her as he had claimed; she was sure. And her optimism for the future flared again, fanned by the expression in his eyes as he brought her drink.

They stood, chatting quietly while they sipped their drinks and nibbled on tiny sandwiches and vol-au-vents, but Sarah noticed that Louella, dramatically beautiful in her red gown, was morose and silent, staring into the depths of her glass, which she twirled incessantly between beringed, scarlet-tipped fingers.

§

'Hey, Briggsy,' said Inspector Kingston with easy camaraderie, pushing his chair back. 'Good of you to come. How are you going?'

'Oh, you know,' said Detective Briggs, leaning on the desk and giving the inspector a hint of a wry smile. 'Plodding along: one foot after the other. Percy Plod: that's me.'

'Percy Plod? You, *never!*'

'Well, thanks for the vote of confidence. How are things with you?'

'In a tangle.' He shook his head. 'Riles is thoroughly confused, and I'm not much better.'

'I can see *that* from the mess you've made of your blotter,' said the detective in an indulgent voice. 'But if it's any help, you can leave Sergeant Riley to me.'

'All right. But I don't know what he'll say about that.'

'Very little, if I know him.'

'Wise man.' He met the detective's steely gaze and held up a warding hand. 'All right, Briggsy, that'll do! No need to look at me like that. *I'm* not one of your crims. Now, what's this complication I've been hearing about?'

Detective Briggs began to study a bronze paperweight. 'It's appearing more and more likely that there is a hit-man involved, so we're looking for two crims, not one.'

'Oh, Lord,' groaned the inspector. 'So that means we're back to square one: or worse!'

'Not quite. You can wash Mr Mainwaring out.'

'I've never considered him.'

'Haven't you?' Detective Briggs raised an eyebrow. 'I have.'

The inspector gave a shout of laughter. 'Everyone's guilty until proven innocent, according to you, Briggsy.'

'Of course. That's how I always get my man …' Detective Briggs spent a moment in consideration. 'Or woman.'

'So, now we're looking for a man or woman rich enough to pay a hit-man or woman, as well as the said hit-man or woman?'

'That's about the size of it.'

'So, we can forget the jackaroos, the cook and the overseer …'

'Not the overseer. He can lay his hands on any amount of money. His family own Wanda. He's only here because he and his father don't see eye to eye on management, and he's still training as a manager. But don't you worry, he's set to take over when his father retires.'

'And the same goes for David Canley, I take it?'

'Yes. And a number of others, as well.'

'Including Louella Richmond?'

'Maybe.' Detective Briggs made a moue. 'But I'm not convinced.'

'What's up with you, Briggsy?' demanded the inspector, slapping his palms down on the desk. 'She's my front runner: fits both profiles. She'll only have to give me the slightest excuse, and I'll be down on her like a ton of bricks.'

Detective Briggs shrugged but said nothing.

'And there are plenty of people can tell you how much she hates Miss Johnston.'

'Yes, but that's just why …' Detective Briggs looked out the window and made a small exclamation. 'Headlights: Someone's moving! I'd better get back to my surveillance. I'm sorry you couldn't trace Bryant. I've got a feeling he's mixed up in this somewhere. My nose tells me something is going to break tonight.'

'I hope you're right. As long as it is the crim that breaks this time and not that poor little girl again.' But he spoke to the empty air. Detective Briggs had gone, striding away with grim purpose. A rueful smile crossed his face. *My best detective*, he thought. *If Briggsy can't solve this case, no-one can.*

§

The woolshed had been transformed into a huge garden, or so it seemed to Sarah, entering at Devin's side just as the band began to play a romantic waltz. The seating areas were cleverly transformed into bowers; the illusion being created by the use of potted trees and shrubs to divide them and trellis-like backdrops, to which were fixed branches of glowing golden wattle.

Artificial silk and plastic flowers were intermingled unashamedly with real ones and cascaded luxuriantly along with ferns and tropical climbers from hanging baskets suspended from the rough beams of the ceiling around the edges of the dancefloor. The members of the band appeared to be seated amidst the trees of a veritable forest, and colourful bunches of huge crepe-paper flowers adorned the rafters, nodding their heads in the light breeze as they looked down on the no-less colourful company below.

Sarah was struck anew with the preparation and energy that the Outback people expended on any gala social affair. She marvelled at the joy with which they received a formal occasion such as this. There were no glum faces here; the air positively hummed with good humour and gaiety. It was as if they grabbed desperately at any chance of the society of their fellows, and having done so, were determined to make the most of it. There was no sloppy dressing, either. For the Outback women—who, in these times, spent most of their days working beside their men in felt hats, work shirts and shorts or jeans, feet encased in sturdy workboots—it was a heaven-sent opportunity to feel feminine again. There was a touch of luxury in taking out a beautiful dress that was only occasionally worn or, if the season and time permitted, in buying a dazzling new creation to be seldom worn but greatly treasured.

It was wonderful, too, to transform sun-browned, tired skin and hair with facemasks, make-up and hair treatments, until, at last, unrecognisable as their workaday selves, they shone at the ball in an array of dazzling finery, enjoying the compliments of their menfolk and the chance to show themselves at their best.

The Outback people are an extrovert, friendly lot, thought Sarah, *warmly welcoming strangers as well as old friends and battening down to have a really good party.* But she was beginning to understand their philosophy: Life was short, and opportunities to enjoy the company of others few; so wholehearted enjoyment of a 'do' provided the safety valve for a life too often fraught with problems of drought, sickness and isolation and, in these difficult times, just plain overwork, as a man and his wife tried to maintain a station that 'in the old days' had employed several jackaroos or ringers plus bore maintenance and household staff.

As they made their way to the bower that had been reserved for them, Sarah was hailed by a beaming Jim and Jacqui. She and

Devin halted to wait for them, while the others went on to their table.

'Hello, Sarah,' said Jacqui, looking her up and down. 'Wow! What a dress! You look like a fairy princess.'

Sarah laughed. *Trust Jacqui to always say what she thought!* 'Thank you, Jacqui. But never mind me. I believe you have something to show me?'

Jacqui, pretty and feminine in fuchsia crepe de Chine, smiled happily; her soft, plump cheeks flushing to an attractive pink as Jim, an arm about her waist, held out her left hand for their inspection. 'It isn't as grand as yours, Sarah. But it's still nice, don't you think?' she asked, dimpling.

'It is lovely, Jacqui,' said Sarah, admiring the brilliant-cut solitaire diamond that sparkled in a dainty, unusual setting—just right for Jacqui's small plump finger. 'Congratulations to you both,' she added, kissing first one and then the other. Devin kissed Jacqui and heartily shook Jim's hand.

Jacqui looked up at her fiancé, a world of love in her sparkling brown eyes, as they shared some private lovers' message. Sarah thought again how happy and right they were for each other and wished with a pang that her own engagement could be like this. Then, as people seized the opportunity to congratulate the popular couple and surged around them, Devin caught Sarah's eye and gently drew her out of the crowd.

He stood for a moment, looking down at her. 'You look beautiful tonight, Sarah,' he said quietly, and before she could compose her chaotic thoughts enough to speak, he steered her onto the crowded dancefloor, holding her lightly in his arms.

Finally, Sarah was dancing with Dev—a slow waltz that made

her feel as if she were made of fragile, scintillating glass that the electrifying touch of his hands charged with thousands of volts and, at any minute, might cause her to shatter into a million tiny rainbow fragments. She looked up wonderingly into his face. His expression was serious, even stern, in repose, but when he caught her glance, he smiled and held her fractionally closer. She knew then that she had been wrong: the glass she was made of was not going to shatter, but melt, instead. Too soon their dance was over, and the magic drained away when he released her.

Sarah was caught up in a social vortex, as first one and then another must dance with her. Occasionally, she caught a glimpse of Devin, dancing with different women, and once, her heart contracted painfully when she saw Louella gliding gracefully around the room with him.

Sitting at the table after an energetic dance with John Andrews, Sarah was waiting for him to bring her a drink from the bar and wondering how long it would be before Devin could dance with her again, when a voice spoke from behind her, so close, it made her jump. 'Excuse me, Miss Johnston. I'm sorry to disturb you like this, but I came to tell you that Mrs Brennan has taken one of her turns and is asking for you.'

'Oh!' Sarah's momentary fear evaporated in the face of this much greater emergency. 'I'll come at once. Where is she?'

'I'll show you, Miss. She was on her way home because she felt tired, she said. Decided to take one of the vehicles and drive herself so she wouldn't worry anyone, but she didn't quite make it to the carpark. She said to fetch you—that you'd know what to do to help her,' said the stockman, eyes downcast as usual. Only once had he ever looked directly at her, and Sarah still shivered at the memory, though she told herself that it had just been a trick of the light. This was just Col who worked here, was always respectful but shy and, by all accounts, a wonderful and reliable stockman.

'Of course,' she said, gathering up her stole and bag and hurrying to the door. On the way, she met John Andrews, returning with their drinks. Briefly, Sarah explained what had happened and that she must leave.

'Oh, that's too bad! Would you like me to come with you?'

'Oh, no. There's no need, thanks. I shouldn't be away too long.' Outside the door, Sarah turned to the stockman. 'Where, now?'

The man pointed to a clump of trees a little way from the edge of the carpark. 'Down there, Miss. See them trees?'

Sarah nodded and hurried in the direction he had indicated, intent on reaching Aunt Fay as soon as possible.

The tall man behind her flexed long fingers. His eyes gleamed momentarily as he watched her, before striding along behind her with leisurely long steps that easily kept pace with her hurried, shorter ones.

It wasn't until Sarah had almost reached the trees that several realisations hit her at once with the force of a sledgehammer. She stumbled and then walked on while she tried to think what to do—her mind in chaos. Fear feathered her skin, causing the hair to rise on the back of her neck.

Aunt Fay was not here, never had been here. Sarah knew that now. She had been with Bill Richmond, and if she had gone home, it would have been with him in his car. Sarah tried to force her numbed mind back to the ballroom. Bill and Aunt Fay had not been there for some time; she was sure of it. Sarah recalled his promise to take Devin's aunt home the minute she was tired.

Then, Sarah realised something else: she was alone in the dark with a man she was afraid of, and no-one would think to look for her because they would believe her to be with Aunt Fay. It had been a ruse to get her away from the protection of the crowd, and like a fool, she had fallen for it.

Sarah turned on wobbly legs to face the stockman, whose tall, menacing figure suddenly loomed over her: a dark shape in the moonlight that trickled through the tree canopy and distorted his features so that his face became an evil mask. Sarah tried to scream, but no sound would come. Then, swinging round, she tried to run away, anywhere, so long as it was away from the sinister figure who, as she now knew, meant her no good.

As in her dreams, Sarah's legs would not seem to work properly. She could hear him gaining on her. Really terrified now, she darted in and out through the trees but stumbled in her fragile high-heeled sandals. Before she could hit the ground, Sarah was jerked roughly back and around to face her attacker; the delicate material of her dress tearing under the strain.

In a kind of detached, blank horror, Sarah saw the man draw thin lips back from his teeth in a snarl—an inhuman gleam is those hard flat eyes—and knew with the certainty of despair that this was the face of her dreams. Only now, when it was too late, were the features revealed to her.

Then, as those iron fingers fastened around her throat—causing a welling, rising pain—Sarah knew that the nightmare that had tormented her for so many nights had been a vision of her own death. And she had not heeded its grim warning.

Chapter Twenty-seven

'You know, Fay, I was always set on having Dev as a son-in-law. It is a pity Louie didn't know her own mind. Too young, I suppose.' Bill Richmond sighed and sipped his coffee, a sad, faraway expression on his kindly face as he thought of the mess his beautiful daughter had made of her life. 'Louie has always been so headstrong, and I had hoped …' He sighed again. 'That Dev would be a steadying influence on her. But … Not to be.'

Fay replied to this with an unintelligible murmur. She could not tell Bill how grateful she was that Louella had not married Devin.

They were sitting in the lounge over coffee, and Fay had been relieved to be able to relax and enjoy her beverage in peace and quiet away from the noise of the ball. But the conversation was becoming awkward, and her coffee suddenly lost its flavour.

'But I like this little girl of Dev's; I really do,' said Bill in a different tone. 'Such a nice personality. And pretty, too. Like you,

"

Fay,' he added, surprising her.

'Yes,' she agreed, ignoring the compliment. 'I think Sarah is right for Dev. She will make him a good wife.'

'Indeed, she will.' He hesitated a moment, then stumbled on, 'Fay … we've known each other a long time, haven't we?'

'Yes, Bill, dear. For more years than I care to think.' *I know what's coming. And I can't handle it. Not tonight!*

'Fay …' Bill's voice held a rough edge of loneliness and longing. 'Won't you marry me?'

'No, Bill. I am sorry, but I can't. I am needed here.'

'That's what you told me all the other times I asked. But, Fay, just consider: the children will have Sarah and Dev. They won't need you here all the time. And, perhaps, I can redeem the promise I made to you all those years ago.'

'Yes, but Dev and Sarah will need some time to themselves. Besides …' She gave him a reproachful stare. 'You broke my heart—*all* those years ago.'

'Fay, I've always loved you. Ever since you first came home from boarding school.' His face softened at the memory of her as a sixteen year old; her dark hair confined demurely in two long, thick plaits wound around her small head; her eyes glowing jewels in her sweet little heart-shaped face. She had been soft and feminine and, in his eyes, was no less beautiful now than she had been then.

'But you *married* Esmé,' she pointed out with gentle irony.

'I am so sorry, Fay. But I couldn't help it. Esmé was so beautiful, I … When I woke up in that hospital bed in France and saw her bending over me, it was like …' He flicked a biscuit crumb off his frilled shirt front. 'I lost my head for long enough to get married … Oh, don't get me wrong: I did love Esmé; I really did. But, deep down, I've always loved you, Fay.' He reflected sadly that it hadn't been long before he discovered that the love he thought he'd found in his whirlwind wartime romance was an infatuation that did not outlive his first wild passion for Esmé, nor his next sight of Fay.

'Poor Bill, you've had such a hard life, haven't you? With poor, dear Esmé becoming ill so young. Yes, and so sad that she felt she had to kill herself, like that.'

'Fay, please! I will never believe that Esmé killed herself.'

'Won't you, dear? Well, I can understand that. But, Bill dear, she was so depressed …' Fay put a hand on his arm. 'If she didn't do it herself, who could it have been?'

'I don't know.'

There was a heavy silence. Fay broke it after a little while with a wry twist to her usually smiling lips. 'I have a damaged heart, you know. Something I didn't bargain for. I think it best we leave things as they are.' Her eyes flashed. 'As *you* decreed all those years ago that they should be!'

'*Fay?*' At her change in tone, he slewed around in astonishment to look at her.

But the eyes that looked back at him showed no animosity, just their usual gentle kindness. 'Bill, dear, we've run out of time. Don't you see that it's all too late?' She smiled and rubbed his arm. 'You don't need another invalid on your hands, dear. You really don't.'

§

Devin escorted Elisabeth Andrews to their table, where Sarah and John should've been waiting for them. His eyes narrowed a little, and he felt a vague stirring of unease when he saw that John Andrews sat there alone. Unconsciously, he quickened his pace, so that Elisabeth stumbled in her stiletto heels as she did her best to keep up with him. She had been chatting with him and wondered at his palpable lack of attention and the suddenly grim set to his mouth. Devin was usually the soul of courtesy, unlike many others she could think of, and she wondered even more.

John's eyes lit up with a smile when he saw them. 'Hello, there. Been having a good time? Can I get you a drink?'

Devin cut him short. 'Sarah! Where is she?' he demanded, a sudden chill of dread striking at his heart as he waited numbly for the answer.

'No need to worry, Dev,' he said, looking closely at him. 'She's gone to aid your aunty. Had a slight turn or something. I offered to go with her, but she said she'd be all right with that new fellow of yours. What's his name? Col. He came to get her. She said she shouldn't be too long.' But these last words were spoken to the empty air. Devin had gone.

John met his wife's startled gaze, shrugged and went to the bar to get her a drink. *Queer, the way Dev went off like that,* he thought. *Maybe I should have insisted on going with Sarah. But it's not as if I let her go alone. She was escorted by one of his own men, for God's sake!* Irritably, he dismissed a vague feeling of guilt and made his way back to Elisabeth with their drinks.

§

The dark mist that had risen before Sarah's eyes receded as the cruel fingers slackened their grip. She drew a deep breath and tried to swallow the hard lump that had risen painfully in her throat. Staring up into eyes that were dark, menacing pools, she managed just one word. 'Why?' she whispered. She tried to frame more words, but they just would not come.

The man smiled—mocking, evil. 'Why?' he mimicked, adding in a savage undervoice. 'Because you're beautiful, that's why! Because you're a stuck-up bitch, that's why!' Suddenly, his mood changed. 'Yes, you're beautiful, all right,' he muttered, gently stroking her throat and bare shoulders, making her shudder with repulsion and fear. His long fingers moved upward from their exploration of the torn neckline of her gown, entwined in her hair, yanking savagely so that she gasped with the pain. He laughed. His employer had not known how only too ready he was to carry out this particular job, having desired Sarah since he had first seen her. And his bizarre lust could only be satisfied in one way … 'Don't think I haven't noticed you, walking about with your nose in the air, showing yourself off. Think you're too good for the likes of me, don't you?' he said on a rising note of anger. 'Good enough for the Boss, eh? Well, I can make you so he won't ever look at you again,' he sneered and slapped her hard across the face, so that her head snapped around on her shoulders. Dimly, through the sudden shock and pain, Sarah was aware that he was enjoying this. She could feel the almost tangible waves of madness emanating from him as he exulted in his power to maim and destroy.

Here was a deranged mind that, out of its twisted mania, obtained a macabre satisfaction from inflicting pain and terror on women. Sarah knew that he was deliberately prolonging the torture—playing with her as a cat does a mouse—and when he finally tired of it, would swiftly put an end to her existence. *But, what will he do to me, first?* The thought stabbed at her mind like a rapier. He would torture and kill her for no other reason than he thought her beautiful. She almost laughed hysterically. *What a reason to kill!* And then, she thought in stark terror, *I must get away!*

Fear, which had paralysed her, now lent her the impetus to struggle and break away. She kicked him hard on the shin and twisted out of his grasp. But, before she had taken one step, he caught her and spun her around to face him.

'You little bitch,' he panted, reaching for her throat. 'You won't get away from me this time!'

Sarah tried vainly to loosen the agonising grip of those iron-hard fingers. Then, just as a rising blackness threatened to overcome her, she felt herself falling. Thankfully, taking great pain-filled gulps of air through her bruised and strained throat, she lay, unable to hear or see anything except the buzzing in her ears and whirling, flashing points of light behind her eyes. She felt a prickling sensation and knew, with a sense of wonder, that she was not dead, after all. *I'm alive! I'm alive!* The thought filled her with joy. To be alive when you thought you were dead was a miracle: an incredible, joyous miracle.

Presently, other sounds intruded on her senses and painfully turning her head, Sarah saw two men struggling together. One was her attacker. The other was ... 'Dev!' she gasped and sat up, holding her throat. *Dev! He's here. He saved me.* She knew a moment of fear for him, and then she saw that he had the upper hand, and the tension and fear seeped out of her like lifeblood from a mortal wound.

After a time, Sarah crawled to her feet and stood, propped against a tree, too weak from exhaustion to move or speak. Her eyes were huge in her ashen face; a livid mark becoming evident on her cheekbone. Her lovely gown was torn and dirty, her hair in disarray and a chilly breeze ran ghostly fingers over her bare flesh, but she neither knew nor cared. Her eyes and mind alike were fixed with painful intensity on the man who was meting out a primitive justice to a now craven individual who bore little resemblance to the powerful thug who had attacked her.

§

When Devin ran out of the woolshed into the pale moonlight, he could not, at first, see anything. 'Where?' he'd asked himself desperately, fists clenched. Then, as his eyes adjusted, he saw a flurry of movement by the trees near the carpark. *Someone running? Sarah?* He set off at a dead run himself, and when he saw Sarah in the murderous hands of Col Jones, a towering rage, such as he had never known, filled his heart and rose up before his eyes as a red mist. He stretched out a hand to the back of the man's collar and plucked him bodily off her. A well-placed blow behind the ear, delivered by his other fist, sent the stockman sprawling.

Devin was waiting. 'Get up,' he said. 'You're going to tell me why you did this, if I have to beat it out of you.'

The man shrugged and stood up.

Devin hit him again. 'Tell me,' he said.

Jones swayed on his feet but said nothing.

Something was happening to Devin. As he gave free rein to a glorious anger, all the years' pent-up frustration and despair were released in a great flood that battered the wall of bitterness he had built around his heart. Under this tremendous tide of rage, it weakened and fractured, until it fell, stone by crumbling stone, to leave him free, at last, to love again.

He loved Sarah; he knew that now. And this insect was going to pay for hurting her. He gave the stockman a wicked punch on the jaw and another to the ribs, which sent him to his knees. 'Tell me, you parasite!' he said fiercely, hauling him up to stand on his feet.

The stockman evaded his eyes and dumbly shook his head.

'Why did you do it?' Devin waited for an answer, and when there was none, gave the man another punishing blow.

Jones staggered a little, spitting blood and then mumbled the one word: 'Money.'

'Whose money?' asked Devin.

The stockman shrank away from his raised fist, and a malicious expression came over his face. He pointed to the edge of the light.

Cautiously, Devin turned his head and saw, among the gathering knot of onlookers, a tall, shadowy figure in a flame-red evening gown, holding a hand to her mouth in shock. And even as that incriminating finger pointed her out, she drew back into the shadows and vanished.

'You rotten *cur!*' Devin turned back to the cowering stockman in renewed fury. But whatever he might next have said or done was interrupted by a calm voice.

'I'll take over now, Sir. You go and see to Sarah,' said Mrs Crampton, stepping out from behind a tree. In her hand she held a deadly .38 revolver, and it was pointed straight at Jones's stomach.

Devin looked at her in surprise, then turned to where Sarah was leaning against a tree trunk and gathered her into his arms. Holding her close, he said, 'Oh, my poor darling! Are you all right?' Then, in a whisper, 'I love you so much!'

Sarah whispered back. She was in Dev's arms, and he loved her. Could anything be more all right than that? The terror of her ordeal and the pain of her swelling cheek and bruised throat were alike forgotten. She was too engrossed in Devin to notice that Mrs Crampton, in a most professional manner, now had Jones up against a tree—his face pressed to its trunk, arms held high while she searched him thoroughly for weapons.

'Mrs Crampton,' said Johnnie from behind her. 'You've done a good job, but I'll look after this blighter now, while you go and fix up Sarah's face. I don't know where you got that gun, but you'd better be careful not to wave it about too much. It could be dangerous.' Then he thrust the barrel of his shotgun against the back of Jones's neck with two ominous clicks. 'You make one wrong move, you mongrel, and I'll blow your flamin' head off,' he growled. 'And if I get a cramp in my finger, and the gun goes off by accident, I don't think anyone'll mind much. So, you just walk very quiet to the quarters.'

Mrs Crampton looked at Johnnie and the shotgun, opened her mouth to speak, closed it again, then, pocketing her revolver, walked slowly across to Devin and Sarah. 'Let me have a look, Sarah,' she said gently, inspecting Sarah's face in the light of her torch. 'If we get ice onto that cheek quickly, you probably won't bruise much.' She smiled. 'But I don't think I could say the same

for your assailant.'

Chapter Twenty-eight

Devin wrapped his coat tenderly about Sarah's shoulders and held her close. 'We'll go home now,' he said. 'Are you coming, Mrs Crampton?'

'Yes, Mr Mainwaring. I'd better get an icepack onto that bruised cheek. I'll go and bring your car over, if you like?'

'Thank you. It's at the far end of the woolshed. The keys are in it,' he called after her rapidly retreating form.

Nestled in his arms, Sarah said, 'It's all over now, isn't it?'

'Well … not quite. But it will be, soon. How do you feel?'

'Oh … fine.'

'Really?'

'Really! Thanks to you. But I wouldn't want to go through it again.'

'No, indeed. We must make sure of that.'

Sarah was about to ask him what he meant when Mrs

Crampton drew up beside them. She supervised them into the back seat and then into the sitting room, bustling away to return a short time later with a tray of coffee and a packet of frozen peas wrapped in a handtowel. 'Hold that on your cheek for a while, Sarah,' she ordered, busying herself pouring coffee. 'This will do us all good.'

'I don't take sugar, thank you, Mrs Crampton,' said Sarah, watching in something approaching horror as the home help spooned liberal amounts of sugar into her cup.

'You do this time,' smiled Mrs Crampton. 'Doctor's orders!'

Sarah meekly accepted the steaming, aromatic brew and sipped distastefully, but to her surprise, she began to enjoy the warm sweetness as the liquid trickled down her sore throat, soothing the damaged tissues and filling her with a pervading warmth.

They finished their coffee in silence—Sarah still bundled in Devin's coat. Devin was seated beside her on the settee, a protective arm encircling her.

Mrs Crampton gathered up the coffee cups. 'Keep that icepack on her for a bit longer, Mr Mainwaring. I'll take these away, and then I'll ring the inspector, shall I?'

'Yes, do that,' said Devin absently, his eyes on Sarah.

What it is to be young and in love! Mrs Crampton smiled a little, her glassy eyes surprisingly empathetic. Obviously, he was too preoccupied to attend to her. *As is proper*, she thought. *And now it is up to me to see that their story has a happy ending.*

Devin, his soul released at last from its lonely prison of bitterness, looked upon Sarah with eyes filled with love and tenderness, and she, entwined in his arms and basking in the warmth of his regard, had finally found the elusive thing for which she had so restlessly yearned.

But Devin still had something to do. Reluctantly, he forced himself back to the problem they had yet to overcome. 'Sarah, I hate to have to tell you this, but it seems that Jones wasn't acting alone—that someone may have paid him to … remove you. We don't know the full story, yet.'

'I can't believe it!' she gasped, her heart pounding and her throat suddenly aching desperately. 'Why? And who?' She gave another gasp. 'Then, Reuben was right! He said there was someone jealous out to get me. Dev, is it …? Can it be … Louella?'

'I don't know. I can't credit it, really. But if it is, I can promise you this: she will never be allowed to hurt you again.'

'But … What are you going to do?'

He stood up, took her hands and lifted Sarah to her feet. Then he folded her in his arms. 'That, my darling, is something that you can safely leave to me and the police. Come, you're tired. I'll see you to your room.'

Outside Sarah's door, he stopped and turned her towards him. He crushed her to him and kissed her hungrily, making her already overwrought senses swim in an ecstasy of delight. A slow, burning fire spread through her, and she melted into his embrace, responding with all her being to the demands of his lips. Her bruises and her stiff, aching throat went unnoticed in the clamouring insistence of their love.

Stifling a groan, Devin released her and cupped her head in his hands, tilting it back with his thumbs against her temples. 'Soon,' he said, his voice vibrating with passion, 'we won't be saying goodnight at your door.' He kissed her again—a sweetly tender kiss that pierced her with a delicious ache, causing tears to spring to her eyes as he said softly, 'Goodnight, my darling. Sleep well.' Then, making a superhuman effort, he tore himself away and strode off down the hall.

When Sarah found herself on the other side of the door, Mrs Crampton was standing by the window. 'I thought I'd just help you out of your dress and see you to bed, Sarah,' she said kindly. 'I hope you feel better now?'

'Yes, thank you.' Sarah's voice was still a hoarse whisper.

'How's the throat?'

'Sore!' Sarah smiled ruefully. 'I suppose I am lucky that that's all that's wrong.'

'My word, you are! A couple of analgesics will help the throat a little—help you to sleep, too.'

'Oh, look at my dress,' mourned Sarah.

'I don't think it will be worn again,' said Mrs Crampton, casting a critical eye over the torn and dirty garment.

'Oh!' gasped Sarah, putting a hand up to her throat. 'My pendant! It's gone!' She turned tragic eyes on her companion.

'Just a moment,' said Mrs Crampton, diving a hand into her apron pocket and searching around. 'Is this what you're looking for?' She handed Sarah the pearl-and-diamond pendant and its broken chain, along with her two jewelled combs. 'I saw it fall when I … I mean, I saw it on the ground when I went for the car … in the torchlight,' she amended, but Sarah, delighted to see her precious pendant, hardly heard her and, in any case, did not attach any significance to her words.

'Oh, I don't know how to thank you, Mrs Crampton. This pendant means so much to me. I would hate to have lost it.'

In her competent way, Mrs Crampton set about making Sarah comfortable, then went into her own room, leaving the door fractionally ajar.

Sarah closed her eyes, exhausted, sore yet full of joy. What was a bruised throat against the fact that Devin loved her? *Dev loves me! He loves me!* She found it hard to believe that her dreams had come true. The warmth of his arms, the loving pressure of his lips stayed with her as she drifted off to sleep. The fact that there was still a murderer loose out there didn't seem to weigh with her at all.

Mrs Crampton, seeing that Sarah was asleep, checked all the doors and windows and slipped noiselessly into the hall, locking the bedroom door and pocketing the key.

§

The inspector looked at Jones's bruised face and then at Devin's skinned knuckles and became suddenly severe. 'Come outside, Mr Mainwaring. I might charge you with assault, too,' he said when they were clear of the bunkhouse.

'Inspector,' said Jim, waiting outside with the other men. 'There are six of us here who will swear we saw that fellow fall off his horse.'

The group mumbled and nodded in support.

'Yes, and I'll have you all for perjury,' instantly retorted the inspector, fixing Jim with a hard eye. He glared at him for a long moment, then suddenly relented. Perhaps a vision of Sue's battered face had visited him, so he said in a milder tone, though his eyes were still snapping, 'Well, if he fell off his horse, I don't suppose we can blame anybody else for it. I'll have to think about it.'

'Thanks, Men. Jim.' Devin's eyes met Jim's for a long moment. 'If the inspector's finished with you, you can go along now. I'll see you all tomorrow.'

'Sergeant.' The inspector jerked his thumb towards the quarters. 'Handcuff the prisoner and escort him to the police vehicle. These men need their bunkhouse.'

'Yes, Sir,' said Sergeant Riley, nodding to the constable.

Jones was lying on a bunk with his face turned to the wall. Johnnie sat on a chair facing the prisoner—his shotgun across his knees. He grinned at the police. 'About time,' he said. 'Honest citizens having to do your work for you!'

Constable Smith flushed at this dig, but the sergeant, showing no sign of having heard it, was busy with the handcuffs.

Outside, Mrs Crampton came hurrying up to the inspector. 'Good morning,' she said, brisk but accurate; it was well past midnight.

'Ah, Briggsy. You're just in time to throw some light on a point of discussion, if you will? But first, let me introduce you. Mr Devin Mainwaring, this is Detective Briggs of the Special Task Force Unit.'

Devin smiled. 'I thought so.'

'How did I give myself away?'

'You didn't, until tonight. It was your revolver and the way you handled it.' He smiled a little. 'Not to mention, the way you frisked Jones …'

'Oh …'

'Detective Briggs!' The inspector recalled the officer to her sense of duty.

The detective turned her strange eyes on him. 'Yes, Sir?'

He cleared his throat, feeling somehow small-minded and mean. 'Detective Briggs: did you see Mr Mainwaring hit the prisoner?' He felt as though he was being impaled and pinned to the wall as the glassy, light eyes of the detective considered him for a few moments before swivelling towards Devin.

The inspector sighed and experimentally flexed his fingers. Yes, he could move again. *If ever you felt like getting on the wrong side of the law, one look from Briggsy would set you straight—that was certain.*

Detective Briggs spoke concisely: 'I saw the prisoner hit Miss Johnston and then attempt to strangle her. I also heard his threat to kill her. Before I could come to her aid, Mr Mainwaring reached the prisoner and pulled him off her.' There were things the police were not allowed to do in pursuing the course of justice, and it had given Detective Briggs quite a deal of satisfaction to have heard the prisoner's confession, but no need to tell the inspector that. She perceived that he was about to question her further and threw in her bombshell: 'I also heard the prisoner state that he attacked Miss Johnston for money, and he pointed out his employer.'

There was a long silence, finally broken by the inspector. 'Well, come *on*, Briggsy: who was it?'

'I am not satisfied that the prisoner was telling the truth, Sir.'

Detective Briggs turned to Devin. 'Mr Mainwaring, would you go back and check on Sarah? I locked her in, but if she wakes up, she may be afraid on her own.'

Detective Briggs was holding out the key, and much as Devin wanted to know if she'd seen exactly what he'd seen, he knew Sarah must not be left alone. When he was out of earshot, she said a name.

'I said it was her all along! Didn't I? Didn't I? Well: What are you waiting for? Send Riles off to arrest her.'

'Whoa there! Whoa there!' said the detective, holding up her hands. 'It could be someone else. There were a whole bunch of people with her. It could have been any one of them. We've only got his word it is a woman. And quite frankly ——'

'I see your point: how could you trust the word of a creep like that?' He slapped his hands together in frustration. 'Then, who? Who else?'

'I don't know. There's something more you should know. I got the lab results. There was poison, but it wasn't in the bottles. They think it was in the ice cubes: thallium.'

'Oh, Lord! That puts a whole new complexion on it.'

'I thought you'd see that.'

'Any ideas?'

'Nothing I can prove. It is well known in the household and possibly to others that Sarah likes to dilute her alcoholic beverages with ice cubes. You don't know what poisons could be lying round in an old shed on these stations. Thallium: colourless, odourless, tasteless; they put it on pumpkin seeds to bait rats.'

'So, it could still be that Richmond woman. Why don't we just bring her in?'

'Look, just give me twenty-four hours. If nothing breaks, I'll go and arrest her myself.' Detective Briggs looked thoughtful. 'But I'd bet my left you-know-what that it's not her … If I had them, that is.'

The inspector tried to suppress a fit of ribald laughter. He failed. 'Oh, you've got plenty of those, Briggsy,' he told her between gasps. 'No need to worry about that.'

Detective Briggs regarded him in withering silence.

'Don't *do* that, Briggsy,' he said with feeling. 'Okay, be it on your own head, or whatever part of your anatomy. You've got twenty-four hours. But I don't need to tell you not to mess it up.'

Detective Briggs gave him another measuring glance before she turned away.

'She never has, Sir,' said Sergeant Riley, finally moved out of his stolid silence to defend his colleague.

'True,' said the inspector. 'My apologies.'

'Thanks for the bouquet, Riles,' said Detective Briggs—her steely gaze softening. 'But nothing is set in concrete.' For a moment, her light eyes glowed into his. 'I'd better get back. Stay ready for my call.'

Chapter Twenty-nine

Devin sat in the darkness of the verandah outside Sarah's door. He heard the detective before he saw her; rising, he held out the key. 'I'm in a quandary,' he said when she stepped onto the verandah in front of him. 'Do I call you Mrs Crampton or Detective Briggs?'

'Whatever you like, Mr Mainwaring. I answer to many things.'

'I need to know who you saw.'

Detective Briggs did not pretend to misunderstand. 'The same person you saw.'

'If she comes back tonight, I will be looking for some answers from her.'

'I've no objection, as long as it doesn't run along the same lines as your interrogation of Jones. Not that I believe it will.'

'I've never hit a woman. And I don't propose to start now.' He made a wry mouth. 'She'll deny it, of course.'

'Yes. And it might just be the truth. Don't forget that.'

'I have an idea that your boss is after her hide, no matter what!'

Detective Briggs inclined her head. *Typical man,* she thought. *Can't see past the end of his nose. But I can't tell Mr Mainwaring that!* 'You mustn't blame him. It is the most obvious solution,' she said, adding slowly, 'and possibly one we've been led to by a very clever operator.'

Devin digested this in silence. 'I take it you have a reason for saying that?'

'I do, but I don't want to go into it right now.'

'Fair enough.' Devin nodded. 'By the way, Detective, thank you for your support and your, er, discretion.'

'That's all right,' said Detective Briggs, taking the key with a wry smile. 'It did my heart good to watch you deliver a bit of good old-fashioned justice to that thug.'

When the detective had gone into Sarah's room, Devin went to the lounge, poured himself a whisky and went back to sit on the verandah.

§

'Dev! You waited up for me,' said Louella in pleased tones as she stepped onto the verandah. 'How nice!'

'Come into my office. I want to talk to you.' He rose and ushered her down the hall. 'I suppose you know what's happened?'

'I heard that Jones attacked Sarah and that the police have

him. Is she all right?'

'Not too bad, considering …' he said, pouring them both a whisky and handing her one.

'Jones!' she said. 'I had no idea.'

'Didn't you?' he said, looking into his drink. 'Well, I'll need to be convinced of that.'

'Of course I didn't!' Louella put down her glass. 'Just what the *hell* do you mean?'

'I'm talking about these repeated attacks on Sarah. Someone paid that creep to do away with her, but fortunately, he made a muck of it. Now look, Louella, I don't want to say anything offensive, but …' He raised his eyes from the whisky. 'This business has your dibs all over it.'

'But it isn't me! Darling, *do* give me some credit! I mean, I may have said in the heat of the moment—and I freely admit it!— that I'd like to murder the girl. But I didn't *mean* it. I'd never do anything as disgusting as that! *Please*, you have to believe me!'

'I only wish I could,' he said, remembering her denial of her attack on Gracious Lady. 'But the evidence is stacking up against you.'

'But it's a set-up! I'm being set-up!' She took a deep breath. 'No wonder you don't want me if you think I am capable of doing something like that! Look, I know I was a bitch at first, but I have accepted the inevitable. Honestly! I mean, have I been giving you trouble lately? I've even apologised to Sarah and tried to make amends … But that *stupid* woman!'

'Detective Briggs.'

'Oh, she's a *detective*?' Louella thought this over. 'But then she must have spilt the drinks because she thought they were poisoned?' She read the answer in his eyes. 'Oh, I see! I've stopped being a bitch because I'm set on doing something so much worse! Was there poison in the drinks? *Was* there?'

'I don't know.'

'Well, if there was, *I* didn't put it there! No, darling, no! You *have* to believe me.' Her eyes searched his face. 'You don't, do you?'

He shook his head. 'That monster pointed straight at you.'

'I don't know why he did that. Maybe he was shifting the blame? Please, Dev …'

'It doesn't matter what I believe. It's what the police believe. I didn't tell the inspector what I saw, but Detective Briggs saw it, too. If you want to avoid a long prison term and hurting your father even more dreadfully than you have already, I suggest you get out of here right now and don't stop until you get to Rio de Janeiro or somewhere else that doesn't have an extradition treaty with Australia.'

'You're *nuts*, Dev!' she told him furiously. 'I haven't committed this—this *heinous* crime!—and I'm not running away as if I had!'

Devin watched her storm out with a grim set to his lips. There was no doubt that Louella did sound convincing, but … It was frightening but true that she hadn't completed her purpose: Sarah was still alive. His brow furrowed. *If it isn't Louella, who else can it be?*

§

Aunt Fay was walking down the hall holding a glass. She stepped aside as Louella almost cannoned into her, blinded by tears, and put a restraining hand on the young woman's arm. 'Come into the sitting room, dear. I don't like to see you so upset. You mustn't go out like that. You'll have an accident.'

'Oh, Aunty …' sobbed Louella. 'Dev thinks I'm the one behind these attacks on Sarah. He doesn't believe it wasn't me.'

'I believe you, dear.' Aunt Fay spoke soothing words for a little while until Louella calmed down. 'I'll tell you what,' she said, holding out the glass. 'Why don't you take this to Sarah, and I'll speak to Dev right now.'

'What is it?'

'Soluble aspirin. The pain in Sarah's throat has woken her, and I told her I'd bring her some aspirin to gargle.' Aunt Fay smiled. 'Call it an olive branch if you like. If goodwill is your intent?'

'Of course it is, Aunty. I *told* you.'

'Good. Go on, then.'

Louella took the glass, went to Sarah's room, knocked and entered. 'Here you are, Sarah, this is for you. As far as I know, it is *not* poisoned.'

'Miss Richmond,' said Detective Briggs, rising from her chair by the window and crossing the room in two strides. 'I'll take that, thank you. Dear me! How stupid to try the same thing twice!'

Louella and Sarah watched in shock as the detective took the glass and emptied its contents into a specimen jar. Before either of them could speak, Aunt Fay came in to stand beside Louella.

'I'm sorry, dear,' she said, taking her arm in a biting grip.

'And so you should be, Ma'am,' said Detective Briggs, dislodging the claw-like fingers. 'Because it's not Miss Richmond I want. It's you. Come along, now.'

CHAPTER THIRTY

'What made you suspect her, Briggsy? She seemed like a sweet little old lady to me,' said the inspector.

'All that sweetness and light?' Detective Briggs screwed up her eyes. 'Nah,' she said. 'It had to be too good to be true.'

'I suppose that's how she got away with it for so long.'

'Yes, she hid it well, but … mad as a meat axe if I know anything about it. She's a jealous old cat, and I'd say she's been nursing a grudge since the old man next door jilted her for your favourite suspect's mother.'

'Nursing a grudge? What? For forty years?'

'Say thirty-odd. She concealed her grievances behind that sweet exterior, and nobody saw what was bubbling away underneath.'

'Except you?'

'I had a reason.' Detective Briggs studied the floor. She looked upset. The inspector did not press her. After a moment, she began to speak again: 'Somewhere along the line, all that jealousy and anger turned to madness. I'd say she saw a way to pay him out and get rid of two potential household rivals in one go. I've been going over the cold-case death of Mrs Richmond from eight years ago and expect to bring a charge of murder against her—not that it'll do me any good—she'll have to plead insanity. I have also been looking into the death of Oscar Brennan …'

'Whew! Black widow, in fact?' exclaimed the inspector. 'You know, Briggsy, I always said you were my best detective. If it had been left up to me, I'd have arrested Louella Richmond.' He looked at her. 'You didn't like her as a suspect. Why not?'

'Because I had the feeling that someone was there in the background, trying to make it look like her—a bit too convenient, if you will. And because she doesn't have the right character profile for a cunning killer.'

'An elemental woman …'

'That's very perceptive of you.' Detective Briggs regarded her boss in surprise.

'Not me. That's the overseer's take on her.'

'He's right. She's spoilt and temperamental and wants a good kicking, but she's all up front: nothing underhanded, and rather too obvious about going after what she wants. I did think Miss Johnston's controlling ex-fiancé could have been behind it for a start, until I realised it would have to be someone who knew all the movements of the members of the household.'

'I still don't know how you lit on the aunt. Louella Richmond was the one who hired Jones, after all.'

'No, her father did. At Mrs Brennan's instigation. Did you know that?'

'No, I did not.'

Detective Briggs nodded. 'I thought not. Don't be surprised if we find out that Jones is Bryant. Mrs Brennan got in touch with him and recommended him to the neighbours when they needed a man. I think that is the explanation of the attack on the housemaid. She'd left him years ago because of his brutality, and he was paying her out. I believe that was the reason the old lady took it so badly. She expected to see one person lying there, and to find out that he had broken her trust and attacked Mrs Bryant was enough to send her off in a heart turn. It almost ruined all her plans. But she's nothing if not dedicated, as we've seen by her persistence.'

'Well, that's the easy part. Now we have to explain it to the family.'

'To two families.'

'God, yes! It just gets worse.'

'We'll split the difference,' said Detective Briggs, getting up to leave. 'I'll explain it to Mr Mainwaring, and you can talk to the Richmonds. It will do you good to eat humble pie.'

'I don't know *why* I put up with you, Briggsy!'

'Of course you do,' said Detective Briggs, turning back from the door, her boiled-gooseberry eyes glowing with amusement. 'You say it yourself: I'm your best detective.'

§

Aunt Fay was seated in the back seat of the police car driven by Sergeant Riley. Detective Briggs stood by her at the open car door, waiting for the family to say their goodbyes.

The children had kissed and cuddled her, promising to write. Sarah stood in the background, either ignored or unseen by her would-be murderer. And now it was Dev's turn.

He leant in the car and put his arm around her shoulders, murmured a few words and then asked the question that had been burning at his brain since his painful interview with Detective Briggs: 'Aunty. Why?'

'You wouldn't understand, dear. I tried to take care of you and the children as best I could. To stop you being hurt. Louella has just no manners, and Sarah, though kind to the children and pretty, has no breeding. Neither of them good enough for a Mainwaring of Medora Downs, I am afraid.' Her gentle blue eyes met his. 'Really, dear, I had nothing against Sarah, but she had to be sacrificed to stop Louella. It *had* to be done. And both, as I said, not good enough for you ...' She looked away. 'And Bill, poor Bill ...'

'What about Bill?'

'Nothing ... That's all finished,' she said, returning her limpid gaze to his face. 'I'm sorry I failed you, dear. I am afraid I made a bad mistake: I chose the wrong instrument.'

Devin let his arm fall and stood back; his air of helpless grief so pronounced that the detective, like others before her, felt a strong urge to try and comfort him. 'She can't help it, you know, her condition,' she said. 'It's a mental illness—a form of dementia. She'll go to a secure nursing home and be well cared for. You have no need to worry.'

Sarah, looking as shocked as she felt, went to Devin and put her arms around him. He held her to him, grateful for her loving gesture.

'Try to remember what she was like before she became ill,' said Detective Briggs, looking on them with approval but handing out Dutch comfort. 'This isn't really your aunty, you know. I am afraid she left a long time ago. Before the death of Mrs Richmond.'

'My God!' said Devin, white to the lips. '*My God!*'

Detective Briggs shook her head. 'She won't be held responsible. The nursing home will take care of her. And you,' she said, including Sarah in her smile, as she got in beside Aunt Fay, 'will take care of each other.' Her glance went to the children, standing on the steps with Mattie. 'And the bright future.'

§

Mattie, her face closed and eyes swollen, served them a late breakfast that neither Devin nor Sarah could eat. Sarah helped the children pick at scrambled eggs and toast, knowing that only the breakfast rule kept them from asking a lot of awkward questions.

Just as they were finishing, Louella came in, tear stained and obviously in shock. 'I have to see Dev,' she whimpered, pushing back a dishevelled lock of hair, totally unlike her usually *soignée* self.

'Of course,' said Sarah, seeing that the other girl was labouring under distress. 'I will take the children into the garden.'

Louella seemed not to hear her, demanding, as soon as Sarah had left the room, 'Is it true? Can it *possibly* be true about Aunty?'

'It looks like it,' said Devin in a tight voice. 'Sit down. Coffee?'

'Oh, I *can't* believe it!' exclaimed Louella, waving a negating hand.

'Join the club.' He took a deep breath. 'How's Bill taking it?'

'Badly. It beggars belief, but they're saying she killed Mummy …'

'I know. I'm so sorry.' He shook his head, baffled. 'I just can't take it in. Aunty …'

'Poor Dev. And poor Daddy—losing both the women he loved—one to the other. And I've lost you.' She gave a pathetic, wavering smile. 'Daddy and I, we made the same mistake—carried away by the moment.' She put a hand on his arm. 'Dev, I've *always* loved you …'

He gave the ghost of a wry smile. 'Not enough to prevent you from embarking on a series of torrid affairs, from what I've heard.'

A little bit of the old Louella came back. 'Torrid? Would you have called them *torrid*? I suppose they must have been if you heard about them here, in your magnificent isolation. In fact, without exception, I found myself *utterly* bored to death. Maybe that's why there were so many.'

'Poor Louella. One day you might surprise yourself and find someone that doesn't bore you to death.'

'I live in hope.'

'But don't look at me. I plan to lead a very boring lifestyle—

at complete odds with your jetset ideas.'

'Yes, I gathered that.' There was a little silence, then Louella burst out: 'I *will* have that coffee if it's still on offer?' She took it with a gesture of thanks and raised it as if in a toast. 'I do wish you happy, Dev.'

'Thank you.' He gave her a straight look. 'Bill will have been devastated by this. Why don't you take him to Paris and Rome, show him a good time at all your favourite European haunts?'

'I'd love to! Yes, I'd love to, but ——' Her brow creased.

'I will look after Emerald Hills for you.'

'That's very good of you, Dev. You're a brick.' A hint of malicious amusement entered her eyes. 'Even if you are set on becoming a boring old married man.'

'Put those pretty claws away and go and console your dad. Sarah and I have some things we need to say to each other.'

'Oh, I'll bet you do,' she said, finishing her coffee. 'I'll just *bet* you do.' But when she left, she waved in a friendly manner to Sarah and called out, 'Dev wants you.'

Sarah sent the children to the kitchen to Mattie before retracing her steps across the lawn to the house.

'Do you want me?' asked Sarah, still unable to trust Louella's word.

'Can you doubt it?' he asked, holding out his arms.

Sarah went into them. 'Louella seemed very upset.'

'She was.'

'Oh, poor Louella, her *mother* … Dev, it is all so horrible. I can't, *can't* believe it.' Tears welled. 'Aunt Fay was always so kind to me. Could the police have made a mistake?'

'They don't think so … And from what Aunty said to me before she left, well … I don't think so, either.'

'Aunt Fay!' said Sarah, her face crumpling. 'Oh, but Aunt Fay!'

'I know, my sweet, I know. She hid it so well beneath all that soft, feminine kindness. I never guessed … Awe-inspiring, really.'

'Heartbreaking.'

'That, too,' he agreed, holding her close. 'But it would have been more so had she succeeded in her objective.'

'She tried to make it look as if it was Louella.'

'And she almost succeeded in getting rid of you both.'

'Was it because … Did she hate Bill for jilting her all those years ago? Or us because of you?'

'I have no idea, my darling. How do you fathom an insane mind? Poor old Aunty: she really lost the plot somewhere along the line.' He sighed. 'You know, I think we will have to try and forget this monstrous thing, put it behind us and get on with our lives.'

'I don't know if I can,' she said, incurably truthful. 'I think that will take a lot of strength, strength you may have, but I don't feel that I have.' At that moment, she forgot her own horror at the thought of the children's distress. 'Oh, Dev, what will we tell Naomi and Adam? I've fielded their questions for now. But they will have to be told *something*.'

'See? I knew you were strong. One of the many reasons why I love you. We will tell them that Aunty has an illness that affects her mind and has had to go away for treatment.'

'The truth, in fact.' Sarah softly kissed his chin. 'One of the many reasons why I love *you*.'

'Mrs Fay?' said Mattie when she was told; her magnificent eyes fulminating. 'Never, in all my born days, have I *ever* heard anything like it!' And that was her first and last comment on the matter. She took immediate refuge in her breadmaking.

Mattie had liked Mrs Crampton from the first, recognising that under all that brisk efficiency, there dwelt a kindly woman with a razor-sharp intelligence and a wry sense of humour. She had not been surprised that she had turned out to be an undercover cop named Detective Briggs, and she never thought to question her judgement, accepting her competence as a detective just as she had everything else. But she was shattered.

Reuben, in common with the other men, did not comment— just ducked his head and went to work out his grief in the garden.

Jim was, for once, rendered speechless.

The Medora Downs tragedy shocked the entire district. Life would never again be the same.

§

'Refresh my memory,' said Inspector Kingston. 'What was the lab report on the glass? Was it aspirin or poison?'

'It was both,' said Detective Briggs. 'Thallium again: enough to kill a horse.'

'Good God! She was serious, then?'

'Oh, my word, yes! She was deadly serious, but only, it seems, if she could implicate Miss Richmond.'

'Well, Briggsy, we've got you to thank that it's not a murder case. Accept my compliments for a job well done. Even if it did take you out of your comfort zone.'

'I don't know,' said Detective Briggs, a thoughtful glow in her glassy eyes. 'For a bush camp, it wasn't so bad.'

The inspector laughed. 'Well, you can tell them that. They'll be here soon to pick up Mrs Bryant.'

'All right, I'd better go and get her. You have Jones ready behind the viewing glass. I want to get this over with as quickly as possible.'

'Right!' said the inspector, jumping to attention as she left the room. 'You're the boss, Briggsy.'

'Huh!' scoffed Detective Briggs, poking her head around the door. 'That'll be the day!' She popped her head around the door again. 'I wish you'd told me that a month ago.'

'Get outta here, Briggsy!' said Inspector Kingston, not quite managing to smother a grin. 'Haven't you got work to do?'

§

At this moment, Devin and Sarah were about half an hour from Mount Isa, having set off hours earlier in response to Inspector Kingston's telephone call.

The children had gone for a sleepover at Ilona Downs; a welcome respite for them from the strange loneliness of their house without their aunty. Mattie had offered to take them because, she said, with another of her fulminating looks, Dev should not be allowed to go to Mount Isa on his own.

Seated beside Devin in the Range Rover, Sarah could not help turning her head from time to time to look at his handsome profile. Sometimes he would sense her regard and look down at her briefly—his smile making her heart turn over—before turning his attention back to the road.

They drew up before the Mount Isa Police Station and were ushered in to find Sue, Inspector Kingston and Detective Briggs sitting at a table littered with disposable cups and the remnants of a tray of takeaway cakes and sandwiches.

Inspector Kingston came forward to meet them and shake hands with Devin. Sue was very pale, but pathetically pleased to see them, and Detective Briggs rose to greet them with an expression of warm recognition in her prominent eyes. 'We're just having coffee after a stressful but enlightening experience,' she said. 'Will you join us? I *do* know how you like it.'

'It was my ex,' said Sue when they'd finished their coffee and sandwiches. 'I'm sorry, Boss. And I'm so sorry, Sarah, for what he did to you.'

'Please, Sue, don't apologise,' said Sarah. 'You're the one he hurt the most. I am fine now.'

'None of this was your fault, Sue,' said Devin. 'But do you know how he came to make contact with Aunty?'

'He rang up one day, asking for you. And I answered the phone. Said his name was Jones, but I recognised his voice. I told Mrs Fay, and she took the phone, told me not to worry any more—that she would deal with it.' Sue looked stricken. 'But then, when I saw him in the men's dining room that day …'

There was a long silence, broken by Detective Briggs. 'You've been very brave, Mrs Bryant, closed our case for us,' she said, pressing her hand. 'But I don't doubt this has been very tiring for you. I think you should let Mr Mainwaring and Sarah take you home now.'

Tears coursed down Sue's cheeks. She tried to stem them with her fingers, and Detective Briggs plucked some tissues from a box, handed them to her and placed the box in front of her.

Sue glanced briefly at Devin, then hid her face in the tissues. 'I am afraid that you won't want me back after what's happened,' she sobbed.

'Of course we want you,' said Devin. 'Make no mistake about that! Medora Downs is still your home, Sue. We've all missed you, but Mattie's lost without you in that big kitchen of hers.'

'You'll be quite safe, Mrs Bryant,' Inspector Kingston assured her. 'Your ex-husband is behind bars awaiting trial. He won't get bail. Not only that, but some other very serious assault cases in three states may be brought home to him, which will put him away for a very long time—possibly life.' He thanked her for her assistance, said goodbye to all three and left them in the capable hands of his detective.

Detective Briggs escorted them to the Range Rover, tucked Sue in the back with her luggage, spoke a few kind words and stepped back.

'Mrs Cra—— I mean, Detective Briggs, I never thanked you for looking after me so well,' said Sarah. 'But I hope you know how grateful I am!'

The tall detective waved away her thanks. 'Not at all: just doing my job. If I don't see you again, I wish you every happiness for the future.'

'Of course you'll see us again,' said Devin, holding out his hand. 'You have to be at our wedding: come hell or high water.' His crooked smile held warmth and gratitude. 'Let's face it, if it weren't for you, there wouldn't be one.'

Chapter Thirty-one

Sarah went alone to Ilona Downs to pick up the children, leaving Mattie and Sue to catch up in the kitchen.

She was greeted by Elisabeth Andrews. 'Come in, Sarah. How nice to see you. I hope you will like the surprise I have for you. The children have arranged a little party.'

'Lovely!' said Sarah. 'Thank you.' She looked around for the children.

'Out on the back verandah,' said Elisabeth. 'Come through.'

The children rushed to hug Sarah as soon as she stepped through the door. When she looked up, her gaze travelled over the table laden with party food and drink to two people rising from cane chairs. 'Wendy! Jo!' she gasped. 'How wonderful! Oh, I must be dreaming!'

'When those dreadful things happened over at Medora Downs, I rang Wendy and told her she ought to come,' said Elisabeth. 'I thought you and Dev might need some support.'

§

Later at Medora Downs, the girls were making the bed in Jo's room, having already done Wendy's. When they finished, Jo said, 'Sit down and tell us all about it, Sarah.'

Sarah complied, but when she came to the description of Aunt Fay's arrest, she burst into tears. 'I'm sorry, I ——'

'Come on, Sarah. Pull yourself together, old girl,' said Jo, giving her a friendly shake. 'You've got to be strong. Dev and the children need you.'

'I know,' said Sarah, wiping her eyes. 'But I can't believe it! Mrs Crampton—I mean, Detective Briggs—was so certain when she made the arrest, but I really feel that she must have made a mistake. Aunt Fay was always so kind to me. She said I was the daughter she never h … had, and she made me a beautiful ball dress, and she—she was making my wedding gown. I don't know what I will do now …'

Wendy and Jo looked at each other, asking simultaneously, 'Has she finished it? Is it finished?'

'I don't know. She wouldn't let me see it.'

'Now, don't you worry,' said Jo. 'This is one thing Wendy and I can see to for you. If it isn't finished, we'll do it. You just point us in the direction of the sewing room and concentrate on taking care of Dev and the children.'

At the door of the sewing room, Jo turned to Sarah. 'Okay, we'll take it from here. See you later.'

Sarah's grateful smile as she left them said more than any words.

'This is a very professional-looking sewing room,' said Wendy, looking about. 'I'll take the wardrobe; you look through that material-and-pattern cupboard. There won't be that many wedding dresses … Hang on, I've found it. Oh, it's beautiful,' she breathed, taking it down from its hanger. Then, she made a sound between a muffled scream and a whimper and held it out to Jo. 'Look, it's a *shroud!* Well … not a shroud. *You* know what I mean.'

'I do,' said Jo, grimly surveying the lace-and-satin construction. 'It's a dress at the front and a winding sheet at the back.' She saw her own horror mirrored in Wendy's face. 'We can't let Sarah see this! You can change it back, can't you?'

'There's plenty of material,' observed Wendy through tight lips. 'Did you find the pattern? Then, of course I can. You just keep Sarah away.'

'Dev can do that. I'll help you. I can start unpicking while you make up the back. You know,' said Jo slowly, 'if that odd detective saw this, it would explain why she was so sure when she made her arrest. A fine job we did getting Sarah away from one would-be murderer, only to let her fall into the clutches of another!'

'I know. It beggars belief. Elisabeth says nobody can credit it.' Wendy shook her head. 'Insanity is a crazy thing.'

Jo burst out laughing. 'Wendy, you fool! Do you realise what you just said?'

Wendy began to giggle helplessly and, for a few seconds, tension ebbed.

Sarah opened the door and looked in. 'What's so funny, you two?'

'Nothing,' said Jo, bundling up the dress and holding it behind her. 'Go away, Sarah. You can come back for the fitting. We'll yell out when we're ready.'

'Yep,' chirped Wendy. 'Don't call us; we'll call you.'

'Very funny!' retorted Sarah. But she shut the door and went away.

'Whew!' said Jo. 'Come on, Wen, we'd better get our skates on. We've got to get this thing looking like it's meant for a wedding and not a funeral before she comes back!'

§

Sarah awoke early on her wedding day and went out into the garden. In the dim half-light of dawn, she floated across the lawn like a spirit from another world. Her pale-gold hair and ivory silken dressing-gown billowing out behind her reinforced Reuben's impression of other worldliness, and understanding her need for solitude, he silently retreated to his flat, determined not to encroach on her meditations on this, of all mornings.

The ancient cactus at the bottom of the garden attracted Sarah's attention because it was clothed in shimmering white globes the size of saucers. As she approached it, Sarah reached out a hand in wonder at the display of beauty before her. In awe, she counted them: twenty-one glorious, creamy blossoms—glistening in the soft, crepuscular light—adorned the harsh plant that she had often thought so ugly. How could such a tough, spiny thing produce anything so exquisite as these fragile, ephemeral moonflowers with their elusive, haunting perfume? They were as soft and delicately beautiful as the cactus was tough and ugly. Even the name conjured up visions of beauty and mystery.

Sarah looked more closely, touched the fairytale blooms with reverent fingers and studied the multilayers of cream, ruffled petals, each one a fabulous wedding gown—still finding it hard to believe that such a thing existed. There was something so pure, so spiritual about them; even a sadness, as Sarah knew that the first rays of sunshine spelt their deaths, that they could never be seen in the light of day. Even now, as she watched, they were beginning to close and fold their delicate, silken petals as the light grew stronger, sending to flight the purple morning shadows.

Sighing, she turned away. Sarah could not, would not, watch the demise of the fragile moonflowers but would retain, forever, the precious memory of how she had first seen them: perfect, shimmering in their purity, each one a glorious testimony to nature's generosity.

Silently, the slender, wraith-like figure glided back across the awakening garden and vanished into the house, conscious of a wonderful sensation of awe and privilege that nature, in its own inimitable way, had presented her with an inspiring and unforgettable wedding present.

Now in her room, Sarah climbed back into bed, feeling as unreal as she had looked to Reuben out there in the garden: a shade floating across the lawn. She lay dreaming. *This is my wedding day.*

Later, Jo and Wendy would be bringing her breakfast in bed as they had promised. Then, pampering and bullying her, one would do her make-up and manicure, and the other would dress her hair. But for now, the time was her own. It was six o'clock, and a little after eleven, Sarah would be joined in holy wedlock to the man she loved.

§

Adam, heart-rendingly solemn in his burgundy waistcoat and trousers, snowy ruffled shirt and jaunty bow tie, preceded Naomi, dainty in white organza, down the carpet that had been placed on the lawn between the rows of guests to form an aisle. Behind them walked Sarah, ethereally beautiful in her lace-and-satin gown between her two friends, who each took an arm, leaving her to stand with Devin at the altar.

Sarah looked up at him, saw the tender, possessive smile that lit his eyes and knew that this was the moment she had been waiting for all her life. In a dream, she made her responses and, in a dream, lifted her face for his kiss.

Mattie, in the back row with Sue, wiped her eyes with her handkerchief.

Reuben, on her other side, nudged her and whispered, 'Gone soft, eh, Mattie?'

'No such thing! It's just a speck of dust in my eye, that's all.'

Reuben cackled soundlessly. 'Musta been a whirly wind I didn't see,' he observed. 'There's quite a few with the same trouble.'

Mattie sniffed, but deigned no reply.

Detective Briggs sat with her husband of twenty years—the burly Sergeant Riley. He smiled at this exchange, looked at his wife and said, 'What about you, love? Is that a tear I see in your eye? Or just a speck of dust?'

'Don't give me that crap!' she whispered. 'You know me well

enough!'

'Yes, God help me, I do,' said the bravest man in the Queensland Police Force, softening his words with a grin.

Detective Briggs gave him an inscrutable glance from those amazing eyes, then she tucked her hand in his, sat back and watched the rest of the ceremony with a little enigmatic smile on her lips.

All the district had been invited and everyone came, with one exception: the Richmonds were still in France, having been welcomed with open arms by Louella's cousins, but they sent a handsome wedding present—a week on a glorious, privately owned island off the Barrier Reef.

§

Standing on the beach outside their villa, Sarah glanced up at the finely carved profile of her husband as they watched the sun set over the water, and she thought how strange it was that she, Sarah Johnston—no, Sarah Mainwaring now—should be in this place, at this time, beside this man who was her world. Briefly, all that had happened during the winter touched on her mind, but only briefly. Their love had transcended all the evil, the jealousy, the bitterness, the obstacles in their path, and would carry them from this new beginning to the end of their lives.

In silence, they watched the blaze of crimson glory slowly fade into soft pinks and greys while the blood-red path on the water turned to gold and then dull pewter.

'So beautiful. Yet, it doesn't last,' sighed Sarah.

Devin smiled indulgently at her regretful tone, gathered her close and kissed the tip of her nose. 'Don't fret, my darling,' he said. 'There'll be another one, just like it, tomorrow.'

'And all our tomorrows,' said Sarah, raising her eyes to his. 'Oh, Dev …'

They shared a kiss of deepening passion—of sweetness and promises—and turned, arms about each other, to cross the empty beach to their villa.

About the Author

Anne Rouen

Anne Rouen—the nom de plume of Lynn Newberry—is the award-winning author behind the successful historical fiction series, *Master of Illusion* and, more recently, a set of standalone contemporary historical fiction romance and suspense novels set in the Australian Outback, starting with *Winter at Medora Downs*.

Lynn is a retired Australian country woman, currently living in the North-West region of New South Wales. A graduate of the University of New England, she is a former teacher, dressage rider and cattle breeder. A life on the land, including eleven years in Outback Queensland, has mixed nicely with her penchant for writing romantic suspense in historical settings.

Lynn has recently exchanged her farm for a delightful small acreage on the edge of a village, where she writes full time. As horses and writing are her greatest passions, Lynn now embraces an idyllic lifestyle, since she has time to delve into the historical research she so loves.

Writing as Anne Rouen, Lynn self-published her historical romance/mystery series *Master of Illusion* with great success, winning four literary awards across the entire set. Book I (*Master of Illusion Bk I*) and Book III (*Angel of Song*) achieved Silver (2014) and Bronze (2016) respectively in the *Global Ebook Awards* for *Modern Historical Literature Fiction*. Book IV (*Guardian Angel*), the final in the series, was awarded Silver (2018) in the same category and Bronze (2018) for the *Global Ebook Awards Best Ebook Cover*.

Lynn also achieved a Highly Commended in the 2011 Rolf Boldrewood Literary Awards for her short story *The Scent of a Criminal* and a Commended in the 2018 *Thunderbolt Prize for Crime Fiction* for *The Min Min Light*.

You can find more information about Anne Rouen and read her blog at www.annerouen.com.

Other Books by Anne Rouen

Master of Illusion—Book One

Master of Illusion—Book Two

Angel of Song (Master of Illusion—Book Three)

Guardian Angel (Master of Illusion—Book Four)